AVID

READER

PRESS

A SHORT WALK THROUGH A WIDE WORLD

a novel

DOUGLAS WESTERBEKE

Avid Reader Press

NEW YORK   LONDON   TORONTO
SYDNEY   NEW DELHI

AVID READER PRESS
An Imprint of Simon & Schuster, LLC
1230 Avenue of the Americas
New York, NY 10020

First Avid Reader Press hardcover edition April 2024

AVID READER PRESS and colophon are trademarks of Simon & Schuster, LLC

Simon & Schuster: Celebrating 100 Years of Publishing in 2024

For information about special discounts for bulk purchases, please contact Simon & Schuster Special Sales at 1-866-506-1949 or business@simonandschuster.com.

The Simon & Schuster Speakers Bureau can bring authors to your live event. For more information or to book an event, contact the Simon & Schuster Speakers Bureau at 1-866-248-3049 or visit our website at www.simonspeakers.com.

Manufactured in the United States of America

3   5   7   9   10   8   6   4   2

Library of Congress Cataloging-in-Publication Data has been applied for.

ISBN 978-1-6680-2606-9
ISBN 978-1-6680-2608-3 (ebook)

To Amy Dawson,
for giving me the best advice ever

To the Cleveland Public Library,
without which this book would never have been

"Beyond the Wild Wood comes the Wide World," said the Rat. "And that's something that doesn't matter, either to you or me. I've never been there, and I'm never going, nor you either, if you've got any sense at all. Don't ever refer to it again, please."

—KENNETH GRAHAME, *THE WIND IN THE WILLOWS*

A SHORT WALK THROUGH A WIDE WORLD

1

A Marketplace

The paper is clean and white—she hasn't drawn her first line—so when the drop of blood falls and makes its little red mark on the page, she freezes. Her pencil hovers in her hand. Her heart, like it always does, gives her chest an extra kick. She drops the pencil. Hand, like a reflex, goes to her nose. She feels the wetness creeping through her sinuses, tastes the brine in the back of her throat. It's a trickle now, no more than a nosebleed, but in moments it will be much worse—and here, of all places, just as she'd sat down.

It's too soon. It's bad luck. She'd hoped to sleep in a real bed tonight, not hammocks or hard ground, and in the morning have a bath, a proper bath in warm water, with soap. She'd hoped to add more entries to her book, like *tinder* or *flint* or *paper*—but how to draw a piece of paper on a piece of paper so that others will look at it and say, "Oh, I see. A piece of paper."

She'd hoped to try the food. Look at this market—taro preserves, steamed crab claws, curried prawns wrapped in sheets of bean curd. No, this will have to wait, too, for another time and another market. The list of things she won't do is even longer than that—what list isn't?—but there's no time to dwell. The bath can wait. She'll find a bed somewhere else. The list is gone. Now is the time to get the hell out.

But the marketplace is alive, the people friendly, and the river right there, a shiny tearstain through the green, clogged with colorful skiffs and fishing boats that can whisk her away, no effort at all. This is Siam, a watery part of the world, all jungle, seasons measured by rainfall. She knew as soon as she set foot here that rivers would be her mode of escape.

That old man, selling fish—such a kindly face, weather-beaten, but a glint in his eye still. He will help. Quickly, she slings her bag over her shoulder and cradles her book in the crook of her arm. She picks up her walking stick, as tall as she is, and moves through blue hairs of incense smoke and burning charcoal. She moves past fishmongers and cloth merchants and tables made of bamboo. The old man smokes a long, thin opium pipe, surrounded by racks of dried fish, dried squid, and dried octopus—anything that was once wet now hangs dry, the old man perched among the racks like a caged bird. She doesn't know the local language, but the French have colonies to the north and the British have influence to the south.

"Please," she asks in her accented English, "a boat? Do you know where I might find a boat? I need a boat."

The old man doesn't understand. He hadn't noticed her before, just looks up and there she is, the tallest person in the market, with dirty blonde hair and blue eyes, looming over him. The walking stick in her hand, long and straight, makes her look regal, like a venerable Buddhist nun or an emperor's daughter. Nothing about her suggests the West—no corsets, no bows, no high lace collars, only local fabrics and a laborer's straw hat—but she will never blend in here, not in this market, not in this country, where she's at least a head taller than everyone else.

She sees the baffled expression on the old man's face. She smiles so that he might lower his guard. She rarely blends in anywhere. It's more rare that she tries. Her appearance invites curious looks and lots of questions. It's the best method she has of meeting people, but it's not working on this old man.

He begins chattering in a language she can't understand. There's a shift in his demeanor. It happens all the time. He's mistaken her for a rich foreigner instead of a poor one, instead of someone who has slept in the tops of the jungle canopy and bathed in hidden rivers for the past three weeks. He tries to sell her a stick of dried pomfret. The way he's gesticulating he might be trying to sell her his whole stand. She raises a single alarmed eyebrow. She's wrong about this man. Her instinct has failed her. It rarely happens, but when it does it's downright unnerving. It's her instinct, her ability to size up a stranger with a glance or two, that's kept her alive until now.

And then the pain strikes—a terrible, venomous pain—a weeping pain, like an ice pick through a rotten tooth. It drives straight down her spine, from the base of her skull to the small of her back. She shudders as if electrified, then stiffens up, crushing all the slack out of her body. The old man stops his chattering, watches her face turn cold and pale, watches her lips form sound-less words. He's afraid she might topple over in front of him. But she doesn't topple. She doesn't even cry out. She clenches her jaw, her body, and shuffles toward the next stall, a jagged limp in her step.

"A boat!" she calls out to anyone. Many turn to hear. None understand. "A boat, a boat, a boat . . ." She chants the words as she limps past vendors and their stands, as if tossing lifelines from a sinking ship to those onshore. Another stab of pain and the first sparks of panic fly through her brain.

She approaches a woman by a firepit, stirring a yellow curry in an iron wok. She opens her book to the page newly decorated with a drop of blood. Not easy, with all her muscles twitching.

The pages are full of little drawings, hundreds of them, a

collection of useful things—bananas, beds, parasols, horses and carriages, needles and thread, locomotives, clockfaces, and candlesticks. She flips through pages with rattled hands until, finally, she finds the little pencil sketch of a boat, of several different kinds of boats—sailboats, steamboats, luxury liners, and canoes, so there can be no mistake.

"A boat? *Bateau?*"

No response from the woman. Do they know Cantonese here? China is not so far. She'd been in China only a month ago, or so it seemed, cutting through the jungle with a worn-down machete. Now she's here, south, begging for her life on a riverbank.

"*Syún?*"

Still the woman doesn't respond, only stares. Does she know the local word? She'd picked up a few. She'd thought that much ahead. *Touk?* Was that it?

"*Touk?*"

But instead of answering her, instead of engaging in some kind of pantomimed conversation as people usually do, the woman drops her big wooden spoon into the curry and silently backs away.

And now she knows she must look very bad. She looks at the handkerchief in her hand. It's entirely red. The noises of the market have, bit by bit, gone mute, as if she's underwater, which could only mean that she's bleeding from the ears, too, and, of course, her mouth is full of blood. She can taste it. She licks her teeth and it pools over her lips and then, to her shame, she knows it's been dripping down her chin the whole time. She must be a terror to behold.

The pain advances; her entire head is an exposed nerve, a jagged blade scraping the inside of her skull. A terrible pressure builds up against her eyeballs and the ice pick that skewers down the small of her back drives straight into her left leg. She stifles a scream. When she walks, her leg drags behind her like a dead animal.

She wipes her face with her sleeve. It only smears blood across her cheeks. She scans the market for fishermen, ferrymen, anyone who might take her away. She holds out the picture of the boat for all to see.

"Boat! *Bateau! Syún!*"

No one comes to her aid, but they do stare, fascinated and afraid. She looks rabid, crazed. She looks like someone who can't be saved. Why would a diseased woman want a boat? To die in? A floating coffin in which to lay her dead body? Would they ever get their boat back? And she can't explain because this is one language too many. She's learned plenty by now—Arabic, Spanish, Mandarin, and Cantonese, even more, even a little Circassian, for God's sake—but she can't learn them all.

Then she hears—yes, it is—English behind her, somewhere in the crowd, a small clear voice.

"Mama, that lady needs help!"

She turns and sees the child, a little golden-haired girl above the crowd, above a sea of black hair and conical hats, as if suspended there in her white sunny blouse and pinafore dress—but no, actually sitting on someone's shoulders, near enough to see, but too far to help. British? American? They will understand her. She holds out her red-stained hand, as if to wave, but in another moment the girl is swallowed up in the marketplace.

A new pain, a vulture in her womb digging itself out. She doubles over and falls to her knees. In one terrible cough, she sprays so much blood on the ground that the crowds swarming around her gasp in unison and back away.

Her hat falls off and her walking stick clatters to the ground. She tries to control her breathing—carefully, because even the smallest breath tempts the gag in her throat. She picks up her walking stick, hugging it close to her chest. She leaves the hat. The hat is not important. She can get a new hat. She climbs to her feet, wipes her mouth, approaches the men in the boats by the shore, unloading fish, selling melons and plantains. They see her coming, see the blood, the stagger. They'd flee but they're trapped against a logjam of boats.

"*Je dois avoir un bateau, s'il vous plait . . .*" she says.

Some of the fishermen point. Some shoo her away. It's not like anything they've seen before, this sickness. She stumbles along the shore and the crowd parts before her.

"Someone . . . please . . ."

She trembles, her own little earthquake. People scramble up the riverbank to get out of her way. Some choose to flee into the river, up to their knees in mud, up to their thighs in water. Now there are no more people in front of her and she's standing on a dock that extends past the boats and into the river.

A ferryboat full of people has just cast off, chugging upstream, clouds of thick black smoke from its funnel. Over the noise of the engine is that same voice, the shout of a little girl.

"Come here! This way!"

She looks and sees two blond-haired children in white—in white of all things, a perfect lambswool white—waving to her from the stern of the boat.

"Here!" they shout. "We'll help you!"

She tucks the book into her sash, wobbles, and almost falls over again, but she focuses and fights her pain and untaps the last of her strength. She runs the length of the dock, clutching her walking stick in her hands. She runs and when she reaches the end, she doesn't stop or slow down, but leaps into the muddy river. She leaps and swims with all the power she has left to catch that ferry with the powerful steam engine. And everyone in the marketplace rushes to the shore to watch.

The crowd holds their breath and the children egg her on. She swims and swims and she manages to catch up to that ferry before it can find its speed, all the while her walking stick in one hand, her bag dragging behind her. The people on the ferry, amazed by this feat, reach down and lift her up by the arms and pull her into their boat.

Then she is sprawled on the deck, sopping wet, in a puddle of river water and diluted blood. She clutches her walking stick tight to her body, the way monks clutch their prayer beads. She looks up at her rescuers, her fellow travelers. Panting, she asks them, "Oh, *mon dieu* . . . Are we moving? Are we underway?"

The two children, a boy and a girl, stare down at her, and their father, too, a big vault of a man with a New Zealand accent, kneeling beside her. He says, "Yes, yes. We're moving."

Relief. Reprieve. No more blood, not from her nose, her lips, or her ears. The pain has already faded away. She can breathe again.

"*Dieu merci*," she tells them and smiles. "I am aweigh."

2

A Riverboat in Siam

The Holcombes have seen many things in their travels—lakes of acid, scarifications, whole fermented swallows at the bottom of their soup bowls—but this diseased woman is at the very top of their list of stories to tell when they get back home. No more than thirty, but a seasoned traveler by the look of her, she'd been stumbling through a marketplace covered in blood, but then jumped into a river fully clothed, only to emerge cured, any sickness she might have been carrying simply washed away.

Now she's leaning over the side of the boat, dragging her clothes in the water, scrubbing out the blood before hanging them on the railing to dry. Magically, the clothes in her backpack are perfectly dry. She tells them it's a trick she picked up, the careful way she twists the sealskin pack shut. But they are thinking, that's no trick one picks up in Indochina. Where does anybody find sealskin in Siam?

Her book is soaked through. It was retrieved from the river but the pages are sodden and beyond repair. Sad, as it is full of precious little pictures she's taken a long time to draw, little sketches of scissors and mail and shoes and eggs. The children are concerned, but she sighs and shrugs it off. It has happened before, she says. She's often getting wet, it seems. She says she will start a new book as soon as she has the paper.

"Are you New Zealanders?" she asks Emily Holcombe, the children's mother. Her husband and two children have gone to fetch drinks from the tea vendor in the cabin. "I love New Zealand. There's a country I wish I never had to leave."

Emily is young for a mother of two, much younger than her husband. Her clothes—long dress, long sleeves, raised collar—are unsuited for the weather but eminently fashionable. She's a product of Western high society, yet here she is, on a common ferryboat, sharing space with the locals, trekking through the jungles.

"What brings you to Siam?" the woman asks Emily in her accented English.

Emily sits and stares, hard-pressed to answer.

"I . . . My husband is on business. Textiles . . ."

"Is this a good place for it?" she asks as if nothing has happened.

"You were covered in blood."

"I was."

"I . . . We all thought you were going to die, right there in the market."

"I did not die."

"But you could have."

"I could have, yes, I suppose. It comes and goes. I must have been a fright."

"Watching someone bleed to death in front of you is a bit of a fright, yes."

"But now I am on a boat traveling down the river and all is well."

"Is it?"

"It is."

And then Emily remembers the articles. Because, like all ex-patriots, she reads her native language at any opportunity she gets—newspapers from home, the London *Times*, a train schedule, anything she can get her hands on—she recognizes the woman and can't help but gasp a little.

"You . . . you are that . . . you are that French lady . . . Audrey . . ."

"Aubry Tourvel."

Aubry holds out her hand and when Emily Holcombe shakes it, she feels a little thrill, the thrill of shaking hands with someone who has been talked about in the London *Times* and the *New Zealand Herald*. She can't wait to tell her children or, even more so, her husband, who might better appreciate it.

But just as Emily is about say something else, their conversation is abruptly ended. Her husband and two children return carrying cups of tea and plates of scallion pancakes.

The children are named Sophie and Somerset. Aubry has thanked everyone onboard for plucking her out of the river. She's made sure to pay the captain her full fare. But there's no question that it's these two children who have truly saved her life. They're lovely children—polite, soft-hearted, obedient to their parents—but not so much that they didn't shout and wave their arms to her. Aubry doesn't think they're twins but she can't tell which of them is older—neither can be more than eight or nine. They come at her, beaming.

"Here you are! We have things for you!" says Somerset.

"Are you well? You seem well! You seem better than before!" says Sophie.

The children are so carried away they look ready to climb onto her lap. Their father shouts, "Back! I said back! You're too close! Everyone take five steps back!"

"But Vaughan," says Emily, "this is the French lady, the one in the papers."

"Who?"

"The lady we read about. In the papers."

This only flusters him. His head pivots back and forth, as if he doesn't know which offender to turn to. "Just . . . everybody keep back!"

Vaughan Holcombe is a big man with broad swimmer's shoulders and close-cropped graying hair. Very handsome, Aubry thinks, in his slightly worn tweed suit. She can't possibly dislike such a handsome man who has raised his children so well. He puts down a cup of tea and a plate of scallion pancakes on the bench beside her and she thinks it's a kind gesture, but when she looks up at his face, all she sees, all she feels, is the blunt force of his glare.

"Now they may be admirers of yours but I don't know you from dirt," he says. "What was that back there? TB?"

"No."

"Malaria? Diphtheria? Typhus?"

"Nothing like that."

She can hear the patience draining from his voice. "Then what exactly was it like?"

Aubry doesn't mean to try his patience. She only means to answer him honestly, so she says, "It was like a great hand coming down and squeezing the life from me," which is accurate, but stupid. It's not what he wants to hear. She knows it as soon as she says it.

For several moments, he stares at her, very still. She wonders what they do with madwomen in Siam.

"I told you, Vaughan," says Emily. "The French lady from the papers. You've been traveling the world since you were a young girl, isn't that right?"

"Yes."

"Around the world . . ." Emily urges her on.

"Yes."

"Around the whole world?" asks Sophie.

"Several times."

"Alone?" asks Somerset.

"No, not alone. Not always. I am traveling right this moment with you."

Mr. Holcombe shakes his head. He's unsure what to make of all this. Worse, his outrage has been sidelined by chitchat.

Emily presses on. "I am Emily Holcombe and this is my husband, Vaughan, and my children, Sophie and Somerset."

"All right, stop! Everybody stop!" says Vaughan with a voice like grinding gears. He's trying hard not to cause a scene. "There's a cholera epidemic three villages away and you're all chattering like schoolchildren on a powder keg. What is this . . . this thing you have?"

Suddenly, she's ashamed. Aubry looks down at the floor-boards. She's been singled out and chastised, like she's a little schoolgirl again, and others are staring now, too. But worse, it's her own nonchalance that's brought it on.

"I don't know," she tells him.

"You don't know?" he says, eyes widening.

"No one does."

"Then you damn well shouldn't be walking around in public with it, should you?"

"It's mine," she says quietly, her head bowed. "It's only mine. I haven't given it to anyone and no one's given it to me."

That—that explanation, that submission, whatever it might be—drains the hostility from Vaughan's voice. A silence descends. There's still the chug of the engine, the chatter of the locals, the froth and rumble of the propeller below—but among this little court in an aft corner of the boat, silence. Emily and her children want to take Aubry's hand and console her. Even

Vaughan's broad shoulders have slackened. But Aubry doesn't dare look at their faces.

"Oh, Vaughan," says Emily. "Now look what you've done."

Sophie leans forward, so low Aubry can't miss her there by her elbow, peeking up like a little garden fairy. "Have you been to Tahiti?"

She lightens Aubry's mood, this little girl who doesn't care who's angry at who, just wants to know. Aubry's so glad to have been rescued by children this bright.

"Yes."

"Have you climbed any mountains?" asks Somerset.

"I have climbed many mountains."

"Have you crossed a desert?"

"And prairies and oceans and swamps and jungles."

"Extraordinary," says Emily Holcombe.

"But isn't it exceedingly dangerous?" asks Sophie.

"Oh yes. Exceedingly."

"Then why do you do it?"

She gives Mr. Holcombe a cautious peek, not wanting to stir his anger again, but he stands there like a marble statue, arms crossed, as if waiting for her explanation. If he wants an explanation, thinks Aubry, he certainly deserves one. But the children deserve one even more.

"Well, I'd tell you, but I can tell you're not interested."

The children protest, "No, no! We're interested! We're interested!" in such a wall of sound she can't tell one voice from another.

"But you're not *really* interested," she says again and feigns disappointment.

"Yes, yes! We are! We are!"

"Well, you did pull me from the river, I suppose. Perhaps after a sip of my tea."

15

The children lean forward in their seats. Aubry reaches for the cup of tea and takes a long, exaggerated sip.

"That was good," she says. "Maybe another."

She takes another, much longer sip this time. She spends most of her life alone, following a thin and lonely trail across uninhabited prairies, or coastlines, or mountaintops. But once in a while she is lucky enough to spend some time with a family, a collection of kin who reminds her of home. They wait breathlessly, these children, eyes pleading with her. Even Vaughan takes a seat on the bench beside his wife, to hear her out.

When she finishes her long playful sip, she looks around slyly and says, "I left home forever when I was nine."

Which she did, holding her mother's hand, her whole family with her, heads low, all of them walking her to a hotel because she could never stay another night at home again.

"Where's home?" asks Somerset.

"Paris."

"Is that where you got it?" asks Vaughan.

"From a well."

"A well?"

"I think. I can't know for certain, but I think it was a well."

"Contaminated water," says Vaughan.

"You shouldn't drink dirty water," says Somerset, shaking his head.

"Oh, I didn't drink it," she tells them.

They look at her, confused. "Then, what did you do?" Sophie asks.

So she tells them.

3

Home

The well was a strange one, made of smooth gray stone, not a random collection of rocks that had been gathered and stacked like a country well, but a few large stones, chiseled as smooth as a river bottom, squeezed so tightly together a sewing needle couldn't fit between them. They were not only carved to fit, but, from above, the lip of the well had been shaped into a face—two white eyes chiseled in one end, a tiny beard in the other, the circular rim forming the mouth, complete with lips and teeth. The mouth was a perfect O—a scream? A cry for help? A beast lunging up from the depths to swallow little children whole? The effect was garish if not freakish and perhaps even a little satanic—but the three sisters loved it.

Each of them had a precious gift in their hands. Pauline, the oldest sister, had a gold chain, borrowed from Mother when she was eight. Like everything else she borrowed from her mother, it had gradually become hers. She wore it to a fancy party their parents threw one evening, again to church the following week, and again to her cousin's wedding. She fancied herself a darling of Belle Époque fashion. It probably wasn't true gold—unlikely her mother would've trusted her with anything more expensive than a good hat—but Pauline had grown attached to it, and now she was holding it for the last time.

"This is so the socialists will stop planting bombs in public buildings," Pauline said and held out her hand. She took a last look at her chain glinting in the sunlight and let go.

The chain fell, into the mouth, past the lips and teeth, dropping silently down the long black throat. They listened carefully. The splash could barely be heard. Was there a splash at all? Even at that moment, they couldn't be sure.

Sylvie was next, the middle sister, with her tattered cloth doll limp in her hands. She had other dolls she played with more, liked more, but this was her first doll. It was so old she couldn't remember where it came from. Like her parents, or her bedroom, or the toes at the end of her feet, it had always been there. But she was ten years old now. The doll had been collecting dust on her bedroom shelf for a long, long time. She would miss it, but she also knew it would make a meaningful sacrifice.

"This is so Dr. Homais may finally discover his cure for syphilis," said Sylvie. She held out her hand but couldn't let her doll go. It was staring back at her. She felt the tears welling up. But she would not let Dr. Homais down. More important, she would not be outdone by her sisters.

She closed her eyes and turned her head. Her hands unclenched and the doll fell softly as snow. They listened. This time there was a sound, but not what they expected—not a sound like water but like a bundle of feathers against a large metal gong. What was at the bottom of this well, anyway? And why was it here, hidden in a courtyard between empty apartment buildings in Paris? It was sheer chance they had found it at all coming home from school one day and Sylvie's doll had paid the price.

Finally, there was Aubry, the youngest of them. She held her gift tight to her chest, stood still, and stared down the gullet of the well. She didn't say a thing.

"Hello?" Sylvie urged.

She didn't move.

"What are you wishing for?" asked Pauline.

"That Mrs. Von Bingham's baby doesn't die of her sickness," Aubry told them.

"Ooooh. That's a good one," said Sylvie.

"But I don't want to throw away my puzzle ball."

She'd discovered it only a week earlier, lying on a dead man's front walk. She was coming home from school and saw the horse-drawn cart parked outside what she'd always presumed to be an abandoned home. But it was not abandoned—two men were carrying out a body on a stretcher, hidden under a white sheet. A group of children from her school were gathered across the street and Aubry joined them.

"Who was that?" she asked.

"My mom says it was an old man who never left his house," answered a classmate. "She said he couldn't speak French so he never came out."

"He was from Africa," said another.

"Where in Africa?"

"I don't know. Africa."

"You muttonhead," said one of the older girls. "He was from America."

"That's not what I heard," said the oldest, a boy not known for saying much at all.

"What did you hear?"

"Somewhere else."

One of the youngest ones shrugged and said, "He's dead now."

They stood there and watched until the cart rode off with the body.

The next day, while walking the same route home, she noticed the house again, locked up, all the shades drawn, as empty of life as a gutted fish.

Then she saw the ball. It sat silently on the front walk at the foot of the steps, as if it had rolled out the door all on its own. She had heard of those wooden clogs the Dutch wore and thought, Who would want such an uncomfortable contraption? Now here she was, staring at a wooden ball, wondering why anyone would want a ball made of wood.

There was wind that day, gusts that scattered sunlight through the trees. It swept across the street and must have caught the ball in its breath because it rolled toward her, just an inch or two. Aubry stood there and watched, a little amazed.

The air inhaled, then blew again. The wooden ball rolled a few more inches, then a few more. Soon it was halfway across the yard, angling straight toward her feet. She did not know what to think. It seemed wrong to take the ball. It felt like stealing, even if its owner—whoever he had been, whatever part of the world he had come from—was no more. But the ball was rolling toward her, all on its own. This was an invitation if there ever was one. She looked up and down the street, made sure no one was looking, and snatched the ball away.

Not sure what to do with a wooden ball, she rolled it down the street and kicked it along. It was a dirty, dusty thing, but when she kicked it into the wet grass, it looked different. Up close and wiped clean, one could see the series of flat wooden surfaces, polished smooth, shiny from lacquer, with grooves that slid against each other in every direction. It was actually rather handsome.

But Aubry had never been impressed by handsome. Still not

knowing what to do with the thing, she kicked it into Mrs. Roussel's yard and promptly forgot about it.

The next morning, heading off to school, it was at the edge of her yard, where the front walk meets the street, as if it had been waiting for her all night. Someone must have kicked it into her front yard just as she had kicked it into Mrs. Roussel's. She scooped it up and carried it all the way to school. When she got there, she tossed it into the playground. It seemed better suited for a playground than sidewalks and streets.

Walking back home with her sisters, her knapsack seemed a little heavier—not much—perhaps it wasn't even the weight, but the unfamiliar bulge she felt. She stopped to see what it was.

The puzzle ball, in her knapsack. Who had put it there? What kind of joke was being played here?

She turned to Sylvie. "Did you do this?"

"Did I do what?" She seemed genuinely ignorant. Aubry turned to Pauline, showed her the puzzle ball.

"Did you?"

"What are you talking about?"

"Someone put this in my knapsack."

They came close to take a look at it in Aubry's outstretched hand.

"It's pretty," said Pauline. "Keep it."

But Aubry said, "You can have it," and put it on Pauline's windowsill when they got home.

When she went to bed that night, there it was, on her floor in the middle of the room. She dragged everyone into her room—first Sylvie, then Pauline, then her parents. She pointed, finger wagging. Everyone professed innocence. No one knew how it got there. Someone was tricking her, she was sure. They seemed to think it was Aubry playing a trick on them.

Since she couldn't get rid of the thing, she tried to open it instead. Maybe the answer lay inside. She really tried, twisting and turning the layers, groove against groove. She banged it against cobblestones and tried prying it open with a kitchen knife. All week she tried but no matter what she did, it wouldn't open.

One morning, Pauline found their father's newspaper on the breakfast table and began reading. "Terrible things are happening in the world," she said, aghast at the headlines. "It's 1885! You'd think people would know better! We must do what we can and bring it to a halt."

"How?" asked Sylvie.

Pauline thought about it. She was the oldest sister and the smartest, too. If anyone had answers, it was her. "Remember that well we found?"

"Yes."

"It's a wishing well, right? We could make a sacrifice."

Aubry loved the idea. "Yes!" she shouted, knowing immediately what she would be giving away.

"She means you!" Sylvie cried to Aubry.

"I don't mean *her*!" Pauline shot Sylvie a look. "That's horrible! I mean like the old days. I mean things that are important to us, to each of us, to prove that we take the future very, very seriously."

"Aubry is important to us," said Sylvie, not quite catching up to Pauline's meaning.

"We are not sacrificing Aubry!" said Pauline definitively.

On the day of the sacrifice, Aubry brought her puzzle ball, the puzzle ball that had yet to open up, to unlock its secrets, but now that she stood before the open mouth of the well, it was the unknowing that made all the difference.

"We agreed, Aubry," said Pauline. "It has to be something important or the wish won't come true."

That made sense. Certainly, dropping trash into the well

wouldn't work. Only things with value. That was the difference between a good sacrifice and a bad one. Just ask Cain. Just ask Abel. And what could have more value than Pauline's gold chain, or Sylvie's oldest doll, or—it turned out—Aubry's puzzle ball?

How had it ended up in her backpack? In her room? She was certain it held a secret she had yet to find. If she tossed it away, she'd never know. She suddenly wished she'd brought anything else—her toy mouse, her favorite dress, her little spyglass—but not this. She felt as if the whole thing had been some kind of trap, as if she'd been set up, the way this foolish thing seemed to follow her and cause so much trouble.

Pauline and Sylvie were staring at her. They'd done their bit. It was too late to go back. They expected big things from Aubry or, at least, not childish things.

"But . . . but it's stupid!" Aubry blurted out, stamping her foot. "My puzzle ball falls into the well, rots away, and her baby will die anyway! It makes no sense!"

"It's a wishing well!" cried Pauline. "It has to come true!"

"A wishing well, you know," said Sylvie, gently.

Aubry could feel the tears coming, the knot in her throat, a mix of anger and shame. "No! It makes no sense!" was all she could say. It was inexcusable, but she ran off with her puzzle ball still clutched to her chest.

4

A Riverboat in Siam

"Did the baby die?" asks Sophie.

For a long time, Aubry says nothing. She is not there on that ferryboat with the Holcombes, but far away in a childhood that is long over. The Holcombes do not press her. They wait, patiently, knowing some things take time to say, if they are ever said at all.

"Yes." The word seems to slip from her lips, quietly, absently. It almost passes by unnoticed. The Holcombes remain silent.

She inhales and straightens in her seat, not once looking up from the floorboards.

Another sip of tea and she goes on. "I first became sick that night."

5

Home

"I don't think I can eat this," she tells them.

Her mother glanced at Aubry's plate. She had spent most of the day on the onion soup alone. She worked hard on dinner. She always did and, as usual, her youngest child had turned her nose up at it.

Earlier that year, her mother had been summoned to school because Aubry had picked a fight with her teacher. Her poor mother had never heard of a nine-year-old picking a fight with an adult before—never mind a teacher—but Aubry had managed it. She'd called him incompetent, right to his face. The entire class was cheating, Aubry explained, and somehow, this incompetent teacher had managed not to see the notes passed around, the silent lips mouthing answers to each other. He didn't notice at least five other students peeking at answers written on their arms and thighs, hidden under skirts and shirtsleeves. Aubry was the only one who didn't cheat and was given the lowest mark. How could he justify this, Aubry asked him, a single eyebrow arching up her forehead. She demanded an explanation. She demanded justice!

"Dear God," her mother could be heard saying. "Only nine years old."

The teacher had turned to her mother in a manner that said, *Please, do something about your child.* She apologized for Aubry's insolence. What else could she say? It was time Aubry learned that insubordination was not a path to success.

It took Aubry months to forgive her.

And her father, when he saw her push her dinner plate away, was even angrier. Of his three daughters, it was always Aubry causing a fuss. Pauline, the oldest, was diligent, hardworking, with the highest grades in her class. She had ambitions unusual for her sex and had a good chance at achieving them. Sylvie was quiet, softhearted. She knew how to share before she could walk. She would rather give up her favorite toy than watch a classmate go without. She was the easiest child to raise and, frankly, the most lovable of them.

But Aubry was a terror. She might have been the prettiest, but she was also the most stubborn and the most proud. Everything they had—the house, the furniture, that orgy of food on porcelain plates—she took for granted. That same week she'd made a scene at a department store when her mother refused to buy her a hat she'd taken a liking to.

"But you promised me a present!" Aubry shouted.

"Does it have to be right here? Right now?"

"But you promised me!"

Aubry at church, bouncing in her seat, kicking her legs, openly sighing, letting everyone know how bored she was. Her parents' faces burned with shame.

Never mind that her sisters had come home angry this afternoon because she'd backed out of a deal they'd made. Their father had had enough. She was spoiled—there was no question—and something had to be done about it.

He hardened his jaw and said, "Aubry, I believe this will be the last . . ."

But one look at her face and his anger died. She'd gone pale. Her hands were shivering and she couldn't stop them.

"What is it?" he asked her.

"I don't feel right" was all she could say.

Her mother and father looked at each other, then back at Aubry.

"Is it your tummy?" asked her mother.

"It's everything," she said.

She grunted, then moaned. Her shoulder spasmed, arm bumping the table, rattling the silverware. She shook, stiffened, then shook again. It was all so fast, so unexpected. All anyone could do was watch it happen.

She fell from her chair. Her father, catching up to the crisis, leapt and caught her before she hit the floor. Her mother and sisters bolted upright. She lay in her father's arms, her little body contorting.

"Pappa, may I lie down somewhere?" she asked in a soft tremulous voice, as if she were three again.

"Yes, of course," her father said. He was already carrying her away to the next room.

"Pauline," said Mother, "fetch your shoes. Run and bring Dr. Homais here at once."

Pauline spun in a circle, then remembered her shoes were always by the door. Mother followed Aubry and her father to the next room, muttering out loud, her hands flapping in the air.

Sylvie, left alone at the dinner table, standing there, overwhelmed.

"What just happened?" she said to an empty room.

Her father put Aubry down on the parlor sofa, his hand brushing her hair. Her mother rushed to her side.

"Is it better lying down?" her mother asked.

"A little," she said, but then spasmed again. Her father kept brushing her hair. He brushed and shushed, very gentle, because he was, at heart, a very gentle man—but the pain looked terrible. Aubry's body twisted like rope, legs kicking.

"Let me see what I can find," he said and he rushed to the pantry to find medicines.

Pauline, at the door, watched her sister convulse, so terrified that she'd forgotten her orders. Then, as if slapped across the face, she tore herself away and ran out the front door to fetch Dr. Homais.

Aubry gasped for air. So much effort to draw such shallow breaths, as if an anvil lay on her chest. Her body spasmed so hard it could have broken bones. Her mother, tears in her eyes, leapt on her daughter, held her tight in her arms to keep her from ripping apart.

Then it ended. Aubry was stiff, but the spasms had gone. She could hear it, around her, all these voices choked with fear.

"Mother," she whispered, her eyes wide and full of alarm, "what is this?"

Her mother could only hold her close, shush in her ear, and make promises she prayed she could keep. "Shhhh . . . We will find out and make you better," she said. "Shhhh . . ."

Another series of convulsions struck and Aubry gasped. Her windpipe knotted up, lungs without air. Her arms and legs curled and twisted, hands became claws. Her terrified mother held on to her tight and refused to let go, feeling her little girl rattle against her chest, listening to her choke until her eyes rolled up in her head and she fell unconscious.

6

Home

When Aubry woke up, she was in a carriage, wrapped in blankets and her mother's arms. The night air felt cool. She heard the horse hooves clopping down the cobblestoned avenue. "Am I going somewhere?" she asked her mother. Oh, the smile her mother put on.

"We're taking you to Dr. Homais's office."

Aubry looked and there he was, seated in the cab across from them, Dr. Homais himself, a paunchy, bespectacled man with red cheeks and a few gray hairs still clinging to his head.

"Hello, Aubry," he said. "I am Dr. Homais. At my office I have all the proper instruments and medicines. So make no mistake, I'm going to take very good care of you."

"I feel better already," she said. If someone else had said this, it would have been mere politeness, but Aubry meant it. She was already feeling better, even without Dr. Homais's instruments and medicines.

"Good, Aubry," said her mother, who didn't understand. "Very good."

By the time they arrived at Dr. Homais's office, Aubry was fine. Dr. Homais examined her thoroughly and found nothing wrong. They waited another hour in case the symptoms returned. Meanwhile, Dr. Homais researched his textbooks and Aubry sat on the examination table swinging her legs, also reading Dr. Homais's textbooks, drawn to the ghastly pictures. Her poor mother sat in a corner and stared—first at Aubry, then out the third-floor windows, at nocturnal Paris, soft and glowing with gaslight.

"So her symptoms were . . . let's see . . ." Dr. Homais said, checking the notes he had scribbled down, glancing between them and his textbooks. "Involuntary muscle spasms . . . shortness of breath . . . Was there excessive perspiration?"

"Oh, it was awful, Doctor," said her mother. "We flew into a panic!"

"Yes, I see." There was a trace of skepticism in his voice that didn't go unnoticed. It hardly mattered. They saw what they saw and it was terrible.

An hour later, Aubry was bored, still on the examination table. She was no longer swinging her legs but examining Dr. Homais's instruments instead.

"The thing is," Dr. Homais said, sitting beside her mother, talking low so Aubry couldn't hear them, or so they thought, "is that unless she exhibits these symptoms here and now, I really have nothing to examine, no way to make a prognosis. You understand?"

"I understand," said her mother, defeated.

They put on coats, were packed into a carriage, and sent home. Dr. Homais came with them, skeptical but cautious. Aubry was no longer wrapped up in blankets or in her mother's arms. She was feeling fine, not even tired, considering the hour and all she'd been through.

But as the carriage turned familiar corners, her skin began to prickle. Her stomach began to churn—not much, but her body clenched up and she quietly prepared herself, just in case.

"Are we headed home?" she asked.

"Yes," said her mother.

"I can feel it."

When the carriage came to her house, she did not want to step out.

"Come on," said her mother. "Aren't you excited to be home?"

Her mother took her by the hand.

Aubry was afraid, but said nothing. Had her mother seen her eyes in that dim gaslight, she'd never have pulled her along, tugging at her hand all the way down the cobblestone walk toward the front door. It was already open, her father and sisters gathered there anxiously. Her mother led, then hauled, but Aubry was deadweight, like pulling a sledge.

"What is it?" she said.

Aubry pulled back like a nervous dog, caught in the flickering light for her whole family to see.

"Oh my God!" cried her father.

Sylvie screamed.

Her face was dripping in blood, from her nose, her ears, her mouth. Her mother gasped—she'd had no idea. She let go of Aubry's hand and Aubry buckled over, clutching her stomach, coughing up a lungful of blood and vomit onto the front steps.

"Dr. Homais! Dr. Homais!" cried her mother, but Pauline was already ahead of her, racing to the carriage.

Aubry was on her hands and knees, quivering over a black puddle, strands of red saliva swinging from her chin. Her father snatched her up, leaving behind small bloody handprints on the cobblestones. He carried her to the carriage where Dr. Homais watched, open-mouthed. Her mother and father piled inside, Dr. Homais urging the driver on. They forgot all about her two sisters on the front lawn in their nightgowns and slippers. But they refused to be left behind, not with their baby sister so ill.

They chased after the carriage. Before the horses could break into a gallop, Pauline leapt onto the splash guard, clinging to the rear iron, and pulled Sylvie up behind her.

Together they rode, wordlessly, through the Paris night, watching home recede behind them.

7

Home

The combined strength of Dr. Homais and her father couldn't re-strain Aubry. They threw their weight onto her as if to flatten the girl out, but her arms spasmed and her legs kicked and her spine twisted beneath them all the same. Her shoes flew off, yet they couldn't wrench her from her coat, she flailed so violently. She screamed, coughed, and spat. The examination table was slick with blood and everyone's clothes were stained red.

It wasn't just convulsions. It was Aubry, slippery as seaweed, pushing them away, trying to escape. Her father saw but didn't understand. He was thinking the sickness must have invaded her mind. He thought this was Aubry's insubordinate streak flaring up at the worst possible time.

Huddled in a corner of the room, Aubry's mother clutched Sylvie and Pauline in her arms, the three of them sobbing. Pauline was frightened, but she watched it all. She needed to see. She needed to know, she told Aubry later. Blood had splattered her nightgown, too. But Sylvie, too gentle for the sight of it, buried her head in her mother's clothes and covered her ears.

Dr. Homais thought Aubry might bite her own tongue off, so he wedged a piece of wood between her teeth. She lashed out as if they were drowning her in a bathtub. Her muscles were hurtling, her spine arching and collapsing, over and over. And still they held her down. She couldn't move, couldn't speak, but kept looking for a way out. She caught sight of the window behind Dr. Homais. There, breaking across distant spires and rooftops, a sunrise burned up the night. She reached for it but her father slapped her arms back down.

Aubry never knew where she got the strength, but she sucked in air and braced herself. She gathered what she could of her muscles, her body anchor-chain taut. She hardened herself there on the table, stuck in a horribly twisted shape, backbone wrenched, fingers curled—but she had halted the fight, the spasms, the thrashing.

For a few moments, her body was a fist, her breathing shallow but controlled. The room went quiet, nothing more than the gurgle of blood in the back of her throat. Her father and Dr. Homais exchanged glances, not quite convinced. Then the doctor ran to his medicine cabinet, fumbled through medicines, clamps, and needles.

She looked into her father's eyes, then at the window, then at him, then at the window.

"What?" he asked her, trying to understand.

He followed her stare, looked over his shoulder at the breaking sunrise.

And before anybody could react, Aubry broke free of her father and ran to the door.

"Aubry!" screamed her mother.

"Grab her!" shouted Dr. Homais.

But she'd already swung the door open wide and bolted down the stairs. Sylvie—Aubry would never forget—stood in the doorway, shouting, "Run, Aubry! Run!"

8

_____

Home

She ran, while the sky was still pink and the city still asleep, while dew still beaded on the grass and wet the cobblestones, rinsing the blood from her bare feet. She took a sharp turn, sprinted down an alley, face and hands still smeared with blood. There was no saving her coat or blouse, stained red, but she didn't care because she was free and running and shedding her sickness behind her. Every step made her breath flow easier, made the pain slip a little farther away. She knew this would be her strategy from now on. She would outrun it. She would stay ahead of this illness and never let it catch her again.

She ran all the way to a wide boulevard, somewhere she'd never been before, and sprinted the length of it. She was alone, airways clear, the bleeding stopped. Her bones were looser with every step. She laughed through her tears, felt better than ever, ran faster than before.

But then she heard her mother's voice, behind her, calling out, "Aubry! Aubry! Where are you going?"

Aubry had been spotted, but she didn't care. Ahead, at the end of the boulevard, a small fountain. She ran to it, sank her hands in the cold water, scrubbed them clean. She watched the blood dissipate and felt unquestionably good.

Then her mother caught up to her.

"Are you mad? Are you trying to kill yourself? Is that it? Do you want to die and break my heart?"

"I'm not going back there."

Her mother grabbed her by the arm, as if to drag her all the way back to Dr. Homais's office.

"I'm not going back! I'm not!" Aubry screamed at her, trying to wrench her arm free. "Look at me! I'm not sick anymore! Do I look sick? I feel fine!"

Her mother looked Aubry up and down, bloodstained from head to toe.

"Oh, you look wonderful."

Aubry broke free anyway and washed her face until the water ran clear from her skin. She turned and showed off her clean, healthy face.

"I am not going back. It will kill me. That place will kill me."

They were both on their feet, facing each other, ready to battle. Instead, because neither of them knew what to say next, Aubry took a breath and calmed herself. Her mother was amazed. Aubry had never taken a breath to calm herself in her life. This was not the daughter she knew. Aubry could be as fierce as a beaten dog. Her tantrums were legendary. Fighting was in her nature.

Instead, Aubry said, "I'm going for a walk. Mama, walk with me."

Her mother looked around suspiciously, as if a trick were being played on her. She looked at Aubry, really looked, but Aubry was fine, disheveled, nothing more. Aubry's mother was thinking that this was no longer her little girl. That Aubry had been left behind at the family dinner table. That's what pain does. It shatters everything. She'd seen it with her own mother, the stroke that destroyed her. Pain rewrites your future, how you think you're going to live your life. It gives you a whole new way of looking at comfort and happiness. To a headstrong nine-year-old it was an apocalypse. She thought she'd better get to know this new daughter of hers, so she gave in and they walked.

They came to a small park, green and tidy, elegant facades of apartment buildings on all sides.

"Mama, where is this place?"

Her mother hardly looked up. They'd walked in silence the entire way, her mother's head filled with fears.

"I'm not sure. Boulevard de Beauvillé?"

"Why haven't you taken me before?"

"There are many places I haven't taken you. I can't take you to them all."

"It's pretty, don't you think?"

"I'm not in the mood for pretty."

"I am. Let's sit on a bench and look."

They found a park bench and sat. Her mother stared at the ground, weary, despairing. But Aubry was looking up. Behind her, the sunrise sent light radiating across the rooftops and the topmost leaves of the trees. Before her, a row of townhouses caught the sun in their windows and flared. Reflected light shone back on her face and felt like a bath in warm oil.

Aubry tugged at her mother's hand.

"Look," she said.

Her mother squinted into the golden light that spotlit them both. For a moment, they were transfixed, taken elsewhere, witnesses to a place they could not name.

Then, back in Paris, they heard her father's voice.

"Aubry! Josette!"

Her mother turned, saw him coming, running across the park with Pauline and Sylvie in tow. Her mother raised a hand, with a small, sad smile that made him pause.

"Your father will not understand," she said.

"It'll be hard," said Aubry, "but he will."

"Then I don't understand."

Her father approached the park bench, saw Aubry patting her mother's hand, and was confused. Of the two of them, Aubry was the collected one and her mother, who hadn't had so much as a sniffle, the patient.

They were all there, her father, Pauline, Sylvie, all of them panting. They sat on the park bench across from Aubry and her mother, as if this were a simple family discussion, though Pauline and Sylvie were still in their nightgowns and all of them were splattered with blood.

"What are you doing here?" her father asked.

"I look good, right?" Aubry said. "Much better."

"She does," Sylvie agreed.

"That doesn't mean you can just run off like that," said her father.

"No," said Aubry. "I'm better because I ran off like that. Have you been here before?"

"It's Caillié Parc," said Pauline. "Catherine Duguay from my etiquette class sometimes brings me here."

Aubry looked over at her father. "I can't go home again. You know I can't."

"What are you talking about? I know no such thing!"

"You saw what happened."

"But that's not . . ." he began, then started over. "There's no . . ." And still he couldn't get anything out.

It was such an outrageous thing to say, even in hindsight. The clear-eyed logic of a nine-year-old. Everyone sat in stunned silence, except Sylvie, who said, "When Mrs. Noland got sick her doctor told her to travel."

"She was asthmatic!" said her father. "She needed somewhere warm and dry!"

"Maybe Aubry needs somewhere, too."

"Like where?" asked her mother.

Another long silence. Aubry noticed all eyes were on her, as if she knew—but then, maybe she did. "Anywhere," she said.

"For God's sake," muttered her father. "Listen to you. You're not Hippocrates! You're a nine-year-old girl! What do you know of it?"

"I don't think anyone knows more of it than me," Aubry said. Her voice was small, especially small for Aubry, but it contained no doubts. It was as if she were speaking for the whole family. She turned to Pauline. "Pauline, would you pack me some clothes?"

Pauline hesitated. She didn't want to agree, but what she'd seen—the blood, the pain—and something in Aubry's show of mettle, too—made her concede. "Yes," she said.

"Sylvie, would you bring me my puzzle ball?"

"Of course."

"Oh wait," said Aubry, reaching into her coat pocket. "Here it is." The puzzle ball had been in her coat pocket all along, though she couldn't remember bringing it.

"This is ridiculous," said her father. He could see the situation slipping from his hands, if he'd ever had a grip at all. He thought it was madness, but his or theirs, he couldn't tell.

"I don't think I can carry much more than that," Aubry said. Even she was amazed at her composure, her foresight. She still is. People look at children sometimes and wonder how they do the miraculous things they do. Aubry looks back on herself and she has no answer either, but she'd felt pain, life-altering pain, and never wanted to feel it again. She'd felt fear and didn't like that either, not one bit. Already, she understood the way she used to live was over. She didn't know in what way, or to what extent, but she knew she would adjust. She would have to. In a sense, her spoiled, headstrong personality was perfectly suited to this—who else could make such impossible decisions but a stubborn nine-year-old, a little girl who knew next to nothing about the world?

"Dear Lord, Henri," her mother pleaded to her father, but he only stared at the ground, deep inside himself, trying to figure out what to do in a world he didn't understand.

"Where are you going to stay?" asked Pauline.

"Right here," said Aubry.

"On a park bench?" snapped her father.

"No . . . I don't know."

"Look," said Pauline, and she pointed. "There's a hotel over there."

They all turned and saw it, looming at the far end of the park.

"And then what?" her father kept saying. "Eh? What about tomorrow? And the next night? What then?"

9

A Riverboat in Siam

"You were right," she says to Mr. Holcombe, who is leaning forward in his seat, who listens without interruption. No one moves. They let the big engine chug its black smoke, let the river flow beneath the hull under their feet. They let the wash of green jungle float past.

"You were right to be cautious," she says. "I've lived with this so long I forget how it seems to others. You were right to protect your family."

Mr. Holcombe's eyes lower a moment, but he shows no other reaction, just the kindness of his silence.

"Did you stay at the hotel?" asks Mrs. Holcombe.

"I did. For two days."

The question hangs in the air until Sophie asks it.

"Why not three?"

10

The Art of Exile

The hotel was a pleasant one. They could have gone to the dining room for breakfast, with its embroidered woodwork, mirrors, and skylights, but they chose to stay in their room instead. Aubry was eating at the secretary when the drop of blood landed in her porridge.

"Mama," she said, as if she were apologizing. Perhaps she was.

A half an hour later they were marching down the street looking for their next hotel. Three days after that, they were looking again. And so it went, staying at a new hotel for two, three, or—if they were very lucky—four days, until the pain hit like a sledgehammer to her spine and they were forced to move on.

They met with doctors in different hotel rooms, visited hospitals they passed along the way. How many doctors in that first year alone—forty? Fifty? More? It was a year of needles and probes, of pills and powders that came to nothing. There was a doctor from Italy who carried a jar of medicinal maggots in his suitcase. There was a Spanish doctor who believed electricity to be a cure-all and was eager to try his patented electropathic prod. One taste of that and Aubry refused to see any more doctors from Spain. Most frightening of all was a fellow Frenchman who wanted to drill a hole in Aubry's head. He claimed it would relieve pressure on the brain, and his office gleamed with surgical knives and hammers. Her parents, in their desperation, briefly considered it. If Pauline and Sylvie hadn't pleaded on her behalf, what might have happened then? All forgotten now, those doctors, their names and faces, their diagnoses, theories, their confusion. She was in the newspapers already. People were talking. Every doctor in the city wanted to be the one to cure Aubry Tourvel. As if the disease wasn't torture enough.

The best way to survive some things, thought Aubry, was not to understand them.

Their stays formed a circular route around Paris until even Paris became too small. They spiraled out of the city and into the outskirts. They didn't want to travel so far from home, but there was no helping it. Soon, it was clear—Paris was to be something in Aubry's past.

Her sisters, her father, had kept up for a while. They visited Aubry and her mother in whatever hotel they were at, but her sisters had school and her father had work. As Aubry's escape took her farther away, she saw them less and less. When she did see them, on weekends or holidays, she'd always ask what they were learning. They didn't want to tell her. They knew Aubry missed school, friends, even her horrid teachers. Everyone understood she would never have the education other children did. Her mother tried to tutor Aubry in math and reading. She tried to lead discussions on classic literature, algebraic methods, the history of Rome, but had no knowledge and no passion to teach it even if she did. She'd been an average student at best, and most of that forgotten long ago.

One winter morning, her mother received a letter from Pauline and Sylvie—both back home helping their father maintain the household. They wrote to tell her that Mrs. Von Bingham's baby had finally died of her illness, but not to tell Aubry. She never asked why, but did as she was told. It would be another six years before Aubry found out, by then, too late to grieve, too late to be forgiven.

Another winter morning. Her mother thought maybe Sylvie was right, maybe a warm dry climate was just what Aubry needed—blue vaulted skies, clean white air. Even the great composer, Chopin, had gone all the way to Majorca to find relief from his tuberculosis. Why shouldn't they?

They set out immediately for Provence, stopping in Bourges, Lyon, Valence, and other cities along the way. The temperatures grew warmer, the air more pristine. They patiently waited for her symptoms to improve. When they had to leave the first few hotels after two, three, or—if they were very lucky—four days, they didn't see it as a setback because they knew these things took time. They traveled the southern coast of France, through Italy, and, three years later, found themselves in Croatia, following the Adriatic coast, exhausted and almost penniless.

11

A Riverboat in Siam

"And then?" asks Sophie. "Did you go farther?"

"Yes."

"And farther?"

"Yes."

"And farther after that?"

"And even farther."

12

The Art of Exile

There was once a carriage ride in some nameless town in the Austro-Hungarian Empire—at least Aubry thinks it was there—after days of rough travel, nights of sleeping hard in strange beds, after hours of counting what was left of their money and haggling with the locals over the price of bread—where she remembers her mother, bent and weary in the back of the cab, breaking down beside her, not for the first time.

"I don't want to take you to Athens or London or Stockholm," she said. "What I want is to take you home. I want to watch you play with your sisters. I want to tuck you into your bed and stay up all night with Henri and talk about what lovely children we have . . ."

She didn't say any more after that, just cried quietly to herself in the back of the carriage until they arrived at a cheap boarding-house and slept like the dead.

"What did you do?" asks Somerset.

"I left a note, said goodbye, and stole away in the middle of the night," she tells them.

Emily's hand goes to her mouth. Time passes. No other movement than that, not until Sophie rests her hand on Aubry's arm.

She looks at Aubry with big round eyes, but Aubry doesn't dare look back.

"There was no cure," she explains, "and I couldn't go to school, and our money was running out, and I realized I had become a terrible burden to my family. My poor mama. She was so worn out."

The act itself wasn't so hard. It wasn't as painful as hearing her mother cry herself to sleep all those times. It wasn't nearly as hard as that. No, once she'd decided, she simply did it, quickly, efficiently. That's what her sickness had taught her.

By then, she was twelve. She wasn't a child anymore—at least, she didn't think so—but neither was she grown. She wrote a short simple note, leaving it on the pillow next to her mother. She can still see her face, calm, almost smiling, escaped to dreams of home. Some things stick to memory, images mostly, like that one. She gathered a few of her most precious things—her puzzle ball, her coat—and shut the door quietly behind her. How her mother must have panicked the next morning, the next week, the next year. Aubry hoped her note would console her but how could it? Even a twelve-year-old knows that. How long did her mother linger in that village, searching, waiting for her daughter to return? What was going through her head on her long trip back to Paris, alone?

Aubry looks up. Past the ferry railings, protruding through the Asian jungle like arrowheads shot through a green hide, are a series of golden pagodas, drifting by, glinting in the tropical sun.

"Your poor mother," says Emily Holcombe.

"I did my best," Aubry says. "I wrote whenever I could, told them where I was, where I was going. She was suffering." Something about the pagodas, the way they catch the sunlight in their gold and radiate it back, transfixes her. "I could live with many things, but not with that."

"I couldn't have either," offers Mr. Holcombe.

"Did you ever see them again?" asks Sophie.

"Oh yes. They would send me money if they knew where I was going to be, and sometimes we would rendezvous."

Those were happy days, meeting on the beaches of Dover, or a village in Spain, once in the Azores, where Aubry rushed down the docks and into the arms of her parents and sisters. They would gather around and, because Aubry always lost track of the years, she would ask them, "How old am I?" And they would answer her—nineteen, twenty-two, twenty-three, twenty-eight. Today, her best guess is thirty, but only her family knows for sure.

Those days came later. They'd adjusted by then. Before that came the hardships, the not-knowing.

"Those first days," she says to no one.

She could tell the Holcombes about living homeless in the streets of Croatia, about stealing food left out for stray cats in Montenegro, about smelling so foul she was chased out of a market in Greece. She could tell them how she once stole a fish carcass from a restaurant's trash bin but lost it to an angry neighborhood dog. She could tell them how she learned not to beg because in some places beggars were beaten, or jailed, or worse. She could tell them about sleeping in alleyways, sleeping in sewer drains, sleeping uncovered in the wilds, in the rain, without fire, without hope, and the pools of blood she sometimes left behind. She could tell them all these things.

But she doesn't.

She doesn't tell them about that first night, the night she abandoned her mother in that little inn somewhere near the Adriatic coast. She doesn't tell them how she stepped onto the cobblestone street, took a deep breath, and picked a direction. She doesn't tell them how her hands trembled. She'd been planning her disappearance for weeks, maybe months. You'd think she'd have built up the courage by then, but she hadn't.

Yet she kept walking, toward the low coastal mountains she could see even in the dark, looming over the village. Her feet led her and she didn't question it. Her heart pounded and her body shook, but she kept going. An hour later she was walking up a steep wooded trail. An hour after that, the sun was just beginning to rise. She turned around for the first time to see how far she'd come, something she'd promised herself she wouldn't do. She could see the town below but had no idea where the inn was. It was for the best, she thought. She might just stare at it the rest of the day, lose her nerve, and go sobbing back into the arms of her poor mother.

Instead, she kept going, mindlessly, sleepwalking through a pine forest. To retrace her steps was to tempt the disease. There was no going back, not ever. She made her mind a blank and walked the rest of the day like that.

When she finally stopped to rest, she was exhausted and hungry. She'd brought some bread but had eaten it all. It was the middle of the woods, and dark, and she didn't know where or when the next village would be. Suddenly she was terrified.

She had no idea how to fend off wolves or bears. She didn't know how to build a fire, hadn't even thought to bring a match. She climbed a tree and half-slept in its branches. She wore all her clothes to keep from freezing and still shivered through the night.

In the morning she wondered if it was too late to turn back. It hadn't been more than a day at that inn. Perhaps she could squeeze out another day? Two? She imagined retracing her steps, even as she continued deeper into the mountains. She imagined a tearful reunion with her mother, even as she spotted a new town in the distance. She thought about her mother sharing a pastry with her for breakfast, even as she stood on the streets of this strange new city and wondered where she was going to find something to eat.

She didn't know how to beg, but she'd seen a thousand beggars by now, and every time wondered if that was in store for her. Now she wandered the streets and, with as little thought as possible, held out her hand. Don't think, she told herself. Just act.

Nobody put a thing into it.

It wasn't a small town—three church steeples, a small lake in its center. People were everywhere and they all avoided her— avoided her eyes, her outstretched hand. A new fear came over Aubry—fear of exile, starvation, of having no plan that might keep her alive. She'd known this fear would come, but now it was here, fully arrived, and it was worse than she'd imagined. It hollowed her belly out. It numbed her brain and dried her mouth.

She remembered the days of being proud, now that she was sitting in the mouth of an alleyway, holding out her empty hand to disinterested strangers. She'd once believed that it was possible to control the world, to make it bend to her personal sense of justice. What a child she was. How foolish she'd been, how haughty. She had friends back in Paris who never fought with their teachers, who would be going to the best schools and getting the best jobs, while she was begging on the streets of an unknown city. Now she knew, without a doubt, that she did not command the world, but was at the mercy of it. It's a lesson most people learn at some point in their lives, but the realization that the world is a bigger and more powerful thing than you are, learned in such a merciless way, was a lot for a proud twelve-year-old girl to come to grips with, so suddenly, and with such little room for error.

She lingered in that village for two more days, hardly ate more than a few nibbles, slept behind a hedge of bushes. At night, she curled into a ball, and wept like a winter storm. Then her illness came and chased her away.

The countryside was different. Here, she followed dirt roads through poor farming communities and looked into the eyes of every passing stranger. One old man handed over a fistful of lamb jerky, patted her on the head, and walked on with his mule in tow. Aubry was speechless. She couldn't even thank him, just stood dumbly on the road and watched him lead his mule away until he was gone.

Another man gave her a handful of leeks from the pack of vegetables he carried on his back. She didn't make the same mistake twice. She bowed and thanked him with the few words of Croatian she'd learned.

Days later, she caught the attention of a boy plucking olives from his family orchard. He smiled at her, said something that sounded friendly. For a moment, she thought she'd captured his heart, but then she understood—the boy was strong and handsome and she was weak and dirty. All she could capture was pity.

So she rubbed her belly.

He ran to the barn and came back with two apples and a pail of milk so fresh it was still warm. His father came over to see this vagabond for himself and brought her some bread. Then his mother, in an elaborate pantomime, offered Aubry a bed in their stables. Aubry thanked them through her tears. She was asleep before nightfall, stayed like that for another day and a half—a day and a half without fear.

Then there was the painful twist in her gut, the stiffening of her spine. Because there was no way to explain, she stole away while the family was busy in their kitchen.

If she could do it again, she would go back and thank that family, thank them on her knees, but there is no retracing her

steps. Once she had been, there was no way back, every departure irreversible. But at least she'd learned to avoid the cities and
embrace the countryside.

That much she could say, so she did, and explained to the
Holcombes the art of exile.

13

I Have Learned to Hunt

She tells the Holcombes all she has learned about the kindness of others: that she survived on charity for a long time, that she received the most generosity from the poorest homes, the best trash from the richest. She tells them how she learned to forage the forests, but warns them how little is actually there.

There was once a family who invited her into their small home in the highlands of Nicaragua, where she sat with a long-married couple, their seven children, and a pair of grandparents. She shared a simple but generous meal with them though they could hardly afford it. She tried to leave them money, do some chores for them, but they refused. "The way we see it, you have traveled all this way to meet us," one of the grandparents explained.

"Had you?" asks Sophie.

"Perhaps it was true, in its own way. The more you move," says Aubry, "the more available you are to chance and little wonders."

At this, Mr. Holcombe nods in agreement.

Aubry knows there are dangers out there. She's not naïve. Wars are as common as bad weather and she is mindful to avoid them. There are desert nomads in North Africa who dogmatically enslave all non-Muslims. There is an island in the Bay of Bengal where outsiders are attacked on sight.

But even after subtracting all that, there is a lifetime of world left to explore.

Mostly, she tells them how far she walked, day after day, until her feet burned, until her muscles went numb, and then grew strong. She tells them she can now walk from dawn to dusk under a torrid sun without breaking a sweat, the vast distances she can go without getting hungry, without eating more than a few scraps a day. She remembers days without water, weeks without food, and the strength she had still astounds her.

She tells them how she once begged a scrap from an Ottoman fisherman. He knew some French and asked her what she had to give in return.

"Nothing," Aubry said.

"What kind of trade is that?" he said, but gave her a fish anyway. She ate in front of a hungry alley cat, tossing it the bones, but she'd taken his point—from now on she'd need to find something to offer.

She found an empty butcher's shop and stole a knife. She scurried through backyards and stole a broom. She went to a quiet spot in the forest and whittled the broom handle into a sharp point. Now she had a spear and spent months learning it.

She walked and threw and walked and threw. She speared tree after tree. She threw distances that were farther and farther. She learned to be swift and light. Her aim improved but her spear became blunted. She constantly whittled it back to a point. She experimented, charred the tip of her spear in fire to make it black and hard and that helped, slathered it in tree resin and that helped even more.

"If you ever need to know," she tells Sophie and Somerset, "the best way to make a wooden spearpoint is to whittle it down, rub it in bird fat, toast it in a fire, then find a river stone and polish it to a sheen."

One day, after a dozen attempts, she speared a fish and cooked it. The next day, she speared and cooked another, even remembered to gut it first. It went on like this for weeks, skewering fish in streams, spearing birds out of trees.

She even speared a rabbit in mid-leap. She still remembers the feeling she had—a clean hit, right through its middle, punching the life from its tiny body. She stood over it, amazed, as happy as she'd been since before the illness took her. To this day, she remembers it as one of the most perfect strikes in all her life. But mostly she remembers it was the day she finally felt unafraid.

She caught so many rabbits, fish, and birds she was able to peddle a few, earn some money for new clothes, some sweets, and, by the time she arrived in Greece, her first letter home.

"I have learned to hunt," she wrote to her family.

And this letter, at long last—she can't express how she felt. It'd been a year—no, even longer—maybe two, since she'd left her mother, a year or two of her family living in ignorance and worry. The letter was a cure-all, like a light in a cave. Now that she was a hunter—now that she could trade—there would be many more.

She noticed fishermen with their harpoons and admired the iron points. She decided her spear must have an iron point, too, but she would need more money. A wild boar would do the trick, she thought. How foolish she was. A wild boar. The most dangerous animal in that part of the world, and Aubry, only half-grown, set out to kill one.

The watering hole was hidden in the mountains. Even the locals didn't know of it. But Aubry knew, and when a family of boars came along, she aimed at the big one—not a small one, not a practice boar, but the biggest one she saw. She waited for her moment, then threw—and missed. The boars ran into the thickets and trees, vanishing like echoes. The next day, she missed again. For three days, she missed.

On that third day, the boars turned on her. She dropped her spear and ran, scurrying up the nearest tree. She waited there for hours, but the hunt wasn't wasted. She studied that boar, grunting in circles around her tree. Many ideas came to her. One stuck.

On her fourth day—how lucky to have a fourth day!—she stalked right up to that boar—that big powerful male with the tusks curving out of his head—and pelted him with rocks. The boar charged. Aubry ran, the boar shrieking at her heels. She ran, leapt, grabbed the hanging bough, and lifted herself to safety, the boar growling beneath her.

But in the tree limbs were her spear and a bagful of rocks. She began a barrage, pelting that boar, whipping him into a rage. This was what she wanted—an angry thoughtless boar. She climbed as low as she dared and took aim with her spear. When the boar was as perfectly positioned as he was going to get, Aubry dropped from the tree with the spear pointed downward like a railroad spike. Even without an iron point, it slammed through the boar's skull, nailing its head to the earth.

She butchered it on the spot. She didn't have proper tools. She didn't have experience. The work was exhausting and took hours. She stripped it of its hide, scraped away the blood and viscera, and draped it on a rock to dry. Slicing cuts of meat was only slightly easier. Soon, she felt her own blood pooling in the back of her throat, the pain building in her joints. She worked through it, just long enough to gather her efforts and march to a new town at the foot of the hill. There, she went straight into its market, carrying the weight of a dismembered boar on her back.

The meat sold right away, fresh, straight from their own mountains. After the meat, someone else bought the hide. After the hide, someone else bought the tail. Aubry had no idea what anyone would do with a tail. Someone else bought the bones and someone even bought the teeth. The skull she left behind, though she probably could have sold that, too. These Greeks had a use for everything. She sold that boar for half its worth—what did Aubry know about selling boar? But her pockets jingled with coins and that was all that mattered. She took her money and went hunting for a blacksmith.

The iron point was narrow and sharp. It was fitted into a hole bored into a new shaft by a local carpenter. She'd wanted a spear-point with a barb in its side, but that would've cost more, so she had the idea of carving the barb into the wood instead. She was so happy with her new spear that she wanted to go back to that Ottoman fisherman, to hug him and thank him for his advice—but, of course, she could never go back.

14

A Riverboat in Siam

Sophie and Somerset are delighted with Aubry's stories of survival and all eyes fall upon her walking stick. She reaches back, lays it across her lap.

They have a corner of the port stern to themselves, in the shade of the lower deck. The walking stick is long and straight but one end bulges slightly, as if carved from the knot of a tree. With no eyes upon them, the Holcombes watch Aubry give the end of her walking stick a twist. The tip disconnects, slides off like a scabbard, revealing the black iron spearpoint hidden inside.

"Is that it?" asks Somerset in a low whisper. "Is that the spear you made?"

"Well, let's see," she tells him. "I have replaced the shaft many times—I am always breaking things—and gone through five spearpoints. Is it the same spear? It looks the same. But I don't know. Is it the same spear? You tell me."

Their fingers all caress the dark iron, thinner and finer than they'd expected, as black as bottled ink. Occasionally it catches light like a starling's feather, an oil-slick rainbow on its blade.

"Be careful," Aubry warns them. "It's very sharp."

"It's actually quite beautiful," says Mrs. Holcombe. Their

58

heads all lean to see the sinuous sweeps and hooks of the three-sided point. Their voices have fallen to a hush, as if speaking over a religious relic.

"I am very particular," explains Aubry. "I track down the best craftsman I can find and have it made to very exact specifications. This was made by a woman, the daughter of a renowned Japanese ironsmith. The barb is now here, part of the iron instead of the wood. Down here at this end is the hole where I can thread a line if I am hunting sharks or seals. The shaft is carved from Australian ironwood and it's very strong. I don't think I will break this one. I certainly hope I don't."

"Gorgeous," says Mr. Holcombe.

"The newspapers said nothing about wells or spears," says Mrs. Holcombe.

"Newspapers said nothing about shark attacks or puberty but those happened to me, too," says Aubry. "I only have so much time. I can't tell them everything."

"You can tell us!" says Sophie.

"I will try," Aubry tells her. Even as she says it, she knows she won't.

"Maybe," says Somerset, "if we put all the conversations you ever had with every stranger you ever met, we could put your whole life together."

"Maybe that would work. But I'd be afraid to read it."

"Why?" ask Sophie.

Aubry's lips curl, but she says nothing. She recaps her spear.

"We should learn this!" says Somerset to his sister as Aubry props the spear up in the corner—the spear now cleverly disguised as an ordinary, but very tall, walking stick.

"If you do nothing else in life, learn a skill," she tells them. "One useful skill people need. That will get you far."

"Did spear-throwing get you far?" asks Sophie.

"I should say so." Aubry leans forward to tell. "The next time a fisherman asked if I had something to trade, I showed him."

It happened in Andros in the Greek isles when she was fifteen—or was she sixteen by then? In a single fluid moment, she launched her spear across the street into the narrowest tree, nearly splitting it open. The skinny curmudgeon who had mocked her, sitting three inches to the left, was so shocked, so terrified to see that spear flying at him, he toppled over in his chair. The fishermen who witnessed it—the ones who weren't laughing—stared slack-jawed.

That'll shut him up, she thought. Her hunting skills had revived her confidence, if not her happiness. But this wasn't the pride of a spoiled little girl. This was something ferocious, something reserved for children raised in the wilds.

Within an hour, there were no less than a dozen offers of employment, spearing spigolas or fin whales, anything that might fetch a good price at the market. Aubry considered each of these weather-beaten men, studying them closely. She took the offer from the old, grizzled captain with white hair and a chin full of stubble. She never could explain why. She sensed a grace in him, she supposed—something heavy, like knowledge no one wants. She departed Greece on his boat early the next morning.

Later in life, her spear would take her on expeditions with the Unangax, hunting seals from their kayaks in a half-frozen sea. She would race through the African scrub practically naked, chasing ostriches with the Bushmen of the Kalahari. She would fight back a charging bear with the Sámi in cold Norwegian forests, her spear among a phalanx of spears. Her most thrilling moment—leaping from the bow of that big wooden canoe off the New Guinea coast, airborne for an endless moment, calculating how to land her feet on the back of the great humpback whale, her spear sinking into its slippery gray flesh, a geyser of seawater and blood from the blowhole soaking her through.

But before anything else, she would be on that lonely Greek fishing boat, patrolling the Mediterranean Sea with a crew of seven men she couldn't and wouldn't talk to, spearing anything too clever for their nets, anything that foolishly swam too close to their vessel.

"Do you speak Greek?" asks Somerset.

"I do now," she tells him.

But then, she knew not a word. When the crew ate below, Aubry ate on deck. When they ate in the cockpit, Aubry ate on the bow. She could hear them, chattering in their language, talking about her, and she could tell it wasn't kind. She saw it in their sideways glances. She knew she seemed sullen and proud to them, always glowering, and it was true. She'd hardly had a conversation with anyone in years. She lived in forests and caves and alleyways. She was not far from a deaf-mute, cut off from the world, as remote as a buried stone. She lived inside herself, formed her own thoughts, her own opinions. She built her own world where she could think what she wanted, where she was never wrong, because no one could tell her otherwise.

She dreamed of her sisters, terrible dreams, of Pauline and Sylvie, playing games at home while she watched them through a window. She dreamed of her mother cooking an elaborate Christmas dinner she would never eat, of sitting on her father's lap while he talked to others, unaware she was there. Only later, in memory, did she appreciate what she had. She wished she'd been a better daughter, a better sister. She wished she had them back. She'd have given anything, but had nothing to give.

She sometimes had a thought that the same way this boat bore her across the sea, she was the vessel her disease rode around the world. It clung to her back, fingers and toes screwed into her bones, gasping and grinning at all the places she went, a happy demon mounted forever on her shoulders. The thought made her feel used and angry. But everywhere she went, every new sight she saw, she could feel her sickness there, huddling in some dark corner of her mind, clinging to her skull and smiling.

"Look at that!" it would say in its low, bone-shaking voice, staring at the stars over the Mediterranean. "I told you it would be beautiful!"

Then she'd wake, early at dawn, scan the horizon for fish, and occasionally spear one. She tinkered with her puzzle ball, ate apart from the crew, and slept, often on deck in the glacial cold of the open sea.

If the crew ever thought of tormenting her, of raping her or throwing her into the sea, Aubry knew the captain would intervene. He didn't hire her for her company. He'd hired her for her skills. But she had a feral streak he respected. She wondered if he had a daughter back in Andros, or if he was childless and regretful in his graying years. She'd already heard his commanding voice shut down the crew's complaints. She knew he often gave her extra food and a bunk isolated from the others. In return, she speared anything and everything, pulling in stray tuna, a swordfish, and on one occasion a rare Risso's dolphin. On that day, even the crew was spellbound, though no one knew for certain how much it was worth.

It turned out to be worth a lot.

After that, the crew gave her more room on the boat, stepped out of her way when they saw her coming. When she dove overboard to wash at night, they no longer rushed to the portholes to gawk. One or two of them even smiled at her on occasion and she nodded back, curt, but not as coldly as she could have.

One day, she realized she'd actually learned Greek, or the beginnings of it. Listening to all that chatter for so long had made its way into her head. She understood half the conversations she overheard. She paid close attention and in another month or two, she'd learned the other half. She learned to swear in Greek, to insult in Greek, how to curse her ancestors in Greek—not that she would ever do such a thing, but if she ever had to, she knew how.

And still she never spoke to any of them.

They docked in a port not so far from Alexandria, on the far side of the sea. Here, they could sell their catch before it spoiled. It was a market the captain knew well, but Aubry had never seen anything like it.

There was sand, an endless horizon of it. A mild breeze could whip a plume of yellow dust into a clear blue sky. There were short spiky trees and camels carrying furniture on their backs. There were buildings many stories high and smooth city walls the color of autumn leaves. There were those who dressed in suits and ties, shirts and slacks, as if plucked straight off the streets of Paris. But the men with their beards and sun-whipped skin, in their long white vests and red tasseled caps, or red vests and white tasseled caps, were unlike any men she'd seen before. And the women, beautiful with their copper bracelets and crowns, hands painted in kaleidoscopic patterns, some even veiled with droplets of silver coins jingling like wind chimes as they walked past. It was overwhelming. Would these people need someone who could throw a spear? Surely they would.

By then she'd carefully fashioned a wooden cap to her spearpoint so it looked like a walking stick. She tied a Greek scarf around her head to imitate the fashions she saw. She had one small bag she slung over her shoulder and, while the crew was busy unloading their catch, she stepped off the boat without a word of explanation. She was peering into the bustle of the crowds, the dust clouds, the strangeness of the city framing it all, when she felt a hand on her shoulder.

The captain stood there, his gray eyes scrutinizing her. He took her hand and pressed a wad of money into it, more than she had asked for or ever imagined. Then he said something, every word of which she understood.

"Be careful. You are a long way from home."

He stood there, his lips taut, his squinty eyes fastened to hers. He didn't let go of her hand for a long moment, but when he did, he turned away and boarded his boat. Maybe he watched her walk away. Maybe the whole crew did. If so, she never turned around to see.

She crept toward the busy city gates, prodding along with her spear-turned-walking-stick. Caravans of camels passed her by, carrying cargoes from the boats—tanned hides, baskets of agate, sweet cardamom pods leaving trails of perfumed air behind them. The entrance to the city was like an enormous keyhole poked through walls three meters thick. She built her nerve. She loosened herself and allowed the currents of traders to pull her along.

On the other side, sun-baked streets.

She took it all in—towers and spires and minarets, the curves of domes over sharp square walls. She wandered aimlessly for hours. Her scarf blew off her head. A friendly businessman retrieved it and a kind young woman showed her how to tie it properly around her head. She bought an egg pastry and the vendor gave her a free orange as well. She liked this city, wondered how long she'd be able to stay. Then it was late in the afternoon, the sun dropping behind the city walls. She found a spot in a wide city square to quietly finish her dinner. She deduced the points of the compass, where the sun was setting, where it would probably rise in the morning.

Then she caught sight of a building, peeking through a gap among houses. It was tall and sleek, domes upon domes, all constructed on a base of horseshoe-shaped arches—so many arches to choose from, and behind them nothing but darkness. She watched but saw no one go in or come out. She found it odd and inexplicably inviting. She finished her orange and crossed the square, slipping through alleys, moving toward the building.

She climbed the steps and peered into its inky interiors. She could hardly see a thing in that blackness and turned to leave— but a wooden clap against the stone floor made her turn back.

Her puzzle ball was on the ground—having somehow fallen out of her pack—and was rolling lazily through the arches. It came to a stop, half-submerged in darkness, as if waiting for her to catch up.

There was something about that darkness, she had to admit, that was comforting—perhaps the idea of seeing without being seen, and perhaps a little of something else she could not describe—a strange tug at her chest, as if she were being pulled along by a string. She picked up her puzzle ball, and took one last look behind her.

Then she walked into the shadows and, as sudden as a startled breath, disappeared.

15

Uzair and the North African Odyssey

Now comes the point in the story where Aubry must decide how much she's going to tell and how much she's going to hold back. She's told the story of her life to many people in many different ways, but she's never told anybody everything, and there are things she's never told at all.

Does she tell them about what she discovered in those shadows? Does she mention the library, the realm of books and scrolls, more than anyone could possibly read in a lifetime, or two lifetimes, or a hundred? That there was hardly a word written in any of them—just pictures, sketches, drawings? Does she mention the hours, the days she spent looking at them? Does she describe the emptiness, the seclusion, a darkness one could almost bathe in? Can she express the way time seemed to loosen itself? It's important, she knows. It is a defining moment, the time spent in the library, this little introduction to the rest of her life. The things she has seen in the world, things no one would believe, is a long and extraordinary list. But the library is the most extraordinary of them all. How does she explain it? Is there a way? No. They'll think she's mad. She thinks the same, sometimes.

She decides, there and then, and hardly for the first time, that some things are better kept to oneself.

She never does explain to the Holcombes how it happened, but much, much later, when she emerged from the shadows—dear God, how long had it been? She doesn't even tell them that—she found herself wandering alleys, bleary and half-starved, her clothes dusty and disheveled, as if she had traveled some great distance but had no memory of it, as if some freak desert storm had carried her off and thrown her down again without mercy.

But how does she explain?

My God, she thinks, a little further in the story and she'd be talking about Uzair. Uzair Ibn-Kadder, a name she hadn't thought of in a long time, the man with all the cures. And in front of the children! She'd scandalize the whole Holcombe family and never forgive herself.

"I think I am tired," she says instead. "And I'm certain I'm a bore."

"Not to me," says Somerset.

"Not to me either," says Sophie.

"Little girl, little boy," says their mother. "She's had enough of talking for a while."

16

A Riverboat in Siam

The ferryboat reaches a port town where the river finally escapes the jungle and broadens into a delta, full of temples, bridges, and markets. The boat docks. Aubry and the Holcombes disembark, stepping off the plank and into the busy street that runs along the riverfront.

Emily turns to her first. "If you have no plans, you're welcome to join us. We're staying at a villa with plenty of room."

"It's true," says Vaughan so she knows the invitation is unanimous.

"Oh, I couldn't," she says politely, though the invitation makes her happy.

"Please come," begs Sophie.

"You can tell us what you saw in the desert," says Somerset.

"I told you what I saw in the desert."

"Not everything."

How keen this Somerset is, to have an inkling of things that haven't been said.

"Really, it would be delightful," urges Emily. They're so sincere. It would be rude to decline.

"Where is it you're staying?" Aubry asks.

"Bangkok."

Aubry's face crumples. "I've been there." Slowly, everyone understands.

Emily frowns and gives Aubry an embrace. "I'm so glad to have met you. You take care of yourself."

"She can't come?" asks Sophie.

"I'm sorry, dear," says Aubry, lowering eye-level with the children.

"We enjoyed listening to you," says Sophie.

"We want to be like you when we grow up," adds Somerset.

"Oh dear, then I've told it all wrong. But you are good children, and smart, and will figure it out." She pulls them close and whispers into their ears, "Thank you for saving me."

She gives each of them a kiss. Then Vaughan takes her by the arm and discreetly pulls her aside.

"Here, take this," he says and hands her a wad of cash. It's thick, too much to accept.

"No. I can't."

"You can and you will. I won't take it back. If you want to get rid of it, you'll have to find a favorite charity," says Vaughan. "It's good business. You don't become an expert at commerce simply by taking. Not everyone understands that."

She tries to explain that her needs are few, that she can spear her own food, that she can earn her own way.

"Would you look at that," says Vaughan suddenly, cutting her off. "Do you see the size of it?"

He points to the thatched eaves of the boathouse over their heads. Up there, a spider as long as a finger waits, bright yellow, alight in the middle of its web. He turns Aubry around to look.

"Do you see it? Sitting there in the center of that web? Away from all the hubbub, all this noise. It's got its own little world up there. Just look at that." His voice is a murmur in her ear. "Reaching out into its little universe, trying to figure out where it is, trying to understand who is shaking its threads."

Aubry looks at the spider, its black legs and speckled yellow body. The silken threads curve on a breeze coursing through the beams. The spider's legs reach out tentatively, then retract again.

When she turns around she is alone. Vaughan is already walking away with his family. They all turn to wave goodbye one last time, especially the children. She waves back. Then they disappear into the crowd.

She stands there a moment, watching until she can no longer see them. They've been wonderful company, excellent listeners, too. She can't remember the last time she talked so much.

She looks around the busy streets, colorful like the rest of Siam, bustling with people, some riding rickshaws, others carrying baskets of produce on their heads. A motorized carriage, imported from America, haltingly pushes through the crowds, blaring a horn.

She picks a direction at random and walks until the crowds thin out and the streets turn to dirt paths cutting through the green. She could explore the city but she prefers the old beaten roads that stretch into the far distances over the chaos of machines and anonymous crowds. Either way she feels small, but the smallness of the dirt trail is her own.

A pair of wandering chickens follows her a while before scurrying under a stilt house. She takes off her sandals. She's learned to enjoy barefoot hiking over the years. She likes the feel of her skin against the skin of the earth—the joys of short grass like peppermint on her feet, the warm dust of desert sand like a dry bath, the assurance of hard, bare granite. The trail narrows. She tosses a stone ahead as a courtesy to snakes and scorpions so they might make their escape before she arrives.

She walks and walks until she feels it spasming inside her carpetbag—her puzzle ball, fighting, bouncing off her backbone as if trying to burst free. She stops in her tracks, turns around, and retraces her steps. She looks to her right, then to her left, into a grove of thick fig trees standing there, a great wooden knot of trunks and roots and low-hanging boughs.

In the center of all that green is a path, tunneling through arches of twisted vines.

Her puzzle ball stops its clamoring.

She takes a cautious step toward it, cocks her head to peer inside. No one goes in or comes out. It is as if this path has rolled itself out like a carpet, as if it had been quietly concealed in the shadows, waiting in ambush exclusively for her.

If only Sophie and Somerset were here to see this. The answer to all their questions, right here, right now. But it never happens that way. She enters alone, always alone.

She slides between the trunks and vines, under the hanging moss. It's a solitary, soundless place. She knows places like this. She's been to them before. A thrill of recognition runs through her. She follows the path through a cathedral of roots and boughs that ends at a door—an inexplicable door with no business standing in a tangle of trees. It is red and blue and green, bright ceremonial colors, edges embroidered with gold. Aubry knows doors like this, too.

She looks over her shoulder, just to make sure this is her door and hers alone. The stillness of the setting overthrows her. If she wasn't so excited, she might feel a deep peace.

Or a loneliness. Yes, there will be that, too—a profound loneliness only these doorways bring.

Still, her heart leaps as if spurred.

I no longer exist, she thinks to herself. Nobody sees me. Nobody knows where I am. I have disappeared from the world. I am gone. And in a moment, I will disappear further still.

Carefully, she turns the knob, pulls the door open, and steps inside.

17

A Brief Aside

A few years later, Aubry escapes a downpour in the cold south-ernmost reaches of Chile by ducking into a small restaurant on the outskirts of Punta Arenas. Though she has conformed to the local clothing style, article by article, her accent hasn't. She catches the attention of an older gentleman with a long, wiz-ened face like a sea turtle. He has arthritis—swollen knuckles, immaculately clean fingernails, and wears his suit starched and pressed and rigid as bone. He invites Aubry to his table for "a chat," as he puts it. She tells him of her travels, the inability to stay in any one place. This amazes him but not the way it amazes others. Others romanticize her illness. They imagine an eternal holiday, which is ludicrous, of course. Does anyone really want an eternal holiday? A holiday is a temporary break from the routine, a chance to shake off the dust of habit, to experiment with new foods and customs, but then to return, perhaps borrowing from the outside, perhaps rejecting it—but either way, a return. In the end we are creatures of habit who prefer possession, security, the bonds of family. But where are Aubry's comforts? Where are her bonds? What are her routines and what, God forbid, can break them?

This man, this prim Chilean, has a different mindset. He

detests travel. He tells her he'd once fancied a trip to Santiago to see what all the fuss was about. He thought it might do him good. After an uncomfortable carriage ride to the station, where he discovered his train was running three hours late, he became hungry and ordered sweet potato empanadas. To his horror, he discovered these empanadas were not to his taste at all, far too sweet, and the café did not carry his favorite tea—in fact, no tea at all. He was forced to try a sweetened tonic water imported from America, which he'd heard of but never pursued. It was a disastrous meal. He thought if a mere trip to the train station had caused him so much unpleasantness, what horrors might a trip to Santiago inflict? He threw his ticket away and headed straight back home. Why drink foreign beverages when he was perfectly happy with tea? Why sleep in a lumpy, unfamiliar bed in a room that was too hot or too drafty? Why scrounge the streets for worthwhile restaurants when he knew several excellent establishments just around the corner? And really, was there anything in Santiago or Havana or Madrid—any artwork or museum or towering mountain—he could not simply read about in a book? Did he really have to cram himself into a train or a boat for an interminable amount of time to see things that had already been photographed and painted and published for his pleasure a thousand times over?

"Finally!" exclaims Aubry, and spends a glowing afternoon in the company of a defiant curmudgeon. She has, at long last, stumbled upon a kindred spirit.

18

On a Train with Lionel Kyengi

If she had to guess, she'd say she is thirty-four years old—thirty-four and still willing to take a risk here or there—like the time she scaled the cliffs near Conakry to avoid retracing her steps through the city. Or just two months ago, foolishly sailing across the Barents Sea in a mighty storm. She's had similar scrapes in Indonesia, Iceland, and across the skinny half of South America. But here, in Russia, it has caught up to her. She has spent far too long in Nizhny Novgorod. She can already feel it—her disease, fast on her heels, overtaking her.

She dreamt of her sickness just hours earlier, its low, bone-shaking voice growling in her skull.

"Go," it shouted. Outside, the skies thundered and rain came down.

"You can't be serious."

"I said go."

"I said fuck yourself."

"Then I will wake you," it said and she woke to pain, gnawing its way through her gut.

Now she pries her way through the crowds with her walking stick, excuses herself to everyone, to no one. She often feels it coming, a gnawing sensation before the strike, and she is feeling it now. She needs to be on that train before her ears bleed, before her body hammers itself with convulsions. She does not want to make a scene in front of these cosmopolitans. They will gather around and stare, too afraid to touch her, too captivated to walk away. She'll have to break through their wall of gawking faces and run for it.

But where? She is in the center of Nizhny. She's gotten to know it—lilac-scented air, rattling trams, churches and monasteries with colorful meringue-shaped domes, a whole city designed by pastry chefs. She has walked and ridden every inch of it, spiraling into its center.

Suddenly, that cold realization, like ice forming on her skin. To escape she'll have to pass through places she's already been. This could be it, the final sickness, the death blow, and she has arranged it herself. She pushes and squeezes and needles her way through the crowd—daily commuters, moving back and forth, home to work, work to home, like tigers pacing a cage. She fights her way through clouds of smoke and steam, toward the black cast-iron beast, jostling the entire length of the platform to the footboards of the Trans-Siberian Railway.

She climbs into the passenger car and finds her compartment as quick as she can. The man sitting there looks up from his textbook. She does not sit. She stands and waits. The train isn't moving. Why isn't it moving? A conductor outside shouts things in Russian—Russian, yet another language she hasn't had time to learn.

"He's talking about delays," says the man in the seat, seeing her confusion. She glances at him. He is Black and speaks with an accent. Other than that, she hardly notices him. Her tongue tests her mouth for blood.

But wait, he said something about delays, and he said it in French.

"What?" she says.

"The train. It's delayed."

"How long?"

"I'm not sure."

Aubry touches her finger to the corner of her mouth. There, on her fingertip, is a spot of blood.

"I may have to walk."

This surprises the man. "It's far, where you're going?"

"Too far."

She trembles all over.

"Have a seat," he says with urgency.

She shakes her head. "It will kill me."

He is alarmed now. Aubry is sweating. Her color fades with every passing moment. He leaps to his feet. "I'll find a—"

"No!" she snaps. He freezes, midstep.

"I'm sure there's a doctor on—"

"Sit!" she snaps again.

He sits.

"No more doctors," she says under her breath. "No more."

Then the train lurches. She wobbles on her feet. He gets up again to steady her, but she doesn't need it.

They stand there, the man watching Aubry, Aubry staring out the window, the platform sliding by as the train slowly eases out of the station.

The gnawing feeling in her gut is still there. She puts her finger to her mouth again. This time, no blood. Still she waits. The train, now rolling at a steady clip, is crossing the Oka River. She exits the city of Nizhny Novgorod forever.

"I think I'll have that seat now." She plops herself down with a sigh and a thump, inhales deeply to calm her nerves. She puts aside her walking stick, her bag. The man continues to stand there, watching her.

"So . . . you are only well when in a state of motion? Is this the opposite of seasickness?"

She looks at him, really studies him now that she can. He is well-dressed, bespectacled, probably West African judging by his accent. He speaks French and Russian, so is well-traveled and well-educated, too. Mostly, he is displaying a touching concern for her well-being, which is appreciated now that she has a moment to appreciate.

"I can see why you'd think such a thing," she says. "How did you know I was French?"

"You were muttering to yourself in French."

"Was I?"

"It sounded French, whatever it was, the sound you were making." He tries to smile. He tries to appear collected, but isn't.

He is the first Black man she's seen in Russia and the only Black man she's seen in—what? A month? A year? But she is not fond of measuring time, so she reaches into her bag, takes out her puzzle ball, and plays. He sits back down, picks up the textbook he was reading, and opens it up in his lap. But his eyes keep turning her way, the way a detective might examine a suspect. He sits up, folds his hands on the table, and turns to her.

"This is a sleeping compartment," he finally says, as if pointing out a bit of interesting scenery.

She looks up from her puzzle ball and blinks at him, not comprehending in the least.

"A gentleman's sleeping compartment," he specifies.

Her brow gathers in a knot, a single suspicious eyebrow arching up her forehead. She fumbles through her pockets for her ticket. By the time she finds it, he has his ticket out as well and they compare.

"Ah, you see," he explains, face straining with apology. "You are in the wrong car. I don't believe you actually have a sleeper compartment."

It strikes Aubry suddenly, her thoughtless indiscretion. She read the numbers wrong. What made her think she had a compartment? She even sat down and made herself comfortable, blissfully playing with her puzzle ball. Her face burns.

"I am so sorry," she says, flustered, rapidly collecting her things.

"Not at all. Not at all." His eyes, big and round. "I . . . I didn't . . ."

She stands by the door and watches him while he stutters through his incomplete thought. In the end, it remains incomplete. She smiles at him, says "Thank you," and steps out, closing the door behind her.

In the narrow hallway, scenery rattles past windows on one side, compartment doors on the other. She is not sure which way to go, where her seat might be waiting, so she picks a direction and walks. All will become known as long as she walks.

Then she stops, only halfway across the coach. In her hurry, she has forgotten her puzzle ball. She turns back around, knocks politely, then cautiously opens his door.

The man is standing there in silent, astonished fear, eyes bulging from his head. He points to the floor by her feet.

"It moved."

She looks down. Waiting for her by the door is her puzzle ball.

"I'm sorry?"

"It moved. It was there," he says and points to the far end of the long seat opposite him. "I turned around for just a moment and when I turned back it was there." He points to it again, by the doorway at her feet. "It moved."

"It rolled, you mean."

"All that way? So quickly? No. The damn thing leapt after you. I swear it."

She looks between him and the puzzle ball. He can't take his eyes off it.

"It doesn't seem likely, though, does it?"

"I saw it."

"But you didn't. You said you had looked away."

"I swear I saw it."

"But you didn't. Not really. You look a little faint. Would you like me to get you something?" She fumbles through her carpetbag. "I have chocolate."

"I don't understand. What is that thing?"

She reaches down and picks it up at last. "It's my puzzle ball. I've had it all my life. But this is nothing. Here is my spear."

She uncaps her walking stick for him, reveals the shiny black point.

"Mother of God," he says, eyes even wider, "what's that for?"

"For hunting. What else?" she says and caps it again. "Maybe the puzzle ball rolled and you didn't hear it."

"It fell off the bunk. I would have heard it."

"But maybe you didn't. Over the noise of the train. Doesn't that make the most sense? I'm sorry it gave you such a fright. Let me find you something to drink. What do you like? A whisky, perhaps?"

"Nothing. I'm perfectly well."

"Chocolate?" She has found her bar of chocolate and offers it to him.

"No. No, thank you."

There seems to be nothing else she can do, yet she is reluctant to go. "Would you like me to leave?"

He looks at her, perhaps for the first time since she walked back in. "I didn't mean to chase you out," he says apologetically.

"I didn't want you to think I was misleading you, fooling a young lady into unseemly accommodations."

"I never thought any such thing. You are a gentleman," she says definitively, but then raises some doubt. "You are a gentleman, correct?"

"Yes. Of course."

"And do gentlemen share?"

For the first time since they met, he smiles. "We frequently do."

"Then perhaps I should stay. Just for a bit. Until you feel better."

He holds out his hand. "Lionel Kyengi."

"Aubry Tourvel," she replies, and they shake.

They take seats opposite each other and talk politely, about Nizhny, about Russia, and soon enough, Lionel relaxes in her company. They say how nice it will be to have someone to talk to on such a long trip. They are idiots. This is pure scandal and they know it—two strangers of the opposite sex, of different races, sharing a compartment. Still, they keep up an illusion of propriety.

"How do you feel?" he asks.

"Oh, that. It was a passing thing."

"Seemed more serious than that."

"It is. But let's talk about our favorite foods instead."

They have plenty of time.

There is a clatter. Lionel's eyes go wide again. The puzzle ball is on the floor.

"I dropped it," says Aubry, already bending over to pick it up. "It was me."

Lionel gets his breath back.

"Are you still nervous about the puzzle ball?" she says. "Let me show you. Why don't you help me open it?"

She shows him how the panels slide against each other, the various directions they move. After a while, they take turns with it, leaning forward in their seats, foreheads almost touching.

"Left . . . No, that way . . ." she dictates. "No, try this."

Nothing works. They laugh and try again.

"Do you mean you've never opened this?" he asks.

"Never."

He turns the facets along their hidden grooves, again and again, and still it does not give. He grunts with frustration. "Why do you carry this evil thing with you?"

"So I can find out what's in there!"

"Give me a hammer and I'll show you!"

He asks where she found it. She tells him about the dead man, how she found it on his front walk, and explains the wishing well, but not much else. She doesn't tell him, for example, about that day in Cyprus when she was a girl, when it slipped from her grasp and fell to the bottom of a ravine. She spent an hour climbing down and found it perched on the edge of a hole in the earth that went straight down. A rickety wooden ladder was lashed to the inside of the hole, inviting her in.

She didn't go down. She did not have the courage.

Not yet.

"You poor girl," he says. "You never had a chance."

"What do you mean?"

"You love this thing. How were you supposed to drop it in a well?"

"I was. I was supposed to."

"It's like forbidden fruit. Why put a fruit tree in the garden of Eden and then say not to eat? And you, with your puzzle ball. Why give you a puzzle ball and then tell you to throw it away? Of course you wouldn't. You're not the type."

"Can we talk about something else?"

"Why?"

"I don't want to think about it."

"Why?"

"It's the past. What's done is done."

"I don't actually mean to say it was the fault of this thing. That's silly. I was thinking of you. That's all."

They play until a red slash of sunset cuts the sky apart outside their window. By then, they've moved on to other things, like how to spear birds from the trees. She is on her feet, her spear unsheathed, showing Lionel the proper stance, how to aim.

"It's in the shape of the arm. Do you see? Do you see the shape?" He is laughing too hard to listen. Everything is funny to them, as if they both share the same mental disorder. "How can you not know this?" she shouts at him. "I thought all Africans could throw spears!"

"You be careful," he says. "Last time a Frenchwoman held a spear like that, they burned her at the stake!" And they laugh like a pair of drunks.

In the middle of it, she stops suddenly, sobered by a disturbing thought.

"Do you mean I was tricked?" she asks him.

"What?"

"What you said about the puzzle ball. That I was meant to keep it. Does that mean I was made sick on purpose?"

"What? No. Nobody . . . It's a condition, like any other."

"It's not like any other."

"Why would anyone give you a disease?"

"I don't know. I don't want to think about it. But you said it, and now I can't stop."

"No one gave it to you," he tells her as authoritatively as he can.

She closes her eyes, puts her head in her hands, then, after a moment, comes up for air.

"No. Of course not," she says. "No one would."

Eventually, they play themselves out. They recline on their seats. He is stretched out, feet up, facing the window. She is on the other side of the compartment, facing him. Without warning, their window has become full of stars. They've run out of talk, so they pick words, favorite words from any language they know.

"*Yariman*," she says.

"What's that mean?" he asks.

"Slut."

"*Mudak*," he says.

"What?" she asks.

"Shithead."

"*O să-ți smulg capul și-o să-mi bag pula în partea care mai mișcă.*"

"Should I ask?"

"I will rip your head off and fuck the part that still moves."

His jaw drops. "Dear God."

"A barkeep taught me that one."

"And I thought I was worldly," he says, a little disappointed in himself.

She shrugs. "It's a different kind of worldly. What are you anyway? A linguist?"

"An accountant."

"That sounds useful. If I'd have gone to school, I'd have studied that."

"I haven't met any female accountants. I suspect they'd be very good at it."

"What are you doing in Russia?"

"I attended Oxford. I attended the ESCP in Paris. It lends me a certain value. I helped save my home city from bankruptcy and a few other places along the way. I have a friend in the Russian ministry. I think he wants to see what I can do for them in Vladivostok."

"Vladivostok is not a pretty word," she says.

"No," he agrees. "And you?"

"I am moving. Always moving. I move so that I may breathe. That's all there is to it. I have no value at all," she says. "My family sends me money if they know where I'll be. Sometimes they deposit small amounts in various cities, like a little treasure trail for me to follow. But mostly I try to make my own way."

"Do you know what happens to thieves here?"

Why would he ask about thieves? What has she done? "Lionel," she says, a little nervous around the edges, "I thought we were friends?"

"They're put into a cell. Maybe they have a window, maybe they don't. Travel is the three steps from one wall to the other. They may live in that cell for years, depending on the crime, depending on whether they've been forgotten or not. They may die in that cell. The point is, punishment is the inability to move, the inability to see the world around you. It's a universal penalty. What you have is the opposite. You've seen so much of the world it must be a reward. For what, I don't know."

She smirks a little. Everywhere she goes, faces that long to go with her, an urge to move, to see, to feel things that can't be felt at home. She's met people who wished they had her disease so they'd have the excuse to explore. People, everywhere, looking at her with envious eyes, heartbroken eyes, eyes that romanticized her illness into something it wasn't. No wonder the newspapers have always been so interested.

"Exile is also a punishment," she says.

"There are countless exiles who have gone on to live happy, prosperous lives. How many do that from a bricked-up room?" And to further his point, he asks, "Do you think Marco Polo was happier en route to China or in a Genoese prison?"

She says nothing.

"You're a remarkable woman. I hope they name this disease after you."

She laughs and carefully studies this Lionel Kyengi.

"I've learned seven languages, can fumble my way through many others," she says, "and still hardly get a chance to use them. Is it all right if we talk into the night?"

"Until the sun rises, if you like," he says.

"I would like."

And with that, they fall into silence. They stare at each other from across the compartment. Lionel lifts his hand, hesitates, then draws the shade on the door to prevent the eyes of strangers. She opens the window to let in a rush of air.

A closed compartment, a man, a woman, hearts flailing, their lives hurtling over the blue-bathed prairie. They've come so far, from opposite directions, to end up here. Who knew motion could be a place? And who kissed who? She is not even sure of that. She is too busy discovering the hidden talents of her fingers. They are too busy giving each other to each other, infatuated by the tastes of their mouths, their sighs and moans, and how easily clothes fall away.

She loves this body before her, this little miracle of muscle and bone. She's seen civilized couples, so very urbane, so very elegant, their children lined up in rows. None of that is in the cards for her. She lives her life as a hunger in search of a meal. It has been a long time, but tonight, she's found one, and lifts him in her hands to her mouth.

"Tell me," he gasps, his breath sucked out of him. "How do you know? How are you so certain there's no cure?"

She's hardly told anyone the story of Uzair Ibn-Kadder. But this man, who cradles Aubry in his lap, who lifts her toes off the floor, this handsome man clearly needs to know. Once he does, he will never ask such a foolish question again . . .

19

Uzair and the North African Odyssey

Floating in the air was music from some strange instrument. This must have been the call to prayer she'd heard the Greek sailors talking about.

Were they still there, those Greek sailors? How long had it been? Was it too late to go back, to make her amends with the captain and his crew? And where, exactly, was here? She'd just emerged from the endless shadows and the endless books. Her mind still spun from what she'd seen, her thoughts still tangled in her skull. It was like waking from a dream.

She shook her head, tried to focus. She couldn't see the water or hear the Mediterranean Sea raking a distant shore. But she saw mountains, pale brown, standing above the horizon, which was odd because she couldn't remember seeing mountains from the boat. Was it the same city? It seemed different. The streets were narrow and clogged with sand. The walls were dirty and cracked, as if they were losing the battle against the ever-encroaching desert.

There was noise ahead, a commotion of some kind. She heard shouting, cheering. When she came around the corner the alleys opened up. It might have been a marketplace once, but there were no stalls, just a mob of men in its center, hooting and hollering, their backs to her.

She approached, slowly. Where had the red vests gone, the colorful tasseled caps? Where were the women, in their flashing gold and silver? Instead, it was a monochrome of brown and dusty gray and she began to realize she was the only woman in sight. She had the feeling she was elsewhere, that she'd come out the wrong door, into the wrong city. It was nonsense but she couldn't help thinking it.

From the center of the crowd came a sound, something animal, something angry. The crowd of men scattered in a loud caterwaul, laughter on their faces, and in the space between them she saw the lion. It was staked to the ground in the center of the mob, slinging its mane of gold and black, bleeding where the men had been poking it with shovels and rakes. It lashed out, then recoiled, half-starved, like a carnivorous ghost.

She felt so many things at once. Awe at the wild animal, so close. Exhilarated by danger, by the death in its jaws. Revulsion at its treatment, and a sickening dread of what she had stumbled into.

With their long sticks, the men converged again on the poor animal. She stood there, lost, afraid, and wondering how to get back to the sea.

Apart from the crowd was a man, staring at her as if she'd fallen from the sky. He came nearer, white trousers under a black tunic, black tunic under a black headdress, eyes so dark they looked charred. He said something indecipherable in a low and fervent voice. She backed away, but he kept coming. He spoke again, but this time, she swore it was a different language, different sounds, to be sure. But he was too close, and kept coming, and she kept backing away.

"If you don't make a sound, how do I know where you're from?" This time she understood every word. It was French. French! It'd been a lifetime since she'd heard it. "French? Is that it?" he exclaimed. "Good. Now get out of the street!" She was so confounded, she simply stood there, her mouth gaping open.

He grabbed her by the arm and pulled her into an alley, out of sight. He leaned into her, blocking the sunlight. She could see the detail in his eyes. She felt fear, real fear, like a cloak of nails. She wanted to bolt, to make her way back to that library and disappear into walls of books and scrolls. She wanted to find that Greek fishing boat where she may have been miserable but at least she was safe.

The man let loose a torrent of questions: "How did you get here? How did you find this place? Who brought you?"

She pleaded her innocence. "No one brought me! I just found it!"

He let go of her arm, took a step back, reassessing her. "Where do you think you are? The banks of the Seine? The Champs-Élysées? Do you see them out there? Do you see what they're like?"

"Is that a lion?"

"It wandered too close to town. That's what happens when you go places you're not invited."

"What are they doing to it?"

"Being cruel."

"Why?"

"I know many things. I don't know that."

"They must stop."

"You want to bring manners to men like these? You're better off hiding. Eventually they will notice you and they will come for you."

"Why?"

Exasperated, he gestures to the crowd. "These are men with no manners!"

"But everyone was so friendly. Everyone was so kind."

"I don't know what place that is. It is not here. Here, you are a stranger, in a place that does not like strangers. You are alone. You are a vagabond. One look at you and they know you will not be missed. They will see you and they will come for you."

"Where do I go?"

He took another step back, raised his arms in question. "Entirely up to you. There is the desert," he said and pointed into the distance. "And more desert." He pointed, then hesitated. "Or," he took a long breath, his jaw clenching, his mind searching for options, "you could come with me." He tried to be disarming, but she only flattened herself against the wall. "I have a home, a private residence—honestly, not so modest—but it comes with food, a servant, a fresh bath in your own room. Imagine that. You may choose to never look upon me again, but the room—I swear in the name of Allah—is yours." And, for her, he swore it, hands in the air, palms out.

Her eyes narrowed. "I think *you* are coming for me."

"Where will you go?" he said, losing patience with her. "Where will you sleep? Here?" He points to the ground at their feet. "What will you eat? Where is there water?"

"I don't know." She scanned the crowd, studied the faces. "I'll ask him," she said and rushed off, fast enough to lose him, head low, weaving through people, disappearing into the crossroads. By the time he found her again, she had already cornered an old man in a back street.

"Please?" she begged the old man. "Just for the night?"

But she'd frightened him off and he slunk away, shaking his head.

"He thinks you are a whore," said the dark-eyed man, approaching her slowly. If he was impatient before, he had softened now, a little baffled by her, a little amused.

"Do you?" she asked, lit with anger.

"No. I think you're French."

"I am French!"

"Other than that, I hardly know you."

"That's true. You invite me to your home, yet you don't ask my name."

"You would only give me a false one."

"Don't you want to know what I'd invent?"

He smiled—this time, a genuine smile—and succumbed. "May I have the pleasure of your name?"

"No."

"Would you care to know mine?"

"Uzair Ibn-Kadder," she said hotly, and while his mind raced, wondering how she knew, how long she'd known, what a fool he'd been, she spun about, her own little lightning storm, and disappeared into the crowd.

20

Uzair and the North African Odyssey

Hours later, when she heard him come home, the front door swinging open, and when she saw him lighting the ceiling lantern that filled in the shadows, she was waiting, walking stick in hand, as if nothing could be more natural than stealing into a strange house and quietly waiting for the owner to arrive.

He looked up, saw her there, sitting in the chair at the end of the hall. Their eyes held. For many moments he was speechless.

"How did you know my name?" he finally asked.

"How did I know where you live?" she answered.

"That, too."

"You thought you'd been following me. Maybe I've been following you."

He stepped back, mildly confounded, as if appraising the latest in contemporary art. "That is not an answer," he said. "But I'm glad you are here. It means you are not dead, and that would have been a pity. You have a fire in you."

"Enough to burn down this house of yours."

"Please don't. It's everything my father left me."

"What's that?" she asked, as if bored of the conversation. She wasn't bored, but she wasn't going to let him control the questions. He looked around as if he didn't know what she was speaking of.

"That," she said, pointing to the next room with her walking stick.

He came closer to the end of the hall where she sat and peeked around the corner to look. He knew exactly what she was talking about—of course he did—but she could feel him trying to angle a little closer to her, to get a better look and take in this cold courage of hers.

"You've never seen a dinosaur before?"

In the biggest room of the house lay a giant animal skull on a worktable, too big to wrap one's arms around, surrounded by brushes and tools. An enormous horn, as thick as a man's thigh, swept forward from its snout.

"Have you?" she said. She was already in the habit of challenging him.

"Pardon me. I misspoke. These are only the remains of a dinosaur I pieced together. I did not realize you would be so exacting."

"You dug this up?"

"I bought it from a Tuareg thief who stole it from an archaeological site in Ethiopia. Not my preferred method but I got it out of the hands of a criminal. It's a nearly complete skull. Very rare. I filled in the missing pieces with plaster and I think I've managed a passable likeness."

"What's it called?"

"I have no idea. You have a suggestion?"

"Stop cluttering your house with bones."

"Well, you see, my ambition is to be a great scientist. The problem is, Newton devised a most elegant theory of the universe and Darwin for all of life. Even dinosaurs have been discovered by a little girl digging up seashells on a beach. I'm forced to wonder if there's anything else left to learn."

"Oh."

"*Oh?* Is that all? Am I asking the wrong questions?"

Aubry only stared back as if he should know better.

"You're right," he said. "I should be asking how you broke into my home."

But she'd moved on, examining his collection of minerals on a display shelf. She held them up to the sunlight flaring through the mashrabiya window screen. They sparkled pink and green and even black, if black can be said to sparkle.

"Is this halite?"

"No. It's fluorite, but that is an excellent guess."

"I saw a picture of it at the library."

"What library?"

"The one here, in your city, with all the picture books."

"The only library in this city is my own."

That was not true, she thought. This Uzair wasn't so learned after all. She'd been to the other library. She'd left the Greek fishermen, stepped foot on African soil, and discovered the building with the horseshoe-shaped arches. She'd stepped into those inky shadows. She'd seen the library within.

"I spent a whole day there." Actually, it'd been several days. Actually, she'd lost count of the days, absorbed in who knows how many books with who knows how many pictures within, all of them to herself—but she was tired and hungry and feeling cautious. She was in no mood to explain.

"The nearest library is forty miles to the east," he said. "Have you walked forty miles today?"

"Did I?" The question was sincere, though he took it as coyness. There was some kind of misunderstanding happening, some kind of mystery that needed to be solved, but she didn't have the inclination. Solving meant explanations, and she had none of those either. She decided to keep quiet. Ever since she ran away from her mother and slunk her way across the Greek isles, she'd become increasingly stingy about how much she revealed to others, and her secrets were getting bigger and bigger.

"I think you need a drink," he said and left to get her a cup of water from the cistern. She wandered through his big room full of things. The layout of the house was simple, essentially a laboratory with rooms attached. The skull was impressive, but she liked the crystals best. She was especially taken with a honey-colored stone, a beetle frozen inside.

"Amber," he said, returning with her water. "From the Baltic coast."

"You're rich?"

He shrugged. "Everything my father left me."

She took the water. She had already helped herself but she didn't want him to know that.

"And you spend it on this?"

"Wulfenite from Morocco," he said while she inspected his collection, all laid out on velvet-covered shelves.

"Why do you collect these things?"

"So I may study them."

"Why do you study them?"

"It gives me a purpose, I suppose."

She stopped, crisscrossed in the broken window light. "A purpose?"

"The reason I'm here."

She felt something, a vague sense of panic in the back of her brain. She wasn't sure why.

"What is it?" he asked.

"I hadn't thought of that," she said. She collected herself, continued to inspect his gems.

"Cinnabar from Peru," he continued. "Opal from Australia."

She heard a door open and close, saw sunlight flashing from

another room. She caught sight of a servant turning a corner, a young boy, even younger than Aubry. The servant saw her, gasped a little, and lowered his head nearly to the floor before whisking himself away.

"You collect many things, Uzair," said Aubry.

"Yes."

"Are there any other street urchins living with you?"

"I'm a harmless eccentric," he explained. "There are no captives here. Search my home if you like."

"I have."

"And?"

"I found no instruments of murder," she said, then leaned in close so he wouldn't miss a word. "And you'd need one to kill me."

21

Uzair and the North African Odyssey

Uzair seemed uneasy, looking at her across a narrow board of a table. She wondered what would happen to Uzair if someone found out she was here, and what would happen to her. She wondered what her own parents would think—but she'd already been through a thousand situations she had determined her parents should never hear of—eating trash, stealing clothes. Insinuating herself into the life of an older man was one of her lesser violations.

She'd only been wandering the world a few years, and she was still learning ways to survive. This was her, experimenting, using her girlish charms to secure a place to sleep, food to eat. She'd never pushed her luck like this before, but here she was, in the thick of it, pushing. She measured every word he said, every look he gave. This is it, she thought. Let's see how it goes.

In his nervousness, he began to boast about the generous hospitality of Arab people, and not just Arabs, but all the friends he had made in his journeys to Europe and Central Asia. "It could be worse. A little farther south and you might have ended up in Berber hands."

She smirked but said nothing. In Bulgaria, she was accompanied as far as the Ottoman border by a traveling farmhand, who had shown her every kindness, who agreed that people were good and charitable all over.

"But," he had said when their paths finally parted, "beware the Ottomans. Of all peoples, they are not to be trusted."

The Ottomans turned out to be just as kind and charitable as the Bulgarians, feeding her and inviting her into their homes. But when it was time to go, they warned her, "Careful of the Greeks. They are unscrupulous. They will rob you blind."

But the Greeks were generous as well. That's how it was, still is, everyone toasting the goodness of mankind, except their immediate neighbors who are always thieves and villains.

She'd eventually meet the Berbers. They would pluck her from the desert, nurse her, feed her, save her life. Uzair, despite his scientific mind and his far-flung travels, was every bit as provincial as the world around him.

She turned her attention to the meal. Spread out on the knee-high board Uzair called a table were foods she hardly recognized. She was sure some were meant to be eaten. She wasn't so certain about others. He chuckled at her illiteracy, pointed to each of the foods.

"Wood apple," he said. "From Persia."

She pointed to another.

"Mangosteens. From the East Indies."

"What else? Ice from Antarctica?"

"No ice."

"And the dates?"

"They're from here."

She ate more dates with bits of goat cheese, trying not to behave like the starving vagabond she was.

"Did you know your little street urchin is ill?" she said.

"I did not. Is it anything serious?"

"In another day or two she will start to die." She washed down a date with her tea.

Uzair stopped eating. "To die?"

Mouth stuffed with food, she gave a nod.

"What must I do?"

She took a chance on a wood apple, looked at him with surprise, her eyebrow up, as if he were a fool for not knowing. "Do? There's nothing you can do."

"There's no cure?"

"Other than death?"

"Besides that, yes."

"There's travel. And only travel. I'll have to leave you soon." She tore little pieces from her slice of bread, nibbled them, never taking her eyes off him. This was the test. This was always the test.

A dismissive scowl was already growing across his face. "I have never heard of such a disease."

"Whether you've heard of it or not, I have it."

"You're speaking metaphorically."

"Why do you think I am so far from home? Hmmm? Have you even wondered?"

"I was getting to it."

"Ha! And you say you're a scientist."

His face grew stern. "I am a scientist," he corrected.

"Then where is your inquiring mind?"

"Would you agree that things either exist or don't exist?"

She paused, puzzled by the question. "Why would I agree to that?"

"Because there is no third alternative."

"Not with you."

He sat back, studied her carefully.

"Do you ever wonder if you are mad?" he asked.

"Of course I do. I look at you and think, if he doesn't know, maybe I don't either."

He had nothing to say to this. He poured the last of his tea into his belly and placed the empty cup on the table, signaling the end of dinner.

"Let's just see what happens in the next few days," he said.

"Yes. Let's do that," she agreed.

22

Uzair and the North African Odyssey

First thing the next day, as soon as Aubry woke, he was there, holding a strange concoction in a clay bowl.

"Try this," he said.

"What is it?"

"Wormwood rolled in rock sugar. Chew on it. See if you get sick then."

"But you don't believe I'm sick."

"I don't. But you believe it. The mind is a powerful thing. There is an account I read—an old woman from Copenhagen who suffered from arthritis and went to a doctor. The doctor advised her to travel somewhere warm, to move and exercise, to loosen up her joints. She took his advice so seriously, she fled south and never stopped. To Malta, to Morocco, to Cape Verde and beyond. She died when the ocean liner she was on stopped to make repairs, anchored at sea for too long."

"Your leaf is bitter."

"In another day or two, you will see."

"Mmmm," she exclaimed, chewing the horrid leaf. "Is this what they do for fun in Egypt?"

"No, it's not."

"Then why am I doing it?"

"Because you're not in Egypt."

She eyed him suspiciously. "Then where am I?"

"The same place I am. Tripoli."

"I thought this was Egypt."

"You are mistaken."

Her eyes scope out the room as if it had been lying to her all this time. "Where is Tripoli?"

"North Africa."

"Oh." This, finally, seemed correct to her.

"The Libyan Desert," he added.

Now a question, a nagging question, had to be asked. "Is the ocean nearby?"

"No."

"But I came here by boat."

He shook his head. "Not possible." He said, delicately, "Do you think, perhaps, you've hit your head somewhere along the way?"

She couldn't remember that either. Was he joking? Was this Egyptian humor? She could not make sense of this conversation. It disturbed her so much, she decided to push the whole thing out of her mind.

At least she wasn't starving. She wasn't sleeping in a gutter or a ditch. And then there were his books, books of all kinds— some about geology, pictures of gems in full color. One, a biology book, with unsettling photographs of diseased bodies. There was an archaeology book, depictions of the pyramids and other ruins. Books on astronomy, chemistry, and architecture. Uzair was a man of many interests. His collection didn't compare to the library she'd visited a few days earlier, but she didn't care to bring up that place again.

There was also an atlas. She studied maps of North Africa, Egypt, and Tripoli.

That evening, shortly after sunset and while there was still light in the sky, she climbed onto the roof of his house. From here, she could see all around—a mosque, orchards, the market-place, and desert that lay beyond in all directions. But she swore this city was different from the one she had stepped into—no great walls, no spires, and no ocean anywhere in sight.

When she dreamt of the demon that night, its low growl in her ear said, "When you are ready, you will know."

23

Uzair and the North African Odyssey

She'd seen many doctors in Paris, in Rome, in Vienna, but none of them talked like Uzair. None spoke of leaves and herbs. They spoke of needles and knives. None ever thought it could all be in her mind—and what a remarkable idea that was—that she had done all this to herself, somehow, that it wasn't a well, or a punishment for a wish gone wrong—that it was her all along.

Crazy, perhaps, but she was willing to try. Uzair's method was novel and, better yet, pain-free. It was her third day of chewing leaves and she felt cleaner somehow, more alert. She asked Uzair if she could chew on another leaf and, encouraged, he gave her three different kinds to try.

Hopes of a cure were churning again.

She settled in and waited. In the laboratory, there was Uzair, drilling a tiny hole in the piece of amber with the beetle inside, glancing at Aubry over his magnifying glass, scrutinizing her complexion. In the kitchen, there he was again, inspecting her breakfast plate, making sure she was eating. In the hallways, in the study—he was always lurking about, watching her eat, watching her fidget with her puzzle ball.

"What is that?"

"My puzzle ball." She considered telling him about the time

it was swept down a river, only to turn up the next morning in the bottom of her sleeping bag. But then, she realized, he'd never understand. "Would you like to play?"

He waved his hand dismissively. "I have no time for that."

If she needed something from the outside—new shoes, a favorite food—the servant boy would fetch it. Other than that, Uzair let her roam at will, unfailingly good-natured, and always watching. Aubry would fling herself on a carpet or a chair, spread herself out like an unmade bed, half-open eyes perusing his books. She had a kind of power over him, she knew, and she wanted to be better acquainted with it. It was subtle but effective and when she caught him watching, it pleased her.

The servant boy was named Hamza and he rushed home that morning from the market, excited, his words pouring out.

"What's he saying?" she asked.

"Someone has freed the lion. It's gone."

She stood up, just as excited as Hamza. "Thank goodness! But how? It was so angry."

"That's true," said Uzair, rubbing his chin. "How would it be done? You'd need to get close. To do that, you'd need to put it to sleep first."

He has a cupboard full of dried herbs and powders and looks through them. "A combination of opium poppy and mandrake, just a little in a cut of meat, would knock the beast off its feet. A cloth soaked in chloroform"—he pulled out a vial of clear liquid from his desk drawer—"placed in front of its nose, perhaps, while you break the chain with a pair of bolt cutters."

Aubry looked at the dinosaur skull on the table, the box of tools underneath it, the bolt cutters sitting on top.

"The lion wakes an hour later and prowls away into the wilderness where it belongs."

A sly grin curled across Aubry's lips. So Uzair had freed the lion, a good deed in the night. Had he done this for her, risked life and limb for her pleasure? So far, she'd been entertained by Uzair, but now, something in the air had changed. In all her travels, after all the people she'd met, it was the first time she'd felt something like this, a physical reaction, a bodily sensation, and her face went slack with sudden awareness.

On day four, Uzair approached Aubry holding a small jar in his hand. She looked up from her book.

"You mentioned ringing in your ears, which made me think of aural aberrations, which made me do some research. Did you know that there was once a man who heard music everywhere he went? Loud music. Beautiful music, too. He wrote it down and musicians played it to large crowds. But the man went mad, all that music in his head day and night. He wandered off into the desert and was never seen again. All in the mind, of course."

"And?"

"And this." He showed her the jar. "Blue lotus wine, thickened with camphor and mustard seed." He offered it to her. "You need to rub it on your skin."

"Where?"

"Your wrists, perhaps."

She stood and held out her arms, wrists up.

"Show me."

This was such a brazen invitation, Uzair didn't know how to respond. Despite their familiarity, there were barriers between men and women not so casually breached. Aubry was hardly aware of this, but his reaction intrigued her.

Flustered, he dipped his fingers in the jar of pale lotion. "If you would permit me."

He took her wrist and, with the lightest touch, rubbed the mixture on her skin. He took her other wrist and again, with a delicacy that raised the tiny hairs on her skin, repeated the spectacle.

"Where else?" she said.

He shook his head, not sure of anything anymore. "Your feet?" He meant it as a statement, but it came out a question.

She sat in one chair, he sat in another. She removed her slipper and put her naked foot on his lap.

With two fingers, he rubbed lotion on the top of her foot. With his thumb and forefinger, he lathered the hollow of her Achilles tendon. Wordlessly, she removed that foot, offered the other.

"How did you know my name?" he asked her, watching her carefully. "We'd only just met. You couldn't have known."

She thought of telling him, but decided that this was not how the game was played. She said nothing, only grinned a little, the air between them so fragile.

"Is that it, then?" she said, voice hardly above a whisper.

He hesitated, then pointed to himself, the soft parts where the jawline met the neck.

She understood. She leaned forward, lifted her chin, and offered her throat to him. His face was tight with nerves, and she couldn't hold back an anxious, awkward smile.

Her teeth were red with blood.

Uzair bolted to his feet so fast his chair toppled to the floor behind him. "Don't move!" he shouted, his hands pointing, unsteady with nerves. "Keep still!"

Aubry covered her mouth. She hadn't felt it coming but now that it was here, she could feel its rusty claws scurrying up and down her bones. Uzair inspected her, turning her head in his hands, watching her pupils, taking her pulse. Then he ran off to find more medicines. While he was gone, Aubry got to her feet, carefully, like an old arthritic man, and walked to her room to collect her things.

Halfway across the laboratory she stumbled to the floor.

She could hear Uzair and Hamza, shouting back and forth in Arabic. Aubry fought her way back to her feet, every bone cracking, every muscle tearing. She coughed, she shook. When they found her, she was clinging to the giant skull. A hand gripped an eye socket, an arm hooked around the elephantine horn. Tears of blood wept down the icicle-smooth bone. Uzair pulled her away, laid her on the floor.

"Well," said Aubry, "it was a pleasure meeting you, Uzair." Her chest rose and fell, fighting off pain. "Your hospitality is commendable. I really must be going."

"Is this it? This is your illness?" he asked her, amazed and terrified.

"Do you see?" she said. "Do you see that I am dying?" She licked her teeth clean, but the blood pooled in her mouth and turned them red again.

"And you have to move? Is that it? You have to—"

"I have to go. I have to go far," said Aubry, coughing more blood onto her arm. "But I will remember you fondly," she added, stroking his cheek and smiling a red smile.

"Wait," he said, half-panicked, improvising a plan. "I . . . I know a place. I know where I can take you. May I take you?"

But the convulsions had moved in. She lay twisting and jerking on the floor as if she'd been set on fire. Hamza was banged through with terror but Uzair grabbed him by the shoulders and shouted orders.

Hamza ran to Aubry's room. Uzair ran to his study. There, he emptied the cabinet drawers, dumping heaps of dried herbs, small vials of powders and colored liquids into a leather bag. When they returned to the big room, Aubry was gone. They followed drops of blood left across the laboratory floor around a corner, and found her half-stumbling, half-crawling toward the front door, reaching for the locks.

When Hamza looped Aubry's arm around his neck, she felt blindly for his hand and held on tight. He was young but strong and lifted Aubry into the sunlight. He whispered encouraging words and carried Aubry until her legs began to kick, then stumble, then walk. They marched into the open heat of the desert, until the town became a distant shadow behind them.

With every step, Aubry's spine uncurled, her windpipe ran dry, and breathing became easy again. She spat the last of the blood from her mouth. Without water, she scrubbed her hands clean in the sand. Hamza took Aubry by the shoulders, looked her in the eyes to be sure things were all right, and laughed with relief.

Moments before, Aubry had lain in bed with death. Now, she was here, strolling through the desert heat with her new friend, delighted to be a part of the physical world.

Hamza kept glancing over his shoulder. It was over an hour before they saw the dust rising in the air. He turned Aubry around so she could see. Three creatures appeared in the distance, fractured through waves of heat. They could hear the grunting, the soft pounding of hooves in the sand. They came closer, molten bits hardening into the shapes of camels. Uzair rode the first, towing two more behind him.

Aubry grinned. "Now this will be fun!"

24

Uzair and the North African Odyssey

The desert—her first desert—all light and silence, magnificence only matched by the sea. Hot days and cold nights weren't so different from open waters, the rise and fall of the dunes not so different from the swell of waves. She spent the days on camel-back in the shade of the canopy that looped over her head. She listened to the soft canter of camels' hooves, let the stream of glittering desert beneath lull her into a trance. At night she slept in sand that contoured to her body better than any mattress she'd known.

It took three days to reach their destination, three days adrift in the desert, listening to Uzair weave tales of men tunneling deep down to find underground rivers, of ill-fated expeditions by unprepared Europeans, of ancient cities swallowed up in sand-storms never to be seen again.

He offered her wild ginger soaked in sugar and kanna petals to chew on while they made their journey. She had lost faith in his theories after her last onset, but she had to admit, chewing on the ginger for only an hour had made her feel better, and she slept very soundly at night.

"There is a sickness," he explained. "I'm not sure what it is. But you also have a fear of staying still, and the two have become entwined in your head. If I can cure just some of the symptoms, all these terrible fantasies will fall apart as well."

We'll see, she thought.

When they arrived, Aubry was the first to dismount—a big dome-shaped abode to her left, a yellow skillet of sand to her right—and she took in the view.

"Where is this?"

"The edge of the Calanshio Sand Sea," he told her. "As far south as you can go before you burn to death."

She wandered out, scooped up sand like hot glass, let it filter through her fingers. Out there, as far as one could see, raw, empty desert, and a silence like no other. No rustle of trees, no buzz of insects, no birdcalls or gurgling streams. It was a silence that made her question reality.

"Here," Uzair called to her. "I have something to show you."

He led Aubry toward the dome. A mosque? Out here? It seemed unlikely. A storage depot? Would there be food to last a lifetime inside?

He pushed open the door, and a ghostly puff of dust rose from its edges. The darkness inside was a perfect black. As Aubry slowly stepped through the door, she swore she'd passed from desert day into perfect night. She was so disoriented she wanted to go back out and start over, to understand what she was seeing. But Uzair had already closed the door behind them.

She stood still, made sure her feet were well-planted. She closed her eyes, shook her head, and looked again.

Stars. Yes, thousands of stars in a clear evening sky, a sea of incandescent stars you could wade through. She rubbed her eyes, looked again.

The dome was full of holes, thousands, maybe more, little pinpricks of light in a black velvety surface. Some were bigger and brighter, others hardly visible. She recognized constellations. There was Orion's Belt, and there, the North Star. She saw a faint glow, a swash of phosphorescence across the sky—what could only be the Milky Way. How had he done it?

"It even turns to match the Earth's rotation," he said and grabbed a rope, pulling as he walked along the perimeter of the wall. The stars moved, the entire dome on rollers, the sky and all its lights swirling over Aubry's head.

"For a long time I was fascinated by the night sky," Uzair said. "I would skip sleep to study it. I dreaded the sunrise. To cure myself, I built this exact replica."

He put down the rope and his eyes caught hers. "I will cure you, too."

Aubry looked away, up at his sky instead. "It's beautiful, Uzair."

"It took years."

She imagined him a younger man, a boy even, holding charts up to the sky, then up to his dome, lying flat on his back on a makeshift scaffold, meticulously poking holes in his black ceiling, a desert Michelangelo. "What discoveries you must have made," she said.

"No. None, actually. But now," he said with satisfaction, "I always have my stars."

She was dazzled—these past few days, a procession of wonders—dinosaur skulls, rare gems, exotic fruits, desert journeys, and now this. She pondered what might lie ahead for her.

"I've hardly shown this to anyone."

"How can that be?"

"Who else would I show? My parents are dead. You are the most interesting person a thousand miles in any direction. Petty, this need for an audience."

"It's an achievement," said Aubry. "It's meant to be seen."

When Uzair turned to her again, she was lying on the floor,

a girl staring up at the stars. He hesitated, then walked over to her, so slowly Aubry took note. She listened to his footsteps, held her breath. It hadn't occurred to her that lying on the floor—something as innocuous as staring at the ceiling—might be taken as an illicit invitation, but now that it had, she decided to see where it would lead, to find out what new wonder might materialize. She'd pushed her luck so far already. She might as well push it to the end.

In slow measured steps, he circumnavigated her body. With no more preamble than the rustle of his clothes, he laid himself down beside her. Their first attempt had been rudely interrupted. If he was hesitant then, he is determined now. He'd always seemed so sure of himself, arrogant even, but she saw he was nervous, lying beside her like that. This man—this scientist—made nervous by a girl! What power she had! But that was good because she was nervous, too. She'd never been with a man before, not like this, and his trembling hands were a comfort.

He rolled himself onto his side, next to her, against her. His lips lowered onto hers. He kissed her, then moved back, and waited. She lifted her face to his and returned the favor.

He peeled back her blouse from her skin. For the first time, she revealed herself to another. For the first time, another revealed himself to her. It was a sight worth a barrel of gold. The stars above, made so dull, so quickly.

He was broad and heavy on top of her. Beneath his kisses and the scent of myrrh, there were moments she felt smothered, pinned to the floor, as if covered in a mattress of sand. She knew it would be a little like this—weight and strength, power and vulnerability. But she'd been free for so long—hunting, exploring, following her own maps and trails—that this was a shock.

"I want to move," she said.

But he gently covered her mouth and did not let her.

25

On a Train with Lionel Kyengi

A second night together on the train, and again, Lionel and Aubry do not sleep, clinging to each other like an addiction. They watch the moon rise through the train window, feel the rumble of the tracks vibrate their compartment, their cushions, their naked spines. They think about how far they've come in such a short time, and how far there is still to go.

"I'm jealous of this Uzair," he says.

"Are you? Don't be. It doesn't end well."

He turns to her, a sudden understanding in his eyes.

"Do they ever?"

She is silent for a while, just watching the moon. "Vladivostok?" she says at last.

"Vladivostok," says Lionel. "The end of the line."

"Then I will go with you. Vladivostok. The end of the line."

They press together as tight as pages in a book, an embrace so long, night turns to day. Only then, sobered by the morning, does Lionel ask how the story ends . . .

26

Uzair and the North African Odyssey

Uzair spent the next two days grinding herbs, separating powders, boiling his mixtures in a clay oven in the courtyard. He spent hours reading medicinal books, decoding the mysteries of the liver and the inner ear. He asked Aubry questions relentlessly—was there dizziness? How did she know which direction to travel? Was it a sharp pain like a broken bone or a dull ache like a flu?

By midnight of the first day, he thought he had something with potential and handed her a cup. It looked like a simple red tea, but the odor was strong. It smelled like compost and pine resin.

"You will drink this several times a day," said Uzair eagerly.

"Will I?"

"It will increase your heart's contractions, clean your blood, warm your internal . . ."

"Stop. I don't need to know."

"It will cure you," he said.

"And if it doesn't?" she asked, though she sipped it anyway, showing her willingness to try. He was her first lover. This, she imagined, was how you humor love.

"Then I will make something that does," he said, and she decided to believe him. His theories made sense. He was relentless in his pursuit and meticulous as well. These struck her as the best qualities a scientist could have. Let him try, for as long as there is time. He had made a ceiling full of stars. He had a monster's skull in his living room. There seemed to be nothing he couldn't do.

"What is my purpose, Uzair?"

"Your purpose? You're looking for a meaning to your life?"

"Wouldn't you?"

"You are here to help me cure you. I wouldn't be curing you if you weren't here."

"And if you don't cure me?"

"Then your purpose is to suffer." He didn't even bat an eyelash. What a cruel lover he could be.

But later that day, while lying on their backs, watching his stars, he drew from his pocket the piece of amber with the beetle inside. He'd drilled a tiny hole and through it ran a thin gold chain.

She held the necklace up to the starlight. It glowed like honey and the beetle inside glinted green. It was beautiful and she teared up a little at the gesture. It had only been an attempt to find shelter for the night, but what began as an arrangement was now a bond. And if that was true, then perhaps she was not such a manipulator after all. Love legitimized everything, she thought, all actions made clean if they ended in love.

Later, if she ever chose to remember Uzair, it was this moment, as fleeting as it was, that she called to mind.

"That one," she said, pointing. "That one there. It's not a star. It's a galaxy."

"A what?"

"They call it a nebula. The Andromeda Nebula, I think. But it's really a galaxy. Like the one we're in."

"You have it backward. The galaxy is a collection of stars. All stars are part of the Milky Way."

"No. The planets spin about a star. The stars spin about a galaxy. And galaxies spin about the universe."

"What next? The universes spin about . . . what?"

"No one knows. But that is a galaxy."

He got to his feet, looked up at his manufactured heaven, looking closely at that pinpoint of light. From behind him came Aubry's voice: "They say discovery lies in the places no one is looking."

"Where do you get these ideas?"

"From a book."

"What book?"

"In the library."

"Take me to this library of yours."

"I can't."

"Why not?"

"It's behind me now. There's no going back."

"Ah, yes. Your so-called sickness. Your so-called libraries."

"That's a galaxy."

"How can I cure you when you are this mad?"

"If you can prove it, you will be great."

He laughed and appeared utterly dismissive of her, but what she did not know was that Uzair would stay up late that night, reading his astronomy texts, his finger tracing pictures of solar systems and far-flung constellations, quietly mulling the implications over and over in his mind. He would study that book into the small hours and would not stop until she began to scream.

He found her in the hallway, blood leaking from her ears.

When the sun rose the next morning, Uzair, Hamza, and Aubry were already on their camels, crossing more desert. Hot winds kicked up sand that whistled through the camels' legs.

They arrived again at a new destination, but this time it was hard to tell where the desert ended and the house began. No one had lived here for years, sand piled halfway up its walls, windows blown out. Sand had drifted inside, covering the floors, forming small dunes in some of the rooms, challenging the notions of inside and outside. The cupboards were empty and there was no water except for what they had brought.

"Am I to assume," said Aubry, putting aside all pleasantries, "that you are running out of places to take me?"

But Uzair wasted no time moving in. He gave orders to Hamza, who bowed and hurried away. Hamza was not bold. He was an orphan Uzair had caught digging through his trash one day. Uzair had taken pity, offered him the role of servant. Hamza had no family, no education, no prospects. Like Aubry, he was keenly aware that homelessness was only a misstep away. He made himself small, like a skittish cat, and scurried off. He tied up the camels and carried in the provisions while Uzair went to work on a new potion. Uzair found a table that had not been chiseled away by the elements, cleared it off, and began separating his dried herbs again.

Later, Uzair showed Aubry a room deep inside the house, just off the empty kitchen where he'd been mixing his powders and herbs. The walls were bare and there were no windows, but there was no sand either. He'd swept it and cleaned it as well as he could and moved in a small cot he'd found elsewhere. She thought she might prefer the sand, but said nothing and thanked him for the room.

"I'm sorry," he said. "The condition of this house . . . It was intact once, even comfortable . . . when I was a child."

She didn't mind. She found a large room like a miniature desert beneath a slatted roof, watched the bars of light creep across the sand. That's where he found her, after grinding his herbs and boiling his powders. He sat down across from her, holding a jar, the medicine inside still steaming.

"This is it," he said, looking sadly at the jar in his hands. "My last attempt."

"You've tried so hard."

"Would you like to know what's in it?"

"No."

She took it from him, prepared for the worst, and drank. But she was surprised. She was expecting sourness like swamp water.

"It's like honey," she said, grinning. "At last."

He had no reaction, but simply asked, "How did you know my name?"

"The old man told me. Remember the old man?"

"He spoke French?"

"No. He saw you coming. *Uzair Ibn-Kadder*, he said. And once you know someone's name, it's just a matter of asking where he lives."

He eyed her with mock disapproval.

"Well, you offered, didn't you?" she said.

But his mind was wondering over many things. "They used to think the center of the universe was the Earth, then the sun, now the Milky Way." Like her, he watches the play of splintered light on the interior dunes. "But now, you say we are just one galaxy among many. But then what? Does it go on and on? Where are the limits to this?"

"I understand," she said. "The search will go on forever, too. It will be endless, like everything else out there. Do you see? One person had an idea that led to other ideas. It's like a story someone began that keeps on writing itself, long after the authors are dead."

"Have I done something wrong?"

"What? No."

"You're going to leave me."

"I suppose it would be a romantic gesture to stay and die in your arms, but practically speaking, it's a bit of a waste."

"You won't die."

"Uzair . . ."

"I swear you won't."

"Uzair, even being that close to death is nothing I want to go through again."

"You see? You admit it's in your head."

"Did I? Sometimes you make things up, Uzair."

She throws her head back, finishes the last of the drink, then climbs onto his lap and kisses him.

That evening, she stood before him, clothes falling at his touch, scarves and skirts coiling around her ankles. Their bodies arched and writhed, formed high peaks and little deaths. Even after he wrapped his body up in robes and left the room to study his texts, his image remained.

But her sickness was coming, and would not stop coming. She thought of clinging to him as long as she could. She thought of leaving quietly in the night to spare everyone the inevitable. Why draw this out any longer?

But then, as she laid her head down on the cot, she fell into an instant sleep.

"Something is wrong," said the low voice of her sickness, coming to her in dreams. "This is not a natural sleep. He is up to something. Be careful! Wake up! Wake up now!"

But it was far too late for that.

In a lonely part of the house, in a chair surrounded by mounds of sand, Uzair spent the night staring at the walls, dreading what Aubry would do in the morning when she discovered that her door was locked.

27

Uzair and the North African Odyssey

By the time Aubry opened her eyes it was already midday and her little room, windowless and airless, was a furnace. She tried to get up but her head spun, her knees buckled, and she fell back onto the cot. She waited for the sensation to pass and tried again.

The heat was narcotic. Her head whirled as if on the end of a lasso. Was it happening already? Had her sickness come for her so soon? It had only been a night. It rarely happened this quickly. No, she thought. It was Uzair's potion. It had to be.

She got to her feet, swayed a little, but stayed upright and walked the perimeter of her small room just to be sure she had her legs back. Then she went to the door.

It didn't open.

She pushed the door and it stayed shut. She pulled the door and it stayed shut. She shook it, then shook it harder. It was stuck. It had to be. It was an old door and the wood was warped. No wonder, given this bonfire air. She looked to see where it got jammed, but there was nothing obvious. When the door still refused to open, she knocked. Maybe Uzair or Hamza was nearby and could help. She knocked again and again. Then she banged, banged on the door with her fists and shouted.

"Uzair!"

She banged, she pulled, she pushed, but the door wouldn't budge.

"Uzair!"

She waited.

"Uzair!"

Why didn't she call for Hamza? she wondered to herself.

Because it wasn't Hamza who had locked the door, she answered.

A sudden terror, like a black mamba coiling up her leg. All her muscles gathered. She felt the stirrings of panic in the bottom of her lungs, rising, but choked it back down. She had restraint. She had that one thing. She put her ear to the door and listened carefully. Then, after a moment, she whispered, "Uzair? Are you listening?"

She heard nothing, but he was there. She sensed it.

"Uzair, you can't do this. You will kill me. Are you there? Are you listening?"

She waited for a response, for a telltale sound, the squeak of a chair, a breath, a sigh.

"Uzair, you have never seen a sickness like this before. Admit it and let me go. It is the right thing to do."

"But isn't curing you," came his voice in a shredded whisper, "so you can stay, so we can be together—isn't that the right thing to do?"

He was close, on the other side of the door, his lips a finger-length from hers.

"You can let me out the door, or you can bury my body in the sand," she said, fighting to keep her voice calm. "Either way, you will have to let me go."

"No," he said, his words half-choked, tormented by his own

scheme. She could hear it in him, the conflict, the voice that had not quite convinced itself.

"Uzair . . ."

"No, listen to me! Listen! There was a man in Tunis . . ."

"Uzair, stop . . ."

". . . a man who was convinced he was dead. He refused to eat, to drink. His family tried to force him, but no—the dead, they don't eat or drink. They don't feel pain. They don't exist! And in two months, his prognosis came true. Is that what you want?"

"No. Do you?"

"It will not happen. I swear it."

"You can't swear it, Uzair. You've created this story in your head, written it like a fiction. But it's the wrong story, Uzair."

"I swear it!"

"My sickness is real!" He protests, but she speaks over him. "I didn't ask for it, I don't want it, but here it is, coming for me, following me everywhere I go!"

"It is not!"

"It's already here!"

"Stop saying it!"

"In this room with me!"

"Stop it! This has to stop! There are no more places to take you!"

They were shouting at each other. She was very close to losing him. If that happened, she knew he would walk away and not come back. There would be no one to plead her case to, no one to listen to her terror and open her door.

She breathed in air and started over.

"Uzair . . ."

She waited but there was nothing but silence.

"Uzair?"

He slammed his fist and the whole door shook. She jerked backward, saw his shadow pacing under the door. Then the shadow disappeared. She heard his footsteps scurrying away, going somewhere her voice couldn't reach.

28

Uzair and the North African Odyssey

"No," said her sickness, its voice so low that when it spoke in her skull, it shook her lungs. In her delirium she could almost see it, the little demon clinging to her back, bending to her ear.

"This is not how it ends," it said. "Get up."

She came to, screaming, rolling on the floor, trying to wrestle it off her. Her screams were cut short by a terrible coughing fit, coughing that emptied her of air and spit blood on the floor.

She crawled to the door. "Please," she rasped. "Please."

But Uzair had run out into the night like a battered dog, which left Aubry alone in a small windowless room, smeared with blood and vomit and piss. She lay collapsed at the foot of the door, a bundle of stained clothes, scratching at the wood.

"Please . . ." she begged to no one. "Someone . . . please . . ."

She had screamed her voice raw, all through the day, all through the night. She had nothing left in her. All her life she had feared giving up. She knew nothing would end her life with more certainty than surrender. Even those days—those terrible days—when she thought she could not go on, she went on. But this sealed room in an empty desert—sometimes there are circumstances even the strongest and most resilient cannot overcome.

Betrayal, not just a lie but the overturning of reality. She could not overcome that. She thought they were in love, and that love meant care, and compassion, and mercy. She thought all those things, and how wrong she was. Love could mean anything it wanted to. Beliefs crumble like the walls of a besieged city. Strange how reality was constantly pulling its rug out from under her.

But discovery lies where no one is looking.

Blood seeped down her throat, simple respiration so hard now. She thought she could feel her internal organs giving up the fight. She thought she could feel her lungs tiring out, her heart slowing down, staggering under its own weight. Her eyes were supposed to adjust to the darkness, should have a long time ago, but now she sensed her vision growing dim.

Still, she scratched at that door. She would scratch this door forever. Uzair and Hamza would find the claw marks dug deep into the wood and be amazed and ashamed.

Beneath the door, she could see moonlight spilling through a window, forming a blue sheen across the kitchen floor. The desert was out there, her escape route, not so far away, not far at all. It was hard to die knowing how close it was.

A shadow floated past, disturbing the puddle of moonlight. She thought it was a shadow. Or delirium. She heard footsteps, soft on the kitchen floor. She reached her fingertips under the door as far as they could go.

There was a click, slow and quiet and careful. The thick wooden door eased back on its hinges, revealing the kitchen beyond, the kitchen that was so small when she first entered it, but now seemed as endless as the desert itself.

Still, she reached out her hand with what strength she had left. She laid her palm on the kitchen tile. It was true. She was not fantasizing this. The door had opened.

Something coursed through her, like a drug kicking in.

She felt her heart, so faint before, now beating again. Her skin flushed. Her mind sharpened. She found the strength to lift her head, to reach out again, to pull her broken body through the doorway.

She inched through the kitchen, a half-corpse in a bundle of clothes, her breath a blood-clotted rattle, hands quaking every time they reached out and hauled her poor body across the floor.

She passed a pair of sandaled feet that could only belong to Hamza, but Aubry had no strength to thank him, no strength to speak at all. It was everything she had to pull herself along.

Hamza saw a stool in her way, quickly pulled it aside. He watched Aubry slowly make her way across the endless kitchen floor. He was afraid to touch her, afraid he might make things worse. It was much more terrible than the first time. He scurried ahead and opened the next door. Through that doorframe, the desert shone.

Aubry crawled. Her legs were carcass meat behind her. She pulled them over the tile. The open door was just ahead.

It took her so long to cross the kitchen that by the time she wormed her way outside, dawn had begun. The Calanshio Sand Sea lay before her, wide and unbroken. The sun had not even breached the horizon and she could feel the heat as if a stove had been lit beneath her.

She dragged her way through the sand, formed little clouds of dust with every exhale.

Her fingers clawed through powder. This was the farthest she'd been from the house. This handful of sand was new to her, new and unexplored.

Feeling was already returning to her legs.

29

On a Train with Lionel Kyengi

"Let me understand," says Lionel Kyengi. "You crawled across the Calanshio Sand Sea?"

They are, almost surprisingly, dressed, buttoning the last of their buttons.

"No," says Aubry. "I walked most of it."

That was true. Her legs recovered within minutes of entering the desert. She fought her way to her feet, stumbling at first, falling once or twice, but within the hour she was walking again, and making good speed.

"How long did it take?"

"Two weeks, I think." That is a guess. It may have been longer, much longer, but she doesn't want to alarm Lionel.

It may have been the third week of her wandering that a Berber caravan spotted her crossing the Calanshio on her bare feet. It may have been then that the man on horseback rode up to Aubry, amazed to see a yellow-haired, barefoot foreigner staggering alone through the desert, and carried her back to their caravan where they fed her, gave her new clothes, and stared slack-jawed at this girl who had the temerity to be alive in the middle of the Sand Sea.

She spent several more weeks traveling with them before

joining an Afar caravan making their way to the Ethiopian salt flats. It was there, in that searing heat, that Aubry decided she would never be that insolent girl on the Greek fishing boat again, or the provocateur she was with Uzair, manipulating others for food or shelter. She vowed to repay kindness with kindness, charity with more charity. She began there, on those salt flats, where she helped scrape the salt off the dried lake beds in a relentless heat, a heat like weight, like molten lead on her shoulders. It was a heat she had never felt before and would never feel again, and she scraped salt like an act of penitence.

She wondered about Uzair. She imagined him scrambling across the Sand Sea on foot, trying to catch her before she'd gotten too far. Perhaps he'd followed her tracks, her trails of blood, until they dried up or until the heat became too much. She imagined him calling her name over and over, full of remorse, but never finding her. Had he turned around, tried again on camel? Did he punish Hamza for his disobedience or thank him for doing what he should have done? Or did they travel home in silence and never speak of it again?

How were his theories working out for him now? she wondered. He only wanted her to stay. He wanted to pull the sickness out of her head, but all he got was her blood smeared on his floor. There had been three of them trekking across the desert—her love for Uzair, his love for her, and the sickness. Of the three, only the sickness survived.

"Two weeks?" asks Lionel. "Without food or water?"

"There . . ." She thinks about it but the question trips her up. "There must have been something. I don't remember much."

"You don't remember much," he asks in disbelief, "of the Calanshio Sand Sea?"

She shakes her head.

"I have been to the Sahara. I have dug skeletons out of the

sand. Even the Bedouin refuse to enter the Calanshio," he says. "At any time during those two weeks did you burn? Did you blister? Did your tongue swell?"

"Why would it?"

"Because most would. It's called thirst," he says. "Do you get headaches?"

Her brow wrinkles—none that she can remember.

"Fever?" he continues. "Dysentery? How about the common cold?"

None of these things pulls a memory out of her. Hasn't she caught a cold at some point? She had as a child, that much she knew, before the illness. Since then, nothing. She assumed she'd grown out of them, or that her constant struggle to survive, to move, had warded them off. Who has time to be sick when walking the earth?

But wait! She had tumbled into gullies, been swept down rivers with—now that she thinks of it—nothing more than cuts and bruises. Was that true? Now she could recall, once—no, not once. Twice. No, many times. Many times she had twisted her ankle so badly she was convinced the bone had snapped. Yet two or three days later she felt good enough to walk, and did, for hours, for days, forever.

But she won't tell him that.

"Of course I've had a cold!" she says with mock outrage. Then, because she can't help it, she corrects herself. "I'm sure I have."

"Wait," he says. "Have you or haven't you?"

"I'm sure I have," she says as if he hadn't heard the first time.

"But you don't know."

"Of course I know."

"But you're not sure."

"I said I'm sure."

"But you don't remember."

131

"Not at this moment, no."

"Then you haven't."

"I have."

"Describe it to me."

There is a long pause as she considers how to answer. What does a flu feel like? Or heatstroke? Or frostbite?

"It hurts," she says.

"That's an excellent guess."

"Thank you," she replies in a whisper.

"I sensed this about you."

"What?"

"You know so much about the world. You know so little about yourself."

"That's not true."

"You don't count the days. You don't pick a direction. You said yourself you try not to think too—"

"It's survival."

"What?"

"What would you do in my place? Drive yourself mad with questions that can't be answered?"

"I understand. I think I do. But the Calanshio. You have to wonder, don't you?"

She doesn't like what he is saying. She doesn't like the memories that are bombarding her. Did her ankle really heal so quickly? And how?

"Don't look at me like that, Mr. Kyengi," she says. "I assure you I am perfectly capable of getting myself killed."

"Yes, so are we all. But I don't think you are quite as capable as you think you are."

30

On a Train with Lionel Kyengi

Her memories of Russia will be sweet and painful. She will remember dressing morning after morning, undressing afternoons and evenings. She will remember laughter, intimacy, shameless impropriety just before lifting the door shade.

She kisses him—a thousand and one kisses by now—and pulls him to her.

"In Vladivostok," she says, "we will go to the library. I will take you."

"What library?"

"There are libraries all over the world, just for travelers like us."

"There are?"

"Yes. And I'm especially good at finding them."

Before he can ask anything else, the train shudders so hard their bags topple off the seats and her spear falls over. Shadows darken their compartment—black smoke billowing past their window. They feel the train slowing, squealing to halt.

Within an hour, everyone has filed off the train and is wandering the fields while the engineers fiddle and swear at the traitorous cast-iron engine. Of course, people are concerned about the delay, hoping repairs don't take too long, but otherwise they seem to enjoy the respite, stretching their legs among the tall grasses, exhaling in the cool air.

Lionel, alarmed for Aubry's sake, goes to take a look at the problem, finds the engine steam-hissing white smoke and black smoke, sees the glum expressions on the faces of the engineers.

But Aubry takes a walk instead. The grass is so high she can feel the feathery tops tickling her palm as she walks past. She takes a good long look at the landscape from end to end—the tossing wheat, the great solitude of the sky—sizing it up, just in case.

It is day one.

That evening, they spread out a blanket and watch the red summer sunset fade into a soft lilac glow, a sunset so exquisite they assume God is in love, too. But Lionel will not sit with her.

"They will talk about us, you know," he says.

Aubry sighs. Her love affairs are all scandals. She is the stranger who walks into town and steals away a man. It's a lie, but that is how it always seems. There is no room in her life for long engagements. She once knew a beauty from Zanzibar who floated from lover to lover, as light as a feather. She did not care what others thought. Aubry cares, but she's not about to add chastity to her list of sufferings.

"You like the danger?" says Lionel. "The notoriety?"

"I just like you. Now sit."

So he sits with her and they stare upward, watching the stars come out one by one.

"What I've done to deserve this, I don't know," he says.

"I don't either."

"It must be your travels."

"My travels?"

"You are everything I admire about Europe and everything I miss about Africa. I wish I could offer you such things."

"Lucky for you I don't ask for so much. Just kindness."

Long ago she found love but tasted only sand. She hasn't looked for love since, not in words, not in gifts, not in candlelight. But tonight, broken down in the prairies, nothing but the wind swaying the grass—of all places, it is here.

She remembers the trade routes, departing East Africa on a small outrigger loaded with cinnamon, sugarcane, and coffee. She sailed around the Indian Ocean, hopping from boat to boat, shipping small cargoes from island to island, often the only female on board. She speared dinners for various crews, ate with them, laughed with them. She was no longer the sullen girl on that Greek fishing boat, nor the cunning vagrant Uzair had known. She had found her footing at last, was as content as she'd been in years.

The sailors were so often young boys full of love, asking for her charity. But she was broke, with little to give. Oh, she may have kissed a few of them, and sometimes a little more than that, but she was a skeptic and carried Uzair's dead love on her back for years.

What is it about Lionel? His intelligence? His softness? Is it that they are both wanderers, outsiders in other people's worlds? She doesn't know, but the pull is there. She feels a sickness like homesickness, like the pain and the fear she felt that night when she left her mother for good. It is a terrible sickness and also precious to her, like a wild bird that eats only from her hands.

They try not to—someone could happen upon them at any moment—but they inch closer to each other. Their knees touch. Their fingers quietly mingle. They lie in the grass and count stars late into the night. They talk of fanciful things, things that could never be, until, finally, they are routed by the cold.

31

On a Train with Lionel Kyengi

Day two. They share the roof of the train with a collection of other passengers, watching the winds cast shifting patterns through the yellow grass.

Lionel says he saw the puzzle ball move again. He says he saw it roll across the shelf—only inches—but it moved quickly, silently, without the motivation of wind or a moving train. He couldn't sleep the rest of the night, watching it rest in a patch of moonlight.

Aubry tries to calm him, but he is shaken and exhausted. A terrible combination.

Meanwhile, the passengers have spread themselves out, some on the roofs, some perched on hillocks, some picnicking on blankets, others keeping to the comfort of their assigned seats.

It impresses Aubry, this fatalism. These voyagers who had been crossing the country, even the continent, have suddenly been made inert, tranquility compelled upon them. They put up with it well, powerless, mindful of being powerless. There is food, there is water, and they've offered an almost instant surrender. They loll, carefree, in an unexpected hush.

Aubry has watched people grouped on parlor sofas, reading their books, never saying a word to each other. She's seen luckless servants living out their lives in other people's homes, children studying their schoolbooks for hours upon hours only to end up sitting at desks in office buildings for the rest of their days. She's watched monks sitting cross-legged in mediation that lasted weeks, beggars sitting on the same street corners night after night, wealthy merchants smoking hashish pipes, discussing the politics of places they'd never been, bored housebound women listening to radios for hours, to shows set in faraway places they'd never see.

Perhaps her illness is a rejection of the sedentary life, her body rebelling against an inertia that mankind has, over the millennia, eased itself into. Suns and planets constantly revolve. Grass was always growing, seasons always changing. The earth would be empty if the winds hadn't blown the seeds, if the animals hadn't searched for better food, if early man hadn't stepped out of his cave. Wasn't it deep down inside each and every one of us, the nomadic life, the migratory push? The steppe that smooths the land from Poland to Siberia is made for walking. Wasn't she just doing what she was meant to do?

Day three. Lionel is frantic—the puzzle ball, her condition. Inertia is his enemy, too. He gets updates from the engineers twice a day. They are now saying things will be fine once next week's train catches up, which only makes Lionel more anxious. She tries to keep his mind occupied, alone in their compartment with the shade drawn, the puzzle ball hidden from sight. She is determined to make these days memorable for them. It works for the most part. Still, his fingers tap out nervous rhythms on his knee.

Later, while they are sitting on top of the roof in the afternoon sun, he suddenly says, "I'm going to see how things are," jumping to his feet and turning to her. "You . . . ? Are you . . . ?"

"I'm fine," she says.

They clasp hands a moment, then he goes to check on the engineers' progress, jumping from the roof of one car to the next until he comes to the engine itself.

He is only gone a moment when she tastes blood. She's been ready for this. She's been waiting for it ever since the train broke down. Even so, now that it is here, a cloud settles on her brain that no ray of light can probe. In the time it takes to taste the blood, her purpose has shifted from pleasure and joy to brute survival.

She is practiced at the art of leaving. No loss of composure, no tears. She simply gets to her feet, climbs down the ladder, and finds the compartment they've been sharing. She gathers her things and packs them up.

Her puzzle ball, though, she cannot find. Where has her puzzle ball gone? She'd hidden it, but where?

Behind her, a sound.

She turns, sees the puzzle ball slowly rolling across the floor. It comes to a rest at her toes like a pet that refuses to be left behind.

"Don't worry," she says, picking it up and packing it in her bag.

She goes outside and sits in the grass with the other passengers for a little. Next to her is a Russian family—a mother, father, a plump, cheerful babushka, several young children. With the little Russian she knows, she pulls a bar of chocolate out of her bag and offers it to them.

They accept gratefully. Their children love chocolate, all smiles on their faces. The mother digs into her bag and offers her a wheat loaf in return. Such a friendly exchange, no words necessary. It gives her a comfort she will need now that she has to do the hard thing.

When Lionel comes back, finding her on the grass, the engineer's progress report is written across his face.

"It's all right," says Aubry. "Have some bread."

He sits beside her. They share the wheat loaf in the airy silence of the plains. When she looks at the bread in her hand, she can see the spot of blood soaking through the bite mark, spreading outward in a tiny red circle.

The Gobi Desert is south of here. There will be prairie to pass through for a while, but then the grasses will dry up and the Gobi will be waiting for her, cold and harsh and empty. But if she gets through it, then perhaps on to—where? Peking? The China coast? Or the other way, toward Gansu, or Kazakhstan?

Does it matter?

She is perfectly still at first, watching the dewdrop of blood soak through her bread. She takes a breath, leans in, and kisses Lionel's cheek.

"It's time," she whispers in Lionel's ear, then stands up and walks away with her bag and walking stick. Lionel watches her go, baffled at first. He did not think it would be like this, so abrupt, so uncomplicated. He does not quite recognize what he is witnessing. He slowly gets to his feet, watching her. Aubry keeps going, straight into a vast indifference. Even the Russian family is confused watching her go. How peculiar this is.

Then he is running after her.

"Where are you going?" he calls to her. "Stop! You can't walk into that!"

Aubry turns, allows him to catch up, the two of them alone in the tall grass. "Why can't I?"

He stops, stutters. He does not know what to say or how to say it.

"Because I hardly know you" is all he gets out.

"I've rarely known anyone so well," Aubry says and turns to go.

"There's nothing out there!"

She stops and lowers her head. She speaks to her feet because she doesn't think she can look into his eyes.

"The whole world is out there," she tells him. "I know. I've seen it."

"I'll come with you."

She is overly familiar with drinking brackish water and warm blood, with chewing stringy leaves and eating animals raw. On bad nights, she remembers being a little girl, refusing her mother's cooking, and is plagued with shame. She will not allow Lionel to live that kind of life.

"We'll need water," he says. "Let me get water. I won't be long. Just . . . all I need is water. Will you wait?"

"No."

"For God's sake, you'll die out there."

"No," she says, finally looking at him. "You will."

"I'm coming."

"You have work to do. You're going to improve the world, Lionel. My job is only to survive it."

"Stop it . . . Don't . . ." He fumbles through his words. "You say . . . you say you have no value, but you do. You are valuable to me. I like to think we are valuable to each other," he says with a graciousness that brings physical pain to her chest. "What am I saying? Of course we are valuable to each other! What have we been doing on that train all week? What if . . ." and he struggles to catch up to his thought. "What if the reason we're here is nothing more than to find each other and be with each other? Isn't that more important than Vladivostok? Or anywhere else? Isn't it?"

She lowers her eyes, as if humbled, as if ashamed. "You said it yourself, Lionel. You made it very clear. This disease will either kill me or keep me alive forever. And I'm not about to die for you any more than you are about to die for me. Let's be painfully practical about this, shall we?"

They stand there. Lionel looks back at the train, at the water he wants to bring. He looks east to Vladivostok. She looks and what she sees, this lovesick man, wild with grief, cuts her in two.

"Lionel, I want nothing more than to have you with me," she says, prodding the ground with the end of her spear. "But you were put on this earth for a reason." She looks up. "And I wasn't."

She smiles gently to him and thinks if she is fast enough, she can escape before there are tears, before she loses control and makes it that much harder. She turns and walks into the grasslands without looking back. Several times he takes tentative steps, as if to follow her, then looks toward the train, then back to her. He clutches his head in his hands, like a child, his dignity as worthless as a mechanic's rag. Even though he is far behind her now, she thinks she hears him curse before folding like paper and crumpling to the ground.

But she isn't certain because she knows better than to turn around to see.

32

A Brief Aside

"You know," says her new friend, "I thought you'd be quiet and guarded, accustomed to being alone all the time. But you are the opposite."

Aubry met the young lady in a tavern somewhere north of Kanazawa. Aubry has been in Japan long enough to become conversant in the language and has made many friends these past few months, particularly in the small villages that dot the coast. The villages are close-knit farming communities and each has its own character. This village is particularly rowdy. Aubry and the young lady have ended up drunk, flat on their backs on a beach, staring up at the night sky. The young lady, who calls herself Yuki, has heard of Aubry, read about her in the papers, and was delighted to find her drinking warm sake with the locals in her favorite watering hole.

"Dancing with the girls," says Yuki. "Drinking with the boys. Talking to me, a total stranger. You are surrounded by people all the time."

"Does it seem so?" says Aubry, her smile fading a little. She thinks back on her travels. "It's strange, the impressions we make."

She remembers the swamp, somewhere, someplace she can no longer name, and she remembers pushing through it, the swamp where moss grew on all sides of the trees. With her spear she probed the dead stew of leaves and slime, all loosely held together by mangrove roots, making sure no snakes or crocodiles lay in wait for her.

"I've moved through entire countries unseen, unknown," she says. "Like a mist. Or a ghost."

She remembers the claustrophobia of it. There were insects buzzing in her ears, skipping over the water. There was birdsong. But there was a silence, too, as if she were being swallowed whole. She remembers, as if apart from herself, plying through black water up to her waist. She can almost see herself disappearing into the stumps and drooping boughs, her trail, all that is left of her, swallowed up by the pea-green weeds.

33

The Prince

She staggers, blinking. She's in a ravine, a shallow river between walls of rock, canyonlands of some kind, with no idea how she got here. She was climbing the mountains, and then the storm that turned her halfway to ice. She was dying, wasn't she?

But now her memories come back. For a moment she thinks, not memories, dreams. It must have been a dream. It certainly felt like one. For another moment, she's convinced she is crazy. Her feet are on dry ground, in a dry land. The sun is bright overhead. She has crossed the mountains. It's impossible, but she has done it.

She is alive.

The realization stills her. She looks about, takes measure of this place. She is as lost as she has ever been. Quickly, she runs through a checklist in her head: Her spear? Still in hand. Her bag? Slung over her shoulder. So far, so good. Name? she asks herself. Aubry Tourvel, she answers. Age? Forty, she thinks, though she's not entirely sure. If anyone asks, she will say thirty-nine, or maybe thirty-eight, which has an even nicer ring to it. Now where could she be? If she has crossed the mountains, then this should be Nepal, or India. It's certainly hot enough to be India. She hasn't felt heat like this in a long time.

Which way? East? West? She thinks of pulling out her puzzle ball and letting it decide. Her puzzle ball was so good at that. But the last time she saw it, it was on the other side of the mountains. It is gone, forever. She remembers that terrible night, too, and still grieves. It hardly weighed more than a hedgehog, but of all the things she carries, the absence of her puzzle ball is the heaviest.

The river flows southward. Follow a river long enough and there will often be a village, or a town, or a city along the way. A lifetime of experience has taught her that. And so she is following the river when, only a few steps into her journey, she walks into them.

Usually when Aubry runs into a stranger in foreign lands, she is pleased. It's almost always a good thing—someone who can feed her if she's hungry, someone who knows a safe place to spend the night. It has almost always been someone willing to help, and if they weren't quite willing to help, they were rarely interested in doing harm.

But when she turns the bend in the canyon and sees these three men walking her way, she feels a coldness from head to toe. What exactly makes her muscles coil up and her fingers grip her walking stick, she can't say. Something in their eyes, in their gait. It is the way they flinch at the sight of her, then see she is alone, then smile. They do not smile at her, but to each other. These are men who've gone a long time without a woman. These are men making terrible plans.

An instinct triggers deep inside, kicks her in the gut, but it's an instinct she trusts and, at that moment, wholly devotes herself to.

The fog lifts. Her mind sharpens. Her first thought is that they are three and she is one. Worse, the one in the middle is a giant among men. She keeps walking, pretends not to be afraid.

145

She even attempts a grin, but in her head, she is already aiming her spear.

Her second thought is to decide the order. Who first? The giant? The scrawny one? The man with the ghostly pale eyes? She is afraid, no matter how hard she pretends, very afraid, but making a decision helps. Once she does, she is able to store everything else away. In that twinkling, she accepts the probability of death, puts it behind her, and prepares her strategy.

The one on the left, that scrawny one, is suddenly alert. He is looking at her walking stick dragging behind her. She's knocked the cap off somewhere in the dozen or so steps it takes to close the distance between them. Now it's a spear. Can he tell?

They are spreading out. They mean to surround her. She understands, almost immediately and without being conscious of it, that this is a tactical error on their part. They will be easier to pick off when separate.

Her third thought is about all the things they don't know. They don't know that the words they intend to say will never be said—that the threats, the intimidations they are about to make, will never be made.

Her fourth thought kills the giant. She spins her walking stick in her hand and thrusts its iron point through his meaty neck, just as he is about to utter his last words. Instead, his throat fills with blood, which comes spewing out his mouth and splashes on the dirt at his feet.

Because she has dutifully carved a barb into the spear, she pulls the giant by his pain, straight onto the canyon floor, where he collapses like a landslide between herself and the scrawny man nearest the river.

Her thoughts come fast now, a rush of them. She knows the two skinny men will be rushing her from both sides. In a single fluid motion, she rips the spear from the giant's throat and rams the blunt end into the chest of the pale-eyed man. When he doesn't fall—just gasps and looks stunned—she rams him three more times—rat-tat-tat—knocking him backward until his skull hits the canyon wall and his legs give out.

By now the scrawny one has leapt over the fallen giant and is almost upon her. But she knows this, too, even before she spins around and meets him midstride.

Her spear breaks through his sternum and pops his lung. He falls like a buffoon, as if someone has pulled a rug out from under him. He hits the ground, coughing a bellow's worth of blood onto the smooth river rocks.

Thoughts come no longer formed, not even half-formed. She runs on pure reflex now, if she didn't before.

She remembers the pale-eyed man too late. He tackles her from behind, pummels her hard to the ground. She sucks in air. He pulls a knife and aims for her throat. She wriggles, punches, and kicks. His knife misses its target, sticking her just under the collarbone. She screams as he pushes the knife deep inside, but she is faster and meaner and grips two fistfuls of his hair, yanking him sideways.

They roll and she is on top of him, ramming her knee into his groin, twisting his hair, driving her thumb into his eye. He screams and swings wildly with his fists, cracking her in the side of the head. She buckles and he pushes her off, but she clings to his hair and they roll into the river, scrambling to keep above the water.

But it is Aubry who ends up on top.

While he flails with his fists, punching her in the throat, in the forehead, blackening her eye and bloodying her nose, her next thought comes to her. She wrenches his knife from her shoulder.

One more jerk of his hair and he is underwater, flailing and gurgling, the river filling up his lungs. He fights his way up, but she yanks his hair straight to the bottom again and a stream of bubbles erupts from his throat. With her other hand, she plunges the knife into his chest, again and again, until the water boils red, until his hands stop punching and his legs stop kicking.

She lets go of his hair, wriggles off the body, kicks it away. She watches the current sweep him up, carry him downriver in a halo of blood. She remembers the other two, and turns to make sure they are dead.

The giant has expired, all bled out and facedown in the stones, still clutching his opened throat.

But the scrawny one with a popped lung still functions, almost managing to sit up, blood slobbering down his belly. Stiff and drooling like the undead, he unholsters the giant's pistol and tries to target her.

Aubry is undisturbed, watching his hand wobble, the gun swaying in the air. He pulls the trigger but goes wide, the bullet punching a hole in the canyon wall on the far side of the river.

She is wearied and bruised, bleeding from the deep puncture under her collarbone. She gets to her feet and staggers to her spear lying on the riverbank.

Sitting there like a broken marionette, the scrawny one shoots again, misses again. Somewhere behind her, a puff of smoke and a dry clatter of pulverized rock.

She has her spear now, and stumbles toward him. He aims the pistol one last time, fighting through his pain, his lack of blood. But she has one final thought and pledges it to him, running the last few steps and sinking the spear into his gut as far as it goes. He spasms and his arms fly out, the gun firing once more into the dirt.

She steps back. Her heart pounds as if beating something to death. But she is alive and they are dead. She feels a palpable sense of disbelief, as if she is not here, and perhaps this has not happened. Her vision flattens, her focus pinholes. It is surprisingly like being drunk.

She doesn't hesitate, or take the time to calm her nerves. She works quickly, impulsively. Her inner voice is silent, her hands working furiously on her behalf. She pilfers their clothes and satchels, feels half-animal in the process, but now she has found bread and turnips, Chinese coins and paper money. She finds a long string of pearls and wonders who they'd killed to get it. She takes the dead man's pistol and all the ammunition she can find.

Tremors roll from her core to her fingertips. She gets to her feet and turns, ready to keep following the river southward and leave this place as quick as she can.

Blocking her way are a dozen men on horseback, watching her in disbelief. She freezes, stares, her spear aimed at them, her eye black, her lips swollen where the pale-eyed man had punched her, a wound wet and bloody under her collarbone, a gash across her cheek.

Some of them are in uniform—blue turbans and peacock feathers, silver buttons on white jackets, swords at their waist. Others carry rifles. Police, she is sure, or royal guards, who just watched her kill three men, then pilfer their belongings. They will hang her by sunrise.

One of the men dismounts. Unlike the others, he is modestly dressed, comes closer on sandaled feet. But her head is a cloud of adrenaline. If she is to die, she will not go alone. She rushes at him, spear raised.

He raises his hands in turn—no gun, no knife. She hesitates, steps back again, looks for escape behind her. She is hyperventilating. Her vision starts to blur.

"It's over," he says. "You are safe now."

A strange weakness descends upon her. All her thoughts empty into the earth. She collapses to her knees, and remembers nothing else from that day.

34

The Prince

"Get up!" shouts her sickness, the demon in her head. "A palace is waiting to be seen. A man is waiting to be met."

"Fuck off," she says. "I'm sleeping."

But she feels pain, like someone sticking their finger deep into the cut where the knife went in, and wakes. She feels for the knife wound, finds bandages there instead.

Surrounding her are the snores of men, sleeping bodies in the light of a bleached moon. The river is only paces away. Overhead, a blue-black sky framed by canyon walls. Morning is not far behind.

Slowly she unwraps herself from her blanket, grimacing from pain. Her spear and bag are next to her. Why would they not confiscate them? She grabs her things and, barefoot, steals away from the camp, over sand and river stone. She wades through water, turns a bend, and then sees someone in the dark.

He is a tear in the shadows, his white tunic a dim glow against the walls of the ravine. He looks as if he is trying to catch a fish, stooping in the shallow water. Perhaps he hasn't noticed her. She can turn back. It's not too late. She can try to climb the cliffs instead.

But he rises, facing her. She can't see his face, but she knows she's been seen.

"Oh, but you should rest," he says, his voice so clear in the echo of the chasm.

"What are you going to do with me?"

"We're going to take care of you." He comes toward her in no hurry, feet soundless in the river. He holds something wet in his hands. He was not trying to catch a fish. He was washing clothes.

"I'm a murderer," she says.

"I don't know that."

"You saw me. You saw what I did."

"Did those men attack you?"

"No."

"Did you attack those men?"

"Yes."

"Did you believe they were going to hurt you?"

"I don't know."

He pauses a moment. "I see." He wonders what to do, looking at her, looking at the dawn, then says, "This is how it was reported to me by the herdsman who was watching from the top of the cliff. He said he saw three large men surrounding a lone woman in an isolated area of the ravine. He ran and found us on the path. We rode as fast as we could to save you. But by the time we arrived, you had already saved yourself."

She's no longer sure of anything. Her dreams haunted her last night. She trusts her instinct, but instinct is only judgment made as quick as a finger-snap. It is not a measuring stick or a compass. It is an intuition, entirely fallible. If her instinct was correct, she had rubbed a bit of evil off the face of the earth. If it was incorrect, then she was a murderer, and a vicious one at that.

"Will there be a trial?"

"I hope not," he says. "You'd make an appalling defendant."

The sky has lightened, opening its eyes on the world. He wears a hint of a smile, almost imperceptible, but always there. A shaved head and he could almost be mistaken for a Japanese monk.

"Will they hang me?"

"My men are convinced you are Aubry Tourvel," he says to her, only steps away, "from Paris. The woman who wanders the world. Is it true?"

Her breath catches. They know her name. She takes a step back, grips her spear.

"I'm a Prince. I commute your sentence. Instead of a hanging, you are ordered to ride with us, to come to my palace and stay as my guest for as long as you are able, and, if you are willing, to tell me a thing or two about your travels."

In his hand is her shirt, holes in it, bloody. He's been trying to wash it clean, but it will never be clean. There is a lack of guile to this man that has her slowly lowering her spearpoint into the river.

"Have you really been around the world?" he asks her.

"Five times."

"Your feet must be sore. Let's find you some rest."

35

The Prince

They call him Prince Surasiva and he and his men have been surveying his realm for several days now, as is their custom every season. By afternoon, they have left the canyon behind and are crossing a dry, heat-blasted expanse of scrub and rock, of red earth and green palms. Aubry is no stranger to horses, and these are the finest she has ever seen, dappled coats and tossing manes shining against the rusty earth.

They break as the noonday sun peaks. Aubry sits in the shade of trees, wearing a mismatch of clothes donated by the men. A man in his sixties named Krishna, thin but hardly frail, tends her wounds. The Prince joins them. He wears a plain linen robe, a loose pair of clean white pants. So simple. His own escort outshines him.

"How is your eye?" he asks.

"Swelling is all gone," says Krishna. "She's a quick healer, this one."

"So I've been told," says Aubry.

"We read about you in the papers," says the Prince. "One time, a group of us sat in the parlor and wondered what it would be like to be you. Do you remember that, Krishna?"

"Oh yes. Everyone had a theory." He turns to the Prince, remembering. "Not you, though."

"I'd rather not know than think I know and be wrong. There are those, I find, who use their remarkable imaginations to visualize things that aren't there. The world is an epic poem in their heads, something they invent to lend purpose to their lives. But I gave that up. I don't remember exactly when, but I long ago decided to use my imagination to grasp what really is."

A thought comes to Aubry, fully formed. The words just come out: "But then, isn't this belief of yours an epic poem in your head as well?"

The Prince sits up. She's caught him in a paradox, like a swat on his nose.

"Yes, it is," he says, surprised. A smile blooms across his face—an utterly genuine, disarming smile, and then she is smiling, too.

An hour later, they are riding again, the Prince alongside her, the legs of their horses reddened with dust.

"The last any of us heard of you," he says, "you were in Kabul."

"Kabul?" Aubry has to think back. "Yes, I remember Kabul."

"That was only two months ago, according to the gazette. My men are curious which pass you took through the mountains."

The mountains? Does he want to know how she crossed the mountains? This will be a disaster. He will ask and Aubry will have no answer. There is no way to explain.

"I didn't go through them," she says after a long while. "I went over them."

Krishna, riding behind her, translates to the guard. A murmur breaks out. If she'd told them she'd flown from Kabul on the back of a sparrow, they couldn't be more amazed.

"They make such a noise!" says the Prince. "They are asking how you did it."

If she tells them, they will think she is either mad or a liar. Instead, she says, "I don't know how I did it."

"You don't want to say?"

"I can't say. I'm sorry."

It's an odd answer, she knows, perhaps rude, and she is afraid of their reaction. But the Prince says, "It's my fault for asking. I promise never to bring it up again. But please know that if there is anything you would like to talk about, I'm happy to listen."

The road takes them through a village and Aubry is struck by the genuine affection the people have for their Prince. They do not come in cheering crowds, but are quietly gracious to him as he passes, as if he were a close cousin or an old friend.

They spend the night in the house of a prominent family, their horses tethered outside. The family is not rich. Their house is not large. But it is only the Prince, Krishna, a few of the guards, and Aubry. Aubry is given a cot, but everyone else is perfectly comfortable on the floor with pillows.

The Prince and Krishna stay up late and speak to the family at length. They are told that an elderly couple has passed away in the night. It seems a small miracle of some kind that they died together in their sleep, at the same time. They were very much in love, even in their old age.

The Prince decides to stay in the village for several more days. At the cremation ceremony, he tells a story about the banyan tree the couple planted as children, how it is still growing, how it will grow for centuries to come. The people listen and nod their heads. Others tell about the death of the couple's children and the other burdens they had to bear, and even more people cry.

Then the pyre is lit and the bodies turned to ash.

"Why are they burned?" Aubry asks Krishna quietly, watching the embers floating up.

He turns to her. "Are you the same as your body?"

The question baffles her.

"You, Miss Tourvel, have no beginning and no end. Your body, however, does, and when it is worn out, you will have no need for it any longer."

After the sun has gone down, Aubry and the Prince wander the trails through the scrub. Though he promises her a place to sit, they wander for a long time. They talk of family, of strangers, the meaning of friendship and charity.

"Friends?" he says. "That's a tricky thing for someone in my position. I'm surrounded by friends all day long, too many to count, none of whom may actually be one."

"All my friends are acquaintances, passing me by on my way somewhere," she adds. "Just when I might have found one, I have to let them go."

Once past the edge of the village, they turn and watch the smoke from the cremation hang in a low spiral over the houses.

"Have you ever thought you couldn't go on?" the Prince asks her. He is exhausted by the day. There has been so much sadness and so many tears. She doesn't answer lightly. She wants to give him something true.

"Once," she says, "when I was young, and scared, and miserable. No friends. No family. No future. I was on a Greek fishing boat." She sits up. "I was a fisherman, Prince. Did you know that? I killed all kinds of things from that boat."

"It's good to have talents."

"Months, sleeping on a wooden deck. Before that, the forest floor. Before that, drainage pipes. And after? Where? Who knew? I didn't." As she speaks, she can feel that long-forgotten sense of panic return, lightly touching her heart. Or is it her recent panic, her spear sinking into the hearts of others? "I was fifteen, damn sure I wasn't going to see sixteen. Life was pain, Prince. Life was a fucking sadist. I swore. I just swore at royalty, Prince! Why'd you ask me that?"

"I'm beginning to wonder."

She'd have laughed, but in her mind she is afloat in the vast Mediterranean, golden in the setting sun, and it looks warm and lovely and inviting.

"I decided I would go for a long, long swim." And in her head, in that moment, she is leaning over the side of the boat, no land in sight, just beautiful pitiless tides everywhere. She wonders how best to enter the water without making a sound. She doesn't want these Greeks to rescue her. She wants to swim until she can swim no more.

"But then," she says, "right there, staring at me the whole time, was a monk seal."

A pair of shining eyes, a fractured prism of silvery skin beneath the waves—how could she forget? She thought she had earned a fearsome reputation with her spear by now, but this animal was completely unafraid, bobbing at her feet, so close she could have dipped her toe and touched its nose.

"How that animal lifted the fog from me, I couldn't say. But I never considered such thoughts again."

Silence between them. Whether it is the tone of her voice or the mood of the evening, she feels the Prince has divined her meaning.

"A lack of words," he says, "is not a lack of insight."

"No," she agrees.

Aubry wakes twice the next day, the first time well before dawn, the sky just a promise of light. She sits up, swings her feet out of the cot and onto the floor. She is not met with wool carpet or cold tile but, strangely enough, water.

She sees her feet are planted in the shallow river, on the smooth stones, water rushing past. This amazes her. She had fallen asleep in a house, in a village, but she is back in the ravine.

The water, so clear, so pure, suddenly turns red, a river of blood flowing over her feet.

"You are exactly where you need to be," says the demon. "And have done exactly what you need to do."

Then she wakes again.

When the Prince finds Aubry that afternoon, she seems distracted, out of sorts. Something of her still wanders the earth or wrestles in the ravine, but at the approach of the Prince, she brightens. They walk together, sharing the road with wandering cattle.

"Does it overwhelm you? The world?"

She's never been asked that, not in such a way. The Prince, so uninterested in easy questions. "I try not to bring too many things into it."

"You hardly carry anything at all."

"I don't mean that."

"You mean, yourself."

"Myself," she agrees, and for example, adds, "Self-pity."

"Self-doubt."

"I cast it all out."

"It's good to travel light."

"That was before I killed three men."

The Prince says nothing for some time. "That is a lot to carry."

"I had a puzzle ball once."

"Yes?"

"I'd carried that all the way from Paris."

"Did you lose it?"

"I threw it away."

She wonders if he can sense her grief, that there is more to the story than she implies. If so, he says nothing. He continues to visit others, consoling those who grieve, talking soil and water with the farmers, politics with the most prominent families. But, as evening approaches, he is with Aubry again, wandering roads and trails. They are together so often, walking side by side, that some of the villagers begin to wonder about them, smiling impishly as they pass.

"Well?" says Aubry.

"Well, what?"

"You haven't asked me. I leave you all these clues and you don't ask a thing."

"Now we are getting somewhere," he says and smiles. "Tell me about your puzzle ball, and why you threw it away . . ."

36

Hunters of the Plateau

The plateau was bronze, bronze mountains heaped upon bronze mountains. Below the mountains, the foothills were soft and spongy and brown—and they crawled. They crawled away, as fast as they could, disappearing in any direction as long as it was away from those dark imperious mountains.

It was all about distance here—how far the plains could stretch, how high the mountains could climb, how long a horse could last without water, how long Aubry could last without food.

She'd come south through the Kazakh canyons, spent years doing so. She'd roamed the lawless edges of Western China, considered cutting across the Tarim Basin. How harmless places look on a map—a blue squiggle of a river, a yellow dab of desert. On a map, the basin was a desert the size of Spain. On the ground it was the size of the world and utterly devoid of people. She decided to follow old Silk Road trails that circled around instead, ancient routes that skirted the foothills of the Kunlun Mountains and delivered her deep into the expanse of the Tibetan Plateau.

It wasn't so long ago that she'd passed the tiny nameless village nestled between hills, gazing down on it from the mountain trail, all its inhabitants asleep inside their stone and timber homes. She was gliding by, spectral, an apparition at most. They would never know she was there, this foreign woman who never stopped moving. Many of them had never seen blue eyes or blonde hair. As she left the village behind her, many never would. She wanted to get into the low valleys before the weather turned. She needed to hurry.

Time to Aubry was the rhythm tapped out by her footsteps and the changing climate. To the people in the village below, time was measured by the daily routine, the crowing roosters, the udders of their goats, the ripening of their barley. Time was long for the young lovers who waited for night, short for the old men who'd lived past their use. It was slow in the mountain villages, fast in the bustling cities. She'd once floated down the Colorado River and time lengthened like a beard, until the rapids cut it short again. It fascinated her, this malleability. She wondered if time slowed down for deserters facing the firing squad, for sailors in a storm, then sped up again while playing croquet or reading a favorite book. Did time ever stop? Would it wait for you to catch up? Would it hurry on ahead?

And then, suddenly, she was in the low valleys, as if no time had passed at all.

Now she sat on a stone in the soft yellow earth on the lee side of a wall of mountains called the Himalayas. She wasn't young anymore, but she didn't balk at the sight of them, only sat and studied this obstacle before her, calculating the climb, measuring herself against it.

She reached into her bag and pulled out her puzzle ball. She laid it on the ground at her feet, sat back, and waited.

"Go ahead," she told it. "Lead the way."

For a while she simply sat and watched, waiting for it to make the first move. It squatted in the yellow grass. Time passed. These were never quick decisions.

Then it rolled, straight ahead, coming to a rest only a few steps away—but the direction was clear—toward the snow-capped peaks.

That's when the little bird landed on it. It perched on the top of the ball, even pecked at it once or twice. It looked so comfortable atop the shiny wood, it seemed it might make a home there. But the puzzle ball shook and the bird flew off in a wild figure eight, landing again on Aubry's forearm.

What kind of bird was this? Soft and brown, a white underside, a long black beak. It perched on Aubry's sleeve, either completely unafraid or completely oblivious. For a minute or more it clung, so fragile. She could see the rapid beat of its tiny heart through its feathers. Had it mistaken her for a tree? She didn't dare move.

And then, as quick as it arrived, it flew off again, with a chirp, coasting over the dry earth. Her eyes tracked the little bird's flight, watching it loop low to the ground, then pull up—straight into the talons of a large eagle that swooped out of areas unseen. It snatched the little bird from the air and for a moment they were indistinguishable, predator and prey forming a single shadow upon the earth. Aubry's pulse froze a moment and her breath stopped in her lungs. A puff of feathers lingered in the sky.

The puzzle ball, as if struck with fear, quickly rolled back, straight into Aubry's bag that lay open in the dirt, and disappeared from sight.

But Aubry watched the giant bird circle on a curve of wind, then bank to the north on outstretched, dark-tipped wings large enough to hide a prayer wheel, before finally landing on Pathik's arm.

He was a nomad, dressed in a coat and a long red robe. The eagle's wings blew the fur on his hat and ruffled his horse's mane, but his eyes never left her. The amazement on his face was easy to read. Aubry had seen it many times before. A woman, he was thinking, days, weeks, from anything resembling a village. And a strange woman at that. She wondered if he had ever seen a white woman before. Out here, it seemed unlikely.

He dismounted, cautiously, cast his eagle into the air, and approached. Aubry watched him come near, their gazes stuck on each other. He paid no attention to her bag or the puzzle ball inside. He must not have seen it rolling about by itself. Thank God for that. Then they were close. He leaned forward to peer into her eyes.

"*Tapāīle kahāībāṭ āekā hunuhunchha?*" he asked softly.

"Oh, don't even bother repeating it," she answered softly, matching his tone.

He repeated it, this time less like a question, more like amazement.

They stood close to each other, together in a vast wilderness. He muttered more words, to himself this time. She stared back at him. She'd met more than a few Tibetan nomads—but she watched his expression and shared the thrill of seeing something for the first time. She'd been there, too, once, not so long ago, perhaps again soon, perhaps today.

He looked to the ground between them, gestured with his arms, suggested they sit. So they did, face to face, watching each other. Once seated, he remembered his manners. He offered her something to drink from his wooden canteen. She took it, drank something so strong, so sour, she almost gagged.

His eyes widened, afraid he'd offended her, but she smiled, nodded her head, and lied. "It's good. Thank you," she said and took another sip, better prepared this time.

"Thank you," he said.

He'd picked up his first French words, without prompting, thick with accent, but French.

"Very good," she said and repeated it for him.

"Thank you," he repeated back, then tentatively reached for her hair. *"Malāī hun sakkha?"* he asked.

He was a very polite nomad. She let his hand slowly push back her fur-lined hood, let him rub the strands of her hair between his fingers.

"Sunai . . ." he murmured to himself. His eagle circled around them, sometimes flying low and close. They would hear it glide past like a rush of wind. Again, Pathik stared into the blue of her eyes. She leaned into him as well, since they were studying each other close and without shame.

No more than a fingerbreadth apart, they couldn't help but smile—big, silly, childlike smiles that spread across their faces and made their eyes smile, too.

"Tapāīle gharbāṭ dūrai chhan," he said.

She reached her hand out, gave him a look that asked consent. He hesitated a moment, then allowed it. She took off her silk glove and ran her hand through his thin close-cut beard, pretending she'd never seen one before.

He took her bare hand, awestruck by how soft it was. She could see the questions rippling across his face: How had she gotten here? From how far? And why? He carefully pulled the glove off her other hand to see if it was as smooth. It was. He held it in awe.

He saw the material of her collar. She unbuttoned her sheepskin coat, slipped it off so he could see the red sheen of Chinese silk underneath. On her arm, he saw the end of a scar and pushed up her sleeve. His fingers traced the length of an old wound.

"Fell on a cactus," she said.

Then he took off his sheepskin coat, pulled up his sleeve, and revealed an old scar on his arm, too, in almost the very same place as hers.

"*Khukuri*," he said, and she wondered if he'd fallen on a cactus, too.

Then she remembered another wound and rolled up her pant leg. There on her calf, another scar.

Excited, he rolled up his pant leg to show her a similar scar just under his knee. She slapped his leg as if he were her brother, and he slapped her leg back. Again, they were smiling like fools.

Because his coat had been removed and his shirt pulled back, she noticed his necklace, a big tooth of some strange animal hanging from a piece of twine, tattooed with purple patterns—perhaps an ancient script. Perhaps a charm or a trophy.

"*Yo ekā chitwanīko dānta ho*," he explained, holding it out to her.

"Is that so?" she said, and they both laughed at the uselessness of their words.

She showed him her necklace—a beetle trapped in amber, hanging from string. It had once hung from a gold chain Uzair Ibn-Kadder had given her, but that chain had snapped long ago.

He stared, amazed, so amazed she removed it from her neck and offered it to him.

"Here. It's yours."

He protested, shook his head, waved his hands, but she insisted. Perhaps out of politeness—was that the custom here?—he took it, then immediately offered his tooth with the purple etchings. And so two necklaces exchanged necks.

"*Dhanyabād*," he said, humbly.

"*Dhanyabād*," she repeated. He was impressed.

"*Dherai ramro. Dhanyabād.*"

"You're welcome."

Each of them stared at the other. Goodbye seemed out of the question. She was having far too much fun. He sighted the sun and pointed in a direction. Southwest, she reckoned.

"Ma kehi shikār garirahēko chu."

She pointed the same way.

"Well, well, what do you know," she said. "So am I."

37

Hunters of the Plateau

She rode on the back of Pathik's horse, up and down the swells and gullies in the earth, holding fast to his chest. His hunting eagle would cling to his glove while they rode, or sometimes on a perch built into the saddle. Occasionally it would circle them overhead, never straying far.

After a while, Pathik found what he was looking for. He'd been studying the ground for clues, scanning the horizon, always looking. Finally he'd discovered something. He dismounted, crept down to inspect. There were strange animal tracks pressed into the dirt, very large—three sharp talons as long as daggers in each step. This wasn't a leopard or a wolf or a bear. She'd never seen anything like it.

"Are you hunting this?" Aubry wondered in French, out of habit, then pantomimed the question again, holding her spear, pointing at the tracks. He recoiled a bit. He didn't realize she had a spear. Once he accepted that, he turned his attention back to the strange tracks. He nodded, said something grave in his language. All this sobered her. They turned their gaze in the direction of the tracks, wondering where in the vast terrain this creature could be hiding.

They rode more, until the sun grew low, when she suddenly

sat up in the saddle, leaning on Pathik's shoulders. She gave his shoulders a squeeze and he pulled back on the reins.

She dismounted with her spear. Pathik, curious, waited on his horse, watched her creep through the grass, her spear raised and ready. She crept up and over a mound of earth. From where he sat, he could just see her let loose with her spear, then disappear over the rise.

When she returned, she showed off a wriggling, whistling pika impaled on the end of her spear. Pathik laughed, once again enthralled by the strange woman. She hammered the pika into the ground, killing it. That night, though the meat smelled awful, they ate a bit of it by a fire, with tea and pickled cabbage and sour yogurt he poured from a yak horn.

"Hāmīle kahilyai paikā khādainau," he said, chewing bits of meat right off the animal's bones. *"Māsā gandā dhūndhalo cha."*

Who knew what he was saying, but it sounded sweet, so she smiled back and everything felt right.

The next day they followed the tracks to a kill. Aubry dismounted to take in the sight. She was stunned. This thing they were hunting had killed not one, but two wild horses—torn them to pieces and gorged on their insides. There was the amputated head of one horse, and at the end of a dried-up river of blood, its hindquarters. There were legs and ribs scattered about, and the earth, torn up in all directions, was covered in three-toed tracks.

When she turned back to Pathik, still on his horse, he was watching her closely. He seemed worried, perhaps regretful, dragging her so close to danger. She held his gaze, then nodded solemnly and climbed back onto the saddle.

For three more days they followed tracks while it was light, slept around a fire when it got dark, always sleeping within an arm's length of each other, his heart pumping blood next to hers. He'd shown her nothing but courtesy and respect. She began to wonder if she smelled of horse dung and rotten onions. Or perhaps this was just her, alone for too long, melting like sugar at the first genial face.

On their fifth day together they stopped at a hillside. Pathik climbed to a high spot with his eagle, scanning the tundra below.

Then there was the shriek, clear and shrill, like a saw blade on stone. It echoed over the hills. She thought it must be big, thought it must be close, but when she scanned the landscape there was nothing to be seen.

Pathik came down from the hill, eagle perched on his arm. He looked at Aubry, gave her a nod, and readied his horse.

38

Hunters of the Plateau

They followed the three-toed tracks until the sun went down, then kept following by torchlight. They followed them through dust and grass and around a wide hill until they came upon the large deep hole dug into the side of a cliff.

The moon was hidden. The darkness was thick. The dim torchlight shone in waves that lapped at the ground, casting shadows like animals crouched in the gullies. It was so dark she could hardly see the hole even after Pathik pointed it out. She could hardly see the ground as Pathik dismounted.

The horse reared nervously. Even the eagle that seemed unafraid of anything squawked and spread its wings defensively on Pathik's arm. Pathik tossed the bird into the air and it took flight. He tied the horse to a bush. Aubry was half-numb with dread, but slid to the ground anyway, taking her spear from the saddle. Pathik continued to ready himself. He grabbed a coil of rope and his short spear.

The eagle swooped down. Pathik and Aubry both heard it, the swish of air between them, the fleeting shadow in the corner of their eyes. Pathik shined his torch. The eagle had landed on a pile of bones—rib cages, horned skulls, femurs and hooves, all scattered on the ground around the cave, like an overturned graveyard. Some of the animals were big. She noticed yak and donkey and even something that looked like a leopard skull.

None of this deterred Pathik. He planted his torch in the ground. She did the same, watching him carefully, mimicking his moves. She saw him pause, shake off his fear, then carefully approach the hole. He tied a slipknot in the rope and looped it around the entrance. He took the other end of the rope, tied it to a wooden spike, and staked it to the ground. He looked around, double-checked his work. She looked, too, double-checked with him, no idea what the plan was.

He looked at her, as if just noticing she was there. He shooed her away, pointed past the horse. He wanted her to hide, to be safe, but she stood her ground and shook her head. She would not leave the man who had shared his saddle with her for seven days, who had fed her, who had touched her hair, and felt her scars, and made her smile.

He stared back, examined her face for signs of fear. There were plenty, she was sure, but he looked away and went back to his preparations.

From the saddle he pulled a bundle of sticks she'd watched him collect earlier in the day. He wrapped them tightly together, brought them to his torch, and lit them. The flames spread until that bundle was the brightest point in the tundra.

Then he went to the mouth of the burrow and tossed the fire down its throat.

From deep underground, there was thrashing and screeching. Pathik's eagle startled, took flight, disappearing into the night. He took a position, hunkered low with his spear. She watched and did the same, low to the ground, spearpoint up. The earth shook beneath her feet. Dirt crumbled from the edges of the hole.

Exploding from its burrow, wailing and snapping, it came.

The dirt flew. The lasso Pathik had looped around the hole caught the creature and went tight around its long neck as it charged.

Even in the undulating torchlight, it was enormous, taller than any man, bear, or horse. It came charging and the weight of those taloned feet—yes, they must be, she thought, must be talons—shook the ground, snapped the scattered bones, and rattled the heart in her chest.

It roared right at Pathik, who stood his ground—the fool!—spear braced against the earth. Then the rope went taut, the stake held fast, and the creature reeled back, almost pulled off its feet.

It spun in frantic circles, talons clawing at the earth. It kicked up dirt and buried skulls. It spun so hard some of its feathers—it had feathers—came loose and swirled through the air. The horse tried to bolt but couldn't untangle its tether from the bush.

And the creature's wings—huge wings spread like cloaks—beat against the night. The air filled with dust, half-blinding Aubry and Pathik.

Pathik charged with his spear before him, like a human dart, jabbing and feinting and jabbing again, looking for the perfect strike.

Aubry gathered her nerve and moved in low, her spear upraised. She lunged from its other side. It let loose a high-pitched screech. There was a flash of yellow and orange, a sharp crack in the air. Its beak—like two shovel blades colliding with each other—snapped just shy of her head, a noise like a pistol shot in her ear.

She pitched, stumbled backward. The thing came at her, its beak snapping, talons kicking up dirt and bone. The stake pulled from the ground, spinning through the air like shrapnel—a whir in the space where Pathik wasn't looking, just missing his brow. The creature, sensing its freedom, spread its wings and swung in circles. It hissed and spat. Pathik dodged, was clipped hard and slammed to the ground. The creature stomped a torch and the snaky, resinous light was halved.

But then the creature jerked back. Pathik had the rope in his hands and reeled the creature in, pulling hand over hand. The thing leaned sideways, almost toppling, its long thick neck curved like a hook. Pathik kept his focus, wrenched the creature even closer, timed his move, and leapt, grabbing the massive bird by its neck and swinging himself onto its back.

Aubry saw this, saw the danger of it, saw the advantage, too. The creature spun, shook, but Pathik did not come loose. It tried to claw him off, but could not reach. It snapped at him and tore a hole in his sheepskin coat, and still Pathik held fast with a stranglehold, his arms tighter and tighter around its neck.

The thing hissed and howled, beat it wings, then, in its fury, it pivoted straight into Aubry's spear.

The spear sank deep into its side. Aubry pressed it in farther, could feel the spearpoint pushing through layers of meat and tissue. The creature screamed, rage for pain, then shuddered and fell, the bulk of it pinning Pathik to the ground.

Aubry scrambled through the dark, found Pathik's spear. She came at the creature, braced her foot against its breast, and buried that spear into the soft spot at the base of its neck, all the way through to the creature's heart.

Slowly, the dust clouds began to drift away. She grabbed Pathik by his arms and wrenched him out from under the animal. They fell to the ground, exhausted, windless, adrenaline still pumping. Despite her whole body throbbing like a wound, Aubry closed her eyes and completely forgot to open them again until the sky was full of light.

39

Hunters of the Plateau

She remembers her sickness, its low voice whispering to her in the night: "I'm sorry. I did not mean to put you in so much danger. I only wanted you to see."

"Why?"

"That's a fool's question," it growls, patience running thin. "Ask yourself, if you could take it back, would you?"

When she woke, Pathik was butchering the bird. She hadn't dreamt it. Her brain slowly unfurled and she understood, with a terrible pang of regret, that the creature was gone. With all the dust and terror and dying torchlight, she'd never gotten a good look at it, and now she never would. She would never know what it was, what the Latin word for it might be, or the French or English word for that matter.

She looked at the pieces scattered around. The talons had been removed and tossed into a pile. So had the beak, its curved shape useful for something. Chunks of leg were impaled on sticks so the blood could drain out. She saw a wing and pulled it by the tip, feathers outstretched. With both hands, she lifted it higher than her head and still it wasn't stretched to its fullest.

Pathik sliced more cuts from the beast with his carving knife, arms red up to his elbows. When he saw Aubry was awake, he reached into the bushel of feathers he had plucked. From it, he took the most fetching, bright gold and red—from the creature's crest, Aubry imagined—and offered it to her.

She accepted, awed by its beauty, and held it up to the light. It was a creature that no one knew existed, too fantastic to be believed, but here was proof.

Bit by bit, the unrevealed earth rolls itself out, carpet-like.

40

The Prince

She stops suddenly in the middle of her story. She has been acting out the killing of the monster for the Prince, and enjoying the telling, under the moonlight in the dark savanna. She even has her spear out, posing with it, raising it in the air, bringing it down on cue.

But now, after all that, she stops, goes still. Her eyes don't leave the Prince. It's a reversal. Until now, it's been the Prince studying her. "Go on."

"It's not so easy, Prince."

"I can see that."

She watches the Prince carefully, the way one watches a dog sniffing about for a buried corpse.

"You don't understand. People, they confess everything," Aubry says. "There was a woman who told me she once made love to a serpent. There was a man who told me he was sunk by a ghost ship on the high seas." A pause, not sure what she's trying to say. "I don't want to sound like them. Not to you. Not to anyone. It's vanity, I suppose. Look at me. I'm a middle-aged woman sleeping in the wilds. I hardly have the right to be vain. But I suppose I am. Still. After all this time." She shakes her head. "I'm going to finish this story, Prince," she says. "I don't care if

177

you believe me or not. If you don't believe it, just pretend you do. Can you do that? Can you do that for me?"

"I haven't doubted you yet. You think I have, but it's not true."

"Well," she says ruefully, laying her spear gently on the ground, "you will."

41

Hunters of the Plateau

Days later, after a long trek across the plateau, feasting on well-earned meat, they arrived at Pathik's home. It was no more than a pair of black tents woven from yak hair, fortified around the edges with stone and earth. Six horses were tethered nearby. She didn't see any, but all around were signs of cattle—the dung, the trampled earth, clumps of hair caught in the grass.

And overshadowing it all, the frozen mountains, the terrible rise of the earth.

His family gathered to greet him—parents, grandparents, sisters, brothers, children, in-laws perhaps—a dozen or more in all, dumbstruck to see the foreigner sharing the saddle with him.

One of the older women pointed, her face aghast. Perhaps his mother? An aunt? What would they think of her, of this? Pathik wouldn't have brought her here if she wasn't welcome, she was sure. So Aubry smiled, made herself as pleasant and humble as she'd ever been.

But the shock was greater than that, far beyond scandal. She saw it in their faces, the way they huddled together, clinging to their children. Riding on the back of Pathik's saddle was proof of a world wider than they knew—wider, larger, and stranger than any they'd ever conceived.

They were afraid.

The old woman sputtered out a series of words. Pathik replied with words of his own that meant nothing to Aubry except that she heard her name and assumed she was being introduced, or perhaps explained.

Conversation erupted, questions all at once, everyone looking at her. Pathik climbed down, helped Aubry dismount, went into a long story. He pantomimed stabbing. His family looked dazzled. She watched fear transform to bewilderment, then wonder. A woman—she'd later learn she was Pathik's sister—came up to her, smiling sweetly.

"Aubry?" she said as best she could.

"Yes, Aubry."

"Ojal," she said, pointing to herself.

"Ojal," said Aubry, and they bowed to each other.

There were greetings, all at once, everyone bowing, pressing hands together as if in prayer. Aubry copied them, hands together, bowing to each of them. The little children tugged at her strange clothes. The adults admonished them, but she bent down and showed them her Chinese silk and her Russian fur. She heard kind tones, saw broad smiles. Her heart lightened. Pathik's family, this little corner of the world, was like a spring in a dry land and, as it often happened, Aubry was surprised by happiness.

As the night settled in, they ate the bird over a fire of burning yak dung outside the tent. Other strips of meat were drying on racks or had been preserved in wooden jars. Pathik's family chatted, laughed, and told stories. They constantly offered Aubry food and drink. An old woman—a grandmother? An aunt?— inspected the bushel of feathers, showing off her favorites, everyone discussing how much they might fetch at the market so many months from now.

At least, that's what Aubry thought they were saying, plucking from their dialogues the few words she'd learned. She had her feather already, bright red and gold, the most fetching of the bunch. She was already learning phrases, listening for strings of words, repeating them under her breath.

The next day, she woke early with everyone else. She saw the eldest quietly give thanks to the little Buddha on the far side of the tent, so Aubry gave thanks, too. She stepped outside to see the day and followed sounds of singing, which must have carried a mile or more. She hiked until she discovered the young boys watching over a herd of yak a hundred strong, and even more sheep, massed on a hillock like moss on a log. The boys circled them and sang, occasionally pelting a wandering animal with their slingshots. Aubry spent the rest of the morning watching, learning, listening to the songs. The boys gave her cockeyed looks—this wasn't women's work—but she was strange and had killed a monster, so they didn't disallow it. Kunchen, the youngest of the boys, no more than eight, seemed to enjoy her company, even sat with her and taught her more words. She'd always liked children, always felt at ease with them. This little boy was no exception.

When she saw the boys filling their sacks with water at a well, she fished her waterskin out of her bag and went to fill hers, too, Kunchen skipping alongside.

What must he have thought, watching her face turn pale like that, watching her body shudder, her confident stride turn paralytic?

The well was made of stones, large and smooth and gray, fitted together so tightly a needle couldn't fit between them. But more than that, the rim of the well had been carved in the shape of a face, two eyes chiseled into one end, a tiny beard into the other, the gaping maw of the well forming its mouth, complete with lips and teeth.

Aubry looked down at that face, went tight and airless. She did not fill her waterskin. She did not take a single step closer to the well. She only stared at it for the longest time, perfectly still, until Kunchen took her gently by the hand, and led her away.

42

Hunters of the Plateau

That night—moonless, starless—Aubry stole away from the tent while the others slept. She had fumbled her way through supper, silent while others talked. Kunchen had certainly told them she did not like their well and they probably wondered why. But Aubry could not concern herself with that. She had to make plans.

The entire plateau was an endless shadow. She was afraid she would not find the well in such absolute darkness, but she kept the silhouette of the mountains behind her right shoulder, stayed on the high grounds, and eventually spotted it—a silvery ring between gray knolls.

As she approached, her lips began working, silently. Her cold hands reached into her coat pocket and drew out her puzzle ball.

The puzzle ball spun in the air and dropped to the earth. It stayed a moment, then began to roll. It escaped to the left, then to the right. She chased after it in the dark. There was desperation in the way she kept after it, clumsily, like a panicked animal. But she could not let it get away. This was her one chance. Soon she had it again, snatched off the ground, held tight to her chest.

She shuffled to the edge of the well, jaw clenched, breath fast and shallow. What she failed to do at the age of nine, she would do now. All would be forgiven.

"Please," she said, and kept saying. "Please . . ."

Her arms extended outward, the puzzle ball shivering in her hands, held over the mouth of the well.

"Please."

She let it go. It fell past the teeth and lips and mouth, into the well's black throat. There was a stalled moment, then the echo of water bouncing back.

She felt faint. She wrapped herself in her own arms, sucked air back into her lungs. Would this be the end of it? Could she stay, here, in this one spot without repercussion? Would the pain never torture her again? Could she go home at last? It took some time for her nerves to settle. When they did, she heard the sickness in her head say, "That was foolish."

"I didn't ask you," she snapped back.

The sound of her own voice in the night startled her. She had said it out loud. It took her a moment to understand, but it was the first time she had ever heard the demon outside a dream. She felt it close, a presence behind her, just over her shoulder.

Slowly she turned, but the only one she saw was Pathik, and she was damn certain the demon was not him. Pathik had followed her. He had seen everything, even her madness, if that's what it was.

Were the naysayers right? Was everything she had gone through, her sickness, her travels, all in her head?

Pathik came near and she looked him in the eye. If she was mad, then he deserved to see it. Tonight, of all nights, it should be plain on her face. But he only held her gaze a moment before he looked at the well. He understood it was a strange well, perhaps unique among wells, but couldn't imagine what, exactly, it had meant to her.

She closed the space between them, white clouds of breath pouring over each other. She threw her arms around him and held on tight. She felt saved, pressed against his body, as if pulled from a storm-swept sea.

Side by side, they made their way back to the tent in a profound silence. His mouth was full of questions he could not ask. She had no strength to answer them anyway. All the way back, she kept looking over her shoulder toward the well, until she could no longer see it in the night.

43

Hunters of the Plateau

She dreamt she was standing over herself, administering a final cure. She dreamt the demon had all but died and she carefully unscrewed its claws from the base of her skull, leaving its withered body on the plateau to waste away.

She woke that morning elated, feeling on the cusp of freedom. She'd sacrificed her puzzle ball, but look what she'd gained. Once, she was as insubstantial as a ghost, a vapor drifting in the night. Now, she began to feel tangible, legitimate, like something that might stay. It was too strange a thought to be real, but something in her mind, in her body, told her it was so.

She gave thanks to the Buddha, then helped the women churn the milk and skim the butter off the top. She cracked open yak bones to simmer in a pot. She helped scrape cheese that had been forming inside a wooden jar.

She paid more attention to words and conversations than ever. She sensed it was coming, her first conversation with Pathik, without sign language, without pictures or pantomimes. They would talk and learn things they didn't know. They would explain their childhoods to each other. They would make each other laugh and, on occasion, cry. He would teach her how to live in this corner of the world and, when it was time, they would go off together and hunt.

But first, she would listen to the chatter and learn.

After so many chores, she ached for the open sky and stole away to see where the boys were. She sat on a nearby knoll and stitched the hole in the back of Pathik's sheepskin coat where the bird had bitten it through. She watched the yak roam while she worked, the long black hair from their flanks and bellies sweeping the sedge like feather dusters. Here, no kingdoms stood, no invaders stayed. Nothing was grown. Everything was animal— the clothes, carpets, tents, and ropes all woven from animal hair, the fires burned from their shit, the food all milk and meat.

The shadows grew. The herd moved on and she found herself alone. Pathik strode by with an empty water sack and stopped to greet her.

"*Madhesh. Rāmro,*" said Aubry, and Pathik blinked. Then he gave her a little bow and said, "*Yo dherai rāmro cha,*" flashing a big grin her way.

She got up and joined him, reaching down to pick up the empty sack of water. He shook his head and protested, insisting on carrying it himself. But Aubry insisted right back and walked off with it, heading into the gullies where they couldn't be seen.

Pathik looked around to see if anyone was watching, then followed. She would not wait for an elaborate courtship. She was as happy as she had ever been, and this was how she wanted to celebrate.

The well was just over there, such a short walk away, but it would take Pathik over an hour to reach it.

44

Hunters of the Plateau

Later, they straightened out their clothes, tied each other's belts, picked the grass out of each other's hair, and for the rest of the day, they were glowing. They could not speak to each other. They couldn't say with any certainty what was going through the other's mind. All they knew was that they had made each other very happy. So simple, this wordless exchange—a moan here, a kiss there. She hadn't felt this alive in a long time, her senses heightened, air breathing on the back of her neck as if for the first time. She looked at the plains, all weather and distance, as if she had never seen weather and distance before.

She thought about all the men she had loved—not so many, really. How many men had she met? There were millions of people in the world and she felt she must have met most of them. Yet, she could count her intimacies on one hand. Out of so many, so few. What made her pick them from the crowds? Each loved in a different way—foolishly, passionately, quietly, even without words. For every stage in her life there seemed to be a love that incarnated it, that embodied what she needed, whether she knew it or not. In this way she'd been lucky.

They gathered in the night, telling stories, making jokes. An iron pot hung over a fire in the center of the tent, the smoke filtering out a small chilly hole in the canopy. She had seen the yak eating the wild garlic and their burning dung made the air delicate with its scent. Pathik's family was having fun teaching Aubry new words. They would point to an object, tell her the name, have her repeat it, and then laugh at her mispronunciations. They laughed so hard their bellies hurt—Aubry, exaggerating her mistakes to the delight of the children.

Her conversation with Pathik, their very first—it would happen. She had found the well, even had the proper gift for it. She'd bought herself more time, perhaps a lifetime. It was the cure to end all cures. It went back to the beginning of it all, sickness pulled out by the roots. She did not understand how it had happened but, for now, it was enough to know it had. She looked around the tent at the faces full of laughter, thought she could easily spend a lifetime here. It was something familiar, a family gathered together, sharing a meal, the cold weather kept securely outside. And perhaps that's the purpose of travel, to sift out the familiar from the foreign, to unearth those moments that remind us of home.

Pathik, sitting beside her, suddenly looked concerned. He reached out, touched her lip, and showed her the dot of blood staining his fingertip.

It was almost undetectable, her reaction—that moment where Aubry went numb, when her thoughts turned black with dread and rage—because she smiled through it. She made a puzzled face as if the drop of blood were a mild curiosity when, in fact, something snapped inside her, like the coil of sanity, like the wire that held her soul together.

"*Timīlāi sabai thik cha?*" asked the old woman.

"*Timīlāi sanchai lāgchha?*" asked Pathik's sister.

But Aubry laughed it off, said in her halting voice, "*Malāi dherai sanchai cha. Ma yahã dherai khushī chu,*" and everyone laughed, not because she'd mangled their language, but because she'd spoken it almost perfectly. Faces lit up, the children laughed, everyone at ease—except Pathik, studying her quietly. He saw something in her face, in her eyes, that was beyond what he could grasp, beyond, perhaps, what was graspable. Aubry touched his hand and they smiled to each other, but in the back of her mind, she was already making grim calculations.

That night, when the tent was full of snores and only burning embers were left in the fire, she rose from her mattress. The entire family slept in a ring of bodies, the men on one side of the Buddha, the women on the other, among whom she'd found her place.

She put on the coat that she had hidden under her blanket. When she finished lacing her boots, she looked up, noticed one of the children, Kunchen, awake and watching her. He didn't understand what Aubry was up to, but concern was plain on his face. Aubry put her finger to her lips and he said nothing, not a sound. Aubry had just made the poor boy complicit in her escape, but she couldn't think for everyone. She couldn't make this painless for all. She got up and walked to the entrance curtain.

She passed Pathik, asleep in his cot. Standing over him, she hesitated. She felt weak, felt like crumbling. Was she really so unforgivable? What, exactly, was her crime? What could a nine-year-old schoolgirl have done to end up wandering the world in exile, friendless and miserable and without love?

One day she will be old, still walking in the rain, sleeping through the cold, stealing from the gardens of others. The well called her close, not to save her, but to take better aim. Perhaps that is the plan: to neglect her, to watch her heart calcify, to cover her body with wounds so the demon can insert its claws and keep them open forever. Perhaps the goal is madness.

She almost reached down to shake Pathik awake. She wanted to explain. More than that, she wanted to be saved.

But Kunchen was watching.

She pulled herself away, stepping through the curtain and into the night air. Before her were the endless summits. She wanted to ignore them, the spine of winter with white clouds blowing down from their heights, always beckoning, always reminding her that the journey was lifelong. Her spear was waiting by the tent flap, her bag hidden not far away. She grabbed them both and headed out by dim moonlight, toward the black eclipse of the mountains.

45

The Prince

"Why do you stop there?" says the Prince. "The mountains—what is it you can't tell me?"

But Aubry has gone stiff. Her body shakes, muscles tightening like fists. Tears stream from her eyes.

Then blood from her nose.

"If you can make this stop," she cries, "I will tell you everything I know."

The Prince leaps to his feet, takes her by the arm, and quickly leads her away. For the first time, his voice is raised, shouting for help, making commands.

Krishna and his guards are alerted, come running into the predawn. She is carried to a horse and they ride out of the village, barely able to explain their sudden departure to the growing crowd of villagers.

Within an hour her symptoms pass. She is sitting upright in her saddle, perfectly at ease, and a few hours after that, she spots the palace in the distance, sprouting from the red earth, made of the red earth, walls and towers linking hilltops together, reaching for the sky as if finishing the job the hills had only begun. So far, she has only seen the Prince in his simple clothes, with his handful of guards, but this palace puts him in an extravagantly new context.

"What is that?" says Krishna, and everyone turns around to see.

Earlier in the day it was a view of red scrublands with a hint of green hills beyond. Now, it is an ochre haze that wipes out the horizon, and it is creeping closer. They can already feel the wind in their faces.

They ride toward the palace, still hours away. By the afternoon, the sky is the color of rust. Their clothes billow in the wind. Sand scours the road. They grow fearful. It is easy, they realize, to become lost in conditions like these.

The Prince assures Aubry that they are following a river, and that the river will lead them home, but she cannot see any sign of it through the storm. It's a relief when they finally reach the palace walls, though she can hardly see more than the gates, a tall decorative door, the rest obscured by blowing dust.

But once inside—how does she describe it? It will not do to wander the royal grounds in men's oversized clothing soiled by the storm, so she washes in a secluded bath scooped out of a marble floor as though with a giant's ladle. The ceilings of her room, burnished in blue and gold, never seem to stop rising. When she emerges from the bath, she finds a white lehenga and choli spread across the foot of her bed, and a pair of sapphire earrings on her pillow. Outside her door, the palace staff rushes about, closing windows and doors to the storm, and when Aubry joins them, sapphires glitter from her earlobes.

Shuttered, the palace becomes five shades darker. Aubry helps out where she can. Candles must be lit, lanterns hung. Floors must be swept, carpets cleaned. But after a long journey, sleepless nights, and an onset of illness, even simple chores become too much. Exhausted, she nods off in a chair in the long and empty banquet hall.

The Prince finds her an hour later, still in her chair, but awake. A great gust of wind, breathing like a monster on the outer walls, moans through gates and pillars.

"I had a dream," she tells him. "The giant, the one I killed, was whispering in my ear. He said it was wonderful, being dead. He even thanked me. He thought he would end up a ghost wandering the world, but instead, he is a rock at sea and the world is wandering around him." She reaches out, touches the Prince's arm. "I'm not still sleeping, am I? It's taken me so long to wake up, I feel like I haven't quite got there yet."

Another roar of wind. If they listen carefully, the chandeliers overhead chime.

"They say waking up is leaving one level of reality and entering another, the dream world into the waking world. When you are enlightened, it is entering a higher level of reality still, and it will feel much the same. Like an awakening."

"I'm hardly enlightened," she says.

"Tell me again when you're fully awake."

They leave behind their brooms, pick up a lantern, and ascend a flight of stairs. He leads her through halls of sky blue, then hummingbird green, then butter yellow, so tall and wide an elephant could stroll through comfortably. An army of them could fit in the parlors. The masonry frames walls that display scenes from the Vedic texts, painted in all the colors of a floral display.

He points out a mural, a figure cross-legged in a field, beside a chariot, armies to either side of him. "Arjuna meditating," he says. "In other places, people journey outward. Arab pilgrims. Wandering Japanese poets. King Arthur's knights heading off to find the Grail. Here, our journeys take us inside ourselves.

Like that doctor fellow in Vienna who talks about the subconscious."

"I don't know him," she says.

"I had a sister once. She lost her sight. Then her hearing. Her fingertips went numb and food lost its taste. She told me she could sometimes feel footsteps on the other side of the palace, or changes in the wind when she was nowhere near a window. You'd think she could feel a hurricane in Ceylon. When you strip everything away, there is a kind of connection formed with the world, with its consciousness, if it has one. That's what she told me before she died."

She remembers a man from the jungles of Guangxi who described something similar when he ate the mushrooms he carefully cultivated in his backyard. He described it as peeling away layers of personality until all that existed was a lack of self, and in its place, something eternal, the core of consciousness, an infinite sea from which all things are born. He had only stood on the shore and let the waves touch his feet, he said, but someday he would swim.

The Prince turns to her. "Maybe that's what your giant was trying to say."

Later, she is alone, the Prince called away by royal business. She is lighting lanterns in the vestibule when there is a desperate pounding on the door so loud she jumps back. She hesitates but the storm rages outside. Someone is in need. She unbolts and opens the door. A cloud of dust and light billows in her face, blowing out every candle in the room.

Standing outside are twenty or more British soldiers, their khaki uniforms painted in red dirt.

The colonel shouts over the wind, "Is the Prince at home?"

46

The Prince

Soldiers brace against the wind, shielding their eyes, holding on to their reddened caps. They are a pitiful sight. For a moment, she is not sure what to do, but she can't possibly leave them there, huddling against the gale.

"Come in!" says Aubry, and the soldiers enter, bowing and thanking her, sand pouring from their clothes. They wrestle with the wind to shut the door behind them.

"We were caught in the storm. We didn't know where to go," says the colonel. His mustache was gray once, she can see, but now is red with dust.

"I'm so sorry," says Aubry, "but it is not my home to offer. Let me find the Prince." If Aubry seems befuddled, they are equally surprised to find her, a golden-haired Frenchwoman opening the palace door.

She turns to go but the Prince is already there, entering the vestibule. When he sees the soldiers, the Prince stiffens. It is only a moment and no one notices but Aubry.

"My God, Colonel Morton," he says, "were you outside in that?"

"So sorry, Prince. We're all half-blind out there. Would we be able to take shelter until the storm passes?"

"Of course. You can stay as long as you like," the Prince declares. "Where are your horses?"

"Tethered, around the corner and out of the wind."

"We'll get them into the stables."

In the banquet hall, they find Krishna and the others. Aubry can almost hear their hearts bang at the sight of the British, just once, like a metal hammer to their collective chest.

"But I thought you were on your way to Delhi?" the Prince inquires.

"We were, my friend," says the colonel, Krishna handing him a brush to clean his uniform. "But then the strangest thing happened. Of all things, we saw a dog running down the road with a man's arm in its teeth. We chased the blasted animal all the way down a ravine. This wind, it turns out, uncovered three dead men buried in the canyons. We have a new mission now. We are looking for a murderer."

The Prince says nothing. Krishna says nothing. Aubry says, "Let's get you and your men fresh baths, then."

The Prince instructs the staff in Hindi—baths, horses, food. The servants hurry away to do their jobs and Aubry hurries away with them, as if she is preparing for guests, when she is actually looking for a way out.

She grabs her walking stick, her bag, makes for the farthest door in the farthest wing. On the other side of the door, the storm. She opens it. The wind grabs the door from her, opens it wide. Light like a great fire, dust like smoke, debris spiraling through the air. She drops her belongings and reaches for the door, fighting against the wind with both arms, legs planted, back braced. At last, she manages to secure it. An escape through the wilderness is out of the question.

For a long while she doesn't know where to turn. She leans

against the wooden door, her hands feeling the storm through it, feeling all her pathways obliterated by wind. Then she picks up her things and reluctantly brings them back to her room.

Finally, it is dark. The weather still howls. Rooms are found for the British before the Prince visits Aubry in her own.

"Have you ever seen a storm like this?" she asks him. They are exhausted from the long, chaotic day. She lies across the massive bed. Though there is a comfortable sofa against the far wall, the Prince lies on the floor at her side instead.

"No. Never. But it will blow itself out soon enough."

They listen. So many open courtyards, so few doors. The sand flows freely, rattling down corridors, between pillars, in through the north, out through the south. It's like sleeping inside a gently rolling maraca.

"I have to get out," says Aubry.

"They don't suspect you," says the Prince. "It's unlikely they would. But if you run away in the middle of a storm, I wouldn't know how to explain it."

Each of them lies in their own thoughts, staring at the same ceiling.

"You've handled yourself well these past few days," he remarks. "Someone else might have been driven to extremes."

"Yes. Tomorrow I will throw myself from one of your towers."

"But after all you've been—"

"I have a secret," she says, cutting him off. "A secret to survival. I've never told anyone. Shall I let you in on it?"

She leans her head over the bed to look at him. He props himself up on an elbow to hear.

"It used to be that my sickness pursued me everywhere, chased me from anyplace I found happiness—forests, deserts, boats, trains. It will even try to chase me from here, to chase me from you. That's what it does. Then one day . . ." She pauses to collect her thoughts. Her hands clutch the bedsheets. The Prince leans even closer. "One day I had a revelation," she says. "I changed my strategy altogether." She slows down her words so not a single one escapes his attention. "Now, I chase it. Whenever it gets too near, I head out and hunt it down like the mangy dog it is."

The Prince is silent.

"I am nobody's victim," she adds, voice like a steel blade.

But the Prince only stares without making a sound, like a man who's overheard a murder plot. Has she said too much? Suddenly, she understands she has. Suddenly, she feels like the madwoman he must assume she is.

"You don't think?" she says, jarred by her own confession.

"I think it's true," he replies, tactful as ever. "You are nobody's victim." He sits back on the carpet, looking her over thoughtfully. "No, you are definitely not."

47

The Prince

In the banquet hall, everyone remarks on the storm. No one thought it would last through the night. If anything, it has grown stronger with the sunrise, and all are dumbfounded.

"Strangest thing I've ever seen," says one of the soldiers.

"The wind is from the north," says the Prince. "From the west, from the south, certainly, but never from the north. Not even the wind gets over those mountains."

But Aubry bypasses them all, goes straight to the shuttered windows.

"Do you hear that?"

Krishna joins her on her left. "Memsahib?"

"That sound . . ."

A soldier joins her on her right. "Ma'am?"

She says nothing for a moment, only listens. "There's someone out there."

In moments, Aubry, the Prince, the colonel, and others have veiled their faces in scarves and are out the door, into the storm. The force of the wind almost pushes them over. It takes everything Aubry has to keep the scarf on her head. They witness a strange marriage of earth and sky, boundaries erased. The wind is so clotted one could raise their hand in the air and bring down a fistful of dirt.

There is a flash of light in the sky, outlining the clouds of dust as they whirl past, followed by earth-shaking thunder.

"Leave your metal inside, gentleman," says the Prince.

"You don't think that could—"

A bolt of lightning, so bright it can be seen through the sandstorm a hundred paces away. It comes straight down, slamming the earth in a show of blue sparks. The thunder happens instantaneously, like a cannon-shot aimed at their chests. Krishna and two soldiers jump back against the wall. For an instant, a trail of smoke can be seen where the lightning was, quickly disintegrated by the wind.

Aubry clutches her chest in fright, but scans the grounds. She peers through her veil, through angry dust clouds roaring past. She calls out, searching behind rocks, behind clumps of bent-over trees. Soon, everyone is doing the same. Finally there is a shed, some distance from the palace. She opens the door and finds three schoolteachers and five children of various ages, huddled elbow-to-elbow in the cramped space. They shield their eyes from the blowing sand. Aubry calls to the others and together they lead the desperate group out of the storm and into the palace.

From far off, she hears something else, a metallic drone. Even through this wind she can hear it. It almost sounds musical. She stumbles nearly blind down the slope, under a sky like an inverted copper bowl, following the sound all the way to the riverbank. To her amazement, she spots an overturned boat near the shore, hears voices underneath it. There, she finds seven men: a boatman, his son, and five others who clutch at musical instruments, using their overturned boat as a shelter from the storm.

They form a chain of hands as she leads them back to the nearest door. As she ushers them inside, she hears chirping and looks up. Clinging to the rafters are birds of all kinds—owls, wrens, song-birds, even a falcon by itself in the far corner. Predator and prey, all sharing the same space, anything to keep out of the storm. She has never seen the like.

By the end of the day, the colonel has discovered two very embarrassed young lovers hiding in the stables with the horses, Krishna, some village girls cowering against the outer walls. The Prince finds two brothers huddling in a well and a mother and her three daughters beyond the east wall, so delighted at being rescued they offer to cook for all the castaways pulled in from the storm.

Everyone is given water, tea, and tanka torani. Water is heated and baths are had soon after.

Krishna approaches the musicians. "Do your instruments still work?"

They shake the sand out of their flutes, sitars, and tablas, blow, tap, and pluck a few notes from each.

"Good," says Krishna.

But when Private Hayley returns with a seven-year-old boy he found cowering on the lee side of a rock, the mood darkens. The boy's eyes have been so blasted with sand he can no longer open them. The British have a medic with them. Several gather around, including Aubry and the Prince, as the medic lays the boy on the banquet table, soaks his eyes in warm water, and care-fully plucks out bits of debris with a pair of tweezers wrapped in oiled cotton. It is an anxious hour, but finally the boy sits up, able to see again.

"Krishna, do we have anything to drink?" says the Prince. "Something inebriating, I hope."

Krishna and several of the help return from the kitchen with trays of champagne, trays of whisky, trays of mahua. Reinforced, the soldiers dress in their military best, boots polished, and the staff scours the wardrobes for gowns, saris, and suits for all those who have been saved. The floors are swept anew and the banquet table set.

The rescued mother turns out to be an excellent cook and is delighted with the large kitchen. When she discovers she is cooking for British soldiers, she cooks two pots of ulavacharu because she is certain the British will hate it. To her surprise, they gobble down the thick spicy soup, and she doesn't know whether to be angry or secretly pleased.

"My dear memsahib," says Krishna when he finds Aubry alone in a corner of the hall, "in all the commotion, I've forgotten to show you your dinner clothes."

Two of the schoolteachers help Aubry change. They fawn over her outfit, brush her hair, and, with a practiced finger, one of them places a perfect dot of yellow turmeric on her forehead. When she returns to the party, the Prince takes her arm in his and they enter the hall, Aubry in her blue-and-white sleeveless sari to match his blue-and-white sherwani. Why do Aubry and the Prince wear blue? To match her sapphires, of course. The whole damn banquet hall is blue, as if everyone has come to see the earrings.

They enter to the sound of applause. She thinks it is all for the Prince but then she realizes it is equally for her. Aubry has never been applauded before and is not at all sure what she's done to deserve it. Then the schoolchildren run up to her with a plate of chikki in their hands, pistachios trapped in bars of sugar.

"You saved us!" proclaims one of them.

"The Prince says you can't carry much," adds another, "so we made you a sweet instead of jewelry."

"How thoughtful!"

They beg her to try one, right here and now, and she does.

"So good! If you were to run outside, and I were to rescue you twice, would I get more?"

They laugh. "No!"

"Then this is even more special."

She sees her Prince, beset with greetings, people bowing to him, shaking his hand, a sea of pleasantries—her poor Prince, sucked into the riptide of the crowd. She tries to smile to him, to bid him adieu, but he's been whisked away and she's been cut loose. She goes to the champagne table and takes a glass, not to drink, but to keep her hands busy. She roams, swirling her glass, feigning disinterest in life when she is actually listening in on it. This is what she hears:

"My right hand is feeding the British Raj," the colonel hisses to a subordinate, "my other hand is holding up all of Madras, and my third hand is missing!"

"Everyone all over the earth prays to God for victory over one another, no matter what side they're on," says one tired soldier to another. "I'm sure at some point God just shrugs and says to hell with them all."

"Ask yourself, is it going to prevent you from escaping? Is there a risk of death attached to it?" says a handsome guard with a long scar that just misses his left eye. The village girls listen breathlessly, moored to his arm like boats in a harbor. "Is it permanently disabling? Is it disfiguring? If it doesn't fit one of those categories, it isn't important." He downs his drink and the pretty girls sigh.

The British pull Aubry into their orbit. "To the hero of the day," says one of them, and there is a round of toasts and congratulations. Soon her glass is empty. The musicians approach her, too, each of them thanking her in turn, bowing, shaking her hand.

She looks around, faces so grateful, so delighted. The British are not welcome here. She knows that. But tonight, lives have been saved, people rescued, a boy delivered from blindness. The rescued daughters enchant in their crimson and gold. A soldier plays games with the children. At the center of it all is the Prince, the celebration circling around him, and she thinks of going to him, and holding him in her arms, just a little, when no one is looking.

Private Hayley, who rescued the young boy, happens by with a bottle of champagne and refills her glass.

"There are antelope in the verandas." He is as joyful and high-spirited as a fighting man can be. He's had more than his share of liquor.

"And birds in the rafters," she says.

"And monkeys in the boathouse."

"Are you drunk, Private Hayley?"

"That is a relative term."

"May I ask you a question?"

"Of course you may."

"You've killed before, haven't you?"

"I'm a soldier. It's what I do."

"What was it like?"

"The first time? Hard. Very hard. I was sick to my stomach, actually. Why do you ask?"

"I'm feeling very joyful. And I don't deserve it."

"Ah. Your first time was hard, too."

Aubry stiffens. Perhaps he is not as drunk as she thought. She downs her champagne.

Others come by, several soldiers, a guard or two. "To the woman who can't stay still," says one, raising his glass. She lets out a quiet sigh. She wasn't aware it was common knowledge.

"What's this?" asks another.

"She has a condition. What is it called again?"

"We're working on a name," says Aubry. Private Hayley keeps refilling her glass.

"Is it dangerous? Are we in danger?" asks one of the rescued daughters, joining the discussion.

"It's an excellent question. I wonder," Aubry says, and drinks more champagne. No one knows what to say after that.

The girl attempts another question. "Is . . . is there nothing we can do?"

Aubry shrugs. "I walk."

"How far?"

"As far as I can go."

"All the way from Paris? To here?"

"Yes," says Aubry. "The long way."

"Perhaps a compass would help." A soldier laughs.

"Then I would never have found you," she says.

"You poor thing," says the daughter, who looks at Aubry with genuine heartbreak.

"No," says Hayley, trying to form a thought in his stupor. "No, don't think that. She's making a point." Aubry looks at him, a single raised eyebrow. "I've been a few places," he says, the champagne glass waving in his hand. "How do I explain it? You've got to think of the world as something on the tip of your tongue, something you can't quite recall. The more you try, the less you remember. Point is, indirection is key. That's what I'm trying to say here. You . . . you've got to let the world come to you."

Then there is music, the wash of a scale rising above the din of the crowd. Heads turn. Chatter ceases. In the air, the drone of the sarangi, the melismata of the sitar. A flutelike instrument takes up a melody that floats above them all, slow and ethereal, like the evening sky. The guests all watch and listen, entranced by the musicians at the end of the hall, candlelight behind them, their music before them.

Suddenly, as soft as the music itself, is the voice in Aubry's ear.

"I once walked the earth."

48

The Wish

Beside her is a woman. Aubry feels her chest constrict at the sight of her, the beauty of her, her long dark hair, her voice like a scent.

"How far did you go?" Aubry asks her.

"My family and I were fleeing our homes—war, you see." They step away from the others, whispering. "We came south through mountain passes, followed the Arabian coast, crossed lakes so salty you couldn't sink in them."

"How do you know the Prince?"

"We are old friends. When he needs help, I show up."

"Just like that?"

"He may not even know he's in need, but then, suddenly, there I am."

"Does he need help now?"

"He will."

Her arm seamlessly interlocks with Aubry's and then, before she knows it, Aubry is being escorted through the oblivious crowd. The two of them together are breathtaking to behold, whispering close enough to be lovers, yet no one seems to notice them pass by.

"Our Prince once made a birthday wish and I happened to overhear. Would you like to see what I got him?"

Aubry is led through three doorways, into a dark uninhabited wing of the palace. The rooms rattle and moan. Currents of air seep in from outside. Windows are covered, yet curtains billow anyway. The raga echoes down the hallways, mixing with the sounds of the storm.

"Look around," says the woman, holding out a candle, lighting another for Aubry. "What do you see?"

"A palace," says Aubry, her candle flickering. "Furniture. Tapestries."

"The tapestries are dyed wool." She points to the wooden sculptures in the corner. "The emerald inlays are colored glass." She turns, points again. "The clock on that mantel hasn't worked in three years. And his servants—all volunteers from the village."

"What are you saying?"

"The Prince is supposed to collect taxes from the people to pay the British for their protection."

"Protection from whom?"

"Yes, you understand."

Aubry walks along, quietly unnerved for reasons she doesn't fully believe. But later, she has it all confirmed—Krishna, the servants, all locals plucked from surrounding villages, all unpaid, all devoted to their Prince. Later, she will examine the diamonds on his embroidered turban and find every other gem to be a replacement, a bit of glass with colored tinsel coating the back.

The woman leads her to another room. On the wall, a collection of small framed pastels. Aubry leans close, candlelight revealing portraits, landscapes, abstracts, still lifes. These are not ancient works, but fresh and masterful. And the colors—golds like hot molten ore, greens like crushed jade, reds like the fire within fire. A room full of butterflies could not be so enchanting. The woman points to one.

"What do you think of this?"

"It's beautiful."

"It's mine," she says and leads her to another. "So is that one. And this."

Aubry is amazed. One in particular draws her near.

"This one, too?" asks Aubry. She leans in close to a painting of a black river—behind it, a thick jungle, painted in swirling green lines that churn and tangle. In the center of all that green, a tall lean-to made from broad jungle leaves stands, a handful of people under it warming themselves by a fire.

"It was a vision. I'll be nodding off somewhere—in a meadow, in a chair—then I have one. They're like dreams, but I'm always awake when they happen. In this case, I remember I was on a boat, but I couldn't see a thing. Then the mist rose and there it was—a vision of a river at the end of the world. It felt like home. So I painted it that way."

Aubry says nothing, just takes it in.

"You like it," says the woman.

Aubry nods. The woman points to another.

"This one I made the day of his wish."

It is a pastel of three horses, two of them bright red, the third sky blue. The hills they play in as green as a reptile in a rainforest.

"He must have been very pleased," says Aubry.

"I had that vision not far from here—three horses on a hill. But that wasn't the gift. After seeing this, the Prince devised a plan. He began secretly breeding horses and selling them to China and Persia in exchange for gold. The gold pays the British, the people go untaxed, and the poorest of them are fed and clothed by Surasiva himself."

What game is the Prince playing? And how dangerous is it? Her stomach recoils at the thought of her Prince in trouble.

"The plan was your gift?" asks Aubry, confused. "Or was the painting?"

As if she hasn't heard the question, the woman continues. "But the world is changing. Trains and telegraphs make horses obsolete and now he is running out of money."

"What will he do?"

"We shall see." They stand, a little distance between them, facing each other. "I have crossed mountains," she says. "The Zagros Mountains. The Hindu Kush. I crossed them with family and guides and a caravan of locals to help us through, and still we almost died many times over. But you crossed the Himalayas. Alone. I have to ask, what miracle was it that got you through?"

Aubry hesitates, measuring how much to say. "Like no miracle I can describe."

The woman smiles, as if she knows exactly what Aubry is speaking of. She comes closer. "There are things on this earth that only exist because you have beheld them. If you weren't there, they would never have been."

Could that be? Aubry has seen things that no one else ever has, it's true. Does that give them reason to exist at all? *"The way we see it,"* she was once told, *"you have traveled all this way to meet us."* She had made herself available to chance and little wonders. And if one wasn't available? Did those little wonders not occur? Did they lie in wait, perhaps in vain, for someone to happen by and behold?

Aubry feels the woman's grip tighten around her hand, sees the woman's face light up. "Is it your birthday?"

Aubry is taken aback. She has to think. "I wouldn't know if it was."

"Let's pretend," says the woman.

"All right."

"Make a wish."

"A wish?"

"I want to do something for you."

A low moan of wind from outside. Their candles flicker.

"What shall I wish for?"

"Well, don't waste it. Give it some thought."

Aubry doesn't have to think about it. She's been wishing for the same thing ever since the sickness dug its claws in her. "And you will give this to me?"

"When it happens, you'll know."

Aubry doesn't believe her, not at first, but the woman's eyes never falter.

"Have you decided?" she asks.

Aubry nods.

"I thought you had. Now wish."

Aubry closes her eyes and wishes hard. The woman touches their foreheads together, her hands soft on Aubry's face. Their perfumes blend, their senses comingle, and for a few moments they let themselves stay this way.

"Happy birthday," she says. With a slow, generous smile, she turns, walks off, and vanishes into the din of the party.

It isn't until the next day that the Prince tells Aubry the woman's name.

"Qalima," he says, and she asks him to repeat it, slowly, she is so taken by the sound it makes.

"*Qa-lee-ma*," and when Aubry goes to sleep that night, she chants it over and over, like a secret prayer.

49

The Prince

Aubry makes her way back to her room with a thousand thoughts crawling through her brain. What did that woman mean? Was it a true wish? When would it happen? Was it happening already? Of course, these are foolish thoughts. No one can simply wish away their troubles. She'd have been cured long ago if that were the case.

But the party was fun, her spirits up, like a bubble that won't burst. Tomorrow she will tell the Prince of all the people she met, all the things that were said. Her mood is so high she entertains all sorts of ideas.

That woman, so beguiling. Something about her makes Aubry reconsider the world as she knows it. But she's had too much to drink. She's not thinking straight. How many glasses of champagne? Four? Five? More? She lost count somewhere along the way, but surely she can hold her liquor better than that.

The door to her room is open, if that is her room. She thinks it is, ahead of her, at the end of the hall. Her head is a little foggy, but she is certain her door was closed when she left. She walks down the hall, hardly in a straight line. Sometimes the floor moves. It is not her fault.

When she enters her room, who does she see but Private Hayley sitting on the edge of her bed. If she is a little tipsy, he is fully intoxicated, lips parted, eyes focused on nothing at all.

"Private Hayley," she says. "Have you come to say good night?"

He peers closely, making sure it's her. "For the longest time, I thought this was my room."

"I think it's mine."

"Yes. I see that now."

She sits next to him on the bed.

"Would you like help finding your way back?"

"No. I found something more important." At first, she thinks she is going to have to rebuff a drunken paramour, but then he shows her the bullet he holds in his hand. "See that?"

She stares for a long moment. She doesn't understand where this is going. "It's a bullet."

"It's evidence. I found it in the pocket of a dead man at the bottom of a ravine. You know, I thought this was my room."

"Yes, you said that."

"And I thought that was my drawer."

He points to an opened dresser drawer and now she feels it, all her anxieties creeping back, like a slow-tightening noose around her neck.

"And I thought this was my gun."

He picks up the pistol that is lying next to him, the pistol Aubry had hidden in the drawer, the pistol she pilfered from the dead man.

"But then I thought this isn't my gun. This is Russian-made. And it only takes a special Russian-made bullet."

He opens the pistol chamber and slips the bullet into the cylinder, as easy as a sword into its sheath.

"Then I thought somebody here has the dead man's gun. Somebody here must have killed them. So I waited. And it's you."

She experiences a weightless moment, as if the floor has disappeared from under her and all her insides have knotted in her throat.

"But that is my gun," she lies. "I've carried that gun with me since I was a girl. Do you see? It couldn't possibly be in two places at once."

"But this isn't French. This is Russian."

"Which is where I got it." She has no idea how convincing her lies are, but she clings to them like a rock in a fast, deadly river. "A man in Moscow gave this to me, worried for my safety. You understand how unsafe things can be for a young woman, traveling the world alone, don't you?"

"But that's not—"

"You can see why a young woman, traveling the world alone, might carry a gun, just like that one, because a kind old man in Moscow worried for her."

"Yes, I suppose—"

"And can you imagine me killing those three men? Can you imagine me killing anyone?"

He doesn't answer this. His eyes roam the floor, wondering.

"Were those men shot, or were they stabbed?" she asks him, as if she already knows the answer.

"Stabbed."

"Then that is not a murder weapon, is it? And what would a small woman like me stab those big men with?"

Private Hayley shakes his head. This has all been very confusing for him. He looks at her again. His eyes widen. "Your nose is bleeding."

She knows it's true. She can feel it, a single drop running to her lip.

"I'm sorry," says Hayley. "I've done this to you." He pulls out his handkerchief and tries to wipe away the blood. Aubry's eyes close tight while she lets Hayley practice his drunken chivalry. She'd been having such a good night. She'd had her wish granted. She has loved every moment spent with the Prince. She cannot walk away. Not again. She feels her whole body being crushed. It is not sickness. It is despair. It squeezes her so tight, tears form, and for a moment, she is blinded by them.

"I'm so awful," Hayley continues. "I didn't mean to upset you."

"Don't be silly. You've done no such thing. But the truth is I am very tired, and I think I need sleep now. We can continue this in the morning, yes?"

"Of course."

They both rise and go to the door. He turns to her one last time.

"How did you know they were stabbed?"

"I didn't. You imagined that."

He nods as if that makes sense. He walks away, still nodding, one hand on the wall for support. She closes the door behind him. Her room is dark and the palace is quiet except for the wind. It is not even her third day, her joy mercilessly cut short.

But I handled that soldier well, she thinks. I'm a clever one when I'm cornered.

She thinks if anyone can save the Prince from these people, it's her. She likes the Prince. No. Why be coy about it? She loves the Prince. It is vital that she stays and protects him.

But the sickness is coming. She shakes her head violently and the room spins. She falls to her knees and beats her fists on the marble floor until they hurt.

She doesn't want to wander the world. She wants the world to wander around her. What did they call it? The core of consciousness? Yes. That was it. Consciousness, and all it implies. When everything has been stripped down, there will be just her, no beginning, no end, and she will have no need for this sickly, ragged body.

That, or she is simply mad.

In the neat pile of clothes the servants have laid out for her, she finds a cord. It's intended as a belt to go around the waist, but instead, with her free hand and her teeth, she ties it around her wrist, good and tight. The other end she loops around the bedpost and ties to her other wrist, good and tight. She sits herself down on the floor and rests against the bed, lashed to the post with little room to maneuver. Her head still spins. Outside, the storm sweeps the hours away. But in here, the sand scratches its nails against the walls, like a giant serpent coiling around the palace. If she listens closely, she thinks she can hear the universe at its center.

Her hands are trembling and there isn't even pain yet. She has lost patience with her body. Tonight, she will beat it senseless. She will bring it to the edge of destruction. Her wish comes just in time. What is eternal will devour all that is temporary. What is Aubry will destroy what is disease. Then, maybe everything that has been closed will open, and she will see the world as she hopes it exists, and she will step through, and her bones will tell her, *We did not know it could be so beautiful.*

Sometimes her lack of sanity amazes even her.

"I'm going to kill you now," she tells her sickness.

"You can't." Its voice rumbles inside her chest.

"Then you will kill me. But one of us dies tonight."

Silence.

"There is more to see," it tells her. "Much more."

"I'll never know," she says, and prepares herself for the end of everything.

When it finally comes for her—late, late in the night—it comes at her angry.

50

The Prince

She moans, grunts, gnashes her teeth, and writhes on the floor. Blood smears across the marble tiles. Her spine twists like jungle vines. Her wrists bound, she does not flee, only holds tight to the bedframe. Not once does she cry out or scream for help. By morning, she will have lived past her pain, or she will be dead.

But no matter how hard she fights, something escapes—a groan, a limb banging the floor. Despite the sounds of the storm, someone in the night senses something is amiss, and opens her door.

The Prince is not sure what he sees at first. In the darkness, it looks like an animal making a kill at the foot of her bed. So much blood. But then he understands it is Aubry, her body convulsing on the floor.

He rushes in, turns her over, finds her wrists lashed to the bed.

"I won't go . . ." she says, tears and blood tangling down her cheeks. "I won't leave you . . ."

"Help us!" shouts the Prince, hurrying to untie her wrists. The mother and her daughters, just next door, are the first to arrive, gasping at the sight of her. The Prince lifts Aubry in his arms, her bloodstained clothes staining his, and carries her into the hallway. Already others are coming: servants, the boatman and his son, the schoolteachers and the musicians, then the colonel, his soldiers—even the shy young lovers, too frightened to come near, but their faces, torn with pity.

They have all come, every last one.

"What can we do?" asks the colonel.

"She must go," says the Prince and, though tears are clouding his vision, he sees Krishna in the growing crowd. "The boathouse," says the Prince, and Krishna spurs into action.

"Food!" shouts the colonel. "Water!"

The Prince carries her across the grand hall, down the corridors to the southeast gates. The boatman and his son rush ahead and open the doors. An avalanche of air greets them, an upswell of dust that lifts her hair, snatches scarves from the servant girls, fills clothes with wind. Lightning freezes debris whirling in the sky. A spray of sand forces Aubry's eyes shut. For a moment, she feels weightless in Surasiva's arms, in a whirlpool of air—a sense of movement, a sense of nonexistence.

Then the wind gentles. The sand becomes a rain falling on her head. The Prince carries her down stairs, stairs that weave down cliffs, cliffs that hold back the wind. The servants follow with swaying lanterns. They reach the boathouse, a series of long roofs that lead to the river, light swishing across the beams and posts.

The boathouse is swarming with monkeys. Scores of macaques have made a home here, hiding from the storm. At the approach of the Prince, Aubry in his arms, they scatter. They climb pillars. They cling to rafters. They flee into the rain of sand. They make a path for them as if for Rama and Sita themselves.

Krishna is already in the long riverboat, lowering the tiller, untying lines. Aubry, on the verge of unconsciousness, tries to understand what's happening. She sees faces—the musicians, Private Hayley. He reaches for her hand, puts something in it.

"Take this," he says. "It will keep you safe!" He presses it into her palm, tightens her fingers around it before she is gone, carried into the boat.

The schoolteachers hand Krishna bundles wrapped in twine. "Clothes and blankets," they say.

The rescued daughters hand him Aubry's bag and her long walking stick. The servants pass along food wrapped in paper. The British soldiers toss in canteens full of water.

They have come to see her off, those she has rescued, those who wish to rescue her. It is a gift she cannot repay. She never wants to leave them. She wants to hold on to them forever, but she cannot put graciousness like this in her pocket. She wants to stay, but desire is only a sweet, helpless surrender to something greater than yourself.

From the dock, Krishna casts off the lines and gives the boat a push. "Take good care of her, Prince."

Aubry can just see them lined up at the edge of the pier, watching the boat taken by currents. Such anxious faces. She sees the musicians, touching their foreheads in prayer. She thinks she sees the two young lovers, in the back of the crowd, watching, and holding each other tight.

She even thinks she sees Qalima, high up on the cliff, gazing down on them all, but she can't be sure.

The river plies through tall canyon walls on either side. The storm rages in the sky above, raining pebbles down on the boat. The Prince carefully lays Aubry under the canopy on the boat, waves of sand sweeping over the canvas. She is not getting any better. Her teeth are red. She is drowning in blood.

"It doesn't go away," says the Prince, trying not to panic. "Why doesn't it go away?"

The pain grips her spine and twists. She shudders, every muscle taut.

"I have to tell you . . ." she says, fighting for every word. "I have to tell someone before I die . . ."

"You are not going to die."

She sucks in air, takes command of her body as best she can. "This is how I did it . . ." she says, jaw clenched, a steady trickle of blood from her lips. "This is how I crossed those mountains . . ."

51

How She Crossed the Mountains

By midmorning she'd climbed so high that Pathik's tents and herds had all vanished into the distance and the Tibetan Plateau was nothing but a dizzying void beneath her. The thinning air made her lungs feel small but she was still breathing—and she would need every breath she had because ahead of her was nothing but mounds and ridges and spires of rock that never stopped rising. She would clamber over one peak only to find a series of pinnacles and cones still waiting for her, piled on top of each other in a never-ending staircase constructed for giants and gods, but not for her.

By evening she had no idea how far she'd climbed and no idea how far she had to go. She made camp in a shallow cave, made a wall out of snow. She made a small fire in the little tin can she'd carried all the way from the Aral Sea. When she peeked outside, she could see the monster clouds rolling in, gray smoke pouring over the frozen, harrowing summits. She huddled deep inside her cave with all her clothes on and began to worry. All through the night she drifted in and out of consciousness. A blink of the eye that lasted a minute, then two, then ten.

"Don't stay here," said her sickness. "Mountains are meant to be seen."

"I don't give a damn. I'm staying."

"You think the storm is hell and this cave is heaven, but neither is true."

"They're fucking close enough."

"Go. I promise to keep you safe."

"You're trying to kill me."

"I'm trying to love you."

She woke to a suck of air that blew open her wall of snow, her fire out in a heartbeat, the wind dragging her halfway out the cave.

All around her, a blinding, stabbing white. The world, reduced to a blank page. Her mittened hands reached out for something to lean against, but there was only cold and explosions of wind. Out of this wind came stinging ice like waves of pulverized glass, sandblasting her coat, needling her skin.

She stumbled through it. The cold seeped deep into her body, through her skin and muscle, into her heart and bones. Her jaw was numb, frozen in place. Her clothes had become useless to her, glazed in ice. Warmth was impossible to imagine, something she knew existed but could not recall. She was made of cold now.

Leaning on her spear, she forged through knee-high snow, half-blind, until the snow suddenly thinned, revealing a wall of ice blocking her way.

If she pressed herself against the wall, there was no wind. Just a step or two away and the air swung at her again. She slunk along the edge, feeling her way, when, suddenly, the wall was gone and a torrent of wind from around the corner blew her backward.

She slid downhill, unable to stop until her half-frozen brain remembered the spear in her hands. As she slid, she twisted herself into position and dug her spear into the ice, snow funneling down the mountain around her. She skidded to a halt among a labyrinth of boulders, all frozen in place. She rolled herself beneath one, out of the wind, but the cold worked on her like a thick numbing sleep. Parts of her body disappeared from her. She could not feel her hands or feet. She had to look at them to locate them. Her brain became dull, wrapped in a cold cotton. Her vision darkened.

Lionel Kyengi had thought her impervious to harm.

"I assure you," she'd told him, *"I am perfectly capable of getting myself killed."*

"Yes, so are we all. But I don't think you are quite as capable as you think you are."

How wrong he'd been. How easy it was to misstep, to misjudge, to underprepare or overestimate. How easy it was to die.

Still, she fought. She rocked herself back to her dead feet and climbed back up the slope on her hands and knees. Blinded by snow, buffeted by winds, her lips blue, she crawled toward that wall of ice looking for a cave, or a crack, somewhere she could hide from this beating. It made no sense, but the wall of ice seemed a better place to expire than a garden of boulders. It was no more than that.

She could see the wall now, and she knew she would reach it, and that, to her chilled mind, would be some kind of victory.

Then she saw the door.

She didn't recognize it as a door for a full minute, even though she stared right at it. It was a thick black iron door, embedded in the ice, without purpose or reason, and she stopped because she wasn't sure she was actually seeing it. Then, like a machine grinding into gear, she willed her frozen limbs to climb. When she got there, she heaved herself to her feet, banging on the iron. She kicked and shoved, but the door would not move. A thick crust of ice on its edges sealed it shut, so she slashed and chiseled at it with her spear, amazed by the strength she suddenly had, wondering, even in the moment, where it had come from. When it was clear, she threw herself against it. The door did not budge, but she did not quit either, and she threw herself again and again.

Finally the door gave, a little at first, then a lot, enough to squeeze through. She wriggled herself into a narrow slit in the mountain, and collapsed into the shadows inside.

52

Terra Obscura

There was no wind here, though the driving storm outside pummeled the mountain and the darkness yawned around her. There was no more snow stinging her eyes. Relief made her loose and she wanted to sleep. She so desperately needed sleep. But there was an ember in her brain that told her she could still freeze to death, that she probably would, that it was almost guaranteed. She gathered her strength, rolled herself onto her belly, and drew in her hands and knees so that she was off the floor. She could see now that the floor was cold bare stone. She must be inside a cave.

She crawled back to the door and pushed it shut, or as near to shut as she was able, then sat, propped up against the wall. She filled her lungs with air, slowly let her eyes adjust, and peered into the darkness.

Her lungs billowed out thick clouds. In minutes the cave was filmy with an ice-crystal fog. Even as her eyes adjusted, her view clouded up.

She needed to be warm. That was her priority. She took off her mittens, dug into her bag, and pulled out her flint. It was so cold it burned her skin. The piddling amount of tinder she'd brought was frozen, too, and she knew it wouldn't light. She'd escaped one danger only to find herself in another. She put on her mittens, got to her feet—her dead feet that felt painful now. She crept on them slowly and carefully because she didn't want to slip on ice she would not be able to feel.

She inched through the cave, but there wasn't much to inch through, hardly more than a crack in the rock. The thin slant of light from outside wasn't much, but it was enough to see the next door.

It was iron, too, and she went to open it, but before she did, she saw the door next to it, and then the door next to that. Moving through the fog, she counted six iron doors.

She imagined it was some sort of test, choosing the least dangerous door, then shook her head. They were all identical doors. Just pick one.

She reached for the nearest door handle, then stopped, considered another moment, and, for no sensible reason, picked the door beside it instead. She turned the metal handle. It swung open with ease.

There was space and light. The warmth felt alien. Her skin tingled with the impact. The light was so clean it took her eyes time to adjust. When they did, she saw a whole room with shelves and rugs and wooden beams along the ceiling and burning lanterns hanging from hooks. But most of all there were books, all books, so many books that the walls and columns and rows of shelves disappeared into them. Every inch—the corners, the doorframes, the rafters—smothered in books, parchments, and scrolls.

She thought she might be dead, that she lay dying on the mountain slopes, buried in snow, and that this was some kind of hallucination. She even dared hope that this was an afterlife of some kind—but there was searing pain in her feet, and now in her fingers, and she knew it wasn't that.

She stepped inside. The door slowly and silently eased back on its hinges and closed behind her. She didn't see it close. She would never think of that door again. Instead, her mind was occupied with the fruit sitting in the bowl.

In the center of the room was a low, broad table carved from mountain stone, covered in thick fur and stacks of books. Around the table were more stones, chiseled flat, like little chairs, small cushions on top. And placed before one of the chairs was a lit lantern and a wooden bowl brimming with fresh fruit.

But she couldn't eat, not yet. Her hands and feet needed to be saved. She warmed her fingers against the lantern. She saw a little fireplace chiseled into the wall, a pile of dried dung nearby, a black kettle hanging over it. She brought the lantern and considered using the pages of a book for tinder, but then thought, even in her desperation, that these were the libraries. Someone owned these books. How disrespectful it would be to burn them. Then she saw the tinder, lit it with the lantern, and soon had a fire going. She pulled off her icy boots, her sheepskin coat, still frozen stiff. The coat stood straight up on the floor, as if worn by an invisible spirit. She sat by the fire and warmed herself at last.

After some time, she was surprised to find she could walk again, without pain, that her feet were not as damaged as she thought. She wiggled her toes. She walked on furs and carpets. Yes, she thought, completely healed.

She sat on the little cushion on the little chair and looked at the food. Her hands trembled and hunger came roaring down upon her. She split open a pomegranate with a long copper knife that sat beside the bowl. There was a spoon, too, but she scooped out the seeds with her teeth instead and wolfed them down. The juice dripped from her chin and onto the fur, staining it. She would be sorry about this later, but not yet. She cupped a handful of buckthorn berries, crammed them into her mouth. She saw the butter tea and drank it right out of the wooden carafe.

She ate till she was full, then calmed herself and looked around. Only then did she finally turn her attention to the books.

She plucked a book from the pile in front of her. All the pages were ink drawings. There was a word occasionally, scribbled across a page somewhere, but always in a language she didn't know, in an alphabet she couldn't recognize. But words were few and unnecessary.

The next book was full of drawings, too, charcoal this time, not professional at all. They seemed scribbled by a child, but she understood them perfectly well. Here was a picture of men building a grand tower, as tall as any mountain. And here was a drawing of—could it be? Yes, it was—a charcoal drawing of penguins, hopping over a flat icescape.

The next book read like a story. She flipped the pages and followed along. It began with sketches of a family in an ancient city, somewhere in Persia, judging by the desert and the looks of their clothes. Then the earth shook. Houses fell. The ones that didn't fall were cracked down the middle or dangerously lopsided. The family had survived the quake, but then came the unsurvivable thing, the great wall of water hissing toward them. There was nowhere to run. The wall of water stretched from one end of the desert to the other. It collided with their city, leveling houses, sweeping away horses, wagons, and people. The only member of the family that survived was a young girl, who clung to a wooden door for three days, riding the currents, watching her desert, the only world she'd ever known, turn to sea.

She closed the book. All of this told in pictures, just like the other libraries she had known. But this one, here of all places, the most impossible library yet. She picked up another book. It told a story, too—an old man and his son, while staring at a strangely shaped gourd one day, invented a new musical instrument, adding a string here, a sound hole there. It took much attention to detail, but in the end, they had created an instrument—a strange instrument—the likes of which no one had ever heard before. They played it so beautifully that people—hundreds of them, some from faraway lands—came to listen. Few understood the lyrics, but all were moved by the music.

There was another book and another story, drawn in colors, pastels of some kind, a story she found especially moving, about a famous sculptor, crippled by a painful, muscle-wasting disease, who only found relief at night when he dreamed. And when he dreamed, he dreamed that he and God were walking through a garden, a garden that God had planted Himself, and that He had taken the sculptor's pain away just long enough so that he could marvel at His creation and enjoy.

Were these inventions? Were they memoirs? Were they histories? She didn't know, but she liked reading them. She opened another book, this one, it seemed, about an old woman who swam with otters.

Then Aubry fell asleep, her head on the pages, and didn't wake for hours.

When her eyes opened again, she was lying on the floor, on a blanket of fur, with no memory of how she got there. She didn't know if it was night or day. She didn't know when her fire had gone out. It was a genuinely inspired sleep.

The second thing she noticed was the fur on the blanket shimmering in front of her nose. There was a draft coming from somewhere. She put out her hand, felt for the current of air. On her hands and knees, she traced it back to the far wall. It was coming from underneath the lowest shelf. She gave it a push.

It yielded easily, with all its books and scrolls, swinging open into another room. This room was long, like a tunnel, a series of arches telescoping as far back as she could see, into unlit shadows.

And every available inch of it compressed with books.

"Hello!" she called into the shadows, but there was no answer.

She grabbed her things—her bag and spear and the lantern, too—and, because it was still cold, put on her thawed coat. She filled her pockets with what was left of the food and entered the tunnel. It was tall and wide, with icicles dangling from the rock walls, or forming thick columns from floor to ceiling. There was more to read here than was possible in a lifetime.

She pulled a scroll off a shelf and unspooled it, rolling it down the long corridor. It was a story, like the others, about a fisherman who found an extraordinary seashell in his net, dark blue but shiny, like a rainbow at night. He cut it open to see what kind of meat might be hidden inside. What he saw were chambers upon chambers, infinite spirals within infinite spirals. He was found three days later, curled up on the bottom of his boat, muttering incoherently. He had glimpsed the infinite and it had driven him mad. No one else ever saw the shell, not in his hand, not in his net, not in his boat, but he swore to what he saw, his eyes wide and crazy. After a few days ashore, he recovered. A few days after that, he went out to sea again, always keeping an eye out for another shell, but never finding one.

She rolled the scroll up again, put it back in its place, and continued to explore. Soon enough she came to an opening in the wall, like a window, and looked through.

Beyond the window were more and more rooms, more and more shelves, connected by staircases and bridges and ladders. It disoriented her—the endless catacombs, the walls and walls of books, like a library designed by Hieronymus Bosch. She was awestruck at the sight of it. It felt like vertigo. She leaned against the window frame to stay on her feet. She took it all in, this underground panorama, and didn't know what to explore first.

She wandered through the endless branchings of rooms, carrying a lantern with her at all times. Everywhere she went, there was always another one, lit, sitting on a table or hanging from a rafter. When hers began to gutter and die, she would simply put it down and take another. It was as if she were following someone else, just behind their every move. And while some rooms were strictly bookshelves, others had chairs and tables, and even artifacts—ancient vases, skulls of long-extinct creatures resting between shelves, here and there a painting or a map stashed away in a corner. Most strangely, she'd find a room with something to eat—fresh bread on a cutting board, clean vegetables, colorful fruit.

"Hello?" she'd call out. "Thank you for this! Thank you for the food!"

There'd be no answer.

She'd wander, grab goji berries here, drink milk tea there. She wanted for nothing. She would shout into the catacombs every so often, "The milk tea is good!" or "Thank you for the lanterns! I'd be helpless without them!" but the libraries remained silent, just her voice echoing back at her.

Though she wondered how this place could be so devoid of people and still have candles burning and fresh food waiting in bowls, perhaps she didn't think about it as much as she should have. Even at the time, even as she meandered through hallways and staircases, she knew she should be more curious, more concerned. Maybe she should have been frightened, too, but she wasn't, for reasons she never could explain. She was perfectly content to think about nothing but the books and the stories inside them.

One day—or night—or some other nebulous wedding of

time—who knew how long she'd been wandering down here?—she happened upon a balcony. She found herself staring down into a deep chasm of books, a great crack in the earth's crust some tireless engineers had carved up into shelves. From where she was she could see the staircase that switchbacked down the steep cliff face, zigzagging into the darkness below.

She descended the stairs, each step a wooden plank over a shelf of scrolls, and wound down the ravine until the air grew warmer and the geology changed. Where there once was hard granite, there were now bands of crumbly red earth. She entered rooms with clay floors and green trees sprouting from them that held bookshelves in their boughs.

She sat at wooden tables covered with orange silk, with proper chairs. She ate mangoes from ivory bowls. She read more picture books, one about the very last tiger on a faraway island, being hunted by men who wondered where all the tigers had gone. Another about a fleet of ancient mariners who sailed across the ocean on boats made of reeds and rope, who navigated by stars to discover new islands with steep shores and thick rain-forests, the likes of which they'd never seen before.

She wandered through rooms with tree roots dangling from the ceiling, one with a stream trickling across the floor, glacial water so clear she could put her lips directly to its surface and drink. That was when she heard voices, a distant echo, from some indeterminate direction—too far away to make out words, too far away to make out much at all. But it was a voice. That much she knew.

She searched the library for signs of life. She ran from room to room. She found more burning candles and fresh food and hot tea, but no footprints, no fleeting shadows, no patter of running feet. She rushed ahead, making hairpin turns into unexpected rooms, trying to catch him or her or them unaware, but no matter what her strategy, she remained alone.

Still, every once in a while, there was that voice. It echoed down hallways, welled up staircases, always obscure, far away, and indecipherable.

One day—or night—she was plucking mangoes from a grove growing among the bookshelves. She gathered up the fruit, placed them in an empty bowl. She was thinking of the voices, the people who might be attached to them. She was thinking how glad they would be to find these mangoes waiting for them. On a piece of blank paper, she wrote a note and left it on the table beside the bowl.

It said, "FOR THE NEXT."

Then, with her spear and her bag and a few mangoes in her pocket, she headed for the nearest door, which was teak and at the end of a hallway so narrow she had to slink through sideways. She opened the door. To her surprise, there was blinding light.

She blocked the glare with her arm. She took a few steps though the doorway to see what she'd blundered into this time.

While her eyes teared up and adjusted, the teak door quietly closed behind her.

She staggered, blinking. She was in a ravine, a shallow river between walls of rock, canyonlands of some kind, with no idea how she got here. Looking up, she saw the blue sky overhead and felt the fresh breeze.

She was outside.

She had left the library.

She spun around, tried to rush back through the teak door. It was gone. No matter where she looked, nothing but rock walls.

For a moment, she thought it was all a dream. It certainly felt like one. She'd crossed the mountains. Impossible, but she had done it.

She looked about, took measure of the place. She was as lost as she had ever been. Which way? East? West? The river flowed southward. Follow a river long enough and there will often be a village, or a town, or a city along the way. A lifetime of experience had taught her that.

But when she turned the bend in the canyon and saw those three men walking her way, she felt a coldness from head to toe. It was the way they flinched at the sight of her, then saw she was alone, then smiled.

An instinct triggered deep inside, kicked her in the gut, but it was an instinct she trusted and, at that moment, wholly devoted herself to.

She kept walking, pretending not to be afraid. She even attempted a grin, but in her head, she was already aiming her spear.

53

The Prince

"But that . . ." Prince Surasiva trails off, not able to comprehend.

"Can't be," says Aubry. The storm still rages. The wind howls. Blood has dried against corners of her mouth, but the pain persists. "It can't," she says. "Who would build such a place? And how? And why would they abandon it? Why leave all their knowledge behind?" A stab of pain. She twists and writhes, then fights it and wins back control. "Who left the food for me, Prince? And lit the candles? It couldn't have happened! I must have climbed over those mountains! Delusional! Out of my mind!" She convulses, half-crushed. She sucks in air, her head falling back, exhaustion overtaking her. "And yet . . ." she says, her words dwindling. "And yet . . ."

Her eyes roll back in her head, and she falls into oblivion.

54

The Prince

When she comes to, she is squinting, not from sand in her eyes, but from beams of sunlight angling into the canopy. There is no taste of blood in her mouth. There is no pain in her spine, or skull, or joints. But she is tired, so tired she can barely move.

She takes a deep breath and wills her body to sit up. She groans. Her body throbs like a bruise. She finds the strength to rise and step into the first sunlight she's felt in days.

The Prince is at the tiller of the colorful, canopied boat. They snail down a wide river that carves a canyon through the dusty savanna. He is staring upriver at what they left behind. Ahead of them is blue sky and bright sun, but back there, the storm still brews. Clouds of red and orange, shaped like anvils, hover over the western horizon, lightning glinting in their depths. Like the canyon walls, like Surasiva's palace, like the hills and the towers, it is a rising of the earth, in rusty shades of ochre, scarlet, and bronze. Their boat floats on water choked by the colors.

He looks at her. She looks at him. She feels something in her hand and remembers that Hayley put something there. He said it would keep her safe. All night, in a rigor mortis of pain, her fingers have gripped it. Now she uncoils her hand, removes the burlap.

It's her gun.

55

The Prince

The trail has become overgrown. The Prince takes Aubry's arm, slowly weaves their way through tangles of scrub, straight up a hill, to reach the wooden house perched at the top.

"I apologize," says the Prince. They have left their boat behind, tied to the riverbank, and are now circling the empty house. "The upkeep hasn't been . . . well . . . There is no upkeep."

They come upon the stairs to the front and enter the large doors.

The house is open, airy, and tall, made of teak and thatch, but nothing resembling royal. It is little more than a neglected retreat. The foliage outside is untended and overgrown. Trees press close to the walls, turning the rooms dim and green. They see empty cupboards, crates and boxes stacked up and forgotten, only the occasional bit of furniture to sit on—a dusty cot, a dusty footstool, a broken chair.

Aubry opens windows. To the east, views of a bright blue ocean shimmer back at her, just past the palm trees.

"I like it even better than your palace," she says.

"Yes," he agrees. "But it's a long way from matters of state."

She opens more windows. To the west, the storm is a distant

yellow smudge on the horizon. The Prince is looking, too. She knows he wants to go back. He has left his people alone in the middle of a storm, in the company of a British regiment. He is torn between Aubry and his duty, and Aubry, so tired, can't think of what to do about it.

He leaves the window, looks through cupboards on the far wall. He finds a collection of colored sands, stored in a dozen or more corked bottles.

"My sands," he says, delighted. His charm is downright boyish at times. "There are still some left."

Aubry finds photographs, framed, dusty, of various sizes, stacked against the wall. She peeks through them, sees a family portrait of people she doesn't recognize, proud parents and dignified little children, dressed in their finest portrait clothes, standing before the marble staircase of a palace she knows well.

"Is this your family?"

He comes over, takes a cursory look.

"Yes, most of them," he says.

She keeps looking, finds photographs of lavish parties, of cricket matches, of a young man posing beside a fine horse. She finds another portrait, this time just the children.

"Which one are you?"

He points to one of the youngest in the group, a boy of maybe four or five, in opulent attire, a turban encapsulating his tiny head.

"Are these your brothers and sisters?"

"Cousins, too. There were thirteen of us, but they're all gone now."

"Gone?"

"One drowned. One fell off a horse. Disease took the rest. The oldest died in the uprising of 1857," he says, lowering his voice. "But the British don't know that."

He says this proudly, as if he has secret information that might undo the British Empire. It all comes as a shock.

"You are the last of your line?"

"Yes."

"Who will you pass this on to?" She looks around the house, but means everything—his wealth, his lands.

"The way things are progressing, there may be nothing left to pass on." He grins a little as if making a joke, so she might not be too concerned.

But Aubry stands there amazed, watching him go through cupboards, his little bottles of colored sand cradled in his arms. She thought him a kind and decent man from the moment she met him. But he's lost everything he had, sacrificed everything he owned, lives outside convention, defies the easy path in favor of the righteous one. He does it wisely and he does it quietly. He has no parents to praise him and no children to admire him. He simply conducts himself, hidden in society's peripheral vision, where no one knows to look.

"You're a good man, Prince," she says. "The best I know."

He smiles at her, a little taken aback, a little amused.

"I met a woman who granted me a wish."

He stops, turns, looks at her hard.

"She was here?" he asks. He has a haunted look, as if he's forgotten his own name. She hasn't seen him like this yet.

"She was."

"Then things are afoot," he says.

"Are you in love, Prince?" She thinks she knows the signs. Not that she'd blame him. She's met the woman. She's a little in love herself.

But the Prince only laughs.

"Will you fight?" she asks. Again, he says nothing. "You don't seem much like the killing type."

He looks her in the eyes. There is no humor in his face anymore, just a kind of sorrow for someone who knows of killing. Aubry looks back at him with almost the very same expression.

"He may not even know he's in need, but then, suddenly, there I am," Qalima had said.

If he is thinking of fighting, then he is in need.

"The story you said. You must be mistaken," he says. "The mountains are not here."

"Yes. I know."

"We are too far south. The mountains are not for weeks in any direction. And on foot! Not for months."

"I know that, Prince."

"Then . . ."

"Then what? I have no answers either." She can think of nothing else to say. Exhaustion is overtaking her. "I'm tired, Prince. Is it all right if I sleep? Just a little?"

Though the sun is still bright, though she wants nothing more than to spend her every last minute with Prince Surasiva, she falls asleep and doesn't wake up until the next morning.

56

The Prince

Such a fine sleep, long and dreamless, with no voices growling in her head. She wakes fully recovered, sits on the cot, and, for a few minutes, enjoys being free of pain. She gathers her things, makes her bed. Her sickness, she feels, is a long way off. She wants to stay, to hold on to her every last moment here, but she knows it is self-ish. She cannot keep the Prince from his people. It is time to go.

She finds the Prince by the shore, painting the beach blue and red and gold. He is bent over his work, carefully tapping out little bits of color from his bottles.

"You are packed?"

She nods. He continues to layer sand upon sand.

"I envy you," he says. "You are in a unique position. All around the world people are asking themselves, Who shall I marry? How many children shall I have? What is this spot in the back of my throat?" He looks up at her then. "But your questions are outside all of that. You may exist in an entirely different realm."

She shrugs. "I've given up trying to understand. I think I'll just let it all quietly overwhelm me."

He nods, then goes back to his mandala in the sand.

"Did Qalima teach you this?" she asks.

"Yes."

She studies his work, his painting in the sand, large and circular, as long as her spear in any direction. It is both a picture of something and an abstraction. There is a man and a woman walking toward each other in a deep, enchanted night, but the moon is a pattern that blooms flowerlike in unearthly colors. It is a moon that threatens to overwhelm them both.

She studies him, too. With him, she has shared her pain. Look how he carries it, a little bent, a little weary. For her, he does this.

"Do you know what she said to me?" she asks.

"No."

She tells him of that single memorable night when she and Qalima strolled through a sea of green curtains, into rooms adorned with her creations, the night Qalima said, *"There are things on this earth that only exist because you have beheld them. If you weren't there, they would never have been."*

The Prince thinks on this and says, "The world needs you." He taps out a little more sand, careful to keep his colors within their lines. "It wants a witness."

"I've seen enough, Prince."

"This sickness," he asks, "when does it—"

"Whenever it wants," she says. "This whole planet is its playground. It roams. It likes everything it sees—the deserts, the mountains, the oceans, the trees. It wants to be out there, seeing the world. It will only keep me alive if I take it."

"And you—"

"I'm only alive when hunting it down."

"What will that look like, the day you catch it?"

She remembers the Berber caravan and an oasis buried somewhere in the Sahara. She saw desert mistletoe, creeping up from the dirt. In its stranglehold, a desert willow, slowly dying in its grasp. She thought, What that willow needs is a way to strangle the mistletoe first.

He corks his bottle of green, sits back, and inspects his work. He shows neither pride nor disappointment, simply sits down in the sand above his creation that faces the sea.

"What do we do now?" she asks.

"We wait for the tide to come in."

Aubry is shocked. All that effort and beauty simply to be washed into the sea. She thinks frantically of some way to preserve it, but there is nothing to be done. He's painted in the path of the tides and it's only a matter of time before it's gone.

Four years from now the Prince will be dead. He will be arrested and imprisoned by the British for illegal business practices. There will be a prison fire and all the guards will run and save themselves while the prisoners, the Prince among them, suffocate in their cells. Aubry will read of it in the back of a newspaper while crossing the Gulf of Oman on an old rickety steamship. She will remember this remarkable man who lived in the periphery, and died there, too. She will be grateful to have known him as well as she did, to have been his witness, to have given him his recognition before his life had been snuffed out.

"I will miss you, Prince."

"I will miss you."

So they sit together and wait.

Then comes a wave, sizzling its way up the beach. It touches the bottom of his mandala and smears its colors across the wet sand.

"Here we are," says the Prince, "in God's classroom, waiting for our lesson."

For another hour, they watch the mandala bleed into the ocean. When the colors have all but washed away, Aubry takes Prince Surasiva's hand and kisses it. She holds his fingers tight in hers and keeps her lips to his skin. He says nothing, but rests his other hand on her cheek until she finally gets up and walks off, north toward the Sundarbans, across unspoiled coastline that awaits her footsteps.

At nightfall, she stops to sharpen her spear.

"I'm coming for you."

"Good," says the sickness. "I'm waiting."

"I'm going to find you. I'm going to skin the meat off your bones."

"This is why I like you," it says. "More than all the others." Its voice, tender in her ears. "You."

57

An Aside, Not So Brief

"Tell me what you've seen," asked the woman from Hezhou. Aubry had met her on the road out of the Nanling Mountains, exhausted from her journey. The woman had taken her in, fed her, but it was Aubry's spirit that felt crushed. She owned a special misery that no one else could ever know.

What did the woman ask? What has Aubry seen? Too much, was the answer. More than she ever wanted to. Aubry was only twenty-seven, but there was already a long catalog of images. She did not wish to be rude. She would answer as best she could, but where to begin?

"I have crewed with the cinnamon traders from Seychelles," said Aubry, and described the willowy sweep of the sails, the mixed-blood crew, an elegant weave of African and Polynesian and Indian.

"I have built a house in the Hawizeh marshes," describing armfuls of reeds handed down the line to the farmers who braided and bent them into arches, forming the shape of the home, and Aubry, singing songs with the women, sounding out words as best she could, the meanings of which she never did find out.

"Slaughtered whales in the Faroe Islands," and Aubry told her of the harbor, stained bright red under a dark charcoal sky, pilot whales deboned on the shores, whale meat that would get every Faroese through the winter—but not her.

"Have you been to America?" asked the woman from He-zhou.

"And danced all night." That night, around the fire, with the Navajo in their deerskin dresses and turquoise beads, their bands of woven color in the firelight, the moonlight. "And wished I could go back."

In a strange reversal, she unexpectedly felt joy. For a moment—and only a moment—she thought she could relate her adventures all night. Even after she quashed the thought—God forbid she becomes a bore—the joy still clung.

"But you can't," said the woman. "You can't go back."

"No. Everything once. And briefly."

The woman's gaze fell. She poured Aubry more tea.

"I was born in Xi'an. Have you been there? Did you try the soup dumplings? Did you try the noodles?"

"Yes! Just days ago. They were delicious!"

"Oh no," said the woman, stymied. "You are confused. Xi'an is not close to Hezhou."

"Of course it is. I followed the river through the foothills. I climbed down the waterfall that led to the lake. I found a raft and paddled until I came to that big hole where all the water drained out, and I wanted to get closer, but I was . . ."

The woman put her hand gently on Aubry's.

"A hole?"

"Yes."

"In a lake? In the water itself?"

"You must know it. It's not so far. Like someone pulled a plug."

"Xi'an is a long, long journey from here. And there are no waterfalls nearby. And there is certainly no lake with a hole in it."

Aubry's mind whirled. Her body seemed so much heavier, so suddenly.

"Are you . . . ?" Aubry hated to think it. "Are you being cruel to me?"

The woman's eyes widened. "My goodness, no. Why would I do that?"

Aubry could think of nothing to say. Exhaustion was overtaking her. But a realization slowly crept across the woman's face. She took Aubry's hand in hers and leaned in close.

"It seems," said the woman, "that the world you travel through is not the same world we travel through."

My God, thought Aubry. *My God.*

58

With Marta in the Klondike

Near the equator, sunrise is a momentary event. Night, then suddenly day, like flipping a switch. But here, so near the top of the earth, it lasts for hours, a slow migration from deep violet, to rose, to the bright blue of arctic forget-me-nots, all fears dispelled, as if pain were no more. Here, not so far from the pole, it is her favorite part of the day.

How many dawns has she witnessed? How many sunrises have kept her company on her travels? She's no longer young. She's been around for half a century now, so old she now measures herself in terms of centuries, and almost all of it spent wandering. Dawns over warm tropical harbors, dawns over steaming rivers, dawns over smoking volcanoes. There must have been a thousand. Tens of thousands. But who counts these things? She is not a statistician. She is a walker.

"How can you be angry," says her disease, "looking at this?"

"I'm not."

"You know what they say."

"I don't."

"If you can't make your life meaningful, make it extraordinary."

"Then you say stupid things like that, and I'm angry all over again."

It's a boardinghouse on paper, but a saloon in actuality, and a brothel more actually than that. The yellow lamplight feels cozy even from a distance, especially from a distance, a warm flame poking through the cold moon-blue landscape.

This time of year, the mud is carnivorous. In Whitehorse, she had seen entire knee-high boots sucked into the muck, never to be excavated. Horses can die of exhaustion walking from stable to saloon. It is said small children have disappeared, too, their little hats all that remain of them on the glutinous city streets. On the other hand, birdsong has returned. It is early in the season, but there are already flowers in the meadows and on the mountain peaks if you look hard enough.

Tonight, it is good to be out of the cold. The saloon is quiet, the mood languorous. The girls, a dozen of them, hang like bedsheets on the chairs in the back. There is Katie, eighteen years old, discovered unconscious one morning under four inches of freshly fallen snow and the stink of scotch. It was a miracle she hadn't froze to death, but the miracles didn't stop there. An angel had visited her in her drunken stupor, or so the story went, and given her an address in Skagway where her fortune lay waiting. At the address lived a judge who, excited by her visit, exchanged thirty dollars and a fabulous supper for a single night of unbridled lovemaking. She never looked back, still thanks that angel in her prayers to this day.

That one, with two teeth missing from her grin, is Doreen, whose desperately impoverished husband rented her out to neighbors and friends, until he was shot dead by a jealous lover. It was the opportunity she'd been waiting for. She fled Circle City with nothing but a banjo, four dollars, and cleavage as deep as the sea. With this, she started over, vowing never to be poor again.

And then there is Vicki, who arrived in San Francisco on a boat full of young Korean picture brides. She quickly discovered that the husbands they were promised were all poor farmhands in borrowed suits. She understood she could live the oppressive life of a fruit picker or a factory worker, or she could strike out on her own. She made her way to Dawson City, where the men outnumbered the women twenty to one. She learned to saddle up with the most well-dressed prospector in any given dance hall and made twenty dollars an evening while miners were making a dollar a day. At the height of the gold rush she was flush with cash. Her best year netted over nine thousand dollars, not including gold nuggets as big as acorns bequeathed to her in moments of dizzying passion. Back then, many of the richest people in Alaska were prostitutes and madams. But that was more than a decade ago. The gold has since dried up. The authorities have cracked down. Vicki took her considerable savings and today, well past her prime, runs this quiet establishment far from the law, where she still manages to bring in an impressive, if not quite stellar, income.

The door bursts open. The first customers of the evening pour in, men from the mining camp. They aren't drunk, but it's hard to tell the way they're carrying on, laughing, swaggering, waving money in the air.

"I just swindled back a week's worth of pay from Fathead Carson!" shouts a red-haired man in clothes that haven't been washed in weeks. He orders a round of drinks. "Vicki, bring on them girls of yours!" he shouts.

"You gotta drink for me?" she says from a table in the back of the parlor, a low-set voice crackling from a lifetime of cigar smoke. All they can see is her hot cigar tip glowing in the shadows. They cannot see she is sitting with a new girl, a woman who has been around the world many times.

"Especially for you, Vicki!"

"Money to the bar."

The men rush to the bar, hidden from authorities in a secret closet where a gap-toothed bartender hands out whatever illegal liquor he has on hand. Vicki meets them there, goes behind the bar, puffing on her homemade cigar, and helps the bald man collect the money and serve the drinks.

From her corner in the back, Aubry notices a straggler, entering the saloon behind them. At first she assumes he is one of the group, but he keeps himself apart, waiting for the others to disperse before ordering his drink. He takes a secluded seat near the door, hidden in a corner, his Stetson pulled low over the eyes. The rest of him is bundled up in oilskin and fur two inches thick. He's short, so short he'd probably struggle to peek over Aubry's shoulders.

And he's lost, Aubry supposes. She imagines he got a tip that there'd be work at one of the tiny settlements upriver, near the nebulous border between the United States and Canada, where territories and laws become confused. These borderlands are havens for gamblers and whorehouses, one of the few havens left in the Klondike now that Prohibition is the law of the land. It's a place only accessible by footpaths through the black spruce forests, or by canoe if you have the strength for a long upriver paddle. And now here he is, this lonely soul, wandering the muddy streets of a tiny former gold rush town without a name. And that is the last she thinks of him.

But, as Aubry soon learns, he isn't done thinking of her.

He is Marta Arbaroa. He is a she, and she has traveled all the way up the coast by steamship, from Acapulco to Skagway, on an epic search. Soon she will be telling Aubry of her adventures

251

in Skagway, where she stepped off the boat only to be inundated by marriage proposals from sex-starved men who only had to glimpse her female figure coming down the gangplank. An annoying start to her search, but she quickly learned to conceal her gender, surprising hotel owners and policemen with pointed questions. She will tell Aubry how she received a tip from a local and traveled even farther, taking the White Pass Railroad all the way to Whitehorse and back again. Another tip, another journey—this time by foot, three days through dark pine forests, all the way to this forgotten outhouse of a town. After four months of ceaseless travel by boat, horse, train, and foot, she has arrived in a cold hell and stepped inside the sole building that seems to contain life, only to find it is a brothel.

Imagine how the scene must have looked to Marta. She tries to be invisible. This is not her country—she is not even certain what country she's in—but she is damn sure nothing that happens in this establishment is legal. She draws her Stetson over her eyes, peeking at the action, her oilskin coat disguising her shape. Even so, one of the boys peers under the brim of her hat. She hasn't fooled him. He thinks she's one of these cake-faced prostitutes.

"Hello there," he coos.

She says nothing, only glares back, face like a loaded gun. The man backs off, decides to carry his drink to the tables in the back.

It takes only moments for the saloon to go from languid to lively, the men turning drunk and loud, flirting with the girls in their bare-shoulder dresses and thigh-high stockings.

"Vicki," says the man who has swindled back his money, "you got the sweetest girls this side of Dawson."

"And you," returns Vicki, sucking on her cigar, "are the sexiest baboon I know."

"What about the Dutch girl? What's her price?" asks a blond boy, yellow hair drooping over his eyes like a sheepdog.

"Me?" says Aubry, more than amused.

Marta can't believe it. That's her, Aubry Tourvel, among the prostitutes. *How long has she been here?* she wonders. A day? Two? Three? Marta has done her research. Aubry Tourvel is over fifty years old and there she is, drinking with a pack of whores hardly older than schoolgirls.

"What do you think?" crackles Vicki. "Would you pay fifty dollars for this beauty?"

"I sure as hell would!" shouts one of the men.

"Then that's how much she is—fifty dollars!"

Aubry laughs. So do the girls. "No, no, Carl," Aubry tells him, drink in hand. "I know the perfect girl for you. Let me see if the zoo will release her."

This gets laughs, too. The men, more than ever, are won over.

How does Aubry Tourvel compare? Is her skin wrinkled? Of course it is, lines at the corners of her eyes, creases in her forehead. Is her hair graying? Especially around the temples. Yet men ten, twenty, thirty years younger are competing for her attention. Marta is in her thirties and barely looks younger than this woman.

Vicki takes Aubry by the arm, leads her away from the party, over to the bar where they think they can talk in confidence, but where Marta, seated not so far away, can hear every word.

"You know, you can handle your liquor, you're good for business, and I like you," says Vicki. "Why don't you work for me?"

Marta listens, amazed. She wonders if she'll ever get offers like that when she's fifty. If Marta thinks that Aubry, with her upper-class French upbringing and her prominence in the press, would be offended, she's wrong. Aubry doesn't blanch or protest or defend her honor. She almost seems to consider it.

"I like you, too, Vicki," Aubry tells her. "Let me sleep on it."

They refill their glasses and head back to the party. Marta stands and calls after her.

"Aubry! Aubry Tourvel!"

But Aubry can't hear her over the impromptu celebration. So Marta shuts up and sits back, watching the evening unfold.

An hour later, everyone is still there, engulfed in a haze of smoke from Vicki's hand-rolled cigars. Some of the men have found favorite girls who sit on their laps and suck alcohol off their lips. No one has disappeared into a room or slipped out back. Not yet. The men shamelessly flex their muscles and arm wrestle to the delight of the girls. The girls lift their skirts and compare legs, including Aubry, daring the men to choose the most beautiful pair. Poor Marta, exhausted just watching from her quiet corner. But they hardly notice her, so full of drinks and dares and dirty jokes.

"What can I do, Vic? I have this terrible love burning inside me for this beautiful Swedish creature, but she still won't have me!" cries one of the men.

"Have you tried drink?" says Vicki.

So Aubry grabs his mug and downs it. She peers at him closely while her head spins.

"It's an improvement," she says, "but you're still the ugliest man in Canada!"

They all laugh. Even Marta's lips twist into a smirk under the brim of her Stetson.

It's not until midnight that Aubry leaves the saloon. Some of the boys have finally taken a few whores away and others are waiting their turn. The fun has petered out and Aubry is sleepy—a little tipsy as well—but she leaves the saloon in high spirits. She waves goodbye to Vicki and her girls, to the grimy men, still smiling to herself, still living off fumes of joy as she plods through the mud with her bag and walking stick.

Before she knows it, there's a man with a Latin complexion walking alongside her, talking in an accent she hasn't heard in a long, long time.

"You say you will see them tomorrow, but that's not true, is it?" he says.

Aubry glances at him, not comprehending—this is the short man who entered the saloon earlier, but what a feminine voice he has. She looks again.

How careless.

A woman.

But Aubry keeps walking, doesn't bother with an answer.

"You've been here two days, maybe three," continues the woman. "Tomorrow you will have to keep moving."

Aubry stops, standing in the mud, and sizes this woman up. She is no taller than a sunflower, but with big striking brown eyes. She seems rather fragile at first glance, but if that were true, she wouldn't be standing here in a place like this.

Aubry continues walking without a word. One of the boys is following them, drunk and staggering, and she doesn't care to dawdle.

"I'm Marta," says the woman, spry enough to keep up. "Marta Arbaroa with *El Correo Español*. I've been keeping track of you since you arrived in Churchill. I tried to meet you in Whitehorse, but was too late, so I jumped on the train and followed your trail all the way here. It was not easy. Please, will you talk to me?"

"Will I talk to you?" says Aubry. "Of course I will talk to you. What do you want to talk about?"

"How about that man following us?"

Aubry looks at him over her shoulder. He's stumbling toward them, smiling like a Halloween pumpkin.

"Does he frighten you? I'll take care of him," Aubry tells her. She spins around, walking right up to his face. This surprises Marta, makes her nervous. Aubry is no match for this man, no matter how drunk he is. But Marta has a rifle, loaded and ready to be used. She once shot four ptarmigan out of the sky in rapid succession. She can shoot through a knothole from a hundred paces. She remembers that Prohibition was a demand of the women's suffrage movement, a movement Marta wholly supports, and if it comes to it, she will have no regrets shooting this drunken slob dead.

"Where are you going?" Aubry asks the drunk.

"Wherever you are," he says with his alcohol-fueled grin. If Marta wasn't so nervous, she might have found it comical to behold.

"That won't do," says Aubry. "You go home."

"You come with me."

He tries to grab Aubry's arm but her spear comes up against his throat. Marta's eyes widen. Her blood freezes. Her hand goes instinctively to her rifle. The drunkard's smile is suddenly less convincing.

"You go home now," says Aubry. "You are a little drunk and I like my men nice and sober."

He's not sure how to respond. He weighs his options in his befuddled brain.

"Don't think you are faster than my spear," Aubry warns him. "Even if you are, I have this waiting for you." She casually shows him her pistol—the pistol she holds in her other hand, the pistol she has never fired at anyone in her life—but now has pointed at his forehead. "Go home now. Get some sleep. I will wait right here till you are gone."

He still retains a bit of grin. Holding on to it, he takes a few steps back, almost trips, and walks away.

"Keep going," she tells him, so cheerful. "Good night! I'll see you tomorrow!"

Marta, open-mouthed, watches the drunk retreat. He glances over his shoulder like a boy who needs glasses. Aubry's not the least bit rattled. She'd gotten rid of him without so much as a warning shot. She even waves goodbye. Marta isn't sure, but this seems like Aubry's idea of fun.

"Hee-hee! Quick!" says Aubry, tiptoeing back to Marta and tittering like a schoolgirl. "Let's get out of here!"

They bank to the left and, together, flee into the rustle of the forest.

59

With Marta in the Klondike

Aubry has already secured a place to sleep for the night in an empty barn loft an hour downriver. Marta fishes for her electric lamp, but Aubry is ahead of her, pulls an ointment from her bag, scoops it into a tin can, and lights it. A warm flame glows and Marta stares, amazed.

"How long will it burn?" she asks.

"All night."

"Where did you find it?"

"I was taught this by a hunting party in . . . in . . ." She's tapping the floor with her foot, trying to recall, but there are so many places she can't remember anymore. "Oh dear," she says. "Where was that?"

"How many hunting parties have you traveled with?"

"Oh, I don't think I could count."

Marta has her notebook out and scribbles this down.

"So this is a typical night for you?"

"Oh no. This is much more comfortable than usual."

"My God."

"Yes."

"And these men . . . And you, being all alone. Isn't it terribly dangerous for you?"

Aubry considers the question. These men tonight hadn't been dangerous, and she would know. She remembers the three men she killed in India. They were dangerous. She remembers a plague-ridden African village, and a child swept away by the tides, and a terrible fire in a grand hotel, but the memories, and their order, and their meanings all blur in her mind.

"Yes," she says, but then, thankfully, remembers Lionel Kyengi, and her mood turns. She forgets the horrors—instead, remembers kissing Lionel on the train, a whole week with him. How happy she'd been.

"Yes?" asks Marta.

"No," says Aubry.

"No?"

If Lionel were here with her now, thinks Aubry, their bodies would be glowing in the moonlight. "A little of both, maybe."

"That man back there, that drunkard. Have you ever killed anyone before? With that spear? With that pistol?"

"What a rude question to ask someone you only just met."

"It sounds like you have."

"Does it? Well, no. The answer is no, I haven't," Aubry tells her, a little more forcefully than she meant to.

"You seem like you could."

"That's the trick to it."

Marta, pen in hand, stares at Aubry, waiting for more.

"Are you going to write down everything I say?" Aubry asks.

Marta closes her notebook and puts down her pen. "Oh. No. Not everything. But I don't want to forget important details before I return to my editors in Mexico."

Distant howls sound from somewhere in the wilderness, a pack of wolves making mournful noises overhead. They listen for a while. Then, for no reason other than she's a little drunk, Aubry says, "Sometimes I follow the animals."

"What?"

Aubry is thinking of the caribou she followed through the tundra only a matter of weeks ago. She is thinking of the time she followed the wildebeest in a great big loop around the Serengeti.

"They migrate, too. Sometimes I think, why not?"

She remembers walking in the shadow of a hundred thousand Baikal teal, wintering in the Seosan Lakes of Korea, turning the noonday sky dark and kaleidoscopic. She remembers paddling onto the tiny beaches of Christmas Island and the thousands of red crabs crawling ashore at her feet to lay their eggs in the sand.

"How does that work out for you?" asks Marta.

"Sometimes very well," she says, because walking through clouds of monarch butterflies in the cool mountains of central Mexico can only be considered a good thing.

"Sometimes not so well," she says next, because following polar bears around the shores of Hudson Bay so she might eat scraps from their kills was a terrible, terrible, terrible idea.

"I'm coming with you this time," Marta announces. "As far as you go."

Aubry laughs. If she is lucky, Marta will get as far as the inlet. Her feet will hurt. She will be sore all over. The mosquitos will have drunk half her blood. Her questions will suddenly dry up.

"You can't shake me," says Marta.

"I won't have to," Aubry tells her. "But we have quite a bit of exploring to do tomorrow and I'm a little drunk. Let's go to sleep."

"But I've come so far. Please! There's so much I need to know."

Aubry rolls over, turns away from her. "You can ask your questions tomorrow. Good night . . ." She can't remember suddenly. Must be the liquor. "What was your name again?"

"Marta Arbaroa," she says. "That's the last time I allow you to forget."

"I've been warned." So much spunk for such a tiny person. "Good night, Marta."

"Good night, Aubry."

Aubry closes her eyes. Marta, with no other recourse available, does the same.

60

With Marta in the Klondike

They awake with birdsong. It's almost impossible not to, the air erupting with broken melodies. But the birds never sleep in, so neither does Aubry. She expects Marta will not rise so easily, but she does, and without complaint. They break camp and climb nearly vertical slopes until they clear the trees, the floor of brittle needles giving way to orange lichen on bare mountain rock.

Aubry expects this to be the day Marta gives up and goes home. Yet, despite her diminutive size, her breathing is easy, her footsteps sure. Aubry enjoys company in most cases, but she isn't sure how long she can stand this woman asking questions like a little dog yipping at her feet.

"You're hardly the first notable figure I've interviewed," says Marta, in her defense. "I helped make Pascual Orozco famous overnight."

"Careful, Marta. If you talk like that, people might think you're bragging."

"I am bragging! What's the point in accomplishing anything if no one ever knows about it?"

The view opens up—mountaintop views that stretch for miles. Nothing is hidden. Yet Marta stops to unfold a map.

"You're doing it all wrong," Aubry tells her. Aubry doesn't

bother to drop her pack. She is the picture of patience, still on her feet, calmly waiting for Marta to find whatever she's looking for. Perhaps, thinks Aubry, this will be the thing that undoes her.

"What do you mean?" says Marta. "I'm trying to find our way."

"Find our way? We're not even lost. How can we find our way if we're not lost?"

"How will we find Juneau without a map?"

"How did we find this view without a map?"

"You're just walking?"

"There is a beauty to this, you know."

"To starvation? To hypothermia?"

"To wandering aimlessly."

Marta hesitates, then, perhaps out of scientific curiosity, folds up her map and packs it away. "Have you explained this philosophy to anyone else besides me?"

"I assume so."

"Were they as patient with you as I am?"

"No, Marta. You are the most patient of them all."

They walk, Aubry with her spear, Marta with a walking stick of her own. Like true nomads, they walk loudly to flush out whatever might be lying in wait ahead, tapping their sticks, clanging their metal. Aubry thought she'd have to explain why, but wilderness survival is something Marta seems to understand intuitively.

They follow the lithic backbone of the mountains through vistas they will never be able to remember properly, clear skies and distant waters to the south and west, passing rainstorms to the east.

"How much have you told to others?" asks Marta.

Aubry has a collection of memories to choose from, a mish-mash of them. What was their order? Which happened first?

Cape Town or Cape Horn? Did she sail from Cartagena to Caracas or Caracas to Cartagena? Did she know the taste of green coconut before she arrived in Somaliland or after she'd left? Did it matter? If it did, and she can't remember, then what was the purpose of it? If it didn't, then her life is something she can construct at her pleasure, and also a lie.

"I've told everything to everyone. My life is out there. It's just in pieces. You only have to find the hundred or so strangers I've told the fragments to."

"What do the strangers tell you?"

"Strangers!" She laughs. "They tell me everything!"

"Secrets?" asks Marta like a gossiping schoolgirl.

"Yes, Marta," says Aubry, wriggling her eyebrows conspiratorially. She's not one to betray a trust, even a stranger's trust, but then, who are they now that they're so far away? Marta doesn't know them. She'll never meet them or know their names. For that matter, Aubry had barely known them, and what she knows is now far away and long ago. Her travels and all the people she's met during them no longer exist. In the act of leaving, she has surrendered them up, as if to death. The most she can hope for is that their memories might come and go, like a wind chime in a distant forest. Perhaps it's okay to disclose a little to this journalist badgering her with questions. She's walked long enough. Sometimes it's liberating to look back at where your feet have been.

"Everybody has at least one secret that can break your heart," Aubry tells Marta. "Everybody."

She's thinking of the poor woman from Angola, walking beside her while she pulled her donkey down the dusty savanna road. Ahead of them were her four children, three girls and a boy, running and playing, but well out of earshot. "There was a fifth child, too," the woman whispered to her. "But nobody knows because I was young and frightened and drowned her in a river." The tears quietly came down her cheeks. It was something she'd never told anyone. Aubry heard her confession and held that woman's hand all the way back home.

Or the bow-tied Peruvian man on the train who sat next to Aubry on the trip down from Cusco. "I once had an employee who stole money from my business. He begged and pleaded but I wouldn't have it. I sacked him. I blackened his name to anyone who would listen. He hanged himself a week later." Then Aubry remembers the man from Cusco sinking into silence after that. "Turns out it hadn't been stolen. I'd misplaced it. And forgot."

The wealthy American on her yacht with the movie-star good looks—Aubry sat back on the cushions, sunning herself beside this dazzling woman who kept herself hidden behind sunglasses so no one would go blind gazing upon her. She was fondling her pearls, Aubry remembers, with such quiet despair in her voice. "There is this disease that killed my father, and his father, and I think I have the same symptoms," the woman told her, "but I'm too frightened to have it checked." The sickness was coming for her, measuring out her days, and none of her wealth would make it go away.

And that night, in their shallow cave under a rocky overhang to shelter them from the rain, a small campfire to keep them warm, Marta looks at Aubry and says, "You're a walking catalog of dangerous secrets."

"They tell me because I am not real to them. I come and go, and when I go, I am gone forever, secret and all, like whispering a terrible crime into a deep dark well."

"Do you have any secrets?"

Aubry looks away, pokes at the fire. "Silly girl. Of course not."

Marta sits up a little. "Oh, then you do. And it must be big. And it must be terrible."

"No. Not terrible."

"Then what? What kind of secret is so harmless you don't dare tell?"

Aubry raises her eyebrow and laughs a little. "You tell me, Marta. Hmm? You tell me."

Marta smiles, mostly to herself. "No more talk of secrets," she agrees, and they both go silent.

Then Marta turns to Aubry and this time her smile is gregarious, but also more sly. Her gaze drops to Aubry's legs peeking out from under her wool skirt. "But I'm wondering," she says, "you must have the strongest legs in the entire world."

"I do!" Aubry is beaming. She is proud of her legs. "They're like steel!"

"May I see?"

"Of course!" she says, always pleased to show off her muscles. She pulls up her skirt. Marta leans close to touch them, to feel the strength beneath the skin. Impressed, she runs her hand up and down Aubry's leg.

"Like marble . . ." she murmurs. "Like art . . ."

Her hand moves slowly, up her leg a little too far, a little too slow. Aubry freezes and watches Marta carefully, wondering where Marta's hand might go next, and how she will handle it.

Marta doesn't look at her, just her smooth, muscled legs, her fingers softly traveling the length of them. Then, without fuss or shame, she simply removes her hand, rolls over, and goes to sleep.

"Good night," she says.

Aubry watches her in the firelight for some time before wrapping herself in blankets and drifting away to the sound of raindrops and distant thunder.

61

An Unmovable Dream

That night Aubry dreams Qalima is with her, sitting at her easel just outside the cave, painting a watercolor much larger than her usual work.

"Did you have a vision?" asks Aubry.

"I'm having one now," she says. "Look."

Aubry comes so close she steps inside the painting. This doesn't surprise her. What does surprise her is that she is in the library, a grand tunnel of columns and shelves and arches fading into the distance, and it is full of people from many times and places. Aubry is so used to empty libraries that this one, so full of life, astounds her.

Ahead is Qalima, once again, sitting at her easel, painting. Aubry walks up to her, steps into that painting, too.

Now she is standing before a large window that overlooks a black river and dense jungle trees, just as it looked in Qalima's painting back in India. She can even see the lean-to made of big jungle leaves and the campfire still flickering its light inside. Qalima was right. Somehow it feels like home.

She wants to go outside, to see this new home of hers, but she quickly discovers there are no doors to this library and the windows will not open or break.

She knows, suddenly, that this will be her last stay on earth.

She wakes from the dream in the middle of the night. The sky is full of stars. She remembers Qalima and wonders how many birthday wishes she has parceled out, how many people are wandering the world, or sitting in their homes, or working their jobs, waiting and waiting for their wish—whatever it is—to come true.

62

With Marta in the Klondike

Aubry, up with the birdsong, goes down to the stream to wash her face in the icy water. The air is cold, and the water is even colder, but Aubry was once told that the best way to fight cold is with cold. A Swedish farmer told her that, a Swedish farmer who took a cold bath every day, jumping in a pond near his home no matter the weather. He was seventy at the time, and the picture of good health. So every once in a while, she does the same.

She has barely put water to skin when she stops, stock-still at the edge of the stream. She thinks she heard something—a rumble, low, as deep as thunder.

She looks up. Something is moving behind the low-growing shrubs, something large and heavy. A rustle in the bushes across the stream.

She reaches for her spear, but it is not there. It is back at camp, she remembers. Of course it is. Just when she needs it.

Here it comes, plowing through the vine maple and the maidenhair fern, a bear emerging from the forest, head low, shoulders spiky.

It stands there on the far side of the stream. It grunts, glares, pushes hot breath though its black lips and teeth. The bear doesn't like her washing in this stream. It is enormous, savage with long brown hair. A grizzly, she is sure.

She thinks maybe it won't cross this stream, but the stream is no more than ankle-deep. Of course it will cross. It will charge, claws splashing, spray filling the air around it, and be upon her in two strides. It will raise a claw and take her head clean off in one blow.

She marvels at the random nature of death. A careless footstep on a mountain path. Eating the wrong mushroom, one you swore you recognized. An impromptu desire for a cold bath one morning. Such a peaceful morning, too—then, suddenly, a bear—and without warning your whole life comes crashing to a halt.

A movement to her left. The click of a rifle. Marta is suddenly beside her, but more than that, now Marta is in front of her. She steps between Aubry and the bear, rifle raised eye-level, a bead on the animal's head.

"On your feet," says Marta, her voice deliberately calm but the anxiety thick, like something you can smell. "And slowly back away." Her body is as tight as a steel cable, her jaw rigid, transforming the shape of her face.

Aubry rises, steps back.

"Don't take your eyes off him," says Marta. "Just back away. Nice and slow." The bear, for its part, hardly moves. It guards its side of the creek, baring its teeth and looking mean. It could charge, but look how Marta aims that rifle. Look at her poise. If this bear were a little smarter, it would run away while it had the chance.

In truth, Aubry knows never to turn your back on a bear, always to back off, nice and slow, to play dead if all else fails. But Marta, this tiny woman, speaking with the mouth of mountains—how does Aubry not fall in line with that?

They back off, two disciplined soldiers in battle, still alive, and stronger for it. Marta's rifle stays raised all the while until the bear has faded into columns of trees and the rumble in its throat is no more.

At camp, they grab their gear as quick as they can and are off. An hour passes. Though they haven't seen or heard the bear since, their pace hardly slows.

"You could've been eaten," says Aubry, now that her pulse has eased.

"There are the people I would gladly shoot dead," says Marta. "And then the people I would gladly die for. You are in the second half of that equation."

Aubry smiles, ear to ear. It's good to have fans, she thinks.

"Really, Marta. You hardly know me."

Marta looks at her, sidelong. She laughs to herself, shaking her head, as if Aubry has just made the most cynical joke she's heard in a long time.

When they make camp that night, Aubry watches Marta unpack her sleeping bag. She notices that inside Marta's carpetbag is a black binder. She has seen the binder before. She has seen Marta checking her facts, making corrections in its margins. It is full of photographs, clippings, and handwritten notes all about her—all about Aubry Tourvel.

There are many photographs. Aubry doesn't see herself very often, hardly ever. She has heard others call her pretty, but that is different from seeing a photograph of herself—especially when she was younger—and recognizing that there is beauty there.

Aubry has seen this binder before, but only now does she understand that it is, by far, the heaviest item in Marta's whole carpetbag, and that Marta has carried this binder—and all the photographs within—from Mexico City, and halfway up the earth, to her. Aubry recognizes an act of commitment when she sees one, and she has scarcely seen any as formidable as this.

63

With Marta in the Klondike

"Tell me a love story," says Marta.

The next day is a hike above the tree line, in the shadows of sharp mountain peaks, following animal trails through the alpine moss. In the valleys below they can see the dark boreal forests that will lead them to Juneau. The hike is long and arduous and requires legs like pistons, lungs like parachutes. But if Marta is dismayed or depleted, she doesn't let it show.

Sometimes they hike in single file, drifting near and apart from each other, sometimes side by side when the geography permits. Here, on the mountain ridges, the trails are wide and easy, at least until they begin their descent, and they talk freely.

"What?"

"A love story."

"Why would I tell you that?"

"For my readers. They love love stories. Everyone loves love. There must be at least one. In all these travels, one for sure."

Aubry hesitates.

"It's a good question, I think," continues Marta. "How does someone in your situation love? Where do you find love? How do you keep it? How many kinds of love are available to you?"

She watches Marta warily. Marta walks alongside her, so pa-

272

tiently, so at ease. Aubry's had companions in the past. There are plenty who've wanted to follow her, as if she were some kind of prophet, but hardly any last. She has to wonder how long this fiery Mexican is going to stick with her.

"I've encountered all kinds of love, actually," Aubry tells her. "Superficial love. Desperate love. Greedy love."

"So negative. What about passionate love?"

"Yes," she says. "That, too."

"Tell me."

"They're all the same, Marta. They're all doomed."

They walk a little longer in silence, until Marta says, "You think I brag—and I do—but I don't just brag about me. I wrote a story about a ten-year-old boy who saved his entire school when a fire broke out. Imagine that! Ten years old! I interviewed a nun who saved hundreds of children from living in the streets. When I brag about me, I brag about them, too. It is my job to brag about the world."

Aubry gives her a look, but says nothing.

"I want to show off a little. I want to brag about you. I have a feeling that the life you have lived is very, very . . ."

But Aubry is no longer listening. She has stopped cold in her tracks. At first, Marta thinks something terrible has happened—a sudden pain, perhaps the onset of her illness—but no, Aubry is excited. Marta sees it in her eyes, eyes that are focused on the cliff wall to their left. Marta turns and looks. She sees it, too.

A door.

A wooden door in a cliff wall, up here above the tree line, the middle of nowhere.

Aubry is already running toward it, her mood electric. Marta stands there, blindsided. Then Aubry returns, spinning on her heels, and grabs Marta by the arm.

"Come on!" she shouts, and they are both running.

The door is a haphazard thing, a stitched-together patchwork of planks. When Aubry reaches for it, it nearly falls apart at her touch.

"Don't be afraid," Aubry says to Marta. "But hurry, before it's gone!" With that, she is through the doorway, pulling Marta into the shadows after her.

"It's so dark!" shouts Marta.

"No! There will be light! You will see!"

But there is no light. They feel their way along walls that shift and turn. They crash into things. They're not sure what. Marta pulls free from Aubry. A moment later she is turning the crank of her electric lamp. Its light comes on gradually, but soon illuminates a room filled with makeshift shelves, tables made of barrels, scattered bones of little animals.

In the corner is a skeleton, sitting on a chair, still dressed in boots and long underwear, holding a rifle in its stick arms.

Aubry backs away, startled, into old rotten shelves that come crashing down on her head. She tries to stay upright, but doesn't make it, falling on her haunches, staring wild-eyed at the corpse in the corner.

The skeleton doesn't bother Marta in the least. She has covered the civil war that rocked her country, crime scenes, traffic accidents. She shines her lamp on Aubry instead; Aubry, who crouches against the wall.

"I was saying," says Marta, "I have a feeling that the life you have lived is very, very big, but what you reveal is very, very select."

Aubry, covered in dust and cobwebs, breathes hard. Her eyes are wide in the glare of Marta's electric lamp. It's not the skeleton that has unnerved her. It's her undermined expectation.

"Do you think I am a liar?"

Marta hasn't expected that. "No," she says.

"Do you think I'm crazy? That this is, somehow, all in my head?" asks Aubry. "Most people do."

"Once. But I do my research," says Marta, kneeling beside her. "Did you know Sylvie still has a pillowcase stained with your blood? She keeps it to remind herself that you had no choice, that you had to leave."

Aubry takes her eyes off the skeleton, now on Marta.

"You've talked to Sylvie?"

"I've talked to both your sisters. I've seen your old house, your old room. I've been to your parents' grave."

Aubry says nothing, just stares. A strange feeling. Jealousy. Remorse. Marta has been where Aubry will never get to go.

"Where is Pappa?"

"Beside your mother. Pauline said he died of a broken heart after your mother had gone. She said they all died a little after you'd gone, too, which is natural. If we were sisters and I lost you, I'd have died a little as well."

Aubry almost never hears news from home. When she does, it's been cleaned up—whether from her mother, her sisters, her father—they all tried to ease her way. She knows she caused pain. She's just never heard it said so plainly until Marta said it.

"Tell me," says Marta. "How do you want the story of your life to read?"

"My life is not a story you can just write up."

"But let's say it is. Let's say all we're all living a story, whether we know it or not. So what do we do? How do we write it? Hmm? Do you want to be a minor character in your own tale? Do you want to be the villain? Do you want to live out a tragedy? A comedy? It's too easy to steal your meaning away from yourself."

Aubry stands. She brushes off the gray dust, goes to the door where the daylight streams in.

"I suppose I have something to tell you," Aubry relents.

"I suppose you do."

But Aubry stares at the ground. "It's hard."

The electric lamp is already dying, the light flickering, then going out altogether.

They don't say another word about it, not as they exit the door, not through their descent into the trees, not while they make camp, cook supper, or roll out their sleeping bags. Darkness falls, and still they say nothing. They sleep a fitful sleep. Aubry is up before the sunrise, cross-legged in her sleeping bag, watching the sky lighten. Marta is up soon after, watching her.

"Don't take notes," says Aubry. "Not yet."

"All right."

They pick up their gear and begin another day's hike, at first without words, their feet padding across the lichen, crunching over the gravel. Finally, after hours of silence, there's nothing Aubry can do. She's made a promise.

She opens her mouth, and tells Marta everything.

64

With Marta in the Klondike

Marta can hardly contain her excitement. She can't be subdued or moderated in any way. Aubry's never seen her in such a state, agitated, pulling at her hands, pacing the cliff that overlooks Juneau and the Gastineau Channel a thousand feet below.

"A library?" she exclaims again.

"Yes," says Aubry, again.

Marta paces some more, only a misstep from the cliff edge, contemplating this claim of hers. How she can contemplate while pacing and pulling, how she doesn't fly off the cliff right into the muddy streets of Juneau below, Aubry doesn't know, but she's managing it.

"An infinite library?"

"Did I say infinite? I don't know. How would I know? How could anybody ever know?"

Aubry has been reluctant to speak of the libraries, but she has to admit, Marta's reaction pleases her to no end. Watching Marta pace the cliff edge like this, all Aubry's apprehension dissolves into thin air.

"But it was a library?" asks Marta again.

"Yes."

"Straight through the heart of the biggest mountain range on earth?"

"Oh, no," says Aubry, waving her hand as if shooing away a fly. "Not only there. I've been to the library many times. Again and again."

For example, the time she walked the North American Prairies, surprised—as she always is—to find her path ended by a hole carved into the earth, as if some modern industrialist had excavated a perfect square in the middle of the flat, empty plains. It was as deep as a well, as wide as a house. At the bottom of this excavation, where the blue flowers grew, were doors, perfectly ordinary doors, one on each wall.

"I'm not looking," Aubry explains, "but then, suddenly, there's a door."

In Greenland, the ship with the broken masts, white with frost, its ribs crushed, half sunk in the pack ice. She'd wondered if anything useful might have been left onboard and stepped through that companionway hatch, the hatch that slowly yawned on its hinges, back and forth, as if the ship still rocked on an open sea.

"And another . . ." Aubry tells her, remembering the enormous tree in—where was that? Madagascar? Mozambique? What side of the water was she on when she found the enormous tree with the big dark hole in it, pitch-black inside, so black she wondered if there was anything in there—and a moment later, descending a staircase that spiraled down and deep and lower and lower.

". . . and another," she says. "And I go in . . ."

Into the underground passages full of books, past the jungle vines and broad-leafed plants that try and fail to hide the shelves, the shelves that contain the scrolls and parchments and the bowls of split coconuts, all awaiting her company.

"And it's a labyrinth. The paths inside have carried me over jungles and under oceans, to places no one has seen but me."

She crossed beneath the Makassar Strait on a gangplank that stretched through an undersea cave, salt water beneath her, dripping stalactites above. Light seeped in from holes in the coral below and lit her way. Bookshelves hung suspended from the ceiling and she'd occasionally stop to read in the swirling blue light.

"I don't understand," says Marta. "If this is true, why would you ever leave?"

"I don't leave. It kicks me out. I'd love to stay longer, believe me."

She once bypassed an entire desert in the peak of the hot season while grabbing some shade in what she thought was an abandoned mineshaft. A short time later, she was lost, winding through a maze of underground slot canyons, books lining its ledges, shelves of scrolls chiseled into its curves. When she emerged, she was in a conifer forest looking back at the desert. But it wasn't even the same desert. It was another country altogether in some far corner of the earth.

"Look it up," she tells Marta when they finally descend the steep trails, down staircases like cliffs that flatten out in the streets of Juneau. "You have your notes. Where was I two years ago from this very day?"

So Marta immediately goes to the nearest saloon to buy a drink. She will need one, thinks Aubry. Of course, there is no alcohol being served. Prohibition. They forget these things, being alone in the woods for so long. They order two gin rickeys without the gin and catch the eye of every red-blooded male there. Aubry smiles amiably, but Marta flatly ignores them, no more attention than she would give a distant seagull. Marta reaches into her carpetbag for her passion project, her black binder full of Aubry. She flips through the pages.

"Wait. Here," she says. "An article from Adelaide, Australia. You were given a key to the city."

"Yes. And where was I a week later?"

Marta looks at her uncertainly, then searches through her binder again while Aubry sips her gin-less rickey. Marta searches until, suddenly, she finds the answer, but doesn't believe it.

"Paris," she says.

"Paris," Aubry agrees.

How can that be? How does one travel from Australia to France in a week? Marta is confused, and maybe unnerved, but her excitement rises like a signal flare.

65

Terra Obscura

She propped her feet up on the stone railing so that the lava flowing under the bridge could warm her toes. In her hand she flipped a gold coin over and over again, an easy entertainment. Her other hand turned pages. It smelled of sulfur down here but the hot molten light filled every corner of these old underground ruins, like some ghostly vision from the last days of Pompeii.

Aubry had a pile of books and scrolls by her side, heaped up as high as the chair she had discovered in the rubble. She had collected ancient Roman coins, too, and stacked them beside the books.

The book in her lap was drawn by a botanist, she would guess, someone who had traveled the world and produced a catalog of the various flowers he'd discovered along the way.

Here, on this page, a flower, delicate and blue, that only bloomed in winter under the deep snow where no one would ever see. On this page, a flower as pale as a mushroom that only bloomed from the heads of dead animals.

And here, strangest of all, was a flower as big as a Chinese lantern, as red as an open wound. During the peak of the season, it expelled a cloud of pollen so thick and noxious it could anesthetize a horse for a week. Aubry was dumbstruck. Imagine a plant that poured sleep from its petals. Why would it do such a thing? For what purpose? She wondered how this botanist had made his discovery. Did he breathe the pollen himself? How long did he sleep? What dreams did he have?

It occurred to Aubry that she probably hadn't slept for a week. She wondered if she could find these flowers down here, and if she did, would they work on her? Time was a concept increasingly difficult to grasp. How long had she gone without day, without night? It was anyone's guess. A week? A month? When she slept, was it for a full night? An hour? A few minutes? Who knew in the libraries, this palace of illogic, outside time and space, where knowledge is accumulated and stored, then left unread.

She heard a voice, suddenly, from nowhere, it seemed. It called her name: "Aubry! Aubry Tourvel!"

She'd heard voices in the libraries before, but always distant, an echo in a passageway, a murmur behind a wall. They could be whispered, like the slithering of dry leaves over hard ground, or lonely, like a groaning metal gear behind a faraway door. But this, this was new. It was sharp and near. Aubry could hear it clearly, even over the hiss and roll of lava in the aqueduct below.

She jumped to her feet, dropped the book. Gold coins fell and chimed on the stone floor. One or two bounced off the edge of the bridge and fed the lava. She looked around wildly, her trusty walking stick instinctively in hand. At first, she didn't see, but then, across the burning river on a distant bridge, she saw the old woman, a diminutive speck from here, shouting at her.

"Your mother is dying!" she cried. "Go to her! It's safe! Go!"

Aubry grabbed her bag and ran after her—she was not alone! There was another! Who was she? A walker like herself? She called out after the old woman, but she had fled, disappeared into the tangle of shadows and catacombs.

Aubry crossed the bridge, a rampart, crossed a second bridge, then saw the door, the only door, the only possible way the old woman could've gone. She pushed the door open, ran inside, down a flight of stairs, up a flight of stairs, became turned around, disoriented. She looked over her shoulder, back the way she came, but which way was that? She looked ahead. The corridors multiplied, branched out, knotted up again. She didn't know which turn to take. She didn't know which way back either. But she heard footsteps, echoing over her head, scurrying away. She followed the sound of them, through a twisting passageway, down tunnels that got darker and darker, until she was engulfed in shadow.

She stopped, lost and afraid. She couldn't see her own hands in front of her. She turned around and around, but all was darkness. She had no sense of direction, hardly a sense of being, but she could still hear the echo of footsteps. They were different now, no longer scurrying, but relaxed, delicate. She paused to listen. Several now, a series of footsteps. There were whispers, too, reverential words, too hushed to make out, floating in the dark.

This was no longer a single person, but people she was after, a crowd. She felt dizzy, as if peering over a cliff. There were so many questions, and now, finally, the answers.

She took a few cautious steps toward the sounds. She saw a dim crack of light against the floor and pushed open a heavy door.

Out of the shadows and into imperious columns and arches. There were rows of burning candles and people kneeling at pews, hands clasped in prayer. There was a ceiling taller than any tree, taller than the slot canyons or the mast of a ship, as tall as anything man could make, almost a substitute sky. Stained-glass windows cast a borealis of light across the cathedral walls. Dazzled and dazed, she stood still, afraid vertigo might knock her over.

She knew she was no longer in the libraries. Where she was, she couldn't say, but it was a cathedral, in a Christian country. If there was a door back to her river of lava, it had closed up and disappeared. She was banished once again. Regaining her senses, she moved through the worshippers quietly, inconspicuously, through beams of light, and out the heavy wooden doors.

The daylight blinded her and when her sight recovered, she still wasn't sure what she was looking at. It was a city, but she did not recognize it. It was European, though she wasn't sure where. There were wide boulevards with the latest automobiles chugging up and down, honking their horns at obsolete horses and terrified pedestrians. Men wore tweed suits and waistcoats and bowler hats. The women wore sleek dresses and hairstyles were short. The Great War was over. That, she knew. But so was the Belle Époque. Gone were the bustles and parasols and ankle-length skirts of her childhood, the long, carefully curated hair tied up in bows. Everyone wore small hats and slim outfits, shoes instead of boots, pearl necklaces that fell past the waist. Women's legs were exposed from ankle to knee. She even saw women sitting at a café across the street smoking freely, cigarettes burning at the end of long black cigarette holders. It was all new, elegant, fun-loving, and completely foreign to her.

When a couple passed Aubry on the sidewalk, talking loudly, it still took her a minute to realize she understood every word.

This was Paris.

She turned and stared and turned and stared. She ran her tongue around her mouth, felt her lips for blood—nothing. Her knees didn't buckle, she didn't vomit on the street. There was no pain at all. Where was her sickness? Was this Paris or wasn't it? She saw a man reading a newspaper—*Le Petit Parisien*. She was back. There was no question. In a wave of emotion, she had a single thought—to go home again.

She ran down the boulevard before she even knew which way to go. *"Your mother is dying!"* the old woman had said. Aubry asked a paperboy for directions and flew down the streets, cutting off traffic, horns blaring behind her—and still nothing was familiar. There were more shops and cafés than she'd ever seen before. When she turned a corner, there was an enormous metal tower, girders crisscrossing into a tall peak that stood over the roofs of the townhouses. The vision stopped Aubry in her tracks; it looked as if it'd been stitched into the sky with black thread. She remembered now, reading of it in the papers. Eiffel, they called it. She grabbed hold of herself and kept running. All around her, automobiles, pedestrians, street vendors and street beggars, blaring radios, ringing telephones, sooty clouds from distant factories, the clamor of new construction from every direction. Was this really Paris? Could it be? Left turns and right turns, she passed nothing that jogged a memory. She came closer and closer to home and still had to ask directions.

When she found it and stood at the end of its front walk, her home looked different, too. The front walk was paved, the wooden gate remade and painted blue. Vines had begun their slow creep up the brick walls. Other houses had sprung up all around, hemming it in, the city swallowing it up.

How much things had to change before they became new again? When was Paris no longer Paris, home no longer home? Slowly, she walked to the front door. Her hands shook, but not from illness. She knocked and waited, and then was face to face with her father.

66

Home (But Not Quite)

His hair was gray, his face thin and lined. But here he was, shocked at the sight of her, tears in his eyes, embracing Aubry tight to his chest. Then her sisters, too, Pauline and Sylvie, no longer girls but women, both so beautiful, coming in a fever rush from the next room to hold her and kiss her.

The questions came in a torrent. How had she done it? How had she come back? Was she cured? Would she stay forever? And, quick, come see mother while there is still time.

She has lived her life a stranger among strangers. This was the only home she had ever known. These were the only people who had known her. Often, she had whispered their names into forests, into chasms, shouted them off the edges of mountains. Suddenly, she was speaking to them, hands touching, voices warm. Tears flowed all around. Such radiance in their faces. What they'd kept closed like a fist now opened up wide.

The house was nothing like Aubry remembered. The walls were different colors, the furniture all replaced, the carpets new and all of it so simple, so practical in its design, nothing like the elaborate and showy cupboards, secretaries, and sideboards of her youth.

But they hadn't changed her room the slightest bit. Only Aubry, the youngest daughter, could have arranged the room in such a way. To change it was to destroy it. Aubry saw, at the end of the hallway, a single closed door, as if she'd died on that day thirty-five years ago.

She wanted to go in. She couldn't recall certain things—where she kept her pen-and-ink drawings, what dresses hung in her closet, what book still sits on her bedside table. She tried but she simply couldn't remember. What might happen if she were to peek inside? Would her sickness come at her in full force, crippling her right there in the doorway? Would she die, instantly, like a black hood pulled over her head?

A bit of her soul was locked in that room and she was desperate for a reunion. But she knew an ambush when she saw one. She stared at the door and wondered, but never went near.

Her mother was bedridden, her last days, perhaps her last hours, already upon her. She was so frail she could hardly lift her head. But when Aubry entered her room, she turned to look. Aubry knelt beside her. Her mother reached out and touched Aubry's face and held her hand and when she spoke her voice was hardly more than a whisper.

"What have you seen?"

"What does it matter?" said Aubry, kissing her mother's hand, her tears falling on those frail wrists.

"I'm dying, Aubry. It's all that matters."

So Aubry thought about it and bits of memory flashed in her mind's eye—images, sounds, smells—but they were a shattered collection.

"I once held a piece of ice," Aubry told her mother, "until it melted and the spider that was frozen inside came to life right there in my hands."

Mrs. Tourvel's mouth opened in wonder. "Remarkable . . ."

"Did you know there are over two hundred million insects for every person on earth?"

Aubry's eyebrow went up and her mother's eyes twinkled. Whether she was a spoiled little girl, or a sullen teen, or a gregarious adult—or whatever she might be in the future—there was always that eyebrow, the one constant in her, this single trait that assured her mother she was, after all these years and all these travels, still her beloved Aubry.

"How do you know that?"

"I counted."

And they both smiled.

"Do you forgive me?" her mother asked, but Aubry couldn't understand the question. Why would her poor mother blame herself when Aubry was the one who left? What kind of history had her mother created in her mind? Would Aubry ever love someone so much that all their tragedies became her own? Instead of answering, she broke down crying, burying her face in her mother's arms, which was its own kind of answer.

67

Home (But Not Quite)

Sylvie woke up first. The morning sun peeked through the curtains. She got out of her chair to close them so Mother could sleep. After she felt Mother's forehead and patted her hand, Sylvie turned to Aubry. Aubry had slept curled on the divan by their mother's feet all night.

Aubry's pillow was soaked with blood.

Sylvie's scream shook Aubry from her sleep. The pain that hammered the back of her head made her vision blur. It ricocheted to the front and smashed against her temples. She groaned. The room dimmed and spun. Before she could stop herself, she vomited blood on the floor.

"Aubry!" cried Sylvie. "Aubry!"

Pauline rushed into the room, saw Aubry on her hands and knees by their mother's bed.

"Aubry," she pleaded, though she did not want to say it, "you must go!"

"No . . ." gasped Aubry.

"Aubry, you must!"

"You must!" cried Sylvie, tears running down her cheeks.

Pauline took Aubry under the arms, lifted her to her feet. "You can't stay!"

The chaos had awakened her mother. She turned and reached for her daughter. Aubry reached back, fighting to stay at her mother's side, tears and blood down her cheeks. Pauline and Sylvie had no choice. They locked arms around their youngest sister and dragged her away. "No, Mama! Mama!" Aubry screamed. "I'm sorry! I'm sorry for everything! Mama!"

Her father carried Aubry the rest of the way, through the living room, out the door, to his automobile parked on the street. She would've fought if she could, but there was no strength in her. She felt dazed and feverish, no longer part of the world.

"Where are her things?" she could vaguely hear her father say as she was dropped into the passenger seat, her face falling limp against the window.

"I have them," said Pauline, and Aubry thought she heard her sister jumping into the back of the car.

The automobile coughed, then hummed beneath her. They pulled away. Aubry could see poor Sylvie standing in the doorway, her hand covering her mouth, then waving goodbye. Aubry put her fingers to the window, a weak attempt at a farewell, smearing blood across the glass. Her Sylvie, her home, slipped out of view.

68

Home (But Not Quite)

When Aubry came to, they were in a city park, sitting at the edge of a fountain, and Pauline was wiping the blood from her face and hands.

"Did you know I'm studying medicine?" asked Pauline.

Aubry's head still spun. She didn't know that, or maybe she did. Maybe there was some vague recollection there coming to her slowly.

"Look," said Pauline as she pulled a textbook from her bag. "I have fifteen more at home. All because I wanted to cure you but didn't know how." Her throat closed up and she fought back tears. "And I still don't."

"But you will cure many others," Aubry said, slowly waking from her fog. "That makes me proud. Don't cry," she said and held Pauline's hand. "I'm fine."

"I know that. But I miss you."

Their father, who had been pacing the whole while, finally sat down beside Aubry. "We must go back to her. You understand?" Her mother, he meant. He was talking about her mother. She was dying. They couldn't be apart from her, not now. Soon the family would return to her side, all except Aubry, who had to be on her way before, God forbid, it became a double funeral.

"But I had an idea," continued her father. "I called on a good friend of mine and made some arrangements on your behalf. If that's all right."

He drove Aubry another hour in his cigar-shaped automobile, leaving the city behind them. She thought, What a strange way to see the world, if you could see it at all, everything flying by so fast—these streets, these forests, unknown, unexplored, as if they'd never been. What kind of life is that for a street or a forest, or a woman in an automobile zooming past them? A whole world, unacquainted.

But this was just the beginning.

Her father pulled around a barn off some dusty side road and stopped at the edge of a wide trampled meadow. There, standing in the grass, was a single-engine biplane. Beside it was its pilot, a narrow-jawed man in a long leather coat and boots, with a thin mustache and hair parted cleanly down the middle.

"Hello!" he called to them.

"Hello, Remy!" her father said as he approached and shook Remy's hand warmly. They exchanged more words, Remy patting her father's shoulders before turning to Aubry.

"I am Remy Clement."

"Aubry Tourvel." They shook hands and Remy turned their attention to the biplane.

"This is my angel, a Curtiss Falcon, made in America. I have flown her all over Europe, as far as Africa and Arabia. I have cleared my schedule. Wherever you want to go, I will take you."

Aubry looked between him and the plane. "Through the air?"

"Through the air."

She'd never been on a plane, had never seen one so close.

"Name the place," he said.

She touched the aluminum fuselage, ran her hand across the cold metal.

"It beats walking," said her father.

Aubry wasn't so sure about that, but at the sound of her father's voice, she turned, wrapped her arms around him, and clung tight. She hoped they might fuse together at last, into one. She never wanted to say goodbye again. She wished as hard as she could that they would never have to. They embraced so tightly and for so long, Remy turned away.

But then she was kissing him on his cheek, letting him go, and walking back to the plane, half-blind with tears.

"Constantinople," she said.

Aubry would never see her father again.

69

With Marta in the Klondike

Marta emerges from the small general store on Fourth Street, one of the typically waterlogged roads in Juneau. She has just purchased a globe and a red crayon. She sits next to Aubry on the edge of the boardwalk that spans the street ankle-deep in mud.

"So, you entered the library here, near the Ivory Coast," she says and puts her crayon to the West African coast, "but emerged here in the Faroe Islands?"

"I think so. Maybe," guesses Aubry, trying to remember.

Marta double-checks the notes she's compiled in her binder. She draws a straight red line from West Africa to the Faroe Islands. Aubry feels the first tingles of excitement.

"Then you went in here—outside Mecca—and came out here"—she draws another line—"near the Dead Sea."

"More or less," agrees Aubry.

Another line to Easter Island, to Baffin Island. More lines from Palau, from Perth, lines across lakes, across deserts, across oceans. The crayon keeps moving and soon Marta has marked up the entire globe. They sit back and observe their work.

The pattern is symmetrical.

It is like a chain of stars, arms interlocked, circling the globe, like the geometric patterns on Islamic pottery or Aztec ruins. It is not coincidental, not chance. It is a distinct repeating pattern and they look at it for a long time in silence.

"You say this disease uses you to see the world," says Marta. "But . . . I don't know . . ." she says quietly, chasing an idea she can't quite catch. "What if . . . what if this disease wants to show you the world?"

70

With Marta in the Klondike

They're in Juneau, one of the largest ports in Alaska. From here there are boats to Seattle or San Francisco, and from there, the world. In these days of steamships and railroads and even airplanes, Alaska is no longer so remote. Even Mexico is not so far away anymore. But Aubry has already traveled the American West Coast, only three years ago, from Baja to Big Sur to Puget Sound. She needs a new direction.

"Have you noticed?" says her sickness. "It's getting harder and harder to chart a course."

It's true. Several times now she has traveled herself into a corner. She'd come up that river already. She'd sailed to that port before. She'd crossed those mountains to the west, wasn't sure if escape was possible to the south. So far, she has always managed a way out, often by sea, or by discovering some new path through a familiar landscape. But the question looms larger in her mind every passing day—what is left? How many jungles, deserts, and swamps has she crossed? What European city is left to her? What South Pacific island has she not stepped foot on? Her options, day by day, are dwindling, her escape routes fewer.

On the other hand, her sickness is running out of places to hide. It's only a matter of time before she corners it and has her day at last.

"Are you worried?" she asks.

"I'm afraid for you," it says. "You must be more thoughtful in your decisions."

"What will you do when the world runs out? I'm going to have you backed against a wall soon enough. When that happens . . ."

"Do you remember India? You tried to get rid of me then. But I will not abandon you. I swear it."

"Very thoughtful. Please don't stick around on my account."

If she could, she would go west, taking advantage of the summer months while they last. She'd follow the Aleutian Islands to the very end of their reach, hop her way, island to island, back to Russia. Perhaps she could finally arrive in Vladivostok, see if there's a trace of Lionel left in the city records, in the parks and squares, in the cobblestones themselves. But she can't, because a pair of madmen have turned her beloved Russia into a killing field. There are only gulags waiting for her there.

To the dock worker, she says, "I was told I might find a passage to Vancouver Island from here."

The dock worker looks Aubry and Marta up and down, curiosity piqued. "Hmm," he mumbles. "Nothing for ladies. Not today. Unless you want to hop on a cargo boat full of crab."

"Yes, that would work," Aubry says, without hesitation.

But he hesitates. "The two of you?"

"Just me."

"Yes," says Marta at the same instant.

Aubry turns and looks at her, then turns back to the dock worker and says, very slow and clear, "Only me."

"And a passage for me as well," says Marta.

Aubry sighs.

"Have you two thought this out much?" asks the dock worker.

"Excuse us," Aubry says to him, and pulls Marta aside. "What are you doing?"

"I'm coming with you."

"No, you're not. You can't follow me forever."

"Why not? I bet no one has followed you forever before."

"That is true."

"I'll be the first."

"You'll be dead before long," Aubry says, her grip tightening around Marta's arm.

"Then I'll be dead. But I won't be a shirker," says Marta, pulling her arm free. "You survive sandstorms and blizzards. You wander the world and see things that can't be there. You access some massive, maybe infinite library that contains—who knows?" she exclaims, throwing her hands in the air. "All there is!" Then she leans in, not sparing Aubry a barb of skepticism. "If you are to be believed." She straightens up again, begins her ritual pacing. "And yet you think . . ." She pauses a moment. "No, let me ask. Which is harder? Going on an extended holiday or turning away from what may be the most groundbreaking discovery in the history of man? Which is it? Which do you choose?"

"I would go home," says Aubry.

"I would not. I am going with you. I will either confirm that you are a fantasist and a liar, or I will find this library with you. I will take shortcuts through the earth and verify them myself. I will see what you see. I will read what you read. I will live how you live, and then decide whether I want to go home or not."

Aubry has had companions in the past. Many of them. Good companions, each and every one. There was a Mbundu boy who paddled across the Okavango Delta with her, down the Zambezi River, straight across to Mozambique, until the naked solitude of the Indian Ocean, glittering like a pale blue eye, infused him with a sense of stillness, and he stayed on that beach and wandered no more.

There was the old woman, who thought she was younger than she was, who tried to follow her all the way down the Norwegian coast but couldn't quite keep up, abandoning Aubry somewhere near Bergen.

There was the teenage orphan who had once been a prostitute, who'd escaped the brothels of Baku and slunk away with Aubry in the night. She traveled as far as Shiraz before falling in love and settling down with a habitual gambler. She had stuck with Aubry the longest, a few months in all. That seemed to be the limit. Not for the first time, she wonders how long Marta might last. Marta is inquisitive, feisty, spirited, and Aubry has come to like her a lot. She likes her so much she fears that Marta might last the longest, that Marta is following her into the same kind of oblivion Aubry knows too well.

Aubry bows her head. She looks at the planks of the dock as if she's already lost this fight—because she already has. "It will be dangerous for you. In ways that are not dangerous to me. Marta, it's madness."

"Madness?" says Marta. "It's Prohibition in Alaska! We can't even get ourselves a drink! What else is there to do but go for a walk?"

71

On a Boat with Lionel Kyengi

The passenger ship departed Constantinople, black smoke chugging from its single funnel. Her mother was dead, her family, once again, far, far away.

Both decks were packed with passengers, men in suits with Mediterranean complexions, the occasional fez cap, women in skirts and sun hats, hair shortened by bobs and shingle cuts. Aubry pulled out a notebook and began to sketch the receding shores—broad city walls, clay-tiled rooftops that lay like an orange blanket over the hills, the wide Galata Bridge that skirted low over the blue water, the four sharp minarets of the Hagia Sophia.

She sketched for a full hour, if not more, leaning against the railing until Constantinople was too distant to observe and the Black Sea moved in all around. It would take another two days to reach Odessa. Her trip to Constantinople had been six days through the air, leap-frogging across Europe onboard Remy Clement's biplane, stopping only to refuel and to sleep.

But she had flown. The roads, the footpaths, hidden when on the ground, had been perfectly obvious from that biplane. They webbed the landscape. It would've taken hours, even days to follow any of them, but from above they came and went in the time it took to hum a tune. Below her, a thousand houses, a latticework of roads, and all the vehicles that pulsed the length of them, crept across the hills. It was more a kaleidoscopic pattern one might see through a microscope lens than it was life. All the people and families and friends who lived and worked and shared secrets and broke bread had turned invisible, along with their borders and palaces and works of art—and Aubry, her whole life, down there among them, living something she believed to be real, but was, in actuality, also invisible. And this was only the view from the air. Imagine the view from the moon? Or a distant star?

"There are still things to see," said her sickness.

"Nothing can top this."

"This? This is a single leaf on a bare tree. Forests are coming."

She packed away her book and her worn-down pencil. She wove through the crowds on the boat enjoying the sunshine, the cool eastern breeze. She was thirsty and with a little of the money her father had given her, she thought she would buy a sweet salep from the vendor in the cabin.

She started to dig out a lira from her pocket, bumped shoulders with a Black man in a suit exiting through the same doorway. She didn't look up. She didn't see Lionel Kyengi brush by, or even hear him excuse himself she was so distracted, fumbling through her pockets. She found her lira and went inside. She bought her salep and drank it slowly in the cabin, sitting down on an empty bench to rest her feet.

But even when cloistering herself inside, she couldn't help but stare out a window, watching the weather, judging the distances. She'd become a woman of the outdoors, like the Inuit she'd known, like the Tibetan nomads or the Bajau people who lived their lives upon the open ocean—inside was a prison, but outside was air, openness, and things beyond the capacity of words. Outside was a religion for those without religion. After a while, she decided it was time to get back into the sunlight.

She got up and strolled the deck. She had the curious feeling of being watched. When she turned around, there, like some kind of mirage, stood Lionel, staring back at her.

His hair was like the early frost of autumn. He had wrinkles scribbled across his forehead and he was much thinner, almost impossibly so, yet age suited him. It'd been, what? Five? Ten? Fifteen years? Could it be more than that? And he still wore glasses and looked handsome in a suit.

"So," he said after a while, neither of them moving, not so much as a hesitant step toward each other, "how was the Gobi Desert?"

She didn't know what to say. She stood mute, something gripping her by the throat. Tourists sidestepped them, hardly noticed the two world travelers colliding once more in the middle of the Black Sea.

"It was lonely without you," she said at last. "It's all been lonely without you."

An attractive Black woman and her two little boys came up behind him. Even before the woman placed her hand on Lionel's shoulder and one of the little boys, the younger one, maybe all of five years, took Lionel's hand, Aubry knew that this was his family, that this was his wife and these were his children, and she was simply a ghost from his past, a momentary rift in time.

Like that, the spell was ended.

"My family," he said, not apologetically, but, though many years have passed, quietly.

72

On a Boat with Lionel Kyengi

Aubry introduced herself. They were Senegalese and they all had French in common—but when his wife, Oumou, asked how Aubry and Lionel had met, Aubry faltered over her words. The look on Aubry's face alone was a warning sign. Lionel stepped in, smoothing things out, but Oumou understood. Aubry was so embarrassed she could hardly look up, but when she did, Oumou smiled to her gently and ushered the children away so Lionel and Aubry might have some time alone.

They sat on a bench outside, near the bow of the ship, their view nothing but a plane of water, the Black Sea sliding beneath them.

"Your family knows, then?" asked Aubry.

"Yes," he said.

"Your children, too?"

"Yes."

It hit her fully, the idea that he had children, that there were little Lionels out there now, raised by him, like him.

"You have children." Aubry beamed.

"Yes."

"They are taking it well?"

"It was hard at first, but they've been very brave," he said.

"My children are . . ." He spoke haltingly, trying not to let his emotions overpower him. "I'm lucky to have such children. You never think it will happen, but then it does. Suddenly there is someone you love more than yourself. Someone you would die for. That's what children do to you. It's an amazing thing. I hear that's what they call maturity."

"How long?" she asks.

"Some doctors say six months. Others a year. Either way . . ." He fell into silence then. So did she. "I should have gone with you," he said at last. "It is one of my most consistent regrets. As happy as I am, as fortunate as I have been, I think about it often. The road we did not take."

"Your life would have been even shorter," Aubry told him. "I went without food or water for a long time. I survived by eating snakes, and not very often. They were hard to catch."

Hearing this, he shakes his head, a half-smile on his lips. "I will die a simple man. All my thoughts have been formed by what I've met in my life. And I've met so little."

Aubry understood that he was showing his children what he could of the world while he still had health enough to do it. It was to be his parting gift, Constantinople, the Black Sea, Europe, beyond.

"You've met the whole world," she told him.

"When I first heard my diagnosis—my sentence, really—I went home and sat very still for a long time. Then I began to look around my room, very closely. I saw things I hadn't seen before, even though I had lived there for years and years." He closed his eyes so he could remember. "I noticed the grain of the lamp-shade and studied it, how turning the light on and off affected its texture. I saw my reflection in the brass door handle and how my image was upended and reversed. I noticed the roughness of the floorboards beneath the rugs, the fine woodwork of my chair. I studied the window frame and saw a little spider that had made his home in the corner—not outside, but in the room, with me. He'd been living there all summer, and I'd never once said hello." He opened his eyes again. "I'd seen London and Paris and Moscow, but I'd never seen that, and I wondered if I'd ever seen London or Paris or Moscow at all. I wondered, do we all live our lives like this, on the surface of things?" He turned to Aubry. "I thought of you, and wondered how you saw the world. I imagined you saw it very closely."

Aubry couldn't imagine she'd been in any one place long enough to be so familiar. But then, she traveled slowly, mostly by foot. It was hard to be more intimate with the earth than that. She walked over it one step at a time, the feel of the sand or the grass or the sod beneath her feet, and she'd learned to read it well. Frayed feathers on the ground told of a lover's quarrel among wild turkeys. A patch of muddy earth told of a hidden spring. Heavy fogs in August warned of a hard winter ahead. But how best to know the world? By the texture of the ground? By the vistas, the weather? Do we know it by the wildlife, the flocks of birds, the odd creature that crosses your path one night? Or by the geology, the gems, the excavations, the bits of amber with beetles inside? Perhaps by the people, the meals you share with them, the customs you learn? Was it their histories, their great achievements—the cathedrals, the art, the fleets and armadas, a simple compass, an irrigation ditch, an animal's tooth with tiny purple runes etched in its ivory? What was the measuring stick by which we say we know?

"Let me show you something," said Aubry and took him by the hand. She led him to the railing, the wind flinging her hair, and pointed to the Straits of Bosphorus far behind them now.

"Do you see the straits?" she said. "That was once a chain of mountains that held back the Mediterranean Sea until one day the earth shook and knocked them down."

She pointed to the water below, to the bottom of the sea.

"And the kingdom that spread over all these plains awoke to see a terrible wall of water rushing toward them, swallowing every man, woman, and child in the city." She pulled him close, so that he would feel the full impact of her words, words she wasn't sure he believed.

"Imagine you have felt the quake," she implored him. "You have come out of your house, or fled the ruins of your city, to see a wall of water a hundred feet high eating up the grasslands, sublime in the worst possible sense. All the flood stories on earth originate here, with the death of that kingdom. Its remains are still undiscovered, right here below our feet. And only you and I know it."

She took a moment to breathe, saw him staring into the water. She cleared her head of that story, looked for another. "Do you like Bach?" she asked him. "In Frankfurt, there is an old woman who doesn't know it, but she has the only copy of a Bach violin sonata that no one has ever heard—and she uses it to line the bottom of her silverware drawer!" Did he believe her? Who knew, but now that she was telling, she couldn't stop. It came out in a rush, one tale after another.

"Why are you telling me this?" he asked, out of humility, and Aubry understood because she had felt the same humility while wandering the libraries and reading the tales and wondering how it was this had happened to her, why Aubry and not someone wiser or kinder or more in need.

"It's all I can give you," she said. "Things no one else in the world knows except us. Would you like to hear more?"

He paused, although she knew his answer. But the power of it—the knowledge, the exclusivity—like forbidden fruit, it overpowered him, made him a little afraid, but euphoric, too.

"Yes," he said.

She clasped his hands, drew him close so they could talk in whispers, the two of them speaking of things no one else in the world knew.

"Have you ever heard of people who hibernate? There is a tribe in the jungles of Africa that can fall into a deep sleep that lasts for days or weeks or even months," she said. "It's how they survive the lean seasons . . ."

73

With Marta in the Congo

The monkeys stare down at them from the trees. They are two women, one carrying the other on her back so that, to the monkeys, they seem one creature. Aubry is doing the carrying and Marta, sick with malaria, is being carried though humid jungle, strangled with vines, gooey with mud and dripping leaves. If Aubry is tired—and she is—she works hard not to let it show. She is soaked with sweat and breathing hard. She's been talking to Marta sporadically, keeping her spirits up with talk of food and sleep and how much better she'll feel when her fever breaks.

But it's late in the day and Marta's been silent for a while. It's during this time that Marta's fevers are at their worst.

"Far enough?" asks Marta, her voice not inaudible, but close.

"I think so," says Aubry, but she carries her a little farther, until she finds a patch of dry earth, and lays Marta down.

"That should buy me a day or two," Aubry says. She can't stay still while Marta recovers. She can't sit in one place during the weeks it might take to nurse her to health—if nursing her to health is even possible in this wet sunless jungle.

"Chills?" asks Aubry.

"Yes."

"I saw a mwasamusa plant back there."

"A what?"

"That's what they called it in Brazzaville."

"What's it do?"

"I'm going to boil you some of the leaves."

"Why can't you get malaria for a change?"

"I said this would be dangerous. I told you not to come."

"Oh, you whine so much. Go back to Canada where you belong."

Aubry makes sure Marta's comfortable on the mossy ground, then raises the hammock they purchased as far back as Calabar, back when they were following trails along the Gulf of Guinea, winding through palms trees and golden beaches, back when sleeping on hammocks was a pleasantry, not a necessity. Now they are in the jungles, deep in Africa's interior, places where hardly anyone, Black or white, has ventured before. This is the second serious illness Marta's contracted in two years, but the worst possible place to be stricken. She tries to keep Marta off the ground, away from the ants and mites. She tries to keep her under the netting that may or may not fend off the mosquitoes that probably gave her the malaria a week ago.

As soon as she has the hammock set up and Marta inside it, cloaked in what's left of their mosquito netting, she goes to find the mwasamusa leaves. She steals through the jungle, through the din of insects, the birdsong, and the howls of colobus monkeys. Anywhere else in the world would be highlighted with vistas and scenic possibilities, but the jungle isn't wide. It isn't panoramic. It's dense and oppressive, thick on all sides with vegetation, choked with fruits and birds. The greenery closes in on you, impossible to see much farther than you can spit. It's a landscape ready and waiting to sink you in mud or garrote you with vines.

Aubry finds the mwasamusa plant. She picks far more leaves

than she needs. Who knows when she might come across one again? Looking around, she notices flowers high up in the canopy, hundreds of them blooming from vines that hold the big jungle trees in a stranglehold. The flowers are big and red, big enough to swallow Aubry's head. They are asymmetrical, with some petals curled in on themselves and others hanging open as if they'd fainted.

They've been lost in this jungle for weeks, but this is the first time Aubry's seen flowers like that, as red as open wounds. Now she notices them everywhere. They hang above her all the way back to camp where Marta waits, sweating in her hammock.

She lights a fire, gathers the rainwater collected in the leaves, and boils it.

"Aubry . . ." Marta mumbles, eyes prying open, just a bit. Whether this is the start of a conversation or something whispered in delirium, Aubry can't tell, but Marta has taken Aubry's hand and is holding it tight. Aubry can feel the fever against her palm. She leans close and holds Marta's gaze. But Marta's voice trails off, her eyelids draw shut, and she says nothing else.

"Do you know what you need?" Aubry says, looking up at the colobus monkeys who have just foolishly leapt into view over her head. "Meat," she says, and she pulls a dart from her bag. She rubs it in a paste she keeps wrapped in leaves. Tied to her walking stick is a hollow pole, as long as her arm. She frees it and loads the dart inside. She uncaps her walking stick—now it's a spear—and loops it around her shoulder. Marta, through slitted eyelids, watches Aubry disappear into the jungle, spear on her back, blowdart in hand.

The monkeys make trails through the trees, just as pigs and deer make them on the forest floor. This Aubry knows. She finds a spot beneath a busy route in the branches above, and hides. This is the wait. This is the hunt. Soon enough, they are here—

a pair of colobus monkeys bounding from limb to limb, black faces shining. She singles one out, takes aim, and waits for her moment. The monkey stops to collect a fig, balancing on the tips of the thin branches, tail curled around a limb. Aubry watches it reach, knows it's vulnerable, and blows.

A racket of screaming and scratching, of breaking branches and falling leaves. She's hit it but doesn't know where—the leg? The side?—but it should be enough. It will be dead any moment now. Except this monkey has no intention of dying easily. It rages, spitting like hot oil. It leaps for a big bough, darting away through the trees. Quickly, Aubry is out of hiding and chasing it, following the screeching above, the trail of falling leaves.

The monkey leaps and leaps, possessed with furies. Birds fly out of its way. Squirrels scatter. She unslings her spear, raised and ready in case of opportunity, never slowing her pace. She leaps over roots, darts between trees. She's not about to lose this meal.

Then the sunlight strikes her, right in her face. She flinches and skids to a stop. She's out of the trees and caught standing in the open at the edge of a meadow. When she looks down, averting her eyes from the glare, she sees men and women coming at her.

There's hardly a stitch of clothing on any of them, just tree bark and leaves. Their skin, as dark as the soil, is painted in chalk and mud. She has scared the hell out of them, bursting through the trees like that, a fiery white woman with a spear raised. Screams go up, shouts of alarm, and the men are immediately on their feet, crying their war cries, pointing their spears at Aubry in a unified front. If she were thinking, she'd lower her weapon, first thing, but she's overpowered by fear, her heart pumping blood that roars in her ears. There are a dozen weapons pointed her way, maybe more, never mind the screaming, the chaos. But they haven't killed her yet. Perhaps the surprise on her face is as blatant as theirs.

Behind Aubry is the rustle of leaves. She doesn't dare turn around, not with a dozen shouting men pointing spears at her, but Aubry sees her anyway—a little girl, not even four years old, perhaps not even three, coming out of the forest, walking right up and standing at Aubry's feet. She stares, curious and unafraid. She's never seen anything like Aubry, skin the same color as the inside of a tree. The tribe screams at her, all of them at once, waving her over. The little girl doesn't even look at them, spellbound by the pale woman with gold hair.

Aubry looks at the girl and knows she's not about to stab anyone with this little child next to her. Children, always getting the better of her. She lets loose a long exhale, her whole body deflating as she lowers her spear and hands it to the little girl. The girl takes the spear in both arms, as if carrying a bundle of thatch, and obediently carries it to her people.

The adrenaline has drained from Aubry, leaving her loose and slack. Now they will either kill her or let her live. She'd known a tribe in New Guinea who'd kill in a heartbeat, a touchy bunch, one misstep all they required. They'd surprised Aubry in a jungle not unlike this. If she hadn't shared her food, she later learned, they'd have skinned her alive and eaten her for her rudeness. One way or another, they get their food.

Then the dead monkey falls out of the tree, as if tossed from the branches. It hits the ground with a heavy thud between Aubry and the ring of men. The tribe gasps, their eyes darting back and forth between the monkey and the white woman who can knock animals dead from the trees.

"I have to get my friend," says Aubry, pointing back into the forest, exhausted and no longer afraid.

Only minutes later, with the help of a dozen of the tribe, Marta is carried into the village and laid out on a woven mat. An old woman—a matriarch? A medicine woman? A priestess?—

hovers over her, chanting, rubbing orange paste on Marta's forehead, Marta's chest, Marta's arms.

Aubry boils tea from the mwasamusa leaves. A tribeswoman nods approvingly and adds a few ingredients of her own—bits of shaved root, something that looks like a crushed chestnut. They are all gathered around, seven or eight of them, occasionally reaching out and touching a strand of blonde hair or feeling the ends of her sleeves. She smiles and welcomes their curiosity.

When the tea is made, the women help her pour it into a gourd. She carries it to Marta at the edge of the village. She weaves her way through mud-and-thatch huts, shaped like cones, sticking out of the meadow like canines. Above her, in the canopy, they've erected wooden platforms and walkways, systems of ropes and pulleys, as if they are mining the trees.

Halfway across the meadow she's intercepted by a group of children who have made a necklace for her—smooth black stones dangling from twine. Aubry gasps and shows her pleasure, stooping down so they can drape it over her head.

"Thank you!" says Aubry, smiling broadly.

She brings the tea to Marta, prone and sweaty on her mat outside one of the huts. The old woman circles her in a slow dance, still chanting, scattering dust, chanting some more. She has painted Marta head to toe with the orange paste in various designs—dots and circles and squiggly lines. She looks like a Christmas ornament.

"She tells me this will help," says Marta, trying to smirk but not able. Her voice is so weak, her eyes unfocused by fever.

Aubry lifts Marta's head onto her lap, and helps her drink the tea.

"No more," Marta says, halfway through the gourd. Instead, she reaches for her carpetbag.

"What is it?" asks Aubry.

"My binder."

Aubry retrieves it, hands it to her. Marta pulls out a folded piece of paper made brittle by time and travel.

"I want to give this to you," she says.

Aubry carefully unfolds it. It is a photograph cut out of an old newspaper, yellowed around the edges, a photograph of Aubry when she was much younger. She is coming down a crowded gangplank somewhere, looking right at the camera, eyes showing white all around.

"What is this?"

"It's you," says Marta. "Do you remember?"

"No."

"It's you getting off a boat in Veracruz," Marta says. "I must have been fifteen when I saw it," she says, then waits a moment to refill her lungs. "You looked so startled. You looked so fragile. Yet you traveled the world." Her eyes close. So much effort to speak. "It's the photo that made me fall in love."

Aubry isn't sure what to say for some time. She folds the photograph up again, very carefully. "Then you should have it. It's not as if I'm going to fall in love with myself."

"Ha!" Marta gets out, hardly above a whisper.

"Get some sleep, Marta," says Aubry, brushing Marta's hair with her fingertips. "Rest."

Marta is silent for a long time. Aubry thinks Marta is asleep, but then Marta says, in a long, slow murmur: "I spent my life chasing things I could not have."

Aubry places the tea beside Marta and sits the rest of the afternoon by her friend's side, occasionally lifting her head to help her drink. The old woman dances circles around them both.

74

With Marta in the Congo

The jungle swallows the sunset and torches are lit. Aubry boils more tea, watching the sky grow dim. She listens to the change in the jungle chorus, the din of daytime birdsong and insect drone falling away to the night shift of frog and cicada. A breeze springs up suddenly, as if in defiance of nightfall, and the torches flicker.

Marta lies on her mat, the tireless old woman still chanting under her breath. She's been at it for hours. How long can this old woman go before she falls over as well? wonders Aubry. What if Marta doesn't recover in the next few days? Will she leave without Marta, after years of constant company, halfway around the world? What if Marta dies here, in the jungle, among a tribe of strangers? Aubry's spent more time with Marta than anyone in her life since she began her wanderings. How does she simply walk away?

But if Aubry stays, she dies. If Marta, sick with malaria, traces off into the jungle with her, then Marta dies. Parting is inevitable.

All this time together, walking, moving, traveling, and no sign of the libraries. It has taken a toll on Marta. Once, they were everywhere. Now they can't be found. They tried to predict the pattern, scoured swamps and deserts for an entranceway, to no avail. Marta still believes. She knows Aubry's no liar, that she appears in various parts of the world without explanation. The libraries, as fantastic as they seem, make some kind of sense. But where have they gone?

Aubry senses a change in the night. Her ears perk up.

The cicadas have stopped. So have the frogs and the crickets. She's never heard a jungle go silent before. It's impossible to miss, like when, after weeks at sea, the engines of a steamboat suddenly shut down. She looks up at the trees, then at the sky, then at other faces to see if anyone is as bewildered as she is.

She's not alone. Heads look up. Children stop playing. The entire evening holds its breath.

Spear in hand, Aubry walks toward the tree line. Behind her, the village is suddenly alive, something ignited. She doesn't know why, but men and women alike arrange things, full of nervous chatter, rushing to and fro.

She reaches the end of the meadow, the edge of the jungle. The torchlight hardly penetrates the darkness beyond. Despite the noise from the village, she thinks she hears a voice. She listens again. Someone has just called out. Someone is out there, far away. No one should be in the jungle when it is dark. She turns to the villagers to try to explain, but they seem to be in a state of irrationality. Spear ready, she is about to go looking on her own when the village children, a dozen of them at least, rush to her. Their eyes are wide. Their mouths are full of anxious words. Their little hands reach for hers. They are begging her to return to camp, to stay in the meadow.

"Shhh. It's all right," she tells the children. "I won't be long."

She turns away and enters the silence.

75

With Marta in the Congo

In the darkness, leaves are bleached of color. She moves through shades of gray and black. Noise from the village, all its torchlight, is swallowed up by the black tangle of limbs and vines.

She hasn't learned many words yet, but she has picked up one that seems to be a greeting, one she hopes is appropriate.

"*Bilawa?*" she calls into the dark. "Hello? *Bilawa?*"

There is no answer. She hasn't heard the voice again since she entered the jungle. She begins to think she's been tricked, lured, like a child in a fairy tale.

"*Bilawa?*"

A wind kicks up, the undersides of leaves flashing like shoals of fish. It breathes through the jungle and ripples through her clothes and hair. It comes and goes, as if the earth is turning in its sleep.

"*Bil...*"

She goes still, not like predator, but like prey. Something ahead, something she can't quite make out. There, beneath a tree, not far away, something is low to the ground, its black fur shimmering in the last of the wind.

She stays still for a long time. When the creature fails to move, she crouches low and approaches, spear raised and ready. It is not moving, whatever it is. It doesn't seem to be alive.

It is a monkey, a colobus, the same kind she hunted earlier, black face, streaks of long white hair. It lies on the jungle floor, but is not alone. Three other monkeys lie beside it, a different species—smaller, red-tailed monkeys—lying in the dirt in the middle of the night.

She prods a small one with the end of her spear. It groans a little, rolls over. It is not dead, only asleep. She doesn't understand. She prods the bigger colobus. It, too, swats at her spear, twitches in its sleep.

Monkeys do not sleep on the forest floor. There is no better way to wake up in the coils of a python or in the jaws of a leopard than to sleep on unprotected ground. They are supposed to be in the trees where it is safe, with their own kind, the colobus with the colobus, the red-tailed with the red-tailed.

Not far away, a sound like someone dropping a sack of laundry. She just sees it, another monkey losing its grip, hanging, then falling from a low tree branch. It drops to the earth, rolls over, doesn't move again. She cautiously approaches, spear aimed.

It's another colobus, long black hair, long white hair—it stretches, yawns, is otherwise immobile. She walks around it. She doesn't want to be too close. What if it has a disease, not like hers, but a contagious one? Giving the animal a wide berth, she looks up, only to find she has almost walked into an elephant.

It is a big male—a forest elephant—slumped against a monster tree. She takes a startled leap back, but the animal is out cold. She can see its mighty rib cage rising and falling, its breath pouring out of its slackened trunk and stirring the fallen leaves. She circled the monkey out of caution, but she circles the elephant out of awe, this grand beast, unapproachable in any other circumstance, now laid before her in the night. It moans slightly, enough to break the jungle's silence, enough to vibrate her bones. Its tusks are pale and luminous in the gloom. The bottoms of its

318

feet, exposed to her, the size of paella pans. Never again will she witness such an animal so close, so vulnerable.

Another gust of wind, blowing over the elephant's skin, slipping under Aubry's shirt. Trees groan. Leaves scatter.

She might have stared at that elephant all night, but for the python that slides out of the tree above her and lands on her shoulders. Its weight almost floors her. It's thigh-thick, as long as the elephant's trunk. She shouts, shakes herself free. The sleeping python unspools to earth, like a vein of melted bronze, and coils up again in the dirt.

It is enough to send Aubry running. She forgets the voice. She forgets everything but the need to be with people again. But now the forest floor is littered with animals. She sees more monkeys. She sees mice and squirrels. Afraid of stepping on them, she swerves left, then right, her path back to the village no longer a straight one. She stops. She has turned herself around. Another wind blows, lifting her hair. She scans the jungle, but no sign of the village.

She closes her eyes a moment, calms herself, then sets out, moving slowly. She sharpens her ears, but cannot hear the village. It was all tumult when she left. Now, nothing but silence.

Then, a patch of light behind the trees. A clearing, she is sure. She heads for it, steps out of the trees and into the tall grass. It's the meadow. She can see torchlight not far away. But where is everyone? Where is the chatter? Where is the commotion?

Even the air is different. It glows. There is something shimmering in the night. Fireflies? Dust?

She moves through the grass, still clutching her spear, and hears a groan. She stops, looks to her left. One of the men from the village has passed out on a floor of chaff and bristle. She leans down, feels for breath. He is asleep, like the animals in the forest.

It's something in the air, this phosphorescent glow. She pulls up her collar, covers her nose, afraid to breathe.

Marta, she thinks. What has happened to Marta?

She picks up her pace, stepping over more sleeping bodies sprawled in the meadow. The village is just ahead.

Aubry goes still at the sight of it. Some villagers have made it to their hammocks, limp in the trees. Others lean unconscious against the huts, still carrying their sleeping mats. One woman lies by a dying fire, her two small children in her arms. It looks like a battlefield, the day after the war. But that's not what it is. It's a collective coma. It's an entire village, an entire jungle, doused in sleep.

Aubry keeps moving through the particle glow. Still covering her face, she peers inside a hut, full of women and children, fast asleep on woven mats. She moves on, looking for Marta. Bodies turn in their sleep—an occasional snore, the odd moan.

Then she sees her, under a lean-to, dormant beside the old woman, their hands clasped together in hibernation.

76

With Marta in the Congo

She wonders how long this lasts, this great sleep. She attempts to wake Marta.

"Marta? Marta, can you hear me?"

Marta's head is no more than a fallen fruit, rocking side to side. Maybe such a sleep is just what she needs to beat her fever, thinks Aubry. She stays by her side for the rest of the night, holding her hand, talking to her quietly.

"I saw an elephant tonight. Up close. I could see it breathing," she tells her.

The sun rises and still the village sleeps. She has tied a scarf around her face. If it is something in the air, then maybe she sidestepped it when she stole into the jungle, with the wind in her favor, but that is conjecture. She is not sure of anything.

She stays by Marta's side most of the morning until she gets hungry and decides to forage for food.

Back in the jungle, this time in daylight, she searches for breakfast. The hush that has fallen over the forest is as startling in the daytime as it was at night. She has no fear of predators, no fear of anything. She wanders past the comatose monkeys. She returns to the elephant and admires it for another hour at least. She gathers the nerve to touch its skin, the texture of an avocado.

She slowly, gently, strokes the animal's forehead and it pleases her to think it enjoys the attention.

The python, on the other hand, she avoids, curled in a tight spiral on the jungle floor.

Farther out, she finds a village boy, maybe twelve or thirteen, asleep at the foot of a tree. Perhaps this was the voice she heard in the night. He is heavy, but she pries her arms underneath him and carries him all the way back to the village.

She doesn't know whom he belongs to or where he's supposed to sleep, but she finds an empty hammock not far from the others and carefully lays him inside. He turns on his side, curling up comfortably, a faint smile on his face. This boy must be having good dreams.

She has collected little more than a few figs and some amaranth. Jungles are usually bursting with food, but perhaps this jungle is more seasonal than others. She sits beside Marta and wonders what will happen first—the sleepers' resurrection or her disease. She suspects her disease. Hibernation is not a short-lived event. She wanders the village a little, looking at the faces. Everyone—the prettiest, the most handsome of them—is even more beautiful when they sleep. But already there is a woman, curled in the roots of a tree, with a spiderweb formed across her mouth.

The sky grows dark. Aubry lights the torches again, keeps the campfires going through the night. She makes sure everyone looks comfortable. If they were caught half-standing, she lays them down. If they are crooked, she straightens them out. She would like to carry the men in the meadow closer to camp but they're far too heavy. The best she can do is roll up some grass and make pillows for them.

She feels Marta's pulse. It's slow. She has never felt such an apathetic heartbeat before. She feels the pulses of others—men, women, children. Their hearts beat like a slow drip in a deep cave.

"You are angry at all the things you lost," says the demon. "Are you angry at all the things you've gained? Knowledge? Insight? Legs with muscle in them?"

"I don't feel insightful."

"You don't look it either. But you are."

Aubry stays awake with Marta for as long as she can, but she's gone two days and a night without sleep and, before long, she is dreaming with the rest of them.

77

With Marta in the Congo

Something wakes her. She's not sure what. Dawn has hardly begun, the sky still dim, and something is not right. The wind has kicked up again, blowing through the meadow, bending the treetops. But louder than even the rustle of jungle leaves is a hiss, a slither, and it is all around her.

She lifts her head, reaches for her spear. Just as she had gotten used to the silence, a new sound emerges, the whole jungle breathing through its teeth. She pulls herself to her feet, settles into position, spear up and ready. She watches the tree line all around, waiting for something to appear.

When it does, it is nothing she expected.

A thick, ghostly fog comes seeping through the trees. For a long moment, she freezes, not comprehending, watching it rise and fall like sea foam, then writhe through the meadow grass from all directions, like so many eels.

The fog glitters in the meager daylight, as if it were full of ice. She thinks it is a reflection of some kind, but it is the fog itself. It glows, like the ocean at night, a roiling phosphorus glow. It closes in, engulfs the first of the huts.

"Marta!" cries Aubry. She scurries toward her friend, shaking her, shouting into her face. "Marta, please!"

The fog exhales its breath over the sleeping villagers, filling the huts. In moments it is creeping over Aubry's feet.

"Marta, wake up! Please wake up!"

Marta not only sleeps, she breathes it in. Aubry can feel it, too, tickling the back of her throat, seeping into her lungs.

Aubry hauls Marta's body along, spear in one hand, Marta's wrist in the other, not sure where to go. They might find safety in the jungle. If she can only reach the trees. But she can't outrun this fog, not while towing Marta's deadweight.

Then comes the massive wave, pouring over the treetops in front of them. It comes down like a waterfall, hits the earth, balloons up in the air, then comes at them. Torches and campfires are snuffed out with a hiss, their dying smoke, the swirling fog, mingling. In seconds it will be upon them. Aubry holds her breath, barely has time to turn away before it swallows her up.

Everything turns gray. She feels her grip on Marta's wrist but cannot see her. She pulls, legs toiling forward. Her ears ring, louder as her need for air grows. She holds on, keeps moving. Her chest throbs. Her eyes bulge and her throat swells. Her grip weakens. She feels crushed, as if sunk in a deep sea, each step more impossible than the last. Her body panics, even if her mind resists.

Her grip gives way, unconsciously. Her vision is a blur, her mind wiped clean by panic. She runs—and only runs—because her need for air has hijacked the rest of her.

And like that, Marta is gone, released on a bed of broken meadow grass, consumed in clouds.

Only half-aware of what she has done, Aubry runs. She needs air, above all else, before she is gone, too.

She clears the fog, gasps, sucking in great gulps of air. Her instinct is to fall, to collapse and breathe, but she doesn't stop moving. She has just enough momentum to stay on her feet. If she can avoid the fate of the others, then perhaps she can return to rescue Marta. That is all the time she has to think on it. A river of fog is slithering on its belly and closing in fast.

There is a marsh at the end of the meadow. She will swim across the marsh, find a stream, a river, some way out of this jungle. Her feet trudge through mud and reeds. She slips, falls, recovers. By the time she reaches water she is blackened with mud, the fog pulsing heart-like through the reeds behind her.

That's when she sees the flowers, the large red flowers as big as parasols. They're clumped in the treetops by the hundreds, spewing their pollen into the sunrise. Their discharge is caught in the wind, tendrils of mist reaching through branches and vines, the hissing sound of fine dust pitter-pattering against jungle leaves.

The entire jungle is engulfed and she remembers—too late—where she'd seen these flowers before. She remembers them in her lap, drawn in the pages of the book from the library. A botanist had drawn them, flowers as red as an open wound, expelling a cloud of pollen so thick and noxious a single flower could anesthetize a horse for a week. What about hundreds of them? What about thousands?

She turns around. The luminous fog—no, the pollen. It's pollen. There's no doubt any longer—is drifting toward her, behind her, ahead of her. She doesn't know where to go but into the marsh, into its center where the pollen might not reach.

She treads deep into the marsh, sinking to her ankles in leaf mush, until the water is up to her waist. She keeps going until she's up to her neck, and then to her chin. The clouds of pollen close in, gleaming white against a dark jungle.

She hears the rush of water, a sound like river rapids. A way out, she hopes. But instead, she sees a hole, a hole in the water where the swamp drains out, as if a plug to the center of the earth has been pulled and all the water is pouring in. It isn't possible, but there it is, deep and black and bottomless, the water funneling away.

It's growing, its edges expanding, the gaping hole spreading across the marsh, threatening to suck her in. She can feel its pull. She digs her heels into the mud to fight it but even the mud disappears under her feet, sucked away with everything else, like walking up a landslide. She thrusts her spear deep into the swamp bottom and holds on, but still the hole comes to meet her. In desperation, she tries to swim. Instead, she is pulled under, tumbling into a wet darkness, the roar of water echoing in her ears.

"The world needs you," the Prince had said. *"It wants a witness."*

Muffled darkness. No sound, no light, no sense of anything anymore. Just the void.

78

An Aside, Brief Again

Around the time of Aubry's fifth birthday, while the family was vacationing on the seashore, her mother spent the evenings reading *Around the World in 80 Days* to all three daughters. They loved the tale immensely, though Sylvie had some concerns.

"But he wasn't really traveling. He was moving as fast as he could. He didn't even stop to see the Taj Mahal. He went right past it."

"That's a good point, Sylvie," says her mother. "Do you think he was just moving for the sake of moving?"

"Yes."

"But it's still an adventure," challenges Pauline. "Think of it! Every moment is a place you've never been!"

"It doesn't matter," says Aubry, sitting in her corner. Everyone turns to her, awaiting an explanation. "We're just going to grow up and have babies. Just like all those mothers in the park. So it doesn't matter what Phileas Fogg was doing because we're never going to do it."

For a moment, no one says anything. Then, with some ferocity, Pauline says, "It matters!"

They were staying at a friend's house not far from Biarritz, on the Atlantic coast, and Aubry liked to join her father when he practiced archery on the seashore.

"Ah," he explains, "but you see, Aubry, sometimes there's more to travel than sightseeing."

"Like what?"

"Sometimes there's just the movement."

"What good is that?"

"It seems to me, things that never move are only half of what they can be." At his feet are his arrows, sharp ends planted in the sand. "But movement is a powerful thing. See my arrows? Like that, they're just sticks." He plucks one from the sand, fits the nock against the bowstring, rests the arrowhead against the bow. "But when I fire one into the air, it's no longer a stick. It's not even an arrow anymore. It becomes something else."

"What?" asks Aubry.

To her surprise, her father aims at the sky over the ocean and frees the nock, as gently as a harp string, and the arrow lets loose. Together, they watch it fly high over the water, dark against the luminous chalk-dust sky.

79

Terra Obscura

When she comes up for air, hands flailing, lungs aching, she manages to grab something tangible. She can hardly see in the dim light, but she purchases a grip and heaves herself onto dry ground.

Now she sees the tangle of roots in her hands, a bank of mangroves that dunk their fingers into the water. For a long time she clings to them, sucking breath back into her lungs.

"Marta," she says. It's all she can think of, her friend she's left behind, swallowed up in an omnivorous fog, her friend who'd come with her all that way to see . . .

This.

She sits up. Beneath her is a floor of knotted roots and tall grass. Above her, a canopy of jungle green, as solid as any cathedral ceiling. And floating in between, books and more books, shelves and shelves of them between the grass and the boughs, carved into the tree trunks, shelves tracing the curl of branches, scrolls dangling from the vines.

She looks for a doorway back, back through the hole in the swamp, a way to retrieve Marta. She leaps into the pool of water, but, inexplicably, it's no deeper than her thigh, a small, shallow, black pool in the ground, nothing more. She feels the bottom but all that's there is her spear and handfuls of mud. She stands, stares into the black water, shoulders slumped, defeated.

"Please," she says, though she knows no one is listening, "let me go."

She resents the books and the scrolls, the whole damn library. She despises its exclusion. She wants to share this place. She wants others to know. She wants Marta to be here, to hold her hand and assure her of her sanity. The libraries, she realizes, are less an honor and more an exile piled upon exile.

She curls up on the mangrove roots and lies there, not moving for a long time, and then an even longer time after that. She no longer wants to read, or walk. She barely has the strength to weep. If she could stop breathing, she'd do that, too. Eventually, though, time passes. She can smell it, the passage of time, like a decaying log, like a low tide. She gets to her feet, and stands there silently, bone-weary. But that can't last either and, after a while, she begins to walk.

What else is there to do?

"You are full of anger," she hears her sickness tell her. "I understand. But it is smoke in your eyes, just when you need to see."

She ignores it and follows a path—or what looks like a path—through the bookshelves. Left, then right, and again, and again. She picks up the pace, a little quicker with every turn. She only wants to leave, to find an exit and see daylight, to find Marta and explain how hard she tried to save her. Soon she's running, turning and pivoting, and turning some more, until she suddenly comes upon a wooden table, carved from a stump, polished to a golden sheen. Next to it, an empty chair, waiting. The tablecloth is nothing more than palm leaves. On the leaves sits a bowl full of tree grapes and horned cucumber.

Next to the bowl is a note that says "FOR THE NEXT" in her own writing.

80

Terra Obscura

The next several years she spends wandering the libraries. Once, she looked for a way out, but that was a while ago. Since then she has become absorbed in her reading and not once has her sickness come for her. She wanders at will, or stays in one place, but when all the books in a room have been read, she always moves on.

This is what happened on that first day: She sat down. She grew hungry. She ate the horned cucumbers. She ate the tree grapes. Scrolls dangled overhead from the jungle vines, but she refused to look at them.

"I knew you right away," her sickness told her. "You love to learn. You hate to be taught. From the first step, it was going to be a long journey."

She made no response.

"Do you remember Katla, erupting over the black sands of Mýrdalsvík?"

That she could not forget, not ever, plumes of fire throwing back the clouds.

"Do you remember that school of tiny fish in the Bay of Bengal that swam in the shape of a shark?"

She remembered that, too.

332

"My life was wasted," she said.

"Nothing was wasted. You wandered the world. You looked around. Soon enough, you were able to see."

Still, she would not read.

"Open one," her sickness gently pleaded. "You won't be disappointed."

It took time, but eventually she gave in, reached up and plucked a scroll from above. She unspooled it across the floor. This is what she saw:

A hunter, tracking his prey across the land. The herds were large, but so was the land, and it took all his skill to track them down. He searched out the urine of the arctic fox first, which would indicate buried caribou meat somewhere nearby. Soon after he'd found shreds of velvet on the rocks where the caribou had rubbed their antlers. He'd found earth stripped bare of lichen and knew that they had just fed. He came to know his prey well, could follow their trail with ease, predict their movements.

By the time he'd found the herd, he knew them intimately. He could lure a caribou closer by tying antlers to his head, imitating their walk, grunting just as they do in rutting season.

Soon he was living among them. He traded his clothes for caribou hide. He learned to eat lichen. He had become his prey, the thing he was stalking, and spent his days wandering the tundra with the herd.

Aubry has been wandering the libraries ever since.

"Think of all the things we've seen," said her sickness. "A dome of stars, a sleeping jungle, that extraordinary sandstorm. Think of all the things we've done—hunted on the Tibetan Plateau, crossed mountains so high even birds couldn't fly over them. But now this, the greatest wonder yet."

Long ago, when she first found a door, she thought, Ah, a library with no words. How strange. How special. But she soon discovered others and she thought it must be an international practice of some kind, libraries for travelers like her in need of a universal language. But then, as she reemerged in other parts of the earth, she began to wonder if it could be the work of a long-lost civilization, an advanced people who tunneled throughout the world, collecting the memories of those who lived on the surface above. It was fantastic, she knew, but she'd reached the ends of logic by then.

She comes upon an expanse of smooth grasslands, the black ceiling above like a low-hanging rain cloud threatening just overhead. Standing in the grass are rows and rows of bookshelves to wander beside, to pluck a book from, to sit down and read as if on holiday. It was as if some great people had laid down their roots here, grown, prospered, then moved on, leaving only their books behind. But she looks at the grass swaying, bright and yellow, at the black-cloud ceiling above, and dismisses that thought out of hand.

"Are you impressed?" asks her sickness.

"I don't understand how this can be."

"Don't be distracted. It's not where the books are kept. It's what's in them." She flips through the pictures. She reads a story of a mining expedition that dug deep inside the earth in search of a rare and perhaps nonexistent gem. She reads of an attempt to measure all the fresh water in the world that drove a team of scientists and businessmen to bankruptcy and ruin. She reads of a poor charcoal vendor who undercooked the monkey he was eating and caused a plague that killed everyone on his beloved island.

She enters a mosque, its dome glittering even in faint candlelight. The weather must be terrible somewhere because a deluge of rain comes straight down through the oculus and pours into a well below. The dome is otherwise dry. She puts her hand in the column of rain and laughs. "This looks like something you'd invent."

"I did."

"Now you're showing off."

She discovers a marsh and poles across in a dugout canoe she finds beached in the shallows. She pushes her way through water and reeds that stretch far over her head, and navigates around libraries built like stilt houses.

Gifts of food and drink, just when she needs them, are always there. So is a change of clothes. If the library is a Chinese court, there is embroidered silk. If she is in an Egyptian tomb, there is thin linen and strings of gold. In a hunter's cabin, she finds a deerskin satchel in which to keep things.

She reads of a couple who built an entire village in the tops of trees, of a young girl who assassinated kings for pleasure.

"I'm never sick anymore," she finally notices.

"Why would you be? I have you just where I want you."

"Where's that? I still don't know."

"At home with the history of the world."

"Why?"

"It's petty, I know, but there are times I just want to forget my manners and brag about things for a while."

"I must tell you something."

"Yes?"

"Sometimes, I hear a voice in my head."

"Tell me."

"He says crazy things all the time."

"That must be aggravating."

"It is."

It comforts her that for every path she's taken during her many revolutions around the world—for every individual footstep, it seems—there's a story. Something once happened, a past

335

that is not hers. And this, it turns out, becomes something of an obsession. That there are a billion souls out there, each carving their own paths through the fears and sufferings of the world, a billion peepholes, a billion mirrors, a billion lives that she has not lived, fills her with a curiosity that borders on madness. She has a voracity that can't be filled, as if she's been tricked into this hunger, purposefully addicted. But there's no stopping it.

Does she notice that she begins to talk to the books as if they were old friends? "Ah, there you are," she tells one, pulling it from the shelf. "That was wonderful," she says to another, "tell it again."

Does she notice what is happening to her? Does she feel the borders of her life slowly inching shut? Maybe. But she's done struggling against it. Let it slowly creep in on her. As long as she has a book to read, she's not bothered.

By the time she's read ten thousand scrolls, and walked uncountable miles, streaks of gray course through her hair and wrinkles etch her face.

81

Terra Obscura

A noise disturbs her reading. A shuffling sound? The clink of metal? It's distant, an echo of an echo floating through the tunnels. She puts down her wine, grabs the candle and her walking stick. She moves through the catacombs, turns and turns until she comes to a door.

In front of the door, on the dusty stones, she notices a gold coin. She picks it up, studies it. Roman. There's another and another, scattered about. Soon she's collected a dozen, maybe more, cupped in her hands. There's something about them that feels so familiar. She reaches out. She feels the thick wooden door vibrate against her hands and feels the heat behind it, so much heat it makes her pause. But then she builds her nerve, grabs the big iron ring, and pulls.

The door, with all its leaden weight, comes open and a hot gust of air billows through. She shields her eyes and steps into a vast open cave floodlit by fire. Immediately she's filled with a nostalgia, one of her scattered memories coming to her all at once.

She is standing on the bridge that spans a river of hissing lava, a hot wedding of fire and rock coursing through a dead subterranean city, like some ghostly vision from the last days of Pompeii.

She knows this place. It's ingrained in her memory. She's walked this place, smelled the sulfur, collected the gold coins, read its scrolls by the soft, sweeping orange glow.

She steps, slowly, from one side of the bridge to the other and she knows, without a doubt but with a terrible unease, what she will see.

Upriver, on another bridge, a young woman is warming her feet over the molten fire, reading from stacks of books, flipping a gold coin in one hand, turning pages with the other. Aubry shudders and stares at this young woman. She hasn't come across so much as a mirror in all her years down here but now here she is, staring at herself. It takes a long time for her to find her voice, to remember her name, she hasn't used it in so long.

She cries out, "Aubry! Aubry Tourvel!" The young woman looks up. "Your mother is dying! Go to her! It's safe! Go!"

The young woman drops her book, amazed, her coins scattering. But the old Aubry Tourvel runs, finds the nearest door, and ducks inside. She finds a corner to hide. There are tears rolling down her cheeks. She bites her hand to keep from sobbing. Maybe it's because she knows what awaits the young woman. Maybe it's because she misses her youth. Maybe it's because she understands how time in these libraries moves in a spiral and she's now utterly lost in its curl. She hears footsteps echoing up and down stairwells, through passageways with no end, searching and searching.

But Aubry knows she will never be found.

82

Terra Obscura

Occasionally she hears voices, not in her head, but other voices, always distant, always an echo, never understood. She tries to ignore them, but once in a great while she will find herself in a perfect crossroads—her ear against a soft spot in the wall, or inside a dome-like room that captures every distant sound. In those moments, if she strains to hear, she can just make out what they are saying:

"Hello?" calls the voice. "Thank you for this! Thank you for the food! The milk tea is good!" And later, "Thank you for the lanterns! I'd be helpless without them!"

Another time: "Aubry! Aubry Tourvel! Your mother is dying!"

Another time: "Please . . . let me go . . ."

But in general, she tries not to listen. She doesn't see the point.

Then comes the moment she finds the book sitting at a table. It's in a curiously empty room. The library is immense, yet she's never seen a completely empty room. There are always books to be found somewhere, until she stumbles upon this—a room with nothing, just bare walls and a stone slab between them. There isn't even a tablecloth or a bit of fur or a banana leaf, just a book and a black pencil, alone together on a slab of rock.

Douglas Westerbeke

When she opens the book, it's blank, every page.

"For me?" she asks. She looks between the book and the black pencil. Her disease is silent. "For me," she confirms.

She gathers both the book and the pencil, leaves the room, and never comes back.

83

Terra Obscura

"Begin at the well."

"Why there?"

"It's where we first said hello."

In the cave with the prehistoric paintings on the walls, she opens her new book full of empty white pages and draws her first picture—three sisters standing around a well, tossing things in. But the youngest sister is angry. She refuses to go along and keeps her little plaything.

The drawing covers two full pages and she's exhausted by the effort.

The next day, or night, she draws her second picture. She sits cross-legged in a tangled garden, scrolls dangling from cornstalks and sunflowers, and draws the little girl very ill at the family dinner table. Her mother and father cry over her as she collapses to the floor. Then she draws the little girl in a doctor's office, feeling happy and perfectly well, and then back home and sick again, and then the little girl running away and, in the next drawing, feeling much better.

Days pass—or not. She measures time by sleep, and whether she's slept for many hours or only minutes, any sleep at all feels like a night to her, so that's how she counts her days.

The years, however, she lost track of long ago.

In a desert canyon, eating flatbread and prickly pears, she draws the little girl and her mother traveling and traveling and still traveling. That alone is seven pages, tiny panels that read right to left, top to bottom, until she comes to her final drawing of the little girl leaving her poor exhausted mother in the middle of the night.

When she's finished, she cries so hard that she doesn't draw so much as a dot or a line for what seems like weeks.

"Because you did things that were hard, you weep."

"Why did you make me walk so far?"

"If I hadn't, you'd have gone nowhere."

She wanders and reads the works of others, studying their art and imitating their techniques. She tries to understand what makes a compelling story, how to better capture faces and moods, how a little smudge can turn a forest into a foggy night, how various turns of the eyebrows can make a character angry or sad or perplexed or playful. Soon enough, she's ready to resume her story. There's much more to be said.

For several more days, she draws herself learning to spear. She draws her bleak days onboard the Greek fishing boat. She rests, then tells the story of Uzair Ibn-Kadder and her escape through the Calanshio Sand Sea, then of her journey across the Sahara with the caravan of salt traders.

By the time she discovers the Persian ruins and ancient gold mines, she's illustrated her journey across the Russian steppe and her nights with Lionel. Although the train ride is only a week of her life, she spends well over a month getting the pictures just right.

"The world was so full of wonders. Why do you include him? What was he to you?"

"He was a wonder."

"But if—"

"And what happened to Marta? Where is she?"

"They found her, staggering out of the jungle, half-starved. She wrote a book about you."

Though it has been many years, she feels a small relief, as if taking off a tight shoe. "That's a wonder, too."

"We had a strange voyage down the Murray River. You should tell that next."

Her face hardens. "I will say what I want to say or there will be no book at all."

She waits for a response, but there is only silence. Satisfied, she continues to draw.

It's in a great blue-and-gold synagogue that she draws the giant bird snapping its beak at the brave Tibetan hunter.

Days after that, there is a sealskin coat and a pair of boots waiting for her at the edge of ice floes. She kayaks her way across the underground bay. She passes shipwrecks, mighty oaken hulls crushed by the ice, crates of books scattered across the frozen sea. Sometimes, if she brushes away the snow, she can make out a caribou hide frozen just under the ice, maps and pictographs etched on the leather.

In an igloo, she draws, to the best of her ability, the sand mandala that the Prince once painted on a beach. The memory of it brings fresh tears to her eyes.

"Do you resent me?"

"I ought to," she says.

"But do you?"

"Shut up and let me finish my book."

Finally, it's under the book tree, pages for leaves, scrolls hanging from the branches, the trunk itself a spiraling bookshelf, that she draws the black fathomless hole in the African marsh that swallows her up for good.

She closes the book.

"Do you see how beautiful it was? None of it existed without you. Your consciousness shone a light on it all."

By now her hair is entirely white, not a thread of gold left. She knows because it sheds on her shoulders and her clothing. She hasn't come upon a mirror in a long time—her dim, fractured reflection in a pool of water perhaps, but nothing more. The last time she saw a strand of blonde was before the age spots covered her hands, before her skin puckered at the joints. Occasionally she wonders what she looks like in her old age but, at the same time, she's glad not to know.

One day, she happens upon an enormous spiral staircase that ascends infinitely up and descends infinitely down, nothing but blackness at either end, and a slow river of air moaning the length of it. The walls that encompass it, however, are a patchwork of shelves at odd, unpredictable angles, and filled with books, so many books, more than she's seen so far, spiraling up and down forever with the stairs. She walks up and up and considers going back down again when, somewhere in the vast in-between, she finds an empty spot on a shelf, just wide enough for one more story.

She removes the book of her life from her satchel and slides it in neatly with the rest. It takes a few moments for her fingers to let go the binding. Then she walks away.

There will come a time, she knows, when everyone on earth will fly around the world and walking will become obsolete. There will come a time when people will fly to the moon and perhaps build cities on the frozen continent or walk on the ocean floor or map the very edges of the universe. Yet we will never know the name of the first person who ever ate a fig, or threw a spear, or kissed. We will never know the story of fire, who first cooked their food and why. We will never hear the music of the unknown but truly great composer who burned up in a fire with all his works in a small Swiss cabin outside of Lucerne. Nor the thoughts of the Persian sailor who was swept overboard in the night, who floated for three days on his back in the Arafura Sea before exhaustion overtook him and he sank into the depths to become food for the eyeless scavengers.

And even these books, uncountable, with all their infinite illustrations, cannot give us a single name. We all die anonymously—if not at the moments of our death, then later. Aubry looks around. Her seclusion is absolute. Her death may be the most anonymous of all.

84

Terra Obscura

Now that her own life is among them, her mania for books has passed. She doesn't read them, she doesn't talk to them, she doesn't even like to look at them. She's exhausted by pictures. They are no substitute for words, just as words are no substitute for the things themselves.

She finds a room that is surprisingly bare—a sofa, a hearth, a place to sleep. She removes every last book, every last scroll, and piles them where they can't be seen in the corridors outside. For several days, she refuses to leave. She does the one thing she's been unable to do since the age of nine. She stays in that room and doesn't move, no curiosity of what may lay beyond.

The days turn to weeks, then months. Her life, she understands, has become dull—wasted some would say, and she would agree. But if you've grown tired of the books, then there's little to do here but waste away.

"What are you doing?"

"Nothing."

"There is more to see."

"I have nothing left."

"You have your spear."

"I have nothing left but my spear."

"And if everything you lost came back to you, would that make you happy?"

"It's not the things. It's what they meant."

"How have you lost their meaning?"

She is silent. She has no answers for questions like these.

"Be grateful," it pleads. "It is better to exist than not to. For that reason alone, be grateful."

"I'm tired. I'm tired of everything," she says.

"You are not ready. I understand. But soon, you will think differently."

She might take a stroll now and then. She might find something to eat, though she's rarely hungry. Mostly, she sleeps.

"I've asked a lot of you. I've taken your childhood. I've taken away everyone you've ever loved. I will make it up to you."

"Now? After all this time? Now you feel sorry?"

"Yes. Just now. I don't know why."

"Because I'm dying?"

"You're not dying."

"I'm not living."

She sits on a chair, as still as the room itself, staring blankly at the walls. Outside the door is a long corridor, dark as oil. But, if she squints her eyes, she can just make out something, a shape, a vague form.

"I can almost see you now."

"Can you?"

"I used to think you were a little demon, clinging to my back, digging into my bones."

"What am I?"

"Not that."

A pause. A stillness. A lack of anything.

"Aubry?"

"Yes?"

"Thank you for taking me with you. It was a wonderful ride."

"You're welcome."

And again, the entire library, dull and motionless.

"Aubry?"

"Yes?"

"Goodbye."

She does not know, at first, what that could mean. She sits in the dim lantern light, looking at the shadows around her, waiting for an explanation, but there is nothing. Minutes ago, silence was a comfort. Now it is jarring.

She thinks of laying her head down. Maybe the voice will return after a good nap. It wouldn't abandon her here, not now, not after all these years. It's the only one Aubry has had to talk to, besides herself. Without it, what will she do? But a long time passes and it doesn't return.

Then, something like a pistol shot resounds through the halls.

She leaps up, blood surging. The echo circles her room. She grabs her spear in both arms and throws herself under a table.

She waits, but there is no other sound, just her frantic breath and the blood pulsing in her ears. It occurs to her, while hiding under the table, that only a crazy recluse would cower like this. Something has fallen over, that's all. She's like a child afraid of the dark. How else to explain an old woman hiding under a table? This does not bode well.

She summons her strength. She climbs out from under the table. She takes a few moments to breathe, to let her nerves settle. Then she walks to the next room.

There, lying on the gray tiled floor, is a book, as if someone has pulled it from the shelf and slapped in down in the middle of the room. Maybe she should be afraid. Maybe she should go back under the table. Someone wants her to read this book. That is reason enough to be scared.

And yet, she comes closer, kneels before it. She feels a shiver, as if she has stepped into an icy cave. She opens the cover.

Drawn in black ink, it is the story of a young man out hunting with a bow and arrows. He discovers an abandoned shack in the woods. The inside is bare, except for the strange wooden ball sitting on the earthen floor. When he tries to pick it up, it rolls away. Every time he reaches for it, it rolls as if making an escape, until it finally drops into a pit dug in the center of the room. In the pit is a ladder, lashed to its insides, and he climbs down to explore.

He finds a labyrinth of books, a vast underground library. It goes on forever. When he opens the books and rolls out the scrolls, they are full of pictures. He wanders and wanders, reading this book and that, stories of people from all over the world. It's like his craving for betel nut—he can't stop. One book after another after another. He loses track of time. He forgets his family, his mother and father, his brothers and sisters. By the time he remembers the world he left behind, it is too late—he is lost and can find no way out.

It ought to terrify him, but he is perfectly content to read, the books so plentiful, the stories so captivating. At first he thinks it is only a matter of days, but then he realizes it has been months, perhaps years.

Worse, the rooms are getting darker. Though there is always a lantern somewhere, he finds it harder and harder to read, harder and harder to see.

He realizes it is blindness, slowly shuttering his light.

Aubry turns the pages, one drawing after another of the young hunter wandering room to room, each room darker than the one before. Finally, the pages become black. Page after page, painstakingly filled in with black ink.

And just as she is about to give up, she turns one last page.

The young hunter's sight has returned, and it is in color—greens and reds, yellows and blues, so vibrant she glances away. She wonders where the artist found such colorful inks. All she ever had was a pencil.

He finds his way out. He leaves the darkness of the libraries, enters the world again with a new understanding, able to see things he never saw before. He returns to his family, who are overjoyed to have him back. A great feast is made, his parents, his siblings, his neighbors, all gathered to celebrate his return.

But, while seated at the table, he feels a presence, just behind his shoulder, like silent footsteps sneaking up on him.

He turns to see who it is . . .

Aubry would read more, but the paper and the myriad of colors on it begin to glow. The colors, already bright, are luminous now. Gently, as if she means to dampen its radiance, she puts her palms flat on the pages of the book.

Light, silver splendors, roaring, rushing, through the paper, into the room, into the air around her—colors thrumming into ears and eyes, colors never before known, that can't exist but do, and the suns and the moons hidden inside

unspool across the sky, and the libraries unspool, too, in their perfect symmetry, spinning orb-like around her—so far away the people wandering the endless corridors, the people who have come before, will come after, and

does she see the long spirit-trail rising from the earth with mouths full of wonder?

does she hear the stories they sing to the scribes, who hand the books to the vassals, who fill the shelves?

and does she know, at last, what knowledge is for?

and the presence behind her, that will either purify or annihilate, and, oh, she means to turn around and face it, but bones are rigid, feeling its misty touch on her flesh and in that

fraction of a moment, all doors are opened, words with no language, language with no words, and all she could ever know is known, the dream of life

ringing around her, with eternity ahead of her,

eternity behind her, and a great

everything in between,

she is turned to ash,

the dust of her

scattered

on the hot

and frigid
winds

in

every

direction

85

The Art of Exile

She sucks in air, thick and wet. She can't see for a long while—the dead do not see—but then, light that makes her cry. Her eyes slowly adjust. She comes to, cowering, the morning light, diffused by the thick jungle, slowly lifting the night. She does not move. She sees the earth, wet and black. Not hard clay. Not red dust. The earth is wet and black.

This is the outdoors. This is air. This is sunlight.

My God, she thinks. Sunlight.

The earth, wet and black. Not hard clay. Not red dust. Wet and black—something to know, if ever something could be known, and that will do for now.

The libraries are gone, forever, she knows, and she doesn't want to know anything more than that, not ever again.

She lies wedged in the roots of a large tree, and, for the rest of the day and all of the night, she doesn't move at all except for the trembling.

The trembling never stops.

Another morning, the dim glow of sunlight through the canopy. She is sitting up now. She has been expelled, expelled for good. But what else? She gets a grip on herself, feels around for her spear, her satchel, finds them in the undergrowth. She lets out a cry of relief, hugs them close. She's been expelled, but has something left.

She breathes deeply to calm her rattled body. The humidity is so thick she feels she's inhaling water. The air shifts, the leaves glinting. Sounds from the jungle encircle her. This is a world constantly moving, constantly changing. Beneath it, all that stays the same, the eternal, the core of consciousness. She has been there. She has seen it. But she never wants to think of it again.

The libraries are gone. That part of her life is done. This part has just begun. Now, in her old age, she must start over.

Perhaps she's right back where she started from. Maybe the curve of time has deposited her at her point of departure. Perhaps Marta is waiting for her, perhaps gray-haired as well, right around the next corner.

"Marta?" she says out loud. It rasps from her windpipe. She says it again—"Marta?"—repeats it until it begins to sound full-throated. She fishes a bottle from her satchel and drinks.

The earth is wet and black. It blackens her hands and soils her skirt. The Congo was red and dusty. This is not the Congo. But where? She doesn't want to know. She keeps her eyes cast to the ground. She is afraid to look up. She is afraid of knowing things. She has already seen too much.

She gets to her feet, clutches her spear in both hands, and cautiously forges her way into the jungle.

Once again, she is walking.

She feels sick. Perhaps it's the humidity. Her body still shakes. She tries to clear her mind. She has to be lucid. She has to be un-bothered if she's to proceed. If there is a trick to survival, that's it. To be unbothered.

Perhaps if she could see herself, she wouldn't be calling for her friend. Marta wouldn't recognize her, if Marta is still alive.

Is anyone left alive? Lionel? Pathik? The Holcombes? Her sisters, Sylvie or Pauline? Is anyone left but her? She almost calls Marta's name again, this time out of fear, but doesn't. She does not want to appear a fool, even to herself.

Her hands still tremble.

She walks until she finds a small village by a river, homes upright on stilts, roofs nothing but corrugated sheet metal. There are children playing in the river, splashing in the mud. There are people in short-sleeved shirts and frayed pants trading goods from canoes to shore. Some have blue eyes and some brown. Some have straight black hair and some curly blond. She recognizes the mix of African and European and Amazonian. Yes, she thinks, somewhere in the Amazon.

She stands, rooted to the spot, silent and unseen. Her first glimpse of people since she was a much younger woman. Maybe she should introduce herself. But, no. Too much, too soon. She sits down under the shelter of the palms and, for a long time, does nothing but take in the view.

86

A Marketplace

She wakes with a start. It's early, before light has filled the sky, lanterns still glowing within the houses, and one of the men from the village is tapping on her knee. He has spotted her there, sleeping at the edge of the jungle. He has taken pity on her and brings her a pair of roasted yams.

But her face is a silent scream. She has seen the invisible, heard the unhearable. She wakes filled with panic, as if the moon overhead has just shattered. She covers her head in her hands and curls into a ball, whimpering. The man, alarmed, backs away, apology pouring from his face.

When he is gone, she recovers herself, slows her breathing. She remembers where she is—the jungle, near a town. She's become a hermit, a tiny crab retreating under a rock. She remembers how she once sought the company of people, shared the road with other travelers, had lovers on trains, danced on table-tops with fun-loving whores. Now she's gone feral. For heaven's sake, she thinks, what am I doing rolled up in a ball, having this conversation with myself? If she is going to be in the world, she must remember how to function in it.

With that, she gets to her feet and follows the river into the village. There, she is confronted by canoes, unloading their cargoes of fish and plantains, by vendors at their simple tables, slicing open melons and aguaje, reselling them in small affordable pieces. Fish are smoking, drying, frying as soon as they are off the boats. Flowers for sale. Spices for sale. A thousand fragrances.

She watches the chaos for a while, hiding behind trees and shrubs. Though her gut sours at the thought of it, she steps out and enters the market. She hears voices speaking in Spanish, in Portuguese, still others in Dutch. She hears an indigenous language she doesn't recognize. Still no idea what part of the Amazon she's in, what countries or coastlines lay nearby. She looks at no one, her eyes, always downcast, afraid to know what the world is up to. She sees a stack of paper on which one of the vendors keeps track of his sales. He has several blank pages left.

"*El papel?*" she says in a near whisper, her finger pointing and quivering.

"*El papel?*" he repeats, confused.

"*El papel, por favor,*" she confirms.

He pulls a sheet for her. It shivers in her hand. She pantomimes a pencil. At this he balks. He only has one. She understands. She reaches into her pockets and finds three gold coins, all of them Roman.

His mouth falls open. Other vendors stop everything to stare at the gold in her trembling hands. They murmur to each other in their various languages. Suddenly, she is sure she has blundered.

The vendor carefully takes one of the coins, purposefully leaves the other two, and gives her all his paper and the pencil in return. He takes her fingers and curls them into a fist around her remaining coins. He looks her in the eye at last, and puts a finger to his lips. *Hide your gold,* he is saying. She nods back, thanking him. But it's too late. As she goes about the market, faces are begging her, goods outstretched in their hands.

Later, she finds a quiet spot to sit in. She's purchased a flat smooth board, lays it across her lap, and flattens her piece of paper against it. With her new pencil in hand, she stares at the pristine white page before her and wonders what to draw.

She thinks of the vision, the light and the colors. The memory of it makes her chest throb and her ears ring. She cannot articulate what she saw, and if it can't be spoken, then it certainly can't be drawn. So what to do? Draw a tree instead? A river? A stone? Nothing seems worthy. The pencil hovers over the page, without aim or purpose.

And then the drop of blood hits the paper.

"Oh no," she says under her breath.

She looks up at the people in the market. They are kind, but they will not understand. The blood is already pooling in the back of her throat.

She hasn't felt this in so long. For years, decades, she wandered the libraries without a thought of it, moving from place to place, every doorway a new country. She'd grown old in those libraries without once falling ill, without once having to scramble down a tunnel or run for her life.

But now, back on the surface, back in the sweep of time, it has returned. The blood runs freely from her nose, down her face. She covers herself with her hand—she has no handkerchief to hide behind—and rises to her feet. She walks toward the vendors, toward the canoes. She speaks as calmly as she can. *"Por favor, un barco. Un barco, por favor."*

The blood is pouring now, through her fingers, down her throat, and the entire market turns to stare. A great hush falls. A few people approach, but as they do, she stumbles forward, coughing a ribbon of blood across the dirt. The people quickly step back with gasps and cries.

"Un barco . . ." she says, struggling to her knees. Inside, her innards pulse and burn. The pain is unbearable. She fights it all

the same, coughing up words. *"Un barco . . ."* she gasps. "I just . . . need . . . a boat."

But no one comes near. She kneels alone in the mud and blood. Perhaps this isn't worth returning to, she thinks, the endless arrivals, the endless departures, and the terrible, exhausting pain. She's too old. She's lived a full life, on her own terms, the best terms she could have bargained for under the circumstances. She has no home, no family, but she knows the world better than anyone before her. That's something. Perhaps she can die here, on this damp patch of earth by a river bank. It's no better or worse than desert sand or mountain snow. She has the choice—right now, this instant—to pick the spot in which to die.

It's an empowering thought. Why not take a little bit of control?

Some people come forward, not too close. Most shake their heads and warn everyone back.

To hell with it, she thinks, and keels over on her side, face sinking into the muck. Her first few cautious steps back into civilization and look how she's botched it, her old body sprawled undignified in the dirt. Already, she can feel the darkness lying upon her like a blanket, soundless, without heat or cold, pressing her into a sleep.

In her last moments, bleeding out in the mud, she thinks: What a world, made for encounters. She should have put down those books sooner. All around her, dimming now, the most copious library of all, a breathing, seeing, hearing library with blood in its veins. Scholars may study, historians may research, readers may read, but nobody knows more about today, this very day, than the person who lives it.

Nobody knows more about her, than her.

Nobody knows more about dying, right now, than she does.

To think that she's her own library, containing nothing but

her, pleases her in the end. She thinks she makes a very good book, perhaps even a magnificent book. She can see it, even more than she can think it—her very last page being filled and the very last punctuation being put down. It's not she who is dying. It's the universe around her, darkening, closing up. It isn't that her body is failing her, but that there's nowhere left for her body to go. The world has run out of space, shrunken down to a vanishing point at the tip of her nose.

"No, no. Bring her here," says a voice. "Come on. Into the boat with her." It is not her sickness, but a gruff, laconic voice. It speaks in Portuguese, and then Spanish. Then all around her are feet. Before she knows it, she's being picked up in a net of arms and carried through the marketplace. Voices of men fuss over her. She hears the splash of water and knows she's being carried over the river. She feels herself placed gently into a canoe. She makes out the blue of the sky, senses the motion of the river, sees the slouching limbs of trees float past.

"Where to?" the voice asks.

She waves her blood-painted hand, pointing in all sorts of directions. Then she's gone.

87

An Idyll for Lost Children

He's an old man with skin like beaten leather and short-cropped silvery hair that looks as if he's cut it himself with a hunting knife and no mirror. He sits in the stern, paddles the long canoe down-river, down the black blood of the jungle oozing snakelike through dense greenery, branching off, widening, narrowing again.

She's packed in the bow with bags of rice and corn flour, plantains and dried shrimp, boxes full of pencils and fishing hooks and wire and string. She leans over the side of the canoe, very carefully. It seems loaded beyond capacity. A wrong move and she's certain the whole thing will capsize. With a cautious hand, she reaches into the water and washes the dried blood from her face.

"Merci . . ." she says, still light-headed, still a rasp in her voice. She has spoken French, though he speaks Spanish. She tries again. "Thank you . . . for saving me."

He stops paddling a moment, regards her curiously. "Is that a lisp?" His tone is so dry, she can't tell if he's insulting her or not.

"No," she answers. "It's an accent."

"What kind?"

"It was French once," she says, drying her face with her sleeve. "I don't know what it is now."

"Huh." He replies without sympathy, or maybe it's his manner. He paddles some more in silence.

She clears her throat. "May I ask where you're taking me?"

"Oh, you know." The tone of his voice, so flat. "Deep, deep in the jungle."

In a single breath Aubry is alert, all her fears returning. She looks around. The river moves past islets of strangled fig roots, thick groves of slime-hung trees. Even if she could swim for it, how far would she get? She feels for her pistol tucked under her belt but it isn't there. Instead, it's at the stern of the canoe, in his hand, pointed at her.

"Mind if I hold on to this?" he says.

Her mind races. How long has she been unconscious? He took her gun, but what else? Her gold coins, too? Had he touched her? Laid his hands upon her?

"I do mind."

"Well, you have a hell of a nerve, then, leaping into my boat, armed, demanding to be taken. You got blood all over my aguaje fruit. What do you got anyway? Cholera? TB?"

"I don't know what it is."

"Probably why it's so hard to cure," he says and pockets the gun. "Name?"

She hesitates. She blinks as if staring into the sun. She has forgotten. He stops paddling. He waits.

Then it comes to her: "Aubry. Aubry Tourvel."

"You're sure?"

"I haven't used it in so long."

He is still, his oar hovering over the water. "You get more interesting by the minute," he says and starts paddling again. He has an accent, too, she notices. He is not from the jungle any more than she is.

"What are you going to do with me?" asks Aubry quietly, crouched low in the canoe.

"Do with you? Oh boy. So many possibilities, you know?"

She has gone from fear of the infinite to fear of this man. Like a switch has been pulled inside her, she lashes out, with all the finesse of a caged animal.

"I don't know," she hisses at him. "I've never murdered anyone. Not like you." She's certain of this now. "I didn't flee my country or hide from the law in a faraway jungle."

He stops paddling, just stares at her, almost daring her to go on. To Aubry, it's as good as any admission.

"That's it," she says. "I'm correct. Who did you kill? Your wife?"

"I left my wife. I don't remember killing her."

"Then who? Why are you hiding here?"

"Did you say, 'I've never murdered anyone. Not like you'? Is that right? Is that what you said?" He rubs his chin, examines her curiously. "So you have murdered someone. Just not the way I did. Do I understand that right?"

She is silent. She's an old fool who talks too much. All those years of silence and now here she is, talking herself into a hole.

"That puts you one up on me," he says, patting the gun tucked in his pocket. "You're sure as hell not getting this back."

She avoids his gaze. When she speaks, he can hardly hear her. "It wasn't like that," she says.

"Like what? I didn't assume anything."

He paddles a few more strokes in silence. She feels around and discovers she still has the gold coins in her pocket.

"Where are you from?" she asks him.

"Rio Gallegos."

"That's a long way."

"You know it?"

Rio Gallegos, she remembers, in Patagonia, thousands of miles south of here. "I know it."

"World traveler."

"Why did you leave?"

"Seemed like a good idea at the time."

"You left your wife?"

"Well," he smirks, "maybe that's not entirely accurate. Maybe she left me."

"Did you point a gun at her?"

"No. I save that for special people."

She sits there silently and waits for more.

"Couldn't have children," he says. Aubry's face is so blank, he assumes she doesn't understand—and it's true. She doesn't. With some irritation, he explains, "I couldn't have children."

In fact, if Vicente Quevedo ever bothered to flip back through his memories—and he rarely did—the last he saw of his wife was through the wet upper-story windowpanes of her childhood bedroom. He was thirty-four years old and she was twenty-six. He had stood in the rain blowing off the South Atlantic, calling her name for over an hour in the cold and dark. She was home, her parents were home, but no one opened the door to him.

"She wanted children more than she wanted you," Aubry says. Vicente throws her a look of disgust. "Am I wrong?" she asks.

"No, but you don't say it out loud!" he shoots back. "Do they have manners in France? Something called tact?"

"I left that behind a long time ago," she says defiantly.

"Well, you damn well better go back and pick it up again!"

"So what?" Aubry jeers at him. "So you can't have children . . ."

"Yeah!"

". . . so you hop on a boat . . ."

"Yeah!"

". . . or a plane and fly off into a jungle?"

"Yeah! No!" he corrects himself, shaking his head. "Weaklings fly. I walked it."

For a moment, her voice freezes in her throat. "You walked?" Aubry is so quiet, so reverential, that his voice quiets, too.

"I walked."

He paddles a few more strokes, feeling her eyes on him, then explains some more: "Quit everything. Headed north. Through the Pampas, through the highlands. Over the Andes—twice. And down the river."

He remembers the lonely trails through Patagonia, the resplendent wealth of Uruguay, the civil wars of Colombia, the lawlessness of the Venezuelan slums.

"But you stopped here," says Aubry.

"Had to."

"Why?"

"They kept following me."

"Who followed you?"

"Damn kids, that's who."

He first noticed them in a dusty tin-roofed town in the Guiana Highlands. He passed a six-year-old boy—that was his best guess, never having had kids—begging at the mouth of an alley. He'd seen so many beggars in his travels he couldn't begin to count them, and most of them children.

But this particular boy didn't beg. He didn't hold out his hands, didn't say a word—just stared at him hard, as if he'd recognized Vicente from somewhere, as if Vicente was his long-lost uncle. Vicente didn't like it one bit. He walked away and put the boy out of his mind. An hour later, he looked over his shoulder to find the boy trailing him, peeking out behind mailboxes and garbage cans.

"Everywhere I went, these little street urchins, staring at me. It was creepy."

"I can imagine," says Aubry.

"No, you can't. You can't imagine."

One night Vicente made camp in the jungle somewhere, on what side of what border he no longer knew, but he had a fire going and yucca roots boiling in a pot. It would have been—should have been—a perfectly comfortable evening, given his newly adjusted standards. But he could still see them, a band of children, from toddlers to teens, homeless and destitute. Their clothes were rags. Some of them didn't have shoes. They formed a ghostly ring at the edge of the firelight, watching him.

"I'd stop for the night and there they'd be," he says, "just past the trees, all night long."

Aubry's not sure if she should believe him. He sounds like a madman. She tries humoring him, but doesn't have the sincerity in her voice to pull it off. "What must you have thought?"

"I thought my wife hired them to kill me."

"How did you get rid of them?"

"What?" Vicente seems genuinely puzzled by the question. "No . . . well, they were young."

They'd followed Vicente through miles and miles of jungle. No matter how fast he walked, every time he glanced over his shoulder, there they were, a band of outcast children in his wake, the older ones carrying the toddlers on their shoulders.

"Some of them couldn't even walk yet," he explains. "If they kept following me like that, I knew they'd get hurt or sick or something."

"Of course," says Aubry.

"So I made camp," he says.

Only then does she start to understand. Her face shifts from smug to surprised. "You mean," she sits up a little, "now you have children?"

"Twenty-three of them." He nods upriver. "There they are."

Aubry turns around. Ahead, where the river splits in two, little figures appear—one, then two, then ten, then twenty—long-haired boys and girls, young and younger, bronze holes in the green fabric of the riverbank. Even from a distance she can make out their big white eyes against their deeply tanned skin, coarsened from a life lived outdoors. They stand sentinel-like on the shore, their reflections shining in the black water at their feet.

Vicente paddles the canoe to shore, angles in. The older kids, up to their knees in the river, help secure it. Vicente unloads food and supplies to the little hands that form a chain, passing the boxes and crates straight into the large open shelter in the center of camp, a wooden frame sheathed in palm leaves and thatch that curves protectively over their patch of earth.

"Here we go," says Vicente as he passes along the crates. "Rice . . . salt . . . dried plantains . . . potatoes . . . beans . . . some aguaje with blood on it . . . Oh yeah," he says as an afterthought, "and an old Frenchwoman."

The children gape at Aubry. They've been gaping all along, but unloading the canoe is a priority. Now that it's done, they watch her step ashore—the only thing to come out of the canoe without their help.

A little girl, perhaps four or five years old, sniffs at her. "What for?" she asks.

"We eat her," says Vicente.

There is a gasp from the children.

A boy, perhaps six, pushes his way to the front of the crowd. He does not care about the old woman, hardly looks at her. "Grandpa," he says to Vicente, "Tulla broke your hammock while you were gone."

Vicente slowly bends down, eye level with the boy. "Are you concerned where I'm going to sleep tonight or do you just want to get Tulla into trouble?"

Tulla, the same age as the boy, rushes forward to defend herself. "Get me into trouble!"

"It's all right," says Vicente. "You're not in trouble. You're going to fix it, Tulla." He turns to the boy. "And you're going to help."

The boy is aghast. "But I didn't break it!"

Vicente drops his voice, talking low and evenly with the boy, out of earshot of the others. But Aubry, standing next to him, hears every word. "Would you rather be known as the snitch who gets everyone into trouble or the one who helps others in their time of need?"

The boy grumbles to himself. "Oh, all right," he says and sulks off.

But mostly, the children are still captivated by the old Frenchwoman, mulling her over.

"But what can she do?" asks a boy, this one older, wiry, maybe twelve.

"Do?" asks Vicente.

"We cook the food," says the boy. "Ollie fishes the river. Moura fixes the roof. I clean the clothes. What can she do?"

Vicente has an answer ready. He has many answers prepared for many situations and is about to launch into one—perhaps a lecture on charity, or allowing people the time to find their purpose, as everyone here at the camp has. And who knows if she even wants to stay with a ragtag collection of ruffians like themselves? Wasn't that awfully arrogant of them?

Before Vicente can get out the first word of his treatise, Aubry knocks the cap off her walking stick, tests the grip of her aged hands, and flings her spear dead center into a tree. A collective gasp, feet thoughtlessly jumping back a step. Even Vicente feels his heart twang like an elastic band. It isn't a thick tree either, but a thin sapling, the narrowest of targets, and it sways from the impact. A tingle of excitement courses through the camp.

"Can you teach me that?" asks one of the girls.

"I could teach you to shoot a gun, too, but your grandpa took mine," says Aubry.

"Good thing, too," he mumbles.

But the excitement is irrepressible.

"She can help us fish! That's what she can do!"

"Or hunt birds!"

"Or jaguars!"

"Look," says Vicente, "I know you're not used to visitors, but the first rule is not to submit your guests to forced labor."

"No," says Aubry, "I don't mind."

88

An Idyll for Lost Children

Aubry and Ollie, the boy who likes to fish—he can't be more than ten—go to his favorite hole downriver before the daylight disappears. They perch themselves on a fallen tree, staring into the river, the boy with his hook and line, Aubry with her spear. Other children tag along but keep their distance, content to observe from the jungle trees, perched in the tall branches.

"This is the best spot," says Ollie. "The big fish come to eat the little fish. The biggest fish come to eat them."

"You know your fish."

Because fishing is not a speedy process, they sit together for a long time, waiting quietly. Sometimes they talk, but mostly they're quiet and very comfortable with each other. Aubry stares at the water, and she swears the more she looks, the more the water seems to slow down for her, as if offering up secrets. She is transfixed. There is a river beneath this river, it tells her, a sound below the sound. It is not words she is hearing but a sensation that is passing through her, a feeling that words are too frail to express.

"Are you really going to use your spear?" Ollie asks.

She blinks, removed from the moment. As if in answer to his question, they see a big fish pass below. She braces her knees, straightens her spine, and lets loose. Her spear drives through

369

the water, sticks the fish through its head. It's a large heavy fish, like a dead python at the end of her line, and she reels it in triumphantly, holding it high for all the children in the trees to see. When they do, they stand in the branches and cheer.

By the time Aubry and Ollie return to camp, they have two big peacock bass and five catfish. The children are delighted. The fish are cleaned and gutted and cooked with rice and peppers. It takes no time at all—the efficient chaos of little hands with assigned duties. They sit under the big lean-to that keeps off the rain but traps the heat of the fire, large enough to shelter all twenty-three children and two adults.

They tell Aubry that on other nights they eat monkey, or tarantulas the size of coconuts roasted over a fire. Occasionally a tapir is trapped in one of their hidden pits. When that happens, they have meat for a month. There are fig trees nearby that sprout fruit all year long. In the jungle there are avocados, cashews, passion fruit, and a tomato garden Vicente carefully supervises. It's a good meal and if Aubry has eaten better food, she can't remember eating with better company. The children are sincere and funny and sometimes funny because they are sincere. They are sometimes moody and sometimes snarly, but never dull, and she talks and laughs and gossips with them well into the night.

When she curls onto her mat under the lean-to, she notices, for the first time, that her hands have finally stopped trembling. She also finds, if she listens carefully to the night, she can pinpoint the croak of a tree frog on the other side of the river. She wonders, Has the jungle always sounded like this? It's like living in a house with the walls suddenly removed, the whole world so lucid, and so much of it. She drifts off to sleep, listening.

But when she awakes the next morning, it's to the sound of screaming.

89

An Idyll for Lost Children

Aubry jolts up on her straw mat and sees the children already gathered around the shrieking little girl.

"Tulla," they are saying, patting her shoulders, whispering to her, "it's all right. Here comes Grandpa."

Aubry rushes forward, breaks through the crowd. Tulla lies on the ground, screaming, white bone sticking out of her calf, blood running down her leg. The broken tree branch that snapped off and tossed her sideways to the ground lay not far away.

"Oh no!" Aubry gasps, but before she can help, Vicente pulls her out of his way.

"I can handle this," he says, and she steps back. He leans over Tulla and studies the leg. Tulla screams. No amount of comforting can take away this pain. "Okay, okay," says Vicente. "You're going to be fine."

Aubry watches, but doesn't know what they can do to help her. She turns to the teenage girl standing beside her. This girl doesn't seem worried. She leans against a tree, watching listlessly, her apathy unsettling.

"She needs a doctor," says Aubry.

"Grandpa's as good as any doctor," says the girl.

"No. A real doctor. And a hospital."

The girl shrugs. Only now does Aubry notice—her eyes are mismatched, one hazel, brown around the edges, the other a pale green. "She'll be fine."

Aubry watches, horrified. Vicente shushes the girl. He concentrates, lips pursed tight, breathing like a bull through his nose.

He closes his eyes. His brows knit up. He builds his nerve and then, all at once, springs to life, grabbing Tulla's leg and pressing down on the bone with everything he has, as if crushing a walnut with his bare hands. He forces the bone back inside. Blood trickles over the backs of his hands. He squeezes her leg until he feels the two broken nubs of bone bump together.

Tulla wails, thrashing in the arms of her brothers and sisters. Aubry can't bear it any longer, covering her ears. All the while blood oozes between Vicente's iron-tight fingers, compacting her little leg back together.

Tulla's eyes roll back in her head. Her screams stop, the pain itself cutting off her voice like a rock jammed in her windpipe. Her mouth gapes open, silently. Aubry's vision smears from the tears in her eyes. She turns away.

Vicente lets go of the leg, falls back, and sucks in air. When Aubry turns back again, wiping her eyes, she sees one of the children pour warm water over the leg, washing the blood away, and another child ready with an ointment that several little hands rub all over the wound.

"Bandages," says Vicente, and a boy, the same boy who'd accused Tulla of breaking a hammock, runs over and wraps her leg up tight, with care and precision. Most important, Tulla is breathing again, breathing as if she'd just run across the continent, but her pain is over.

"You're a very brave girl," says Vicente, his hand on her cheek. "I'm proud of you."

It is hard to see, but Tulla manages an exhausted smile. The children comfort her, rubbing her shoulders, holding her hands. Vicente, drained and muddleheaded, passes Aubry as he walks away.

"We should take her to a hospital," she glares.

"Nah," he replies with a dismissive wave of his hand.

She watches him go to the river's edge and wash the blood from his hands. Her head reels as if recovering from a punch. Tulla may very well die within a week—infection, gangrene, blood poisoning—but not one of them seems concerned. She wonders what kind of madness this camp survives on and what she will do about it.

90

An Idyll for Lost Children

The next morning, when Aubry awakes on her straw mat under the big lean-to, little Ollie is curled under her arm and a warm mist has rolled in, blurring the edges of the jungle all around.

It's a strange morning, curtains of fog exhaling through the trees, sliding through the camp. By the river's edge, Vicente and the little boy who helped wrap Tulla's leg stare into the luminous white.

"Where did you see it?" Vicente asks him.

"Straight ahead," says the boy and points upriver.

Vicente walks up to his knees in the water. Everyone is up now, standing along the shore, peering into the wall of fog.

Then they see it, materializing out of the haze, a shadow, a black hole in the brightness, caught in the lazy push of the river. It slowly drifts toward them.

Vicente wades farther into the black water and white air. Slowly, bit by bit, he can begin to make it out. Too small for a boat. More than a clump of driftwood. It's a small raft, a small raft with a little person on it. He waits for it, up to his waist now. The raft drifts into his hands. On it, a girl, four years old, guesses Aubry, with straight black hair, sitting cross-legged and alone.

"How are you?" Vicente asks her.

"Fine," she says.

"Was it a good trip?"

"Uh-huh."

"Why don't you rest here a bit?"

"Okay."

He picks her up and carries her to shore.

"Little Mouse," Vicente says to one of his children, "why don't you make us a new hammock?"

Little Mouse obediently runs off to start her work.

"She can have mine!" offers a young boy and he rushes off too.

"Let's see what we have for food around here," says Vicente as he carries the little girl into camp. The children gather around her, feed her, ask her many questions. Her name, they discover, is Kuliki.

Later, after Kuliki has eaten, after the children who have been crowding and pampering her have thinned out and dispersed, Aubry and Kuliki finally have a moment alone. The two of them sit together under the big lean-to, picking seeds from cacao beans.

"Your name is Kuliki?"

"Uh-huh."

"That's a pretty name."

"Uh-huh."

"Where are your parents, Kuliki?"

She brushes some flies away from the beans before answering. "I was playing outside and there was a big shaking and all the houses fell down."

Aubry, afraid to ask: "But where are your parents?"

"In the houses."

She is so young, so untangled by emotion. Aubry wants to console her but there is so little to console.

"How did you find this place?"

"I followed the fireflies."

She offers nothing else, but Aubry thinks she hears an accent, something that belongs far away from here.

"Did you always speak Spanish?"

"Am I speaking Spanish?" Kuliki looks up at Aubry, genuinely interested.

"Yes."

"Oh," she says curiously, then goes back to seeding the cacao beans.

"How long have you been on the river?"

"I don't know."

"Did you come from far?"

She thinks about it. "I remember the ocean. And big mountains."

"That's a long way, Kuliki."

"It is?"

"Yes, it is."

Kuliki has no reaction other than to go back to her task. That's as much as Aubry will extract from her this day, perhaps ever. Who knows how long the memories of a four-year-old will last?

During the night the fog condenses into rain that falls in a monotonous downpour, a steady drone that vibrates the leaves and drums the jungle floor. In the morning, the swollen river groans in the language of whirlpools and bursting dams.

Under the big lean-to, it is perfectly dry, but Aubry wanders anyway, walking stick in hand, studying this strange camp, these strange children, so apart from the world. Kuliki is still asleep, but the rest perch in the trees or splash in the river or run circles in the rain. Ollie has gone off fishing. It is best to fish in the rain, he says. The teenage girl with mismatched eyes is leaning against a tree, half-drenched, watching the rain on the big river as if waiting for ghosts to appear.

Aubry follows the river. It is hypnotic watching the currents scour the jungle of its debris—green leaves, brown leaves—no matter. The river sweeps them all away. *Listen*, it says. *Beyond this place, glaciers are filling the riverbeds. Tides are pulling back the oceans.*

Vicente's tomato garden floats on a bed of logs and grass in a quiet inlet of the river where the monkeys and the deer can't reach. When he wants a few tomatoes, he grabs a rope and reels it in. This is where Aubry finds him, on the riverbank, tending his garden.

"It's not as if we don't have room," he tells her. "Ahmee left us a month ago. Isla a year before that."

"Who's Ahmee?"

"Good kid. He's all grown up, out there in the world now. That's how it is. They show up. I feed them, raise them, teach them what I know. I let them go." He shrugs, as if offering an apology. "I do my best."

She helps thread a new hammock that afternoon, then helps cook dinner with the children—Ollie's fish again, with potatoes, mushrooms, and avocados. They gather under the big lean-to to eat, rain pelting the leaves over their heads, a fire to keep them warm.

"Have you been all around the world?" asks one of the children. Word has gotten around.

"Yes."

"How many times?" asks another child.

"I don't know."

"That's a lot of times," says another.

"You think so?" says Aubry.

They are all talking at her now. "I've never been anywhere," says a ten-year-old, glumly.

"You're young. I'm old."

"Did you see everything in the world?" asks a little one.

"Oh, that's an awful lot to see."

"But you might have."

Aubry is about to deny it, but finds she can't. Words get stuck in her mouth.

"Oh my God," says Vicente, "she might have."

"Were you on a mission?" asks Tulla.

Vicente laughs, but again, Aubry hesitates to answer. He looks up at her, curiosity piqued. "So, what kind of mission might that have been?"

She looks at the fire, as if the answer were there. "To see things."

"Somebody wanted you to see," says a little one, nodding her head in utmost certainty.

"Was it hard?" someone asks.

"Yes."

"Did you suffer?" someone asks.

She can't say it aloud. She only nods.

"Was it worth it?"

She looks at the children. She looks at Vicente. It's as if she wants someone else to answer these questions for her. She has trampled this world, walked all over it. She has curled in its lap and eaten its fruit, and only now does she feel they have finally met.

"Yes," she says. "It was."

"What did you see?" asks Ollie.

But Aubry is silent.

"She can't tell us half of what she saw," says the girl with the mismatched eyes, and how she discerns such things, Aubry doesn't know.

"Why not?" asks one of the children.

"She's afraid we won't believe her."

"I'll believe you," says Ollie.

"I'll believe you," says a little one.

Aubry wants to say something, but what? Since she's left the libraries, she's had one foot on the earth, the other in an apparition. Sometimes, when she is alone with the world, she is afraid to turn around too quickly, in case eternity is crouched behind her. But how does she explain? She has knowledge that needs to be shared, and these children are such perfect listeners, but how does one describe color to those who can't see? What she encountered was like a great fire that swept the world. All she can do now is blow on the embers and hope others can make out the glow.

"Why wouldn't we believe her?" asks Tulla. "Wasn't it real?"

Aubry turns to her. "It was more real than real."

Everyone waits to hear her tales, but she has nothing else to say.

"Leave her alone," says the girl with the mismatched eyes. "She doesn't have the words. I doubt anyone does."

"No rush," says Vicente. "We've got time."

"But I don't have time," Aubry blurts out. The children go silent. "I'm not allowed to stay. Not anywhere."

"You have to leave?" says one of them, distraught.

"I'm sorry."

"When?"

"Tonight. Any moment now."

"Tonight?" says Vicente.

"I don't want to go. Really, I don't. I wish it were otherwise."

"When you need to go," says Vicente, very calmly, eating his avocado, "let me know. We'll get in the canoe together and I'll take you somewhere safe." He looks up at her. "But try to get some rest first."

Sleep doesn't come easily that night. Vicente sits down beside her, not too close, but not far either. He doesn't look at her, only stares into the night. He is unobtrusive company.

The rain stops. After the endless drone of raindrops, a preternatural silence descends on the camp, as if the jungle has dunked its head underwater. The evening deepens. Slowly noises return—cicadas chirping, frogs croaking. Together, they listen.

Beyond this place, magma is churning. Magma is reshaping the face of the earth. And she knows it.

When she wakes the next morning on her straw mat under the big lean-to, there are three children burrowed under her left arm and two more under her right.

91

An Idyll for Lost Children

Vicente carefully unwraps Tulla's bandages. With help, she rises to her feet and stands. She is supported by her brothers and sisters at first, but they gradually release her. Soon, she stands on her own. Her leg, though scarred, seems otherwise strong, strong enough to carry her weight with only a small limp. As she walks about in circles, even the limp seems to disappear. Soon, she is running off with her friends to play in the forest.

Aubry has witnessed the entire recovery from beginning to end, and is still unsure of what she's seen. She wanders off, shell-shocked, as if viciously assaulted by a miracle.

"Impossible," she mutters to herself.

The girl with the mismatched eyes overhears her.

"Impossible things in your world," she says, "are inevitable in ours."

Later that afternoon Aubry hears Vicente talking to Shona. Shona is a girl of few words, small for an eight-year-old—if that's what she is—but wiser than her years. That's how it seems to Aubry. When Shona walks up to Vicente that afternoon and says, "You know, we should check donations today," he straightens up and pays attention.

"Nothing there last week."

"There is today," and she says no more. Less than an hour later, Vicente is coiling some rope and gathering company for an excursion.

"There's a place where people sometimes drop off gifts for the kids," he tells Aubry. "It's about four miles from here, but I figure you could use the walk."

"Because I haven't walked enough already?"

He has a grin that always veers to one side. "It's a hell of a story," he says.

"What?"

"Yours. You tell it to anyone out there and they're going to admire you. There's no helping it. Whether you admire yourself or not is up to you."

"All I did was not die."

"And you did it rather well. Come on," he says, offering his hand. "That was an outstanding walk you took, young lady, but it isn't over yet."

He helps her to her feet, and so Aubry joins them—Vicente, Shona, Ollie, the girl with mismatched eyes, and an older boy named Tonuhai. Together, the six of them trek into the jungle.

92

Home

Vicente carries the coil of rope around his shoulder. Ahead are the children who know the way. Tonuhai, the oldest of them, carries a woven basket on his pale blond head, filled with an assortment of things—a small fishing net, a lantern, something wrapped in a banana leaf. They walk through the dark green jungle following a dim path that even Aubry, with her lifetime of experience, can hardly see.

"I've been meaning to ask," she tells Vicente. "How do I look?"

"You look like an old woman with long white hair." It should have been one of his usual caustic remarks, but it isn't somehow. It almost sounds affectionate. "Very lovely, actually."

"Yes?" She is pleased to hear this. "I haven't . . . I don't know what I look like. Not anymore."

"No one here does."

A little late, she says, "Thank you."

"You're welcome."

She hesitates before she says more, then tells him: "I saw something."

He waits for more, but nothing comes.

"A butterfly?"

"A vision."

He looks around, gestures to the jungle. "Did it look like this?"

"No."

"Then what did it look like?"

"Everything." She has stopped in the middle of the trail, so he stops, too, turning to her. "And nothing has been the same since."

He watches her closely. For all his scowl and sarcasm, he is a good listener.

"How . . ." she stammers out, "how did that little girl's leg heal so quickly?"

He thinks about his answer before responding. "As long as things are getting fixed around here, I wouldn't ask too many questions."

Tears are forming in her eyes. He goes to her, puts his hand on her shoulder. It is an invitation and her arms snake around him, timidly, like a frightened girl. She holds him tight and, because she is too scared to say it loudly, whispers in his ear:

"This is my fifth day here. I've never stayed anywhere for five days before. Sometimes four, but never five. Never."

He whispers back, "I don't think you need to count the days anymore."

Then she is sobbing, overpowered by emotions she cannot explain. It is a sense of relief, as if freed of service. It is a kind of sadness, too, as if watching part of her die. It is the sorrow of loss, and the joy of liberation, and she cannot separate them. He holds her close, her head against his. Her body is filled with tremors, but he understands and lets her cry, a long, silent, open-mouthed cry.

"We're here!" shouts Ollie up ahead.

They do not move. Vicente waits while Aubry recovers herself, wiping away tears, quieting her nerves. He holds her by the arm and gently walks her down the path. With Vicente guiding her, she sleepwalks through the jungle, exhausted. The world seems impalpable, the ground beneath her feet hardly there. Insects are trilling in the canopy. Somewhere in the distance, a monkey howls.

And the jungle air, green and humid, warns her that up ahead is the moment language stops.

Vicente gently leans her against a tree, then hurries ahead with his coil of rope. Aubry can see the four of them scrambling to rig a line. There's a long sturdy pole fastened between two trees, and Tonuhai lifts Ollie up on his shoulders to reach it. With a handful of grease he keeps wrapped in a banana leaf, Ollie slicks down the center of the pole where a well-worn notch has been seared into the wood. He throws the rope over and it slides right in. To the end of the rope, they tie the woven basket.

Aubry watches the process, not understanding the plan, staying out of their way. She is no good to them anyway, her unfocused eyes like cloudy water. But she wonders why Vicente is lighting a lantern and what they are going to put in the basket. She approaches, an unsettled feeling in her gut, increasing with every step.

She can feel it before she can see it.

They pull the rope, lifting the basket into the air right over the well that's only just come into view. She slows as she recognizes the smooth gray stones shaped like a mouth, a pair of eyes carved into one end of the rim, a little beard at the other.

Aubry freezes. She cannot force herself to take another step closer.

It's Shona, small for her age, who climbs into the basket. The basket is just small enough to fit down the long dark gullet of the well, but just big enough to hold her weight.

"Take your light," says Vicente.

He hands her the lantern Tonuhai has carried. It glows yellow in her hand.

"Got your net?" he asks.

"Got it," she says, her little form curled into the basket.

"You know what's down there?"

"Some coins."

"What else?"

"We'll see," she says. A few paces away, the girl with mismatched eyes is watching Aubry as if they share some ill-fated secret.

"Down you go, then," says Vicente. Carefully, he and Tonuhai lower Shona past the lips, past the teeth, into the black maw. She sinks and sinks until she is a dim glow far down in the darkness below.

Aubry stays away, backed against a tree, watching and waiting. She doesn't move, only breathes.

Vicente calls down to Shona, "You good?"

"Good!" comes her voice, echoing up the well.

Tonuhai ties off the rope, but keeps his hands gripped on it just to be safe. Vicente and the others peer into the well at the soft glow in the underside of the earth, sounds echoing up—a bit of splashing, the clink of metal.

Behind her, Aubry feels a presence, something just over her shoulder. The skin on the back of her neck prickles. It's like silent footsteps stalking her, coming upon her fast. She turns, peers deep into the jungle, but sees nothing.

Shona's voice comes echoing up the well. "Okay!"

Vicente and Tonuhai pull in the line, slowly, carefully, hand over hand, until she clears the teeth. They swing the basket over the rim of the well, past the open eyes, and onto dry ground.

Vicente helps Shona out of the basket. Her hands are black with mud, the basket dripping with well water.

"What'd we get?" asks Vicente.

She upends the basket and a small treasure pours out.

"Look at that," says Tonuhai quietly.

They huddle around it, picking through the small pile at their feet. They find coins smeared with mud. Vicente pours water over them, cleans them well enough to see they are Chinese and they are gold. Shona holds up a pair of earrings and everyone gasps at the sight of them. They are beautiful, not from around here, but some faraway place. Vicente swears that only sapphires have that color to them.

The girl with mismatched eyes fishes out a piece of amber that glows golden in the light. When she holds it up, everyone can see the beetle frozen inside. Ollie has found a big tooth with strange purple letters etched in the enamel.

"Look," says Tonuhai. "Money." He pulls out a tightly coiled wad of bills from an old leather pouch. Vicente inspects it.

"New Zealand money," he says. "It's like someone sank a Spanish galleon in our well."

The whole while, Aubry keeps coming closer, inching her way forward until she stands over them. She could protest. She could clutch all these things to her chest and run off. She did that once before. But she would just as soon let the children have them. It must be her age. It seems to bring with it such composure.

Then she sees, in the center of the pile, a wooden sphere, its many facets still shiny with lacquer. The girl with mismatched eyes notices Aubry, picks up the puzzle ball, and hands it to her. Aubry takes it, holds it as if it is made of thin glass, thin glass with her own heart beating inside. She sits, leaning against the rim of the well—against that face—and slowly turns the puzzle ball over and over in her hands, wiping it clean with her skirt.

"Worth anything?" Vicente asks her, but Aubry doesn't hear him.

She remembers Marta's globe, crisscrossed with red crayon lines, the pattern they formed. She remembers the vision, burned into memory, the latticework of the libraries, their perfect symmetry encircling her, caught in her orbit. She turns the ball, sliding the planes against each other, snapping the pieces into place, as if the puzzle ball is the world in miniature. She doesn't always remember which came first, Reykjavik or Cardiff, Ceylon or Samoa, but she finds she only needs to close her eyes a moment, and it all comes back somehow, all the paths she forgot she'd taken. Her pace picks up. As the pieces turn faster in her hands, the pattern reveals itself.

Then it clicks.

It has never clicked before, not in all her years of trying. Despite its age, despite the long wait at the bottom of a well, it unlocks in her hands, so lightly, so easily, that her eyes mist up and she has to blink the tears back to see. She pulls the rest of it open gently, like pulling back flower petals.

Inside, hidden in the hollow center that she's never seen before, is a piece of paper, folded up small.

She opens it very carefully, fold by fold. As it opens, colors bloom in her hands. She sees that it's a watercolor, a painting of a black river—behind it, a thick jungle, done in swirling green lines that churn and tangle. There is no mistaking it, nor the hand that drew it.

It's Qalima's.

How did she describe it? It was a vision she had, a river at the end of the world.

She feels the skin on her back goosebump. She turns the paper over. On the back, with Qalima's graceful pen, is written, "HAPPY BIRTHDAY."

But when Aubry turns it back, the watercolor is gone. She turns it over again—perhaps it's a trick of the light—but now that side is empty, too. Suddenly she's holding a blank piece of paper in her unsteady hands. Had she seen it? Was it there? She turns the paper over and over.

The others are staring at her. For how long she's not sure. She stares back, but doesn't really. She is thinking: there are things in this world that only exist because you have beheld them. She's almost in shock over the miracle of her being—how she happened, how she continues to happen. From the beginning, such an impossible plot. It's curious, this gratitude she suddenly feels, spreading through her like a ring of bright water. She wants to cry, but the tears are no longer there.

She stuffs the paper in a pocket. In a silence full of unasked questions, she puts the puzzle ball back together.

A gust of wind stirs the trees.

"A bit of weather coming in," she says.

Another gust that sweeps leaves across the sky and bends the treetops. It's ominous and beautiful, and she's glad to be a witness.

"Right," says Vicente. "Let's go home."

"Let's go home," Aubry agrees.

They gather up their things and drop them in the basket—their basket of treasure, they call it—and head back to camp. Vicente leads. Tonuhai, Shona, and Ollie follow close behind. Aubry tosses the puzzle ball to the girl with mismatched eyes—her gift—and she examines it with a curious smile. Then they hurry to catch up to Vicente and the others. In single file they walk into the jungle and, one by one, they vanish into the shimmering green.

Acknowledgments

My mom often suggested I write a novel, but the task always seemed beyond me. "Those are real writers," I told her. Finally, with a great deal of trepidation, I took her advice. She didn't live to see it finished, but she would have been so proud. If you like Aubry Tourvel, there's a lot of my mom in her, particularly when it comes to children. She was the best mom ever.

Alice Lutyens, who is up to her armpits in clients, took me on anyway. God knows what inspired her. She saw something in this novel, gave me some of my first writerly advice, which was invaluable. Her counsel has always been spot-on and I'm grateful to her and everyone at Curtis Brown who have worked so hard on my behalf.

If I hit the jackpot with Alice, then I hit it again with Margo Shickmanter, my editor. If you like this book, remember that Margo had a lot to do with that, steering me around many landmines, helping to streamline an unwieldy narrative. If I was a reluctant learner at times, she was remarkably patient with me. Along with Margo comes the whole gang at Avid Reader Press—Jofie Ferrari-Adler, Meredith Vilarello, Amy Guay, Jessica Chin, Alexandra Primiani, and Katherine Hernandez. They've been great, keeping me on schedule and holding my hand through the strange new world of publishing.

This novel was born from my days at the Cleveland Public Library. A lot of people took part in its making, many of them

Acknowledgments

unaware—Amy Dawson, Jean Collins, April Lancaster, Dorrian Hawkins, just to name a few. Heartfelt thanks to all of them.

Finally, there's my extraordinary wife, my two highly entertaining kids, my three brothers and their families, my best buddy Angela, Cil, and my ever-attentive, ever-supportive dad, all of whom have been quietly cheerleading me in the background, each in their own way. It's been much appreciated.

About the Author

Douglas Westerbeke lives in Ohio and works at one of the largest libraries in the U.S. He has spent the last decade on the local panel of the International Dublin Literary Award, which inspired him to write his own book.